THOU SHALT NOT KILL

Genocide in Central Africa

BY

REV. MALCOLM SMITH

Milton Keynes, UK

AuthorHouse™
1663 Liberty Drive, Suite 200
Bloomington, IN 47403
www.authorhouse.com
Phone: 1-800-839-8640

AuthorHouse™ UK Ltd.
500 Avebury Boulevard
Central Milton Keynes, MK9 2BE
www.authorhouse.co.uk
Phone: 08001974150

First published by AuthorHouse 2/16/2007

ISBN: 978-1-4259-9827-1 (e)
ISBN: 978-1-4259-6475-7 (sc)

Library of Congress Control Number: 2007901179

Printed in the United States of America
Bloomington, Indiana

This book is printed on acid-free paper.

Table of Contents

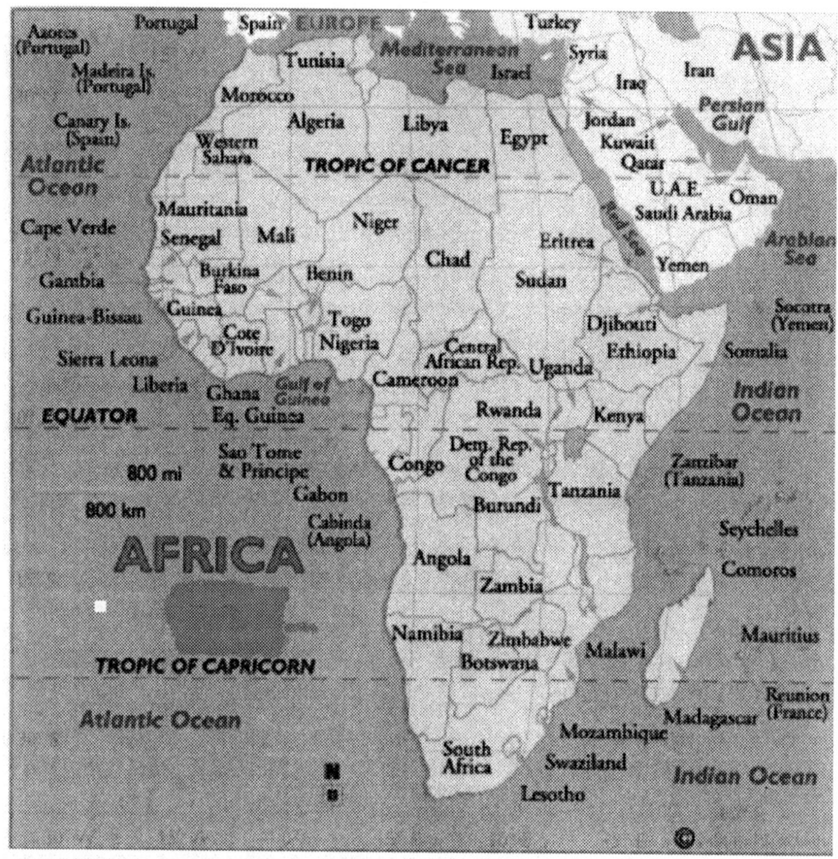

http://worldatlas.com/webimage/countrys/africa/printpage/africa.htm 11/14/2006

Burundi Within Africa

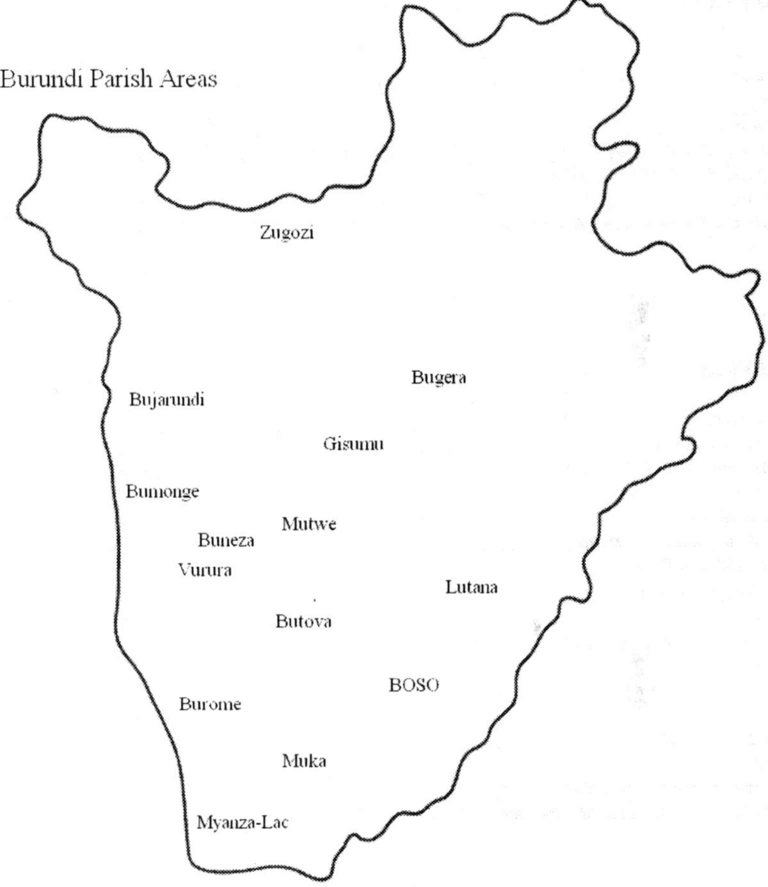

Regions In Burundi

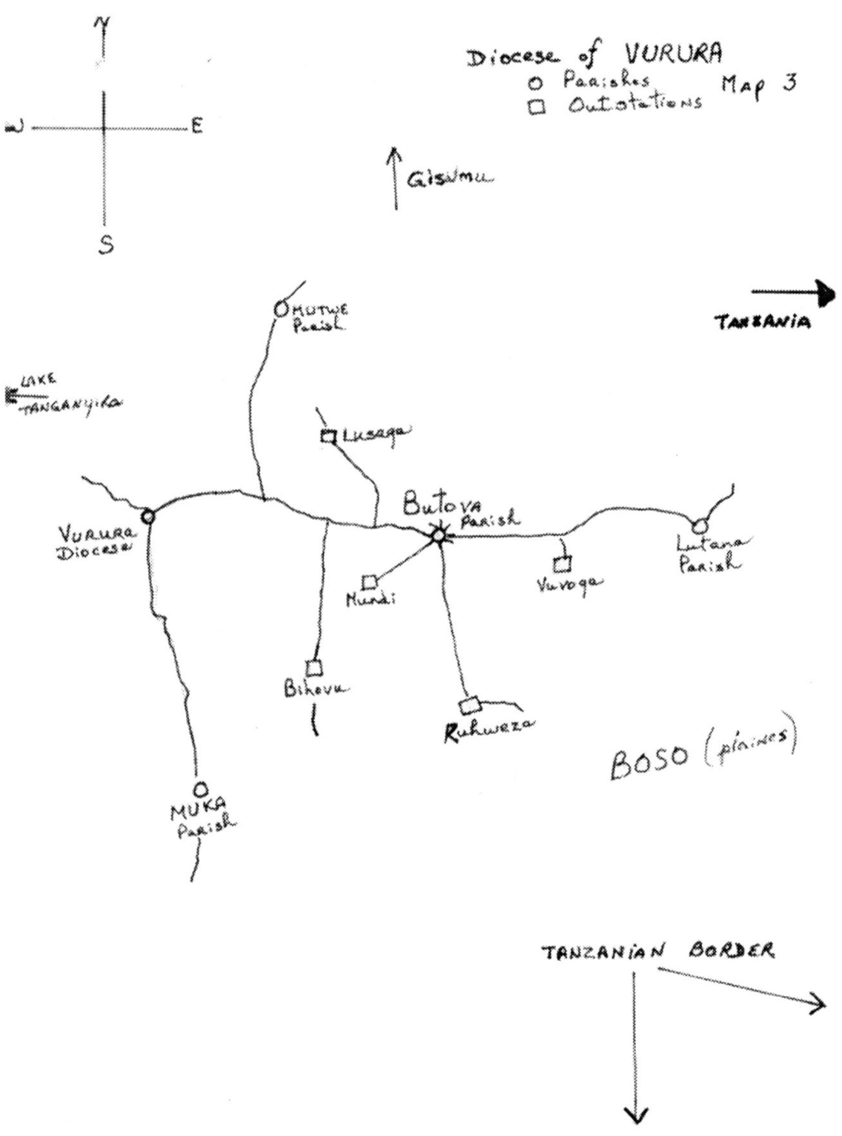

Diocese of Vurura: Parish of Butova

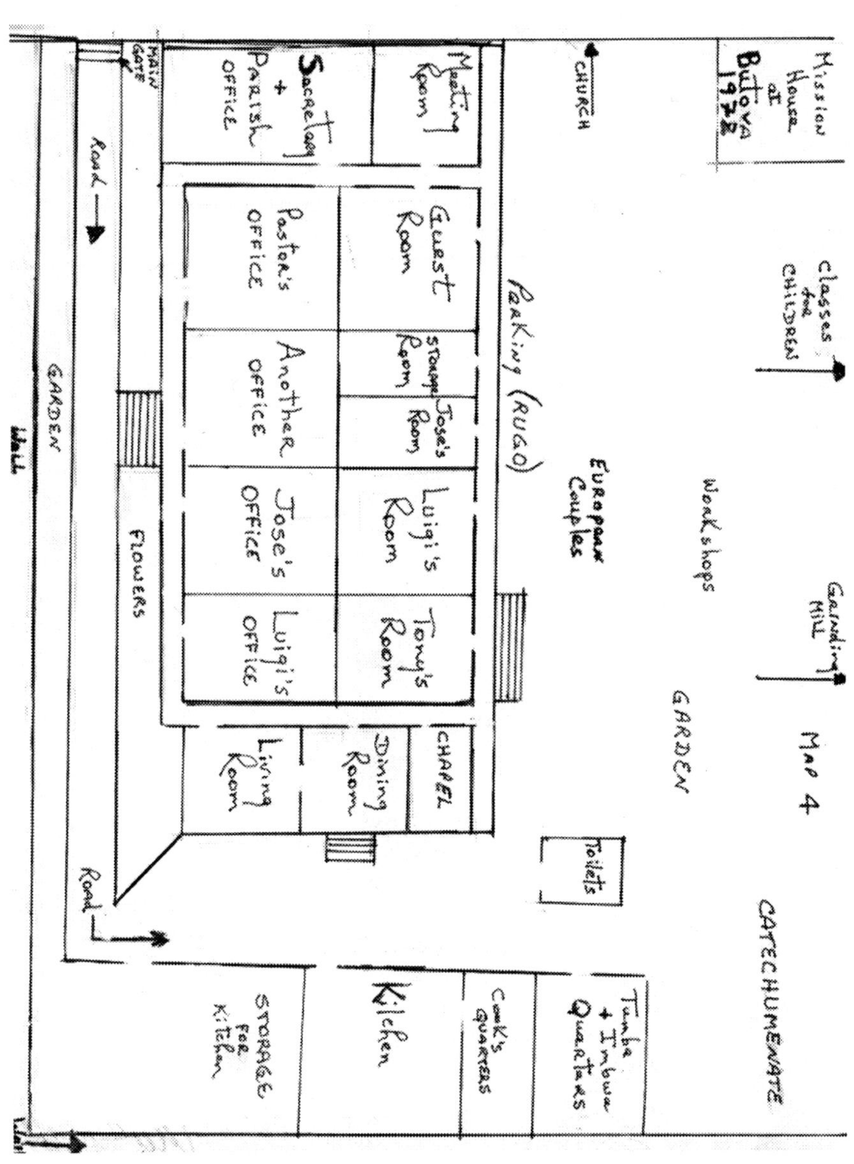

Compound of Butova (Parish House)

Prologue

In May of 1972, one of the bloodiest genocides in the history of the world took place in Burundi, Central Africa. It was alarming indeed because of its rapidity, for it lasted only 22 days! Over the three-week period, from Thursday, May 4 to Friday, May 26, the ruling Batutsi tribe killed over 150,000 Bahutu men and boys. In the beginning, all serving forces of the Bahutu tribe were killed in military camps, on May 3. Thus there was absolutely no opposition to these hideous assassinations, as the Batutsi military occupied all 87 communes throughout Burundi. In the work that follows, I try to explain the situation and describe, in great detail, the happenings all around me, as I pastored a Roman Catholic Church in the southern part of the country.

In this account, the names of both the people and the places have been changed, to allow me the freedom to authentically and honestly explain the happenings as they occurred, without prejudice to anyone. My account is historically and chrono-logically accurate but the change of names gives me permission to explain the events without any intention of improperly accusing anyone. The account is written in the third person, for it is not an autobiography. Rather it is dedicated to all missionaries throughout the world who daily face circumstances that, tragically, endanger their health, morale, faith and ultimately, their very lives.

This story, that, until now, has remained hidden deeply in my heart, must be told so that the truth may be known and acknowledged by the whole world. First of all by you, citizens of Burundi, who were involved in the conflict, and your descendants who have since been born, who need to know more about the events of May '72. Then, by the whole African world, where racial hatred reigns in almost every country of the dark continent. As you examine the atrocities described in this book, may you look into your own situations and your broken hearts and realize there are definitely solutions to political situations that would bring about peace and harmony rather then violence and chaos. May you recognize, in the mirror of Burundi, that you are looking at the same barbarism in the Congo, Sudan, Ivory Coast, Algeria, Sierra Leone, Uganda, Rwanda, and still Burundi today. Somehow, the pressure placed on Burundi by European countries at the end of the month of May, 1972, forced the Batutsi army to halt its killing of the Bahutu. May those of us who live outside Burundi realize the important role that is ours to support those now governing this small Central African country, so that their first priority for everyman will be the respect for human life. Let us do everything in our power to prevent further bloodshed. Enough bodies have been thrown into rivers, too many men and women have been buried in common graves, enough huts have been burned, too many limbs have been severed, enough women have been raped, too many children have been traumatized to allow those who govern Burundi to ignore the fangs of continuous, horrendous genocide. As Pope Paul VI said at the United Nations on October 4, 1965: "Never, never, never again may there be war!" The large catholic population of Burundi did not savor this message in '72 and has yet to apprehend it today.

The African language, spoken by both the Bahutu and the Batutsi of Burundi, is Kirundi. Kirundi is a Bantu dialect spoken by the now 6.5 million people living in Burundi. The root of the word, unlike in English, is at the end of the word and the prefixes are adapted to show people, numbers, classes and things. For example, in the root RUNDI which means "that which is of the earth", one person is prefixed by MU, murundi = one person. The plural, "many people" is contained in the prefix BA. Barundi basoma Kirundi. (Burundians speak Kirundi) As in Latin, the person denoted as the subject of the verb, is contained in the verb: note BAsoma means they speak. The singular would read: Murundi asoma Kirundi (A Burundian speaks Kirundi). Note the verb is in the third person singular, a-soma.

There are 10 different classes of Kirundi words, each having singular and plural prefixes. The adjectives must agree with the nouns. Bagore (women) bane (four) bagenda (went) kwa (to) Bujumbura.

Further any geographical area is prefaced by BU. Burundi is the country of the people. Bubeligie is Belgium, Bulyaya is Europe, Bukanada is Canada and Buamerika is the United States. Of the ten classes, one is for intelligent human beings MU/BA, one is for unintelligent beings MU/MI. Another is for animals; I (singular) I (plural) I-nka (cow), I-nka (cows). Many times in the book, I will use Kirundi words rather than the English, for a two-fold reason. This was the way we normally spoke as missioners, using the Kirundi word even if we were speaking French. Secondly, why translate when we were only using French as a vehicle to explain what the Barundi thought or said about something We would use their own words, the language of the people and the country. We called most people by their Kirundi (last) names: Kabura, Sabimana, Bucumi rather than their equivalent christian (first) names: Maria, Domitila, Paulo.

Barundi do not live in cities, towns or villages. Being in a very mountainous and unleveled country, they live on the hillsides often half-way up the mountain, so that they receive the rain twice: when it falls and when it seeps down from the top of the mountain. The people have banana trees around their homes and a fence to contain cattle during the night. Their main foods are: beans, sweet potatoes, peas, sorghum, bananas, corn, manioc, beef and chicken. They drink coffee, tea, milk (children) and banana or sorghum beer. Most water in infected and a cause of sickness, especially malaria. Many have built immune systems that prevent illness. The women and girls wear blouses and skirts with a long impuzu (sari) covering them from shoulders to feet. The men wear trousers or shorts and shirts or sweaters. Neither gender wears shoes unless they are able to afford this luxury and then buy them (the plastic variety) at some marketplaces. Burundi's national debt to other countries in 2002 was 1.133 billion USD.

Their houses are also built very simply. A pole, hewn from local wood about 3-4 meters high, is planted in the middle of where the house will stand. Posts are inserted in a circle, often 10-12 meters from the main pole and circling around it. The posts are then tied together with cord, and mud is smeared both outside and inside. The central pole supports the whole house and cords and branches are then tied from the center of the cone-shaped roof to the top of the posts making the roof of the house. Hay is then placed from the top of the central pole down to the top of the posts. Heavy rocks are placed on top of the hay, to prevent the roof from blowing off.

The Batutsi are herdsmen and live by the produce of cows, sheep and lambs. When they need money, they will sell a cow or slaughter one, and sell the meat and entrails at the marketplace. The Bahutu are very different. They live off the land and plant and harvest twice a year when the rains do not fail. They plant their gardens and carry the produce to the marketplace to sell and trade. People from different areas cultivate different products. So the market is very necessary in their lives.

The marketplace in Burundi is the center of every district. Normally there are two market-days per week at the town center. People often walk ten to fifteen kilometers to come to the market, and set up areas where they can deal their products. Usually a cow is slaughtered and the meat sold individually by kilograms to those who are interested. The marketplace is also a social arena. Boys and girls come to know each other and sometimes even talk and spend time with each other. When a couple comes to the parish to register for marriage, they will often say that they met at the isoko (marketplace). In fact, only at the marketplace and at church can the young people meet each other.

But famine is still the scourge of Burundi. The rainy season in Central Africa is from October to May with some drought after Christmas. However there are years when the rains are late, or don't come at all. The people cannot plant their gardens and thus have nothing at harvest time. If this happens for an extended time, there is famine throughout the area. Sometimes the lack of rain is only in parts of the country and thus trading at the local marketplace is an excellent response in needy times.

The Burundi countryside is one of the most beautiful and picturesque in the world. The high altitude with huge valleys below give you the impression that you have never disembarked from your airplane. The zigzagged, clay roads that climb high into the green mountains give the impression of a snake crawling on bright green grass. The banana trees, mostly planted around houses, situated half-way up the mountain side, add more color to the scenery. At the bottom of the hills, there is always a marsh or small irrigated area, that allows them to go down and do their cultivating, sometimes even in the dry season. The main roads are usually very narrow. When two cars are crossing, both must slow down to avoid an accident. Often, during the rainy season, the main roads are washed out and bridges, that are numerous, are carried away by the high waters in the brooks and rivers.

Burundi is a very small country, not very visible on a map of Africa. The country has three different borders. Rwanda is to the north and Tanzania straddles the east and southern borders. To the west is Lake Tanganyika and the shores of the Democratic Republic of the Congo. In all, Burundi is only 27,830 sq. km, slightly smaller than the U.S. State of Maryland. The altitude varies from 770 m to 2,670 m above sea level, making Burundi's climate very temperate, between 17 to 23 degrees centigrade throughout the year. The average annual rainfall is about 150 cm. The present population is estimated at 6.5 million, an increase of 55% over the past 35 years since the events of this book. 46% of the population is below 15 years of age. The median age is 16.6 years. 6% of the total population is living with HIV/AIDS.

Of the Barundi population, 63% is Roman Catholic with mass conversions having taken place between 1935 and 1955. Other christian religions are 10%. The Roman Catholic Church of Burundi was established with the arrival of the first missionaries (White Fathers) in 1898. The people sought the catholic faith in large numbers. Many chiefs were baptized and along with them, thousands of their tribesmen. Large churches were built, some 90 meters in length. Some parishes, in 1972, had over 50,000 baptized catholics. An average parish in the Butova area was between 15,000 and 20,000. The churches were built of red-clay bricks that usually were made on the spot. The former church would then serve as the catechumenate. Often, parishes had over 3,000 catechumens preparing for baptism during a four-year period. Most small protestant groups developed slowly and today there are not many congregations throughout the country. The Moslems, 10% of the total population, live on the west coast of Lake Tanganyika near the capital where they own duka (shops) or are involved in other commerce. The final 17% could be listed as animists, belief in one God but with no religious persuasion.

Behind every human being in this book is a real person whose heart contains the love and presence of God but whose body has a tendency towards evil. With great heroism, the grace of inner strength defeats the pangs of evil. But unfortunately, at many other times, the forces of the evil one far overpower the good. The complexity of our human condition and freedom, witnesses evil triumphing over good. In the events that follow, the stories weigh more on the power of sin despite the presence of Grace and the Love of God. It is for each character to realize the gift of freedom and the magnificence of God to allow goodness to be subjugated in many conditions. Each character is a study of good and evil, grace and sin, God and Satan. To those who triumphed, we say: "Praised be God." To those who failed, we recognize God's wonderful gift of liberty.

I wrote this book and chose my second and third names as my character: Anthony Joseph. At the time of the genocide, I was twenty-eight years of age, and a priest of the White Fathers, a religious community founded to implant the Catholic faith in Africa. I had been recently appointed as pastor of Butova parish, in the south of Burundi, where the number of baptized people in our area was 22,000. The story is told through my eyes, my perceptions and my perspectives. It contains a glimpse of youthful enthusiasm swallowed up by the discouragement of people living in hatred.

Fr. Jose Suarez is a Spaniard and also a White Fathers priest in Butova. He has little order and personal discipline and seems to always be doing obnoxious things, but is on fire with zeal for the love of God and his people.

Fr. Luigi Franco is an Italian Missionary of Francis-Xavier and also a priest in Butova. He has been appointed to learn Kirundi there and acclimatize himself to the kirundi culture, to examine the pastoral ways of the White Fathers and then be sent to another parish of the Vurura Diocese.

Luc Grange is a young nineteen-year-old Frenchman doing his military service. He has been commissioned to go to Butova and establish a co-operative there and help people manage economically amid the scarcity of food and the lack of financial stability.

Bishop Bernard Moulin is a Belgian White Father and Roman Catholic bishop of the local diocese of Vurura. He founded the diocese in 1961 after having headed the diocese of Zugozi in the north, from 1949-1961. He has a good sense of humor, tells many jokes, speaks strait-forwardly and acts and makes decisions impulsively, without sufficient reflection.

Monsignor Luduvico Ruyaga is the vicar general and is being prepared to succeed Bishop Moulin. He's very calm and likeable in nature and the obvious public relations man for the Roman Catholic Church. He is a Mututsi and very shrewd.

Other priests in neighboring parishes and playing a large role in the book are: Walter De Winter (Lutana), Angelo Bertuzzi, Pedro Sanchez, Raphael Saturnino (Mutwe).

The Brothers of Christian Instruction are from Quebec, Canada. Brother Alex Labine is the superior of their mission and director of the Teachers' Training College at Butova. Brother Jean-Guy Tranchemontagne and Brother Louis are among the ten members of their local community.

Many Barundi were born in the Bututsi area which was in the south-center of the country: the President of the Republic and leader of the l'UPRONA Party, Etinenne Sabimana (name means: "Pray to God", even though his parents were animists); Arturo Shabaru, Minister of Defense; Tomasi Muhwa (means "Thorn"), Director of the Experimental Farm; Alberto Kizungu (name means: "White Skinned, European"), local administrator at Puma; Samueli Kufa (name means: "Death"), squad leader of the soldiers at Puma; Martino Kupiga (name means: "to Beat or to Strike"), chief of police. Others still lived at Butova: Cypriano Kitwa, the cook; Jean-Bosco Musaba (name means: "Prayer"), the secretary; +Alfredo, +Luduvico, +Osicari, the three cooks of the European couples teaching at the TTC.

Other prominent people working at the church were: +Petero Tumba, trained catechist; +DeoGratias (name means: "Thanks be to God", in Latin) Pungu, catechist and secretary; Yohani Bora (of Mundi), Bora means "Good"; Danieli Rutega (of Vuvoga); Eusebio Bitega (of Lusaga).

Burundi is composed of two mayor tribes: Bahutu, forming 85% of the entire population and Batutsi, 14%. There is also 1% Batwa (pygmies) who live by themselves in the forest and seldom communicate with others outside their boundries. They remain isolated from all community life in the country and call themselves "children". The Bahutu are basically Bantu people who are often short and stocky, with round faces that smile and laugh unceasingly. They are hard workers and draw their subsistence from the land. They eat vegetables and drink banana or sorghum beer. The Batutsi are Hermitic and originate from north-east Africa. They are tall and light skinned with majestic looking faces and long pointed noses. Their features are usually large and impressionable. They live by the money they make on their cattle. They sell cows or goats or their milk and chickens at the marketplace. They do some gardening and live off the produce of beans, millet and manioc. There is some intermarriage between Batutsi and Bahutu but not on a large scale. Usually the man will be Muhutu who will take a Mututsikazi wife.

Both the Bahutu from the now Central African Republic and the Batutsi from Ethiopia, descended to present-day Burundi in the fourteenth or fifteenth century. Even though there was little intermarriage, nevertheless, both tribes lived side-by-side throughout the country. However there is a predominance of Batutsi in the south, whereas the north is almost all Bahutu.

The Batutsi are a very striking looking people with long-thin features (height, faces, noses, fingers, toes). In general, they possess a very serious demeanor. The Bahutu, on the contrary, are much shorter than the Batutsi, stocky, with round faces and have a very jovial temperament. There are 5.5 Bahutu to every Mututsi and thus one area of conflict between them is that, since independence from Belgium on July 1st 1962, the Batutsi have governed and dominated the Bahutu with force. Over the years, most of the military (army) were Batutsi and thus the Bahutu were suppressed continually. Similarly in the field of education, the Batutsi always had places in schools whereas it was rare that Bahutu children were allowed secondary education.

After the First World War, the protective state of Rwanda-urundi passed from the Germans to the Belgians. Belgium, unlike the British in East Africa, did very little to develop life in Burundi. The Barundi became disillusioned with the European leadership or lack of same. Thus, when many African countries were becoming independent in the early sixties, it was obvious that Burundi wanted freedom from Belgium as soon as possible. This was a horrible mistake that a less abrupt severing of ties could have prevented. Burundi became a constitutional monarchy in 1962 and Prince Louis Rwagasore became head of state. When Colonel Michel Micombero took power with a bloodless coup d'etat in November, 1966, he became the First President of the Republic of Burundi. Under his governance, tension grew between the two tribes to the point of arrests of Bahutu and executions in 1969, that lead to the genocide in 1972, described in this work. However trouble between the two tribes has seen hundreds of thousands killed over the past thirty-five years, with 200,000 exterminated in 1993 alone, and 150,000 in 1972, the story of this book.

Jean-Bapiste Bagaza, Micombero's cousin, took power by a coup d'etat in 1976. Seven years later, Pierre Buyoya became president of the Republic by another coup. He led the people to their first democratic elections in

1993 and they elected a Muhutu as President: Melchor Ndadaye. He was assassinated in October. His interim replacement was killed along with the President of Rwanda on April 6, 1994. Within six months, the Barundi had murdered the first two Bahutu presidents. Buyoya took back power in 1996 after another successful coup. When the accords for peace in Arusha, Tanzania, came in 2003, Domitien Ndayizeye was appointer president and after the second democratic election in 2005, the people choose Pierre Nkurunziza who is still president at the time of this writing.

I would like to present the following as a personal witness of the events that took place in the south of Burundi, in May, 1972. Over three weeks, from May 4th to 26th, 1,500 Bahutu were executed in Rutovu where I lived, an area inhabited by 47,000. In all Burundi, of a 850,000 able-bodied-adult-male population, 150,000 Bahutu were murdered. That was 17% of the whole country's population! The truths of this massacre are hopefully explained in this work.

I would like to thank the people who have helped me with this writing. Melinda my lovely wife, who was always helpful, encouraging and visionary, and our little son, Anthony, who was born after this book was started and who allowed me the time and space to write in peace…sometimes! My heart-felt thanks to Bruce Boggiss for his proof reading and many helpful suggestions. "You have encouraged me so much and reminded me that this book had to be written." To Michael Lawrence, who was very helpful with proofing, and helping me to get the book to print. "Michael, your availability as well as your careful guidance to better the story, encourage me to spend long hours getting the work 'just right.' Thank you, Dear Friend, for your kindness and help."

Rev. Malcolm Smith

1 A Month Of Horrors

Fr. Tony Joseph arose with the sound of his alarm at 5:45 am. He groped for his slippers in his dark bedroom and slipped on his bath robe that he had slung over his bed to keep him warm during the night. He could never get use to the cold Burundi nights and especially the chill from the high altitude of Butova. Opening his door and walking down the outdoor corridor toward the small sink in the public area outside the chapel, he began washing his face and combing his hair. He wondered if the natural urge to brush his teeth would ever leave him. Since the running water was germ-infested and had been the cause of many of his colleagues getting dysentery, teeth-brushing would come later in purified water he had in his room. In the distance, dawn was breaking. Tony loved this early hour when life all around him seemed to be birthed anew with the anticipation of the adventures of a fresh day.

Back inside his room, Fr. Tony reviewed his Sunday homily. He felt excited that this was the first Sunday with him fully installed as *Pati Mukuru* (Pastor) of Butova Parish. At the end of both masses, he would tell the people how happy he was to be their pastor and how he counted on them to collaborate in building the parish into the visible expression of Christ's love. He dressed quickly and his mind drifted back to the many Sundays he had spent with Mathias Becker whom he now was replacing as parish priest. Mathias had taught him so much about the work and life among the peoples of Burundi. Both priests always dressed neatly in suit, white shirt and tie when they were at the central mission of Butova on Sundays to show their respect for their parishioners. Even if most of their people were poor and could not afford new haberdashery, yet it was important to them that their priests dress as neatly and as cleanly as possible. He knotted his tie, and brushed his suit coat and smiled as he recalled how he and Mathias used to tease each other about their neatness. Two Sundays previous, the former pastor's last in Butova, Mathias had put his long strong arms around Tony on the steps of the church and asked the people to be loving and kind to his successor. He then hugged Tony and told the people: "Our fathers were on opposing sides during the last World War, thirty years ago when the Germans fought against the Canadians. Yet now we two, a German and a Canadian, work together and live together and love each other as brothers!"

"You, too," Mathias had pointed at the hundreds of people standing before him, "can love those whose fathers hated your fathers. We must break the cycle of hatred and war and bring God's gift of peace to this country, *Burundi Bwacu* (our Beloved Burundi)."

Tony smiled as he felt Mathias' presence even though the former pastor was now far away in Germany. He continued to live on through his words and proverbs and seeds of wisdom that he had planted in the hearts of so many during his past six years as parish priest. Tony was determined to keep Mathias' memory and message alive. The seeds he had sown would continue to take root, grow and germinate into tall trees in this materially and educationally poor country of Central Africa..

After spending some time in the house-chapel re-reading the prayers for Mass in Kirundi, Tony walked into the refectory where Jose Suarez and Luigi Franco, his two confreres, were already eating breakfast and conversing very animatedly. Jose was from Spain and had been in the country for nine years. He was a small man, with a rather dark complexion. His hair was black and curly and seldom combed. He cared little about his appearance and usually wore a heavy maroon sweater in the coolness of the early morning and his dark blue pants often had a stain or two running down them. The only clothing change he ever made was to put on his religious habit over his other clothes. His gandurah (habit of the White Fathers) was usually dark khaki and often carried on it mud and dirt of many motorcycle trips. This Sunday morning, he still had to dress to go by motorcycle to the outstation of Lusaga where he would celebrate two masses for the people there.

"Have you heard the news from Vurura?" Jose asked looking at Tony walking to his place at table.

"What happened?"

"Well, it's not clear but there was some trouble last night and some government officials are dead. Nyandwi has been killed!" Jose said making reference to the local governor whom they both had met many times. He went on:

"They are reporting from Bujarundi that the military camp was attacked and that the soldiers have killed quiet a few of the assailants. The radio report is calling them traitors. They are saying that peace has been restored throughout the country. However they fail to mention any other areas where attacks have taken place. Governor Nyandwi was killed in the capital. It seems that many government officials were invited to *Soirees Dansantes* (Dancing Evenings) in *calabu* (drinking clubs) in Bujarundi and throughout the country and at a given signal, an attempted *coup d'etat* (palace revolt) was made by killing all the officials. All this happened at

8 o'clock last night. *'La Voix de la Revolution'* (radio station) has denied that anyone ever took over the radio station but they did mention that one attempt to control the country via the airwaves failed early last night. The radio is announcing that all citizens are to remain calm for there is peace throughout the country." Tony's eyes met Jose's as he asked:

"What about the President? Is he all right?"

"They keep saying that he is safe and in some secure unidentified place." Jose responded. "Maybe he will come to Butova." President Sabimana, a personal friend of the fathers, would surely be alright if he were to come to his home area of Butova. The three missionaries agreed that it would be nice to host the president at a time of difficulty even though such a happening could have negative repercussions on the mission in a country so divided by tribalism. President Sabimana had been born and raised on Ruhaha, a hillside facing the mission. He loved to return home and did so often. Once he came to the mission over Holy Week and made a retreat in silence by himself.

Tony bolted from the dining area to his room and turned on his radio. It was difficult to pick up Bujarundi and he patiently played with the fine-tuner on his Hitachi. A solemn male voice gave two or three choppy sentences, amid loud wiry whistling sounds, confirming news similar to what Jose had said. Some seconds of instrumental music played for a time that seemed endless to the anxious missionary and then the voice continued with further short, almost incoherent, excerpts. The announcer was telling the people to stay calm, that peace had been restored and the 'culprits' responsible for the mutiny were apprehended and would be punished. He made it clear that the army had everything under control. The broadcast then seemed to become clearer and a strong, very patriotic voice stated:

"Colonel Etienne Sabimana, Clairvoyant Chief, First President and Liberator of the Peoples of Burundi is safe and hidden in an undisclosed location." As was the custom of the people of Burundi, hand-clapping always accompanied the mention of the president's name. When the announcer had mentioned "President Etienne Sabimana" there was a short halt in the speech. Then the hand clapping began, three times three. Tony had heard this kind of clapping many times, countless occasions in the past. Nine claps of unenthusiastic repetition did more to show lackadaisical disinterest than grateful appreciation for the person who was Head of State.

Sabimana was the president of the country and the leader of the only political party: l'UPRONA, that promoted a three fold slogan: Unity, Progress and Work. So anytime the president was mentioned in public, it was expected that all would applaud these three values threefold. It seemed childish and foolhardy, but the government officials demanded that their motto be respected to the highest degree. Tony had snickered as he thought how there was no unity in this country so divided because of tribalry (word invented to change adjective to noun). There was no organized work since there was no industry in Burundi. The men never helped the women with their chores around the *rugo* (courtyard). Most men did little more than look after their own cattle.

"No unity! No work! and No progress!" Tony smirked as he thought of their Machiavellian jingle. This proposed thesis for freedom was more of an antithesis. For a moment he wondered whether the government in general and his friend Etienne Sabimana in particular might have deceived the poor people. Could this, coming over the radio, be another configuration of deception? Tony caught himself thinking that way. He shook his head and murmured: "No! No! No!" He chose not to reexamine the possibility of *kitutsi* shrewdness but rather quietly convinced himself that all would work out for the best. He was an eternal optimist and wanted to see the government putting the needs of the poor people first.

Tony found the sacristy to be quieter than usual that early Sunday morning. Anyone who needed to speak only did so in whispers. There was no *camaraderie* or small-talk. Tony enjoyed the quiet that contrasted sharply with the noisy excitement that greeted each preliturgical gathering on a normal Sunday morning in the parish. He took the time to pray quietly for the country and asked the Lord to give peace to the people of Burundi.

As he vested for Mass, his eyes caught those of Sister Maragarita, a Beneterezia nun who worked full time as choir director and catechetical teacher of the many childrens' groups of Butova. Since there was no place for all the children in the public schools, it was the responsibility of the mission to form classes for those left behind and try to teach them the essentials of hygiene, gardening, religion, reading and writing. Maragarita was a robust, dark-skinned young nun who had been assigned to the parish for the past year. She had bright sparkling cheeks and was a picture of beauty as the sun's reflection created different shades of light on her countenance. Her face shinned like the sun when she smiled. Her habit was all white, starched and pressed to perfection. A red chord, holding a stainless-steel crucifix over her chest, dangled from her neck. Her hem line was rather short and Tony often thought that the religious habits of young sisters 'now-a-days' often resembled mini-skirts more than the long flowing robes of previous generations of pre-Vatican II nuns. The habit she wore this Sunday was relatively conservative running below her knees and she wore a pair of brown sandals that were adorned with flashy pearl-colored beads. Maragarita enjoyed teaching the many groups of children that the parish organized. These programs called *Bana Bakristu* (Christian Children) had been a particularly large undertaking.

However the fathers had all found Sr. Maragarita very lazy and lacking in convictions on certain occasions. At these times, she certainly didn't help them very much. Nonetheless she loved to sing and never missed a Sunday with the choir. But she was often late for her classes or choir practice and set a very bad example. Mathias had scolded her many times, yet she always succeeded in coming up with an excuse, usually blaming others for her tardiness or saying that she had too much work to do for one person. For that reason, the sisters offered another nun, Sr. Anunciata, to assist Maragarita. But alas, she too was often late or absent.

Mathias had mentioned to Tony that Sr. Maragarita was one problem that he would have to deal with as pastor. Obviously it was not time for him to request a replacement, but if Maragarita didn't improve, he would be forced to talk to Mother Gaudentia, the Superior General of the Beneterezia Sisters. He had met the Reverend Mother many times in Gisumu and she seemed to respect the young missionary. Above all he had trouble tolerating Sr. Maragarita's obviously lackadaisical ways. Her attitude reflected indifference to life in general and Church work in particular.. She didn't seem to have a care in the world, least of all about being on time and prepared for class! This Sunday morning, their eyes met in a lengthy stare across the sacristy but then Tony looked away, not wanting to convey the negative feelings he had about her.

As the mass procession began this Third Sunday of Easter, Tony noticed two things that alarmed him very much. He couldn't believe the congregation was so small at the early morning mass. Usually the church filled to capacity about five to seven minutes before the start of the eucharist. But this Sunday indicated there would be less people than even at a weekday mass. In fact, as the procession wended it's way toward the main altar, he glanced at his watch thinking there might be some mistake and that he had begun the entrance five or ten minutes early. But, no, he was right on time.

The second troublesome concern was that as he looked at the faces of those who were in the church and as their eyes met his, he could read panic and fear in everyone, as trauma glumly painted the expressive countenances of all he perceived. Their eyes seemed exceedingly large and their whole faces drawn and droopy. As soon as they would recognize his eyes on them, they glanced away, apparently looking at some invisible object that attracted their attention in the far distance.

Tony recalled the last time he had experienced such feelings. He had driven a young mother to hospital to give birth to her sixth child. The baby was still-born and the mother died on the delivery table as well. He had taken the woman's mother-in-law, the mid-wife, with him to the hospital. So he had found himself driving the mother-in-law back to an African hut on a bright moon-lit night to tell the devastating news to the deceased woman's husband and other members of her family. He recalled how he looked at them, his eyes moving from one to the other and all of them staring blindly into the distant hills made visible by the light of the moon. These feelings of sadness, so dreary and dismal, moved Tony beyond words and now they came back to him as he stared at his parishioners while descending in procession. The common message conveyed that the political events threatened everyone and what had already happened would continue to bring harm and suffering to all the Barundi people. Fr. Tony approached the altar and asked God to help him to celebrate one of the most meaningful masses of his life and, through the miracle of the eucharist, bring stability and peace to the peoples of Burundi (country).

Tony had been looking forward to this Sunday Mass because April 30th was the feast day dedicated to Our Lady of Africa. Over the course of the past week, he had reminisced about the special times he had in the seminary on this day when the White Fathers rededicated themselves in a special way to their patroness: The Black Virgin, Mother of all Africans. His mind quickly recalled the many years in the seminary when he and his colleagues never would think of beginning their recreation before praying an 'Ave' to the Virgin. Every night they intoned the *Sancta Maria* (Holy Mary) at the end of night prayers. He entrusted the political situation to the Blessed Mother hoping she could help bring peace to the country. As he went to the altar he believed in the change of bread and wine into the Body of Christ. Would this be an analogy of the political situation of Butova changing into hope and peace.

Mass lasted about ninety minutes. The parishioners participated by singing and saying prayers and answering invocations loudly. As Tony concluded the Mass, he thanked the people for their support in his new ministry as pastor. He told them that he would always count on their collaboration:

"I am still a child, when it comes to speaking your beautiful language. However if you help me, I will grow up fast and someday speak like Father Matahasi and Bishop Bernardo," he said. They all responded appreciatively and the women started their chant of joy and exultation.

Outside, little by little, the people started to disperse and walk toward the main roads that would lead them to their villages and hillsides. But this

Sunday was very different from the normal joyful dominical respite that the people of Butova seemed to appreciate so much. Tony's eyes smiled at many in the gathering outside church as they exchanged: *"Amakuru maki?.....Amahoro!"* (What's the news? Peace!) But unlike former happier times, there was a long empty stare after their responses and many reflected the fear and panic that was obviously in their hearts. A realization of the stark seriousness of the political situation seemed to be caught up in each and every exchange.

Crossing over the courtyard and walking down the driveway to the priests' house, Tony saw some men with a portable radio. They had gathered together with one man holding the voice box high in the air hoping to get better reception. He nodded to the pastor invitingly, but did not say a word. The radio station was *La Voix de la Revolution*, the Burundi national radio station from Bujarundi and the announcer was saying in slow, simple Kirundi (language) that there had been an attempted palace revolt the previous night. The attack had been toppled by government soldiers but there had been many hundreds of deaths, among them some very prominent government officials. The newsman also added that there was only one area, in the southland, that was still held by the rebels: the catholic mission of Burome. Tony glanced at the men listening to the portable radio. They seemed very alarmed and apprehensive.

The mission of Burome was where Jose Suarez had first been appointed as a young missionary. He often talked about it. The present pastor was a bush missionary in every sense of the word. He had developed his own brand of cheese that had a very revolting odor to it. Every week each of the thirteen parishes in the diocese would send a runner to the diocesan headquarters of Vurura on Thursday and they would pick up all the inter-parochial mail that evening and return home the following day with a trunk of mail carried majestically on their heads. The pastor of Burome was very enterprising and took advantage of the local mails to fill orders of cheese for parishes that desired a stronger aroma than most African cheese makers were prepared to supply. So the stinky cheese accompanied the runner from Burome to Vurura and then, after a night smelling up diocesan headquarters, was dispersed by other runners to the four corners of the diocese!

Burome was not a very significant area of southern Burundi. It was not like Butova that was one of the most political corners of the country. Politicians had been born and raised on many of these hillsides. The President, Etienne Sabimana, came from the hillside facing the mission. Bonaventuro Ruha, who held the three fold title of Ambassador to the UN, the USA and Canada, came from Bihovu, to the southwest of Butova.. The former minister of finance, Paulo Minani and Tomasi Muhwa, the director of the experimental farm were also home grown. Even though Muhwa had a very influential position, nevertheless, he was not in politics. Since he was an intimate boyhood friend of President Sabimana, he had appointed himself political overseer of the Bututsi. In his case, he didn't need an appointment. Friendship with the president and loyalty to the Batutsi cause were all that mattered. Then arrogance took over for Muhwa. Over the next four weeks, he was to show himself as the malicious tyrant of the Bututsi.

Usually after Sunday Mass, Tony would go to the catechumenate where hundreds of adults, learning the Catholic faith, would remain for a further instruction from the priest. Tony enjoyed this time with these very special people who were often quite enthusiastic about learning their prayers and hearing Gospel stories.. Usually they were older couples whose grown children had already been baptized. The church had a rule that if someone were married and wanted to be baptized and become catholic, one had to come accompanied by one's spouse. That presumed an ending of all polygamous relationships before starting the catechumenate. So most catechumens attended as couples even though they never sat together. Rather facing the front of the classroom, the men were on the right side and the women on the left, with the babies and children near them. The catechumenate was usually filled with an equal number of men and women because of the rules for couples.

As Fr. Tony went through the dining room to get a quick cup of coffee, his mind focused on the bleak political situation that had developed in Burundi. The cook, Cypriano Kitwi, heard him in the dining area and came in to see what he needed. Tony told him he only wanted a quick coffee and then he would be off to the catechumenate. However Cypriano told him that he could see out his kitchen window and that there hadn't been a service in the catecumenate since very few people showed up. Even the catechists weren't there. Tony wanted to panic, wondering if this were just a sign that people were petrified and stayed close to their huts. He realized that all the people attending the mass had been regulars who were so accustomed to attending Sunday morning mass that they couldn't imagine doing anything else on the first day of the week.

Tony moved to the table, lifted out a heavy oak chair and sat down to better evaluate the situation. Brother Alex Labine opened the dining room door and came in. Alex said that he didn't have time for a cup of coffee but that he just dropped in to get Tony's evaluation of the political situation. Brother Alex was the director of the Butova Teachers' Training College. The Canadian Brothers of Christian Instruction (they were called f.i.c.: *Freres de l'Instruction Chretienne,* but f.r.i.c. was also the French slang for "money". Thus they got much kidding from other missionaries.) their community had replaced some of the priests of Tony's community, the Missionaries of Africa (also White Fathers), three years previously and the school had instantly become one of the best secondary institutions in Burundi. The brothers were born teachers and became very close to their students. They had three hundred and fifty young men in the four levels and all lived in the big long dormitories behind the school. The brothers had more money for schooling than did the missionary fathers and thus they upgraded the school materially as well as academically. Tony, being Canadian, felt close to the brothers as they all had a common heritage.

However Alex was a rather cold and self-righteous individual. He was one of those educated persons who would let you know that you couldn't tell him anything. So Tony thought it surprising that Alex had come over to question what the priests knew about the political problems. The year before, when Mathias Becker had been in charge, the two communities had quite a problem.

One of the brothers, Jules Caron, taught religion and catechetics at the school. He had approached Mathias to do Sunday ministry in the different outstations. As a brother he could not celebrate mass. However Mathias suggested that on Sunday mornings Brother Jules would go to an outstation, one that would be about two hours walk from the central parish. He would travel on foot with six or seven of his students who would animate the service by leading singing and doing the readings. In this way, the people could receive holy communion during their usual Sunday service that was deprived of the sacrament. These outstations usually had three or four catechists, but they were no priests, no eucharist, no communion. Jules loved the outings and he was doing a loyal service for the priests as well as for the people.

Soon Jules was so caught up in this ministry that he met with Mathias and told him that he believed he was being called to be a priest for the catholic diocese of Vurura. Mathias, in turn, became very enthusiastic and encouraged him to see Bishop Bernard Moulin immediately. Every member of the clergy, especially those closest to the bishop, recognized a common fault the Ordinary had. They affectionately called him *Natura Prima* (primary in nature) because when confronted with a situation, problem, or trauma, the bishop would immediately give a solution. Sad to say, he would often be wrong but, better to err than to be surpassed by someone else! His decisions were quick, straightforward, and often lacking reflection. But this was Bishop Moulin at his forthright, candid best, which seemed to be his only way of dealing with the realities confronting the diocese.

Bishop Moulin was very excited about getting another priest for Vurura diocese. Since he had met the recently-appointed Archbishop of Montreal, Canada, at a meeting in Rome the previous year, he saw an ideal opportunity of asking him to accept Caron for theological studies in *le Grand Seminaire de Montreal.* The Archbishop would probably handle the expenses as a way of helping a missionary diocese. Caron was originally from Montreal and so the situation seemed heavenly-made. Caron would then come back to Vurura as a diocesan priest for Moulin and the catholic church of Vurura.

Jules Caron had said nothing of these plans to Alex Labine or the other brothers of his community. He even thought that Alex would throw spanner in the work of his plans if he knew that the zealous brother had gone over his head to deal directly with the bishop. Besides being the director of the school, Alex was also the local superior as the F.I.C. community had told him he was the one responsible for the entire mission in Burundi.

Mathais had met Alex on the road one day and, thinking that Jules had been sharing all his plans with his superior, had mentioned how happy he was that the situation was working out. Alex was suspicious enough to ask a few pointed questions and was not pleased in the least with what Matthias told him since he knew nothing whatsoever about Caron's plans. Needless to say, he was embarrassed and humiliated to hear all this from Mathias, a person outside his community.

Jules Caron's situation would soon become very miserable indeed. Another brother, Jean-Guy Tranchemontagne often sent roles of film to a Belgian Photo Studio to be processed. Caron decided to do the same. One day Brother Tranchemontagne excitingly opened a packet noting the Belgian return address without checking the addressee's name on the front label. He went right to the photos, believing they were the ones he had taken of his classroom and some of the boys playing volleyball and soccer in the school yard. How shocked was this religious brother, when he looked at the first photo! He recognized the boy as a student in his first year at the Teachers' Training College. The boy was entirely nude and innocently looking out at the camera, shyly. Tranchemontagne was horrified and nervously fumbled for the next photo and it was of another student also posing naked in front of a bed. He quickly went from photo to photo and they were all the same. They were posed in a well-lighted room and most of the boys were students in their first year who were slender in build and looked innocent and bashful. As he flipped through other photos, he was mystified by what he was seeing. Even though these scenes seemed foreign to him, he recognized the boys and even knew each one by name. Jean-Guy understood that there was a mistake in identities and flipped the packet over to the address. Thus he saw Jules Caron's name on the front of the envelope. All at once, like a blindfold falling from his eyes, he realized what had happened. His greatest suspicions were confirmed when he saw three snapshots of a group of students, fully clothed, walking with Jules Caron in the middle of the group carrying the Blessed Sacrament to an outstation!

"*Fils d'une chienne!*" (son of a bitch) the brother heard himself say: "Maudit Caron!"(damn Caron) He flipped over the envelope again and stared at Caron's name on the front label. Going outside from the common room where he had opened the envelope, Jean-Guy found Labine in the courtyard talking to one of the Canadian lay teachers who lived with his wife on the same compound as the brothers. They taught science and geography at the school. The burdened brother went right to Alex and said he had to see him immediately. The two brothers bid the professor *adieu* (good bye) and walked away. The younger man handed the evidence to Alex as he said with rousing anger in his voice: "This will show the bishop that Jules Caron wants something very different from the priesthood, *maudit castor*! (damn beaver)"

The director took the envelope from him and, trying to shake off Tranchemontagne's verbal outburst, opened it suspiciously:

"*Tabarnush*" (French slang for tabernacle) he exclaimed as he looked at the photos and blushed innocently.

"I will take these to the bishop at once" he said.

Jean-Guy added that he would accompany Alex, since the distance to Vurura diocesan headquarters was about an hour both ways.

Tony, on this Sunday morning, looked across the table at Alex and said:

"We should have known something was in the air for the last few weeks," the pastor said. "Ten days ago when we came back from leaving Mathias at the airport in Bujarundi, we were stopped by soldiers at many different checkpoints along the road. There were many armed soldiers searching every car. Now I know what they were looking for. I'm sure the Batutsi government was expecting this for a long time. But, according to the radio, it seems that many government officials were killed."

"It is hard to believe everything that is reported on the radio," Alex replied, "but some of the students are saying that plans to attempt a revolution had been made as far back as during the Easter vacation. The students are anxious and fearful. What is most worrisome is that we don't always know who is a Muhutu and who is Mututsi. Tony broke into a sarcastic smile and said:

"Alex, why don't you ask them?" Tony loved to tease Alex who always was so serious and solemn. He was a true phlegmatic, ever composed and giving the impression that he had every life-situation under his control. Yet when Alex appeared, it wasn't merely to have a chat or cup of coffee on his busy Sunday afternoon. He was business, all business.

Labine went on:

"I want you to know, Tony, that we are sending Jules Caron home to Canada. I have had a long talk with him and if he is to pursue his studies for the priesthood, it will have to be in Canada and outside our community. We are educators and ask our brothers to spend all their time working in the apostolate as teaching brothers. If someone wants to be a priest, we see that as a vocation not complimentary but rather apart from ours and thus he must leave the community," the director said in a pompous tone.

Tony wondered if Alex was going to tell him about the photos. So he thought to himself: "I need a little fun!" Before he could control his tongue, Tony blurted out:

"Maybe Jules can get a job in Canada as a photographer!" Alex looked up and stared straight across the table at Tony:

"You have heard of our cameraman?" the brother superior went along with the sarcasm.

"Yes, I am very sorry for this ghastly inconvenience that didn't need to come about when we are in such difficult times", Tony said seriously. Alex continued:

"Caron has told us that he is a sex-pervert, a pedophile. He has been doing this for a long time, always with boys. The boys were given high marks, clothes or food if they cooperated with him. We want to get him out of the situation before someone comes forth and puts us all in a bind." Tony looked straight at the director of this exemplary school and realized that he had a responsibility to speak the truth that the brother seemed to be avoiding.

"I know that Caron must be accountable for what he did. However he was a brother and member of your community when this happened. You have the moral responsibility to admit the fault, take your share of the blame and examine the psychological repercussions it will have and possibly has had on many of these students. Africans are more affected by immoral sexual traumas than we are from North America. You know, Alex, you sound like Pontius Pilate, washing your hands of the whole affair. There is a responsibility you must claim and own." Tony said staring across the table at Alex.

Alex started to get up from the chair and calmly said:

"We'll see when the superiors from Canada write to us about the problem. Right now, all I know is that the bishop has ordered Caron out of the diocese and we are sending him back to Canada. Let them deal with him when he gets home," the director said over his shoulder as he glanced back at the priest rising from the table to accompany him outside.

Walking back from the gate alone and up the front verandah steps, Tony felt pressure on his shoulders and in his head. Never had he ever imagined that so much could go so badly, so quickly. He entered the dining room once more and finished his coffee. He wondered where the gift of God's grace was and how he would be guided in his new office as pastor. Tony decided to write a letter to the brothers, with a copy to their Canadian superiors and another to Bishop Moulin demanding that they have an open investigation about the whole incident and that it be done with Jules Caron still in the country. He walked outside, along the verandah to his office thinking of all the particular details that he would put on paper. Tony walked briskly as his mind ran at an unbelievable pace. The clear air gave him the opportunity to focus on Caron's case and seek justice toward all the African students. The thought of Caron went through his mind and he spit in disgust thinking of the horrible deeds this presumed 'man of God' had done.

As he approached his office, Tony saw two local catechists who were waiting for him on a bench in front of his door. They exchanged greetings and asked to see him. The pastor invited them into his office and they sat down and told him how depressing everything seemed. They had come to tell him that very few catechumens showed up for the morning service. So they took the few who had come to mass in the church and then the catechumens exited before the *credo* (proclamation of the roman catholic faith), since they were not yet accountable for practicing the faith. Tony affirmed their decision, saying that a small group often led to a very lackadaisical spirit. So it was better that the novices prayed with a larger group of believers in the main church.

"The news is not good," commented Deogratias Pungu the taller of the two men who was also a secretary at the parish on days when he was not teaching in the catechumenate. Deo was over six feet tall and quite thin. He was around thirty-five years of age with shiny brown skin and a permanent frown on his forehead that made everything he said sound so serious. When Deo smiled it was rare and only for a few seconds. Yet he was always in good humor and complimented everyone around him in the office. He had a large pudgy nose and big thick lips and always wore gray pants, a blue jacket and brown sandals. Seldom did anyone ever see

Deogratias Pungu without a piece of paper and pen in his hands. He was both an excellent secretary and an outstanding catechist.

"I am afraid for our country," the other man, with a darker complexion and shiny, starry eyes, added. "The whole country is in turmoil."

Tony realized who was saying all this. It was Daudi Murore, the brother of the president, who had been a catechist at the central parish before the building of the first church in 1940. Daudi often came over to visit the fathers and convey a message from President Etienne Sabimana. It was admirable how one son was a full-time catechist-teacher for the church and the other, president of the country. Both went to daily mass and communion. Yet neither of their parents was baptized!

Daudi Murore was older than his presidential sibling. He was married and had nine children. Murore was dark skinned and shorter than Deogratias and of much smaller build. He spoke with a whispery voice as if he had sandpaper in his throat. Daudi smiled frequently and his whole face lighted up with a twinkle in his eye. He had no facial scars, rather small Mututsi lips and a small pointed nose. No matter what clothing he wore, he was always neat and clean cut. He seemed to enjoy his job as catechist and once, when Tony was preparing the pay envelopes for the catechists, he was surprised to find out that Murore only made 619 frBu per month! (frBu is Burundi francs. 100 frBu then worth $1.00 USD)

Sometimes Daudi would arrive at the mission saying that he had heard from 'the president', as he called his younger brother, and related specific messages that Sabimana wanted the fathers to know. When Sabimana stopped by to see his parents at Piga, he seldom failed to pay a courtesy visit to the mission. The missionaries appreciated the gesture that allowed them time to prepare for the presidential visit even though President Sabimana was very simple and never demanding. The fathers considered him a parishioner and close friend but respected him as the Head of State. Tony asked Daudi if he had heard from his brother since the attempted *coup*. All Daudi said was that he had heard that 'His Excellency' was in the capital since he would be making a speech that evening on the radio.

"I'll be listening" Tony reassured his catechist. Daudi and Deo stood up, shook hands in the Kirundi custom and stepped outside.

Tony's morning saw one person after another requesting a *majambo* or interview or wanting to speak to him about many various subjects. He thus was never able to start the letter about Jules Caron that he wanted to write to the brothers and the bishop. Soon Sister Maragarita was at his door as it was time to start the second mass.

"There is almost no one in the church for the service. Shall we cancel mass?" she exclaimed in a partially distraught voice. He was surprised that she had come to inform and wondered if it was excited anticipation that she wouldn't have to lead the singing if mass were canceled. Then again he concluded that it was just plain uneasiness about the unrest in the country.

"No!" Tony told her sharply, "for if we skip mass, people will feel insecure in the future, wondering if, for other reasons, he will cancel mass."

The nun turned and walked away heading for the sacristy. Tony meandered over to the church and, even if he had been forewarned by Maragarita, he was still surprised to see so few people in the church on a Sunday morning. Normally there were fewer at the second mass than at the first. In fact, those who came to the second mass were the young people who guarded their unlocked houses and cattle while the other members of the family attended the first service. Usually there were two complete hours between both services giving people the time to walk home, relieve those who had stayed behind and allow them time to come for the second service.

After mass, Tony took off his vestments quickly in the sacristy, laid them on the long table and quietly exited by the side door that led to the "*rugo*" of the fathers' house. He walked alone along the trail and unlocked the side entrance to the mission yard. Once inside, he felt some relief. He had prayed for the people involved in the political uprising as well as for those who had been killed and hoped that peace would come to Burundi as soon as possible. He thought about listening to the radio but he decided that might only make him more upset and he had a headache already from all the stress generated by the morning's disturbing news. He went out on the veranda. The day was bright and sunny as the blue sky of late April brought warmth, preparing people for the dry months ahead. However the political situation seemed to become more and more critical as those who came by the mission had bleak and gloomy comments to make. Stories were exchanged and very few persons knew what to believe. Rumor all around triggered exaggerated distress.

After lunch, Jose returned from Lusaga where he had spent the morning celebrating masses, and having a meeting with the parish council to organize help for the poverty-stricken in their area. He came home with stories of gun battles that had taken place the preceding night at Vurura in which many government officials had been killed. Many had been trapped in the local *calabu.* Jose said he believed the conflicts all stemmed from tribalism. The Bahutu had organized *Soirees Dansantes* for the local government officials and then around eight o'clock in the evening, when it was already dark, some young Bahutu men attacked the leaders with guns and machetes. Many prominent officials had died. However Jose said that he had heard that the government was officially announcing that the attack had come from the southern part of the Congo where people resembling short, heavy-set Chinese black men marching into southern Burundi and planning to attack the whole country. Tony asked Jose if he thought it was a plot by the government to decoy the real problem in Burundi which was tribal or racial. These two missionaries had often talked about the political situation in their adoptive country and both agreed that the unique problem in Burundi was the racial hatred between the Batutsi and the Bahutu. However living in the southland, the missioners had no other choice but to take the news about an enemy from without seriously. Jose nodded his head and said:

"I'm sure the government has taken an awful beating. Surely they never thought so many would be killed so quickly. They are now talking about hundreds of politicians being murdered."

2 Signs Of Death

This Sunday afternoon was one of the quietest Tony had ever spent at the mission. After lunch he went over to the youth hostel where the young people normally gathered following the second mass. They met in part of the building that had been the first church built in the early 1940's. The entire church building had been divided into rooms of different sizes and used for gatherings and group meetings. The young people were proud of their center and appointed certain members to keep it clean and in proper order. When they gathered, they would sing, exchange ideas, play games or march to the beat of the drums outside. They wore beautiful uniforms, the girls light or dark blue dresses and the boys blue shirts with light blue bandannas flowing from their necks.

Most of the boys wore khaki shorts that were sold in abundance at the market place for 25 frBu a pair. A few weeks earlier, two men had come to Tony on separate occasions, asking him how much a United States' dollar was worth in kirundi francs. Tony had told both that a dollar was worth about 100 frBu and then asked them why they were inquiring about foreign currency since it was illegal in Burundi. Both told him the same amazing story. They had gone to the market place to buy a pair of shorts for twenty-five francs. When they took them home, and put their hands in the pockets they both found an American dollar bill in each pair! Americans were either trying to help these poor Barundi, or the previous owner had thrown his shorts in the used clothes bin without ever checking the pockets. In both cases, Tony took the dollars and gave them a bit more than the kirundi equivalent of one hundred francs. He had become accustomed to people asking him to change money. When he was going to Bujarundi, people would come a few days before his planned trip and ask him if he would be kind enough to go to the bank in the capital and get new bills for the money that had been burned when it got too close to the cooking fire. Tony knew the ground rules for exchanging money at the bank since it had happened so often. If the serial number was still visible on the front of the note, the bank would take it in exchange. If the number was not legible: "*Nagasaga*!" (good-bye!)

Even the young adults were not doing anything this Sunday afternoon. Tony had never remembered a Sunday when the "*Chiro*" (young people's group) or even members of the youth group that was called "*UGA*" did not come together. He was the chaplain of the *Chiro* as Jose was responsible for the *UGA*. Jose had a puzzled and worried look on his face as he went over to the *UGA* center in a room in the old church. This group was older than the *Chiro*, gathering young people from sixteen years-of-age until they married in their early twenties. He found the room empty and became even more dumbfounded. He said a short prayer asking God to protect the youth of the parish. Never did the thought cross his mind that within four weeks, the tension in the *UGA* between the two tribes would grow to such proportions that, of the four elected *UGA* leaders, three Bahutu would be killed and the fourth, a Mututsi, would testify against them and thus be directly responsible for their demise. These were the young catholic youth of Butova!

Tony was completely baffled as he went to investigate the Chiro area. But worrying about them and the possibility of problems would not help. He walked back to the mission and went to his room. He found a magazine that he had wanted to read for a long time, set up some music by connecting his cassette recorder to a car battery that he had recently charged and lost himself in soft Chopin classics that he had recorded in Canada before coming to Burundi. Tony began to leaf through his outdated *Time Magazine* that had laid around his bedroom for months.

Supper time was at 7pm and Jose was late as he was prone to be. When Luigi Franco, Tony and Luc Grange sat down, they quickly made a pact not to talk about anything they had heard or seen that day concerning the revolution since it would only be rehashing what already disturbed them.

Luc was young, energetic, compulsive and idealistic. He was a nineteen-year-old who choose to spend two years in Central Africa satisfying his French military service. If he had chosen the military option, he probably would have remained in France. Luc's responsibility was to help the poor among the 47,000 people that lived in Butova and the surrounding areas. They existed by the tens of thousands. Mathias Becker had made the arrangement for Luc with a representative of the "*Volontaires du Progres*" (Volunteers for Progress) who had trained him in France. His goal was to start a cooperative, a general store where the members shared the profits equally. Every day Luc would drive many miles in the parish volkswagen van and purchase vegetables, fruit and other needed articles like hoes, soap, Fanta and beer, clothes for women, men, and children, as well as general *kirundi* food stocks of everything imaginable: beans, rice, yams, peas, tomatoes, corn and grain. When he got back to the store, Luc would calculate his costs and then price each article for the members. Even with the added transportation costs, the prices on all commodities in the Butova cooperative were cheaper than anywhere else in the southland where the

Greek and Arab merchants cheated the poor people and raised the normal prices to unusual heights. On many occasions, Luc became angry at these swindlers and confronted them. But it was in vain for he was fighting a winless battle, questioning them on their livelihood. He was a hero for all the poor and was admired by all the BanyaButova ("*Banya*" is the prefix for "the people of" and in kirundi is normally placed on the front of the location which is capitalized). Obviously, Luc made many enemies among the dishonest buyers and sellers and quickly became known to them in their butchered Kirundi as "*Mufranza Butova*" (the Frenchman from Butova).

Yet the cooperative continued to grow and Luc now had hundreds of members. He awaited the dry season when he would host a member meeting and share the yearly profits. He was very proud of what he had already accomplished and daily his passion to help the poor seemed to grow. Sincerity and hard work characterized this young man whom the Africans loved and trusted very much.

After supper was over, the three moved to the common room and a few minutes later, Jose showed up with his age-old excuse: a girl wanted to leave her family and marry a soldier who lived in a military camp. Her parents had told Jose in the afternoon and he had left immediately via *pikipiki* to try to talk her out of it.

This act of chivalry was always a waste of time, Tony thought, because the girl had already made up her mind. He believed that her freedom of intention was more important than following the *Kizungu* (European) outdated laws of marrying within the catholic church. Obviously that was not in the young peoples' plans since they didn't have the finances to get married and throw a big party to celebrate, which was required in their culture. Most couples thought it would be better to live together at first and then, when they were more financially stable and ready to make the commitment of marriage, receive the blessings in the church and complete the religious marriage with a big party.

Finally the four missioners concluded their small-talk with the prayer of compline (night prayer of the church). Tony thought of the people who had been killed especially the leaders and their families that must now be in mourning. He read the scripture from St. Peter who reminded them that the devil goes about as a roaring lion seeking someone to devour. He thought of how the Bahutu rebels, whoever they were, had acted like roaring lions bringing havoc to the capital and the southland. Never did he imagine that the roaring lion would change tribes and devour the vulnerable, simple Bahutu.

After prayer, Tony went to the courtyard to shut off the generator and, as he walked back to the house, looked up into the sky. It was a beautiful star-shiny night. As he gazed into the pale gray hues, he looked at the millions of bright signs of God's marvelous creation and prayed the Lord, Creator of the universe, to intervene and bring peace to his beloved Burundi. His prayer would never be answered.

Monday was the first day of May and the priests anticipated a special celebration at church. They had looked forward to this day since Easter. However it would not be at all what they had expected it to be! This day was always a great feast day in the church since it was the celebration of St. Joseph the Worker. It was a holiday in Burundi, a country where the majority of the population was Roman Catholic. But since this was also the first day of May, the month consecrated to the Blessed Mother, there was a late morning mass organized by the Legion of Mary with renewal of promises.

When Tony first arrived in Burundi, it surprised him that there were so many people in the Legion of Mary. He had once attended a meeting of the legion in Punda, a small outstation in the flatlands to the southeast of Butova, and there were fifty-seven members, most of them men, who came to the reunion. All together there were only 196 people registered in that small outstation! So over 25% were Legionaries!

Throughout the whole parish there were over one thousand active members of the Legion of Mary. Even if their devotion often seemed like catholic heresy, since they believed that Mary was the source and direct cause of all graces, nevertheless all members were asked to work at least two hours per week in the apostolate. The members were invaluable in doing parish visits, ministering to the sick and dying, taking parish census and doing other manual work around the outstations. Tony loved teaching the legionaries and praying with them since their level of commitment was higher than that of the average parishioner. He would often explain to them how to pray the gospel contemplation method or the church teaching on mass or holy week or the reason why their confirmation made them apostles and responsible for building up the church. They would often say in the middle of a strong exhortation:

"*Ego, Egome Pati*" (Yes, Yes I agree, Father) as the priest would go on with the teaching. Tony had prayed in the early morning that a large number would come to the mass and thus would serve as a sign that the trouble was over. But on the contrary, to his consternation, there was only a handful of people who risked the dangers along the roads and trails to come and celebrate the beginning of the month of Mary and the feast day of her spouse, St. Joseph.

Tony started the mass on time and Jose and Luigi concelebrated with him. The new pastor made it very clear from the outset of mass that the keynote theme was: "Peace in Burundi" and asked the people to focus their prayer on peace as he moved rapidly from one part to another. There were so few legionaries, that it was useless to renew their promises to the Blessed Virgin at this time. They would reorganize another celebration later in the dry season. Tony realized that it was hard to pray together when there was no peace in the community. Few realized that there would never be peace in Burundi again and that travel and government sanctions of religious celebrations would soon create difficult impediments. They had come to the end of a marvelous era. The "good old times" of a catholic dominance of the life of Burundi were vanishing before their very eyes and yet they knew it not!

On this day, Cypriano Kitwi began his month as cook for the missionary fathers. Usually each mission had two cooks who alternated the kitchen duties monthly. Each would use the same bedroom close to the kitchen and be available day and night for cooking and serving table. The scheduled cook would work each day for the entire month. Today, a holiday, Cypriano was serving them a dish that they considered his best: fried chicken, mashed potatoes and gravy, with fresh garden green beans. He had baked a cake for dessert.

Cypriano cooked in a small kitchen across a pathway where cars turned going around the far corner of the mission house to park in the back courtyard. The kitchen was far enough from the house that any odors coming from that area would not penetrate the dining room. The mission house was higher than the kitchen, so when Cypriano would cross the path with a tray of food in his hands, he would then climb six stairs to enter the dining area.

As the community was half way through the one o'clock meal, suddenly the door burst open, startling everyone at table. Cypriano entered and looked very anxious. He came over to the table and, as he politely removed the soup bowls and spoons from the table, waited until the fathers had stopped eating and talking. They sensed something was wrong for Kitwi would never disturb them with anything that could wait until they had finished their meal.

"They have come to the kitchen," the cook continued, "and have told me the sad news!"

"What is it, Cypi?" the pastor asked with much concern in his voice.

"People have come from Bihovu announcing that the rebels have arrived in that area and are killing all the government officials and all the Batutsi," he blurted.

Tony was astonished for in his years in Burundi, he had seldom heard an African refer to a tribal name. That was a taboo. Even when the fathers were alone at table speaking French, they would never refer to anyone as a "Mututsi" or "Muhutu" because it was considered too personal. That was used by intimates of the same tribe only. However the priests would call them "*les longs*" or "*les courts*" (he's a 'tall' or he's a 'short') referring to the taller generic Batutsi with long noses or the shorter Bahutu with pudgy noses. The four men's eyes met over the table and Tony said: "I'll go, in case there is need for the sacrament of the sick and 'viaticum' (Latin: "with the journey" i.e. communion to accompany the sick person on the journey back to the Lord).

Luigi who was just learning the language and was having quite a bit of problems understanding the words and grammar added:

"I will go along to accompany you, Tony. Two are better than one and you never can tell what is happening and what fate may be awaiting you."

Tony Joseph was delighted with Luigi's offer. His exterior calmness and serenity merely hid a heart that was pounding and thumping, fearing what lay ahead at Bihovu for him.

"Thanks, Luigi," he smiled at his colleague, "I appreciate your support and courage. I'll get the oils and hosts from the chapel and we'll meet by my car as soon possible."

Both men rose from the table and Luc accompanied them out the dining room door and down the corridor.

"I'll get the keys and bring your car over to the chapel," Luc said wanting to do his share in helping to get this difficult mission on the road.

Both priests soon arrived at the car, with Tony getting behind the wheel. As they drove away, he placed the pix containing several consecrated hosts in Luigi's hands along with the leather case holding the holy oils. He drove away from the mission and down the back road heading towards the hill across from Butova where President Sabimana had built a large home at the summit called Piga. As he got closer to the hilltop, the house seemed much larger than he had imagined it to be. He realized the view from the mission had distorted reality for him. He recalled how President Sabimana had told him that he built this house for his parents. They, however, were simple African people having spent their whole lives in the bush and could not get used to a house with windows that allowed the sunshine to penetrate all day long. They also preferred a grass roof for when the torrential rains would come, they disliked the noise on the '*mabati*' (corrugated roofing). They preferred the gentle sounds of rain on a grass roof. So they had moved out of this luxurious house and into a dark mud-smelly hut where they were more at ease in their *kirundi* ways.

Tony drove past Piga, then continued along the road toward the valley. He wondered if the road would suddenly come to an end and they would have to retreat and take another route. It was the first time he or Luigi had ever traveled this road to Bihovu. However Luc had convinced them that this was the fastest way for he had traveled this exact route two weeks previously.

"Trust me!" Luc had said to Tony, "I know all the trails around Butova and this one can take your small VW but nothing bigger. You will make it!" The priests trusted Luc's directives.

Luigi had a slight smirk of his face as he looked at Tony. It was time for both these missioners to talk about other lighter subjects than the massacres and attacks that they anticipated ahead of them.

"You remember what the bishop always says about trails like this?" Luigi asked and answered his own question, "You don't say 'it is a road and so I'll pass'. Rather you say 'I passed, it must have been a road!'" Both men broke into light laughter with smiles shining forth from their faces. Tony imagined Bishop Moulin telling the story and hitting his elevated right thigh with his right palm as he always found humor to cope with the everyday problems in Burundi. Further, he loved to share his anecdotes in colorful detail.

The two missionaries continued their bumpy journey and conversation flowed rather freely. Then about fifteen or twenty minutes later Tony refocused on the problems that lay ahead:

"Luigi, we really don't know what is awaiting us. One thing is pretty sure. We will probably come into the company of some who killed the government officials Saturday night. We could end up dead as well! I have never felt as anxious and nervous about anything before in my life as I feel right now. That is why I am totally indebted to you for coming along and being a source of strength for me. Would you do me a favor, my friend?" Tony asked.

Luigi looked at the man who was a few years younger than himself and only had two years more experience than he in Burundi yet had the heavy responsibilities of being pastor at this unusual time in the history of Butova:

"Yes, anything, what do you want me to do?" Luigi answered with a tinge of curiosity in his response.

Tony took a deep breath and sighed:

"As we drive along, would you hear my confession? It is not that I have a guilty conscience but if death is ahead of us on this road, I would prefer to have received a sign of God's pardon before dying."

When missionary priests arrived in Burundi, they were amazed at the simplicity of their colleagues when they asked each other to hear their private confession.

Luigi responded:

"You know, Tony, I was thinking of the same thing myself. It has been some time since my last confession and I should have gone last week. But I was alone in the outstation. So let's do it right now."

The two missionaries took a moment of silence to reflect on the God-experience that they were about to share through the sacrament of reconciliation. Then Tony started his confession. It seemed strange, these two adult men, thinking they might be driving to their deaths and yet, in a small car traveling over bumpy roads, they confessed bad intentions, evil thoughts and vain filled deeds that they had done in the past. Tony seemed to be somewhat relieved that the penitential exchange took his mind off the immediate dangers for a few short minutes. He liked Luigi very much and had little trouble letting this warm-hearted and sensitive man into the most intimate parts of his heart. He opened himself and told Luigi how much difficulty he had accepting others and their idiosyncrasies. He often became angry when Jose would be late for a community exercise, be it a meeting, prayer or even a meal. When Mathias had been in charge, there had been less pressure on Tony. But now that the mission depended on his leadership, he didn't know how long he could take this lack of commitment to common good. He explained that when things didn't go his way and he became discouraged, he would give in and seek satisfaction in daydreaming, or excessive food and drink or imagining how life would be better elsewhere. It was both easy and a struggle to explain these faults to a brother priest. Tony presumed that Luigi had the same temptations and would be understanding towards him. But he also felt guilty and this encouraged him to tell all since the unknown ahead seemed so dangerous.

Luigi was very responsive to his colleague. He lived his priesthood in a beautifully simple way allowing his natural qualities to be enhanced by the graces of Christ's priesthood. He looked across the car at Tony who was embarrassingly staring straight ahead guiding the small car as he tried to avoid potholes and large rocks on the road. Luigi responded with a slight smile and beautiful words that would build confidence in Tony:

"Sometimes God wants us to help other people who are much weaker than we are. Jose lacks direction and often acts very impulsively but you must realize that he needs you and sometimes a person fails ten times before he can get it straight. Pray for patience with Jose and God will help you to be an instrument of strength in his life. You are the one who must put aside annoyances and help him realize his potential which at times is extraordinary and at other times seems minimal. However God does not ask us to be successful. Rather He wants us to use the grace He has given us to become better persons. Jose has a long way to go. Yet God has chosen you to be the guiding force in his life to improve his sort," Luigi concluded in a consoling tone that seemed very challenging to Tony.

Then Luigi broke into spontaneous prayer, thanking God for their lives and their priesthood and asking the Lord for grace to be patient. Finally came the words of absolution that Luigi didn't know in French and was just learning in Kirundi. So he spoke them in his native Italian. Tony followed easily since these words resembled the Latin words of absolution he had studied in the seminary.

As Luigi looked across at the driver, he asked Tony if he would do the same thing. He nodded in approval smiling, for this was the first time he would hear a confession while driving a car. The uncharacteristically calm Italian began by saying that this was the first time he would confess his sins in French and wondered if he would find the right words and expressions. Still intensely staring at the road, Tony promised to help him. He remembered with a smile the first time he went to confession in French since English was his mother tongue and French was a language he was just learning in the novitiate, eight years before. He always went to the same priest. Once he had confessed: 'breaking the ruler' rather than 'not following the house rule' and the confessor laughed out loud at the meaning in French. The confessor explained that in French, one would say 'missed the rule'. So Tony realized that following the house rules would not only help him grow in spirituality but also help him avoid embarrassment in the confessional!

Luigi's confession was similar to Tony's. Rash judgments, evil desires, dislike for certain persons. As Tony heard this litany of weaknesses, he wondered how Luigi saw him and if he, himself, were not a cause of Luigi's failures. Yet he knew that Luigi had great respect for him and supported his decisions. So he filled his heart with admiration for this penitent, remembering what he had been taught in the seminary: 'Confession does not show the confessor how bad people are but rather how good they yearn to be!'

Tony Joseph always prided himself as being a helpful confessor. In fact he often kept people a long time in the 'box' giving them suggestions on how to avoid sin and better their lives.

He liked to recall the first time he had heard confessions at Butova. He had arrived the previous day from the language school and in the morning Jose had told him that he was giving a retreat to some local people and he asked Tony to come and help him with confessions around 1pm. Leave it to Jose, on Tony's first day in the parish he planned confessions at meal time and then ran one hour late! The neophyte priest went to the new church and waited in the confessional. He reviewed what he had been told in theology: 'If you do not understand the penitent or cannot make out his confession, you cannot give him absolution.' In came the first penitent who seamed to talk so fast, Tony only heard one never-ending jumbled expression of Kirundi that he could not decipher if his life depended on it! Tony asked him to repeat; "*subira kandi*" and again he understood not a word. "*Genda, kw'uwndi Pati*" (Go to the other priest) he said and the penitent left his box and crossed the church to go to Fr. Jose. This embarrassment continued over and over again. The people, waiting in line, would laugh heartily every time a penitent backed out of the box and crossed the church to line up outside Jose's confessional whose line became longer and longer. Finally Tony, totally discouraged, stood up, took off his purple stole and strolled timidly out of the church, red-faced and embarrassed by the mocked laughter of those he left in his confessional line. He thought that it would be better to say nothing than to express something in Kirundi that they would not understand anyway.

But now, even with Luigi by his side, he felt empty and void. He wondered how his priesthood could be so barren and dry. Did he not care about Luigi who had accompanied him? He consoled himself with the realization that it was his nerves, confronted by the situation that lay ahead, that led him to emptiness. He asked God to bless and protect them and said the words of absolution in perfect French as he blessed Luigi and smiled at his colleague. Both men agreed that this had been a beautiful experience and mutually thanked each other for the gift of absolution and priesthood.

The volkswagen carrying Fathers Tony Joseph and Luigi Franco moved along slowly up hillsides and down into steep ravines, from time to time bumping a rock in the road and finally came to a high-peaked area overlooking the plains of Bihovu. Tony stopped the car and both men got out to view the area. All seemed calm and peaceful and they even heard shouts of children herding goats in an area at the bottom of a hill. They quickly got back into their car and rambled down to the valley. Soon they were within the area of Bihovu and they slowed down almost to a halt hoping that people living in the roadside areas would hear the car and come out to greet them and give them the news of the region. Finally after they had proceeded along for about two more kilometers, they saw a group of men gathered together on the road directly in front of them.

"Well this is it, dear friend. Let's get out and hopefully they'll be friendly," Tony said. "I hope they are as peaceful as they look from here."

He stopped the car a few feet from the group and both men got out and greeted the *bagabo* (men). Tony knew that the African cultural way was to greet first and be informed about the person's health, family, house, cattle and life in general before getting down to any particular business. His *kizungu* (European-ness) or lack of being African seemed to get the best of him and he went from one man to another shaking hands but at the same time already asking:

"We got news that there was trouble here. What do you know about it? What can we do to help?"

There were six men standing in a semi-circle. Some wore coats and another covered himself with a gray blanket. The man who was dressed the best with a black and white checkered fedora on his head and wearing a dark blue coat down to his knees and plastic sandals spoke up. Tony knew him well. Artimo Tanze was a slick and slimy Mututsi who was the head-catechist at Bihovu. Tanze personified the worst of this race of hypocrites. Even when he spoke, his voice always seemed to whisper, giving the listener the idea that he was sneaky and trying to cover up something. Tanze was only a catechist for the pay and since he had lived in this distinct area all his life, he was assured of a paying job that was secure since he knew the church of the Bazungu would always have the funds to compensate him each month. On two different occasions Tony had gone to the Bihovu unannounced and unexpected and found the catechumens all working the private property of Artimo Tanze! Being the catechist in an outstation far from the central mission of Butova certainly had its advantages!

Nice job! Tony had thought. Artimo is being paid to boss people around working for him in his own garden! This guy is a real profiteer!

"Peace has come to this area, *Pati*," Artimo continued, "but the last two days have been a disaster for us. There hasn't been fighting here but news has come today from Vurura and Mutwe and Bumeza that many of our brothers, even government officials, have been killed by those nasty rebels. You must have heard the *induru* (hysterical screams of the women when news of a death arrives) in Butova. I hope the soldiers catch every last one of them and cut them in half before murdering them. They should all be tortured for weeks before they are left to die in their own blood."

Tony Joseph was abhorred at the hideous words Artimo Tanze was using to describe his desire for revenge. Maybe Tony was being influenced by the grace of the sacrament of pardon that he had just received. But probably he mistrusted Artimo or saw through him, realizing the odious racist that he was! In any case the pastor spoke loud and clear for all to hear:

"Artimo, do you know all the circumstances to make such judgments and statements? You two tribes live in hatred of one another and never even try to love and reach out to each other. But you, Artimo Tanze, are the catechist, the man-of-God for the area. Why don't you try to imitate Christ and forgive all who do wrong. Who has the greater sin…those who did these sad deeds because they hate the Batutsi or those, like you, who will not forgive them because you hate the Bahutu? As *padri mukuru* (pastor), I demand that you be a spiritual guide for all and begin a campaign of reconciliation, starting in Bihovu. However all I hear in your voice is hatred. If I hear that you do not change your ways, I am going to relieve you of your posting as head catechist." Tony's voice seemed to raise a few decimal points as he concluded his reprimand.

Artimo Tanze stared long and hard at his pastor. Fury steamed from both eyes as he looked angrily at Tony. He mumbled under his breath but loud and distinct enough for all to hear:

"If Pati Matihasi were here, he would take our side," Tanze managed to say.

"What did you say, catechist?" the pastor yelled at him, letting him know that he had heard his remark and it was totally unacceptable.

"Before continuing to be head catechist here in Bihovu, Tanze, you must come to my office in Butova so that we can review your work, words and actions in your present posting. Your salary will cease until I see you at the mission. Come as soon as you can!" Then the pastor went on about his primary business:

"Have any of you heard how many persons originating from Bihovu have been killed?" Tony addressed the question to no one in particular but looked at all of them except Artimo, showing that a response from him would be totally inappropriate. One by one they started to call out names of Batutsi whom they had heard had been killed the first two nights: "Stanisalasi, Karoli, Bucumi, Gerardo, Rukari, Imamura, Lazar, Simony….." Tony and Luigi listened closely and realized the massacres were real and they had taken their toll on the Batutsi from this area. In the southland of Burundi, the Batutsi were in a majority. In fact this area was referred to as the *Bututsi* (land of the Batutsi). In a few days, every Muhutu would be suspect and the genocide of the Bahutu tribe would reach overwhelming proportions.

The two missionaries got back into their car, turned it around and said good-bye to the men still standing on the side of the road. As they made their way back to the mission, relief was clearly seen on both their faces. Luigi laughed a little as he said:

"Tony, you really spoke strongly to Artimo." Then he broke into laughter and jokingly said: "Do you want to go to confession again, this time driving back home?" he snickered and Tony laughed heartily. The stress of Bihovu was now behind them.

When they arrived back at the mission, President Sabimana's father was waiting for them in the corridor leading from the dining room out into the back courtyard. He, of course, was worried about his son and had heard the news concerning the alarm at Bihovu. Tony and Luigi both reassured the old man that all was peaceful and no one had mentioned the president's name when talking about those who had died.

"If something had happened involving your son," Tony reassured him, "we would all know about it and it would be announced on the radio immediately. He is probably at his palace working hard on papers at this moment. Peace will soon be back. Everything will be all right." Little did they know that this old man had absolutely nothing to worry about. The Batutsi casualties would soon be revenged in the highest degree by the atrocities that would be dealt to the Bahutu over the coming weeks.

Later that afternoon, Walter De Winter, the former pastor of Butova and the man who had built the present church, drove into the yard. He was now the pastor of Lutana, a neighboring parish to the east. He liked Butova and the community of missionaries there so on casual days off he would jump into his car and come to visit.

Another attraction to Butova was the electric organ that they had in their common room that De Winter loved to play. It had been a present from the president when the fathers had baptized one of his children. The baptism saw the fathers not only taking charge of the ceremonies in the church but also arranging the party that took place afterwards in the mission courtyard. There were few areas in the interior of Burundi where a large celebration could take place, so usually the president counted on the mission to handle that part of it and paid them afterwards for all their efforts. He was very generous with his gifts. On this one occasion, there had been three hundred guests invited to the baptism. So he sent along the electric organ that obviously had come from Europe. Every time he came to visit, Tony would play some dancing music and the President of Burundi would get up and dance with different male companions. Women were never part of their group. In fact, the president gave the impression that women were always to be ignored. Sabimana spent all his vacation time away from his family with his old cronies. Yet Tony presumed that the president, when it was time for bed, expected a young Mututsikazi (woman) from the area to be awaiting him. People didn't see this as immoral but rather natural for a man in high authority in the former chiefdom of Burundi. Their culture of polygamy was not washed away by the waters of baptism. In fact the fathers found it more difficult to accept that Sabimana always came to the mission with friends rather than family. But that was the *kirundi* way, male companions only…. women bedmates often. It seemed to insinuate that his wife and children were unimportant. Yet was that not the way he wanted to live his life, without any family responsibility whatsoever, as a free-wheeling bachelor? His way to live was to have a wife to give him children who stayed on home turf in his palace, while he went from place to place in his helicopter acting out his presidential duties and kicking up his heels.

Luigi heard Walter's car from his room and went out to greet him and walked him into the living room. He called out to Tony who came quickly to welcome the former pastor. He was very grateful for Walter's friendship and that it carried on even though a great personality like Mathias was now back in Germany. The three men, one a veteran of twenty-five years in Burundi and the other two rookies to the missionary life, talked about the recent happenings. Since the attempted *coup*, Walter had many stories to tell them and Luigi and Tony responded with anecdotes of their own. Walter told how nervous the other priests with him had become in Lutana. He lived with a Belgian and an Italian. The priest from Brussels was beyond himself, going around the mission making sure the doors and windows were all bolted securely. Walter had built Lutana mission only four years earlier and so he added :

"It couldn't be more secure. You've seen my work. The mission house is all built in blocks, steel doors with a high fence of cement and pieces of broken glass on the top of the wall so that anyone trying to climb in would be cut to pieces." The Italian priest had only been with De Winter for the past two months. He had been sent as a *'Fidel Denim'* (Gift of Faith) priest to replace a Missionary of Africa who had gone back to France on home leave. Walter went on to say how much he missed the Frenchman and the wisdom he had brought to their community. Now he felt very isolated since the other two were beyond rational thinking. He went on:

"If there was an attack on our mission, I don't know what I would do. There would be no sense in talking to these two others since their emotions and fears have gone beyond reasoning. I feel very alone in making all the decisions."

Tony encouraged him to remain calm and told him that he knew he was wise and strong enough to always make the right decisions in times of crisis.

"Maybe that is the reason why you are there with those two, so that you can help them to think correctly," Luigi added, using a similar line that he had spoken to Tony in confession earlier.

Walter De Winter did not accept the back-handed compliments. He said that he lacked confidence in himself and had no trust in the other two. He stood up and walked to the door. Luigi asked him to stay for awhile longer and he would get his guitar so that they could play music together. Walter said not to bother turning on the motor for electricity:

"I'm certainly not in the mood to play music. Besides I have taught so many of those who have now been killed in the *coup* that playing music would seem disrespectful." He opened the door and the two hosts walked him in silence to his car. He got in, started the motor and rolled down his window:

"Please come to visit us soon. We need encouragement that only youth can provide. You are most welcome any time." De Winter called out as he drove away.

Tony went back to his office and fondly recalled the great meals he had had at Lutana. The Belgian bursar made sure that they ate better there than at any other mission in the country. He himself weighed over one hundred and twenty kilo even living in a semi-tropical climate! He would laugh at himself saying in French:

"*J'ai la bone fourchette!*" (I've got a good fork!)

They always had meat from the flatlands, often sent by President Sabimana who years earlier had been a student of De Winter. The president never forgot his "favorite teacher" as he often fondly referred to Walter. On Sundays he would send a Mercedes to Lutana early in the morning and have his driver bring Walter to where he had overnighter so that his favorite teacher could say mass for him personally. Then the president would leave and hunt from his helicopter! The driver would bring De Winter back to the mission for Sunday masses. Later in the day or sometime during the dusk of the evening, the driver would return with a gazelle that would keep the good fathers on a gourmet menu over the next week.

3. Searching For The Enemy

Luigi Franco awoke screaming, sat up in his bed and realized that he was having a horrendous nightmare. He reached for his flashlight and shone the spotlight all around his room. He knew that this was the after shock of his bad dream and that there was nothing in the room that could harm him. So he shut off the lamp, turned over in his bed and tossed to and fro for half an hour before he finally fell back into a sound sleep.

Tony and Luc Grange were having breakfast and Jose was saying mass in the church when Luigi finally came to the dining room for the morning meal. His face seemed heavy with sleep and he looked tired.

"How did you sleep, Luigi?" Tony asked his confrere amazed that he looked so pale and dismal.

"I had a terrible nightmare" Luigi responded, sitting down and pouring himself a cup of black coffee.

"I was playing music with De Winter in our living room and he made some mistakes on the organ. President Sabimana was there. He got up, went over to the organ, took out a machete and cut off Walter's hands. Then he came across the room to me. I stood up and said I've never made a mistake on the guitar. He didn't listen and started coming after me with the same machete. Then happily I woke up and realized I was only dreaming, but I heard the echo of my screaming: *"Me pugna! me volna!"* (He's stabbing me, he's wounding me). Tony and Luc sympathized with their colleague and both admitted embarrassingly that they had heard his screaming during the night. Luigi kept saying how traumatizing it had been.

Changing the subject, Tony said that he thought it a good idea to go to Lutana in the afternoon to encourage De Winter and the other two fathers as well. He mentioned how sorry he felt for De Winter, living with two men who seemed to be so afraid of the *'coup'* that they gave very little support to the pastor in this traumatic situation. Luc said it would be a good idea and showed interest in making the *safari* to Lutana. Tony appreciated the nineteen-year-old and his mature commitment to be of help to others. He was still a teenager, yet could show these older men a great deal of courage and inner strength. So they decided that Luc and Tony would leave after the noon meal and spend the afternoon visiting in Lutana. Jose came in as they were all getting up from table and said:

"*Zoot*, what was all that screaming about at three o'clock this morning?" They all realized that Jose's room was beside Luigi's and obviously Luigi had awakened him with his shouts.

"It was me," Luigi answered. "I had a terrible nightmare."

"Someone must have come after you with a knife" Jose went on as Cypriano entered and asked him how he wanted his eggs prepared.

"Amaso" said Jose, using the Kirundi word for "eyes". So he wanted them sunny-side-up! Jose loved to joke around with the Africans especially about how they prepared the food.

"What makes you think that Luigi was attacked with a knife, Jose?" Luc asked curiously.

"Well he kept shouting: *'me volna! me pugna!'* said the Spaniard eloquent in basic Italian.

Luigi, embarrassed, did not go into detail telling the story again in fear that he might become more and more traumatized. He never realized that his nightmare was absolutely minor compared to the major traumas that they were all about to witness over the next twenty-five days.

After lunch, Tony and Luc set out for Lutana. It was about twenty-five miles up the road, passing the outstation church of Vuvoga and would take them fifty minutes to an hour. As they talked about the distance while they drove, Tony told Luc that he always calculated by his watch rather than by mileage.

"Sometimes the distance is rather short but the roads are not in very good shape. Other times, during the rainy season, the roads are even worse! You never talk about good or bad when speaking about the condition of the Burundi roads," he said, "you always talk about bad, worse and worst!" Tony then realized that Luc had more experience than he had driving in all four directions to get supplies for the cooperative. The young Frenchman readily agreed with him about the poor quality of the *kirundi* roads.

They entered Lutana mission, the apple of De Winter's eye since he had raised all the funds in his native Belgium, made all the plans himself and then masterminded all the construction. His church was built of solid cement and blocks with plastic colored windows that would let in enough air during the dry season. The roof was in reddish corrugated tile. Yet it would not become extremely hot in the summertime. His *masterpiece* was an electric organ that was given by some friends back in Antwerp. Of course there was no organist in his parish so he himself played before mass as well as at the masses he did not celebrate. If he were the presider, he would play the organ, which was in the front of the church, and accompany the recessional hymn. All the other ministers would march out to the rhythm of his beat. He never went to the outstations for Sunday mass anymore since he preferred to stay behind and play music. As chance would have it, his two curates preferred the outstations since they felt more at ease than at the mission of Lutana where many of those who attended mass were among the most sophisticated people in the southland. Both priests enjoyed the simpler and uneducated folks in the rural areas.

De Winter came over to the volkswagen van that Tony was driving. Mathias had received it from Germany and was kind enough to leave it to the parish when he was called back to his native country to direct White Father missionary activities in the Rhineland. Walter had a big smile of welcome for his two neighbors and invited them into the common room, offering them coffee or a cold drink. Grapefruit grew very well in Lutana and Walter had his own recipe for making grapefruit wine. Since Luc was a wine connoisseur, he opted for coffee but Tony said he preferred a cold drink of home made wine. De Winter came back from the dining room with a tray of drinks He mentioned that he had some important news to tell them since he still had close contacts with many government officials having taught so many in the junior seminary. Many often came to visit *"Pati Wati"* when they were near Lutana.

"I heard some bad news this morning," Walter went on, "the Governor of Lutana came to see me and told me that we are going to be attacked from the southwest. There is a large group of men marching from the southeast of the Congo and are killing all the people that they find along the way. He told me to expect the worst and to do all I can to secure the mission. Have you been listening to the radio?"

Tony and Luc both admitted apologetically with embarrassment that they had not been listening to *La Voix de la Revolution*. Luc asked Walter if he knew where the rebels were going to attack; specifically he wondered if they would attack the south side of Lutana or their area of Butova.

"I'm not sure. It is so alarming!" De Winter answered, then went on:

"But the governor says that he thinks they will attack your area first, probably via the outstation of Ruhweza and then march quickly through the flatlands of the Boso and attack us. I can't believe this is all happening. If they attack the mission that I've built and destroy my lifetime project of helping this poor country, I will be devastated. I will never get over it. The radio told us that these rebels look like black-skinned Chinese people. They are short and stocky and very violent. The governor told me he doesn't know what nationality they are but they wear dark khaki uniforms.

Oh, yes, the radio also said that they have killed many people in Myanza and are now holding Burome." De Winter talked nervously, meandering from the radio broadcast to the talk he had had with the governor. It all sounded very confusing and eerie to Tony and Luc.

"I'm really worried," Tony went on, "what do you think we should do?"

"I'll tell you what we have done. We can't make the mission any more secure so we have all taken the time to write our last will and testament as well as letters to our brothers and sisters and close relatives and friends." De Winter told Luc and Tony.

"I still have my *maman* and I wrote a letter to her that really broke my heart. She lives in a nursing home in Antwerp and doesn't walk anymore. It is sad, very sad. We put these letters and documents in the safe that is in the wall over my bed." Walter De Winter said with a tear in his eye.

"Read us your letter to your mother that we will be able to console you, Walter." Tony pleaded not out of curiosity but rather to be able to support his confrere who was so despondent.

The Flemish missionary, in his early fifties with shiny bright white thinning hair, got up and headed for his room. He soon returned and took an envelope from his vest pocket, withdrew the contents and unfolded a letter as Luc and Tony waited for him with uneasy anticipation. The silence was deafening as they experienced the emotional side of De Winter:

"Dear Maman,

As you read this letter, you will know that I have gone home to the Father having been killed by the rebels that have attacked our beloved Burundi. It is very hard for me to tell you "Adieu, Maman" because since my birth, you have been the most wonderful person in my life. You taught me my prayers when I was young and how to respect people and to be kind to them. You nursed me with your own breasts and when I grew to be a boy and then a man, you always were there to see that I was well fed, well clothed and had all I needed. I will never forget you, Maman, and I know you will never forget me. I know that on the other side of this world, lies a better life with our God. I await his welcoming arms. I know that when you read this, I will already be in the loving embrace of God the Father, and I will gaze on the countenance of Jesus, His Son and my Brother. Bye Bye Sweet Maman!!

I love you,

Your Walter xxooxxoo

Luc cleared his throat and blew his nose to avoid embarrassment as Tony told Walter how beautiful the letter was and that everyone who still had his parents should do the same. Then he thought of his own parents who were in excellent health back in Canada. How would he ever be able to write a letter of *'adieu'* to them? He took a deep breath and sighed wondering why such tragedy was befalling them all in Burundi. He wondered if news about what was happening was reported throughout the world and, if so, what slant did the broadcasters give? He imagined his parents and friends watching television and hearing about the rebels massacring people along the roads. His parents had come to Burundi the previous year and he remembered taking them on a visit to the outstation of Ruhweza where his father had stood up in the church after mass and, encouraged by the people, made a speech to them in his mother tongue. Tony had translated it into Kirundi and afterward an old man from that area came up to Mr. Joseph and spoke to him in very broken English with a heavy accent but clear enough! English? spoken by a Murundi in the heart of the Central African bush? The man said that he had learned his English when he was in Tanganyika during the Second World War and joining the British troops, was sent to fight in Egypt. There, with the Brits, he learned to understand and speak the language of Shakespeare. Tony, imagining a rebel attack on Ruhweza, visualized his parents watching the scenario at home on television. He was filled with anxiety and shame.

Tony Joseph and Luc Grange soon left Lutana to go back to Butova. When they arrived, Jose came to meet them:

"The administrator came to see you, Tony, about an hour ago. He wanted to know if you could drive him around tonight as he needs to visit those on nightwatches." Jose said this with his right hand drawing circles in the air similar to how he imagined the groups of men to be. They had been organized to watch nightly for the rebels throughout the area.

"Did he explain what the night watchers were looking for?" Tony asked Jose.

"He just said that all the *bagabo* have been ordered to come together each evening to protect the country. He added that we, here at the mission, should be ready to help by driving him around in our vehicles. I told him that I don't drive the van since I have enough with my *moto* (motorcycle)." Jose explained. This was the first time Tony had heard about the vigilante watches that were now scheduled to begin that evening. The government demanded that all able-bodied adult men come together in particular areas along the roads to watch for and intercept rebels that might invade the area by night. The government had already announced that they were counting on the areas in the southland to protect the whole country. So Tony got back into his car and drove to Puma where the administrator lived.

Puma, the town center, had originally been organized in colonial times by the Belgians and before them by the Germans. They called it the "*arrondissement*" in French, where the Administrator, Alberto Kizungu, directed all government business for the immediate area. The twelve-bed dispensary was there as well as the small jail and public court. On Thursday afternoons, compulsory political government meetings took place out-of-doors in the same area. Everyone was required to attend under pain of imprisonment. Usually there was no discussion at the weekly meetings, but people had to attend to show support of the government officials who would tell them what they could or could not do.

Tony turned right at the corner of the square and stopped his car at the first house which was that of Administrator Kizungu, who came out when he heard the car turn the corner and stop. The administrator, a tall man with a long narrow face and straight pointed nose that revealed *kitutsi* traits, approached the car and greeted the pastor. His face was scarred with two large markings, one running above his eyes about an inch below his hairline. The other was a three-inch gash that ran parallel to his nose, from his right eye to his chin. Kizungu also had thick large eyebrows and a huge mouth, large lips yet small ears. He was wearing gray pants with a dark blue shirt. When he talked his eyes would close, then open again, as he spoke. Tony surmised that he was always uncomfortable, being under qualified for his position.

The pastor always tried to look favorably on Kizungu but found him to be a devious character. The fact that he had trouble making eye-to-eye contact increased mistrust in Tony's mind. Besides Kizungu was the brother of Bonaventuro Ruha, (no common family name among the Barundi) the Burundi Ambassador to the United Nations, the United States and Canada. Mathias had introduced Tony to Ruha after warning him: *"Il pette plus haut que son trou!"* (He exaggerates!) He cautioned his successor always to be mistrusting of Ruha and all Batutsi who acted like him: proud, arrogant, haughty, stubborn and belligerent. Kizungu was more personable then his famous brother who liked to tell stories about his adventures in the UN and North America and often detailed anecdotes showing him superior to his counterparts in the USA. He had recently written a book which many missionaries jokingly referred to as "the breaking of the eighth commandment!" In his writing, Ruha had brazenly stated that the Batutsi and the Bahutu knew no differences between them. It was the first missionaries who branded some "Batutsi" and others "Bahutu". He strongly denied that the percentage between the two was 14% - 85%. Every book that Tony had ever read on Burundi gave these exact figures, 85 % Bahutu, 14% Batutsi and 1% Batwa (Pygmy). Yet Ruha made it sound as if there was an equal number from both tribes in Burundi and that the people didn't know what ethnicity they were! So it was the missionaries that told them who they were. Ruha was a liar and a hypocrite and was educated well enough to be dangerous. However he stayed in Washington or New York most of the time and when he made periodic visits to Burundi, Ambassador Ruha spent most of his time in Bujarundi. He had long outgrown the African *mihana* (bush).

Tony wondered what sly tricks Kizungu would have up his sleeve since he was cut from the same cloth as Ruha. But then the pastor reasoned that he owed Kizungu a chance to prove himself since he never had shown the arrogance that typified his brother. The law of averages dictated that he be the better of the two brothers from Bihovu. It would be difficult to outdo Ruha in conceit, arrogance and pomposity.

"Pati," Kizungu started, "the government has asked that all able-bodied Barundi men come together to guard against the enemy during the whole night from the first hour of nightfall to the first hour of daybreak. I have already indicated the locations where they will gather in my area. However I would like to go and visit many of these areas tonight and encourage the men. But alas, I don't have any transportation. Could you help me?" Kizungu made a passionate plea.

Tony mauled the invitation over for a few seconds and was thankful that Jose had already given him a warning. Then he answered affirmatively. They agreed to leave at six o'clock which was dusk and anyone traveling to the checkpoints ought to have arrived already.

Tony grabbed a bite to eat in the dining room around 5:15. After telling his companions that he was going to drive the administrator around the *arrondissement*, he got into his car and drove to Puma. Kizungu was waiting for him in front of his *kigo* (enclosed yard) and was talking to two other men, whom Tony recognized as officials who worked at the public trial court just kitty-corner to the administrator's residence. Bidding them farewell, the administrator got into the passenger's side of Tony's car. The pastor was somewhat startled when he saw Alberto carrying a long sword locked in its sheath. He placed it down gently on the floor with the handle openly protruding between the two seats. He looked right at Tony with his dark piercing eyes penetrating deeply into Tony's subconscious mind. The administrator said:

"You never know when we might run into trouble," he went on, "I always keep this sword handy in case anyone would dare attack me as the local civil authority and representative of President Sabimana. Thank God I have only had to use it twice, both times when robbers broke into my house during the night. People think I have lots of money because Ambassador Bonaventuro Ruha is my brother. They don't realize we are not a rich family but have to work hard for everything we have."

Tony listened without making a comment. He recalled hearing about the two robberies at Puma and how, on both occasions, the bandits were seriously injured by a sword. Tony was sure the robbers had not attacked as an act against the government. Maybe Kizungu thought he didn't own very much, but in the mind of the Barundi, he was very rich.

Then Tony thought of Bonaventuro Ruha. He psychologically felt sick to his stomach. Here was one of the most arrogant bastards he had ever met and since the fathers had baptized his child at the mission the previous September, Tony had become appalled with Ruha's attitude. He had a soft job in Washington holding receptions and cocktail parties and attending similar gatherings and having a grand old time in a rich, first world country. He received a large salary to match ambassadors from other countries and had so many embellishments in this position that he thought himself better than anyone else. Kizungu, somewhat younger, was walking in his brother's footsteps. However he had to be more rational, realizing that he lived far away from the land of plenty, in a small village in Burundi, one of the poorest areas of the whole world. How he must have longed to get out of this hell hole and join Ruha in Washington.

Tony decided not to entertain evil thoughts of the arrogance of the Mututsi ambassador and asked the administrator if he had heard any news about the political situation and the attempted *coup*. This was a great opening line for Alberto and he didn't miss the opportunity to justify the night watches, thus explaining to the foreign priest the government's discipline. Kizungu realized Tony was trying to remain totally impartial to the conflict that already had become tribalry between Batutsi and Bahutu.

Kizungu, staring out the front window, dropped his voice and spoke frankly to Tony:

"I have heard on *La Voix de la Revolution* that there are rebels attacking our beloved Burundi from the exterior, in the southwest. They are marching and probably will come up from the flatlands to our area. It is very frightening and many people have come to see me today and all have shown their concern and nervous anticipation. The *bakuru* cannot get a message to us in such a remote place as Puma. So with my counselors we have listened to the radio and are acting according to the information that is coming to us through the media. This is the only way by which the government can act."

Tony Joseph realized how easy it would be for revolutionaries to capture this country. They would simply take over the radio station and direct all operations and attacks throughout the country via the airwaves. He became very anxious when he realized that the voice Kizungu was hearing could be that of the enemy disguised as the government. There was no way of proving that the voices were authentic and a well-planned revolution might see many more government officials killed. Further, if he did come upon the enemy with the administrator in the front seat of his vehicle, he, the local priest and driver, would be killed immediately. Fr. Tony realized that he had got himself into a life-threatening situation. Was it worth his life to offer to drive the administrator to visit his men? Fr. Tony prayed like he had never prayed before, that peace, having been disturbed for now, would be restored after this night. So he drove on with Alberto a very attentive passenger.

"Where would you like to go first, *Monsieur l'Administrateur*?" Tony asked, knowing Kizungu would be delighted by his using the official title. Africans so enjoyed hearing their official titles and the tall, lanky, frightened overseer of Puma was certainly not an exception.

"Drive along the road that goes to Ruhweza" the administrator dictated in a stern voice, taking on a ring of authority he believed his position demanded especially in a time of civil strife and crisis. The two men small-talked for awhile speaking loudly so that the noise from the motor of the volkswagen and the bumps from the road would not drown out their voices.

They hadn't proceeded very far when they saw the first group of vigilantes to the left of the road in an open area that was in the middle of a small wooded forest. Fr. Tony stopped the car and Kizungu, sword in its scabbard but with the handle firmly in his hand, got out. Tony sensed something very strange. He knew most of the men who were at this outpost: Filipo, Evaristo, Emanueli, he even knew them by their Christian names. Did Kizungu think the enemy was so close he had to carry his sword from the car not to be attacked before reaching the men who were there to protect him? Or maybe he wanted to show his power? Did he consider some of them to be the enemy? Tony surmised that Kizungu wanted an excuse to show off his shiny weapon. Surely he knew all these men, even better than the missioner knew them. Yet maybe he didn't trust them? Maybe he had reason not to trust them? A thousand questions and imagined-scenarios went through the priest's head as he walked a few steps behind the administrator, greeting some of the men who had stopped their conversations and came towards the two *bakuru* to bid them welcome.

Alberto quietly took a few men aside and spoke to them but made sure he was not within earshot of the others. Tony didn't know the tribal stock of each man but he could tell with a measure of certainty who was who. It was difficult to know each person's tribal persuasion since the question no one ever dared to ask: "Are you a 'Mututsi' or a 'Muhutu'?" was part of their unspoken taboos. Furthermore, it would be tribal blasphemy if some foreigner ever mentioned the name of either of these tribes publicly. Yet Tony, as everyone else in Burundi, always thought in tribalry terms. The pastor quickly surmised that those to whom the administrator was talking were Batutsi and those who were not invited into the inner circle were Bahutu. With that in mind Tony continued his thought-pattern:

What if?..... What if?.....What if there were no enemy?..... What if? ..... What if the troubles Saturday night, that were still continuing in a certain part of the country, were staged Batutsi insurrections?..... What if? .....What if the Batutsi were now coming together to destroy and annihilate their natural enemy, the Bahutu?.....

Tony flinched, feeling guilty for this innocent yet realistic reflection. As a priest, he had been taught to respect everyone and to try never to take sides, pitting one tribal group against another. But his suspicions remained. If the Bahutu population outnumbered the governing Batutsi 85% to 14%, then surely they should have toppled the regime two nights previously. Tony surmised that probably there was only a small percentage of Bahutu involved. If not, if the whole tribe were involved, the revolution would have been overwhelming since the Bahutu outnumbered the Batutsi almost six to one. He decided to stop daydreaming by night and believe the news that had been circulating via the radio throughout the whole country: "The Barundi must be strong, must unite and must help one another. A common enemy from the southwest is attacking the country." Tony would only be reassured in a few days that there was no enemy from without and that the government was inventing a story to keep all Bahutu in place to prevent them from fleeing over the borders or into the woods. Thus the Bahutu, caught in panic, would believe over a period of three weeks that peace would come if they stayed quiet, non-violent and in their home area. No Muhutu dared to believe that his tribe had become sheep that Batutsi wolves were preparing to attack and devour.

There were road blocks and night vigil shelters all along the road to Ruhweza. As the VW carried them from one sentinel to the other, Kizungu seemed to become quieter along the way. The missionary presumed that there were many things that he chose not to share with him, a foreigner. Furthermore if what he dared think were true, he considered the lack of conversation a sure sign that there was a conflict between the two tribes. Tony wondered if it were *kitutsi* strategy, controlling the movement of the Bahutu thus setting up areas of night vigil whereby the location of every Muhutu would be accounted for daily. Surely none of the Bahutu would ever be able to get away if they had to spend the twelve hours of darkness at the vigil outposts. What *kitutsi* cleverness! They could keep their eyes on their Bahutu enemy at all times, night and day. Tony wanted to shake his head to rid his mind of these repulsive thoughts that seemed so unfair and excessive. He tried to convince himself that such opinions were unjust and fictitious, coming from some inner dislike for the Batutsi *bakuru* and from certain inner prejudices he had against them. He found it difficult to admit to himself that he had these judgments. But time would show that his intuitions and inclinations were justified and impartially correct.

After stopping at numerous checkpoints, the two *bakuru* doubled back over the dark winding road and returned in silence to the administrator's house at Puma. Then Tony drove the final two miles from Puma back to the mission. Darkness blanketed the entire area of the offices, common rooms and sleeping quarters. The gate was locked so he got out of his car to open it using his headlights to guide him as he put his key in the lock and the chain fell to the ground at his feet. He heard Jose Suarez calling out to him, welcoming him back home. Jose told him that he had just shut off the generator and that the others had gone to their rooms.

"Let's sit and talk for a minute." Tony suggested and Jose said that he would meet him in the common room.

Tony parked his car in the back courtyard and came into the living room leaving the watch dogs outside breathing hard at his heels. Jose was already seated and was lighting an oil lamp on a small table beside his chair:

"I'm now convinced that the only enemy of the Barundi is the Batutsi", Jose began by emphasizing both proper nouns, "and the government officials are extremely fearful that the Bahutu have now demonstrated that they want to take over power in the country. This idea that a black-skinned enemy, resembling Chinese men, is totally ludicrous!" Jose said emphatically almost shouting at Tony. "The Batutsi leaders are trying to use the small Bahutu uprisings to create a panic that there is an enemy from without. In this way, they hope to keep the Bahutu in check and make sure there will be no more trouble. And so if both tribes are joined together in defending against a common enemy, the Bahutu will cause no danger! But it seems Saturday night the Bahutu showed they are fed-up and want the power since they have the numbers," the more experienced missionary exclaimed to the pastor.

"Have you been talking to anyone who can help us understand the entire situation?" Tony asked.

"The simple people have been saying how they perceive the scenario. This clarifies the picture for me."

Jose Suarez always called the people by their Kirundi names and spoke as if everyone knew the precise people he was discussing. However Tony was newer and less experienced and had much more trouble retaining the Kirundi names since he seldom understood the significance of them:

"I was talking to Nakuru," Jose went on, referring to someone Tony didn't know, "and he says he can't understand how this enemy from without looks like black Chinese people. He's right and yet he can't even read. He's never traveled to know that black Chinese is a non-entity," Tony listened as Jose made perfect sense. He went on with his philosophical expose:

"Then there is Majambomenchi. He's a smart man. He told me that he knows the Batutsi are so angry that many of their tribe were killed on the weekend that they are mounting a plot to seek revenge on the Bahutu. His son married a Mututsikazi (Mututsi woman), you know. But still intermarriage does not prevent both races from acting secretively and violently," Jose said, predicting the framework of genocide that would take place over the next weeks in Butova.

Tony told his confrere of his long evening of driving Kizungu to all the night watches as Jose moved his head up and down confirming that what the administrator had done acknowledged his theory of this bitter struggle between the two tribal rivals. The two men got up and went to their respective rooms, telling each other that they should pray hard for a solution in the situation. But both men sensed that the acting out of this tribal hatred would probably go beyond the limits of divine grace and intervention! Their people had been created free. If they wanted to usurp that freedom and live in revengeful tribalry, then God would not intervene and settle the score since freedom was a greater power than man's destruction of it.

Tony Joseph slept very badly all night long. He kept waking and imagining conflict between the two tribes. When he rose in the morning, he convinced himself that this was all an exaggeration of his imagination and that the political troubles were all behind them. He went to the church to celebrate the morning mass and to his surprise there was a large number of men waiting for him. The first week of every month was the *Mushaha* (Heart: seat of God's love). Bishop Moulin demanded that all priests stay together at the central mission for the first week of the month to build community life and to give themselves a break from travel. So Mathias Becker, great pastor that he was, had set up a program. Every day of the week they would invite a special group to the parish church for morning mass and then the priests would give a spiritual teaching after the mass and an opportunity to receive the sacrament of confession. Normally on the first Tuesday, the women had their Mushaha Day. On Wednesday more than 200 men attended. Friday was the day for 500 teen-girls and Saturday for the teen-boys. Thursday was always the morning for marriages. So Tony, being the pastor, was in charge of the *bagabo* (men) and he loved to be with them, to talk to them and to pray with them. He also ministered to the *bagore* (women) while Jose would take the *bacobwa* (girls) and the *bahungu* (boys).

The *bagabo* were sincere, honest and straight forward. There seemed to always be many more Bahutu than Batutsi, since many of the men, motivated by *mafranga* (money) worked in small jobs around the mission or at the brothers' Teachers' Training College. They had to come to work anyway so why not arrive early and attend mass and the instruction. Also it was their way of being seen by the fathers and thus staying on the right side of those who could give them money, food, clothing and work.

At mass, the only reference the pastor made to the political uprising was during the prayers of the faithful. He prayed that peace and stability come back to Burundi as soon as possible. During the instruction after mass, he spoke to the men about the gift of "motherhood and parenthood' since it was the month of Mary. He felt rather awkward, being a celibate yet teaching grown men, husbands and fathers, about parenthood. But the parish team had decided on this theme for the month of May. So Tony was relieved that he didn't have to talk about politics.

Throughout the day Jose, Luigi, Luc and Tony met from time to time walking to and from their different offices, rooms or in corridors. It was a nice day, clear and not too windy with bright sun that had shined strongly from early morning. The end of the rainy season had come and the winds would soon pick up. As Tony looked out over the hills, he thought of the day the year before when President Sabimana had invited the Emperor Haile Salasse to his home and His Highness, now an old man, came carrying his little pet dog. Most Barundi who came out to see this dignitary were amused that he would carry a little dog with him for dogs were considered dirtier than pigs in the Bantu customs. Since he was elderly, he fell asleep during the speeches and dropped his little dog on the ground. The dog yelped! Tony wondered if the "big house" as the priests in the parish called Sabimana's home-palace away from Bujarundi would now have special protection if the rebels were on their way to the area. He thought further that if it turned out to be a battle between the two tribes, then maybe the Bahutu in this area would first attack the president's home.

The day seemed to be endless and seldom did anyone speak about the situation of the country. Most Bahutu were afraid to speak about anything whatsoever. They preferred to wait and see what would happen. The simple Batutsi were also very confused for they didn't seem to understand whether this situation was good or bad for them. They felt better talking about their cows, goats, fields and crops rather than discussing politics. However some seemed to give the impression that there would be no further danger. Since the only reported dead were Batutsi, they seemed to believe there was no foreign enemy to fear. Their only concern was the Bahutu tribe that had always lived in their midst but were their natural enemy.

Late that Wednesday afternoon, May 3rd, Fr. Tony entered his office. He sat alone at his desk and tried to prioritize his life. What would be the most important thing he should do right now? He often made a list of what was essential, numbering the functions according to importance and then tried to resolve each one in its logical order. Then came a very simple but frightening thought. If this enemy were authentic and the mission were attacked, it would be vital to leave a testimonial message in the safe. Fr, Tony got up and walked over to the safe, behind the bookcase facing his desk. He removed some books and worked the combination and the door opened at his gentle touch. There were only a few personal papers that he had left in the safe a couple of weeks prior. He thought of the conversation he and Luc had had with De Winter in Lutana and realized that one responsibility had slipped his mind. If they were attacked and killed, some final message should be left to his family. In fact, the ideal would be to write to all family members, friends and benefactors and other confreres throughout the diocese, Europe and North America.

He left the office quickly and found Luc and Luigi. Jose was out saying the evening rosary with some parishioners, on some hillside, somewhere. "Somewhere" seemed always to describe where Jose might be! Tony explained to the Italian priest and the French layman that it would be a good thing to write a last will and testament and any other correspondence that would be sent to families in the case of an attack that they might not survive. Luc brushed it off in his very French style by saying he believed they would be all right. There would be no cause for alarm. Luigi seemed very reserved and introverted and walked away saying he preferred not to think about that part of the dilemma. Tony raised his voice, and asked the two men to come back and gather around him:

"This is something none of us want to do. However I suggest that we take some time before supper to say *'nos adieu*x' to our family and friends in case there will be no tomorrow for us."

As Tony spoke these words, he churned inside. He, listening to himself, put into phonetics what he had been thinking since Sunday morning. Hearing the words come forth from his own lips made the whole situation frighteningly real. Because he was in charge and responsible for others, he could not doubt the importance of this gesture and came face-to-face with the reality of what was happening. He ended the conversation by telling them that he was very frustrated about what was happening before his very eyes but welcomed the opportunity of writing a last farewell to his parents in Canada.

Quickly and briskly, he turned on his heals and headed back to his office. It was six o'clock and Cypriano had turned the generator on lighting the darkened room. Tony went over to his desk, filled his pipe with tobacco and lighted it. This was the pipe his dad had proudly brought to him the previous year when he and Tony's mom visited their son in Butova. As the smoke climbed from this beautiful red large-bowled black-stemmed cylinder, he fondly remembered their visit and the presence in his mind of his dear parents filled his office with warm memories. Tony began his letter considering it was his last to his parents:

Dearest Mom and Dad,

I love you both with all my heart. When you read this letter you will have already heard of my death. Although I do not now know when and how this moment will arrive, I promise you that I will go to my death as courageously and strongly as I have confronted all other adversity throughout my life.

I believe in Jesus Christ because, from the time I was very little, you told me about God and you taught me to love Him and show my love by sacrificing for Him. As I write these lines, I am preparing myself mentally to accept the death God has chosen for me, even the most painful and excruciating of demises. I want you to know that I love God above all things and that I am willing to suffer and die for Him because that is what He did for me. I remember, Mom, your singing a song to me when I was very young and could barely understand all the words: 'Oh how I love Jesus.

Oh, how I love Jesus. Oh, how I love Jesus. Because He first loved me.' I promise you I will die singing these words you taught.

You both have been wonderful parents for me. Mom, I will always remember you holding me on your knee and tickling the front of my neck. Or when I was somewhat older you would talk to Grandma on the phone and I would lie beside you, face down on the bed, and you would put your fingers through my curly hair. Oh how I also enjoyed the Sunday afternoons and evenings we spent at Grandma's house. I love you very much.

I remember, Dad, the afternoons and evenings in the summertime when I would go to work with you on that big diesel engine and we would be shunting passenger cars and preparing the trains to bring down to Windsor Station. Or the time, when I was eight-years old, you let me put my hand on the throttle and drive the steam engine and you had me fill out a time-sheet and I got paid for it! That was certainly before unions! Dad, I want you to know that I was very proud of you and I was honored to sit beside you as I realized that my father was such an important person to have the responsibility of running this train that seemed so gigantic to my young mind.

I thank God for both of you, my dear parents, and what you have done for me to make me happy in this world. I freely chose Burundi but if I had it to do all over again, I would have chosen somewhere else. However I have helped these poor people to prepare their road to heaven. That is worth the sacrifice of my life.

Well, Dear Mom, Dear Dad, I now must say 'Good bye'. I ask you to pray for me that God receive my soul in heaven. I am truly sorry if I have ever hurt you in any way or made you angry or anxious. I ask your pardon and blessing. Please tell all the family and friends I'm sorry for my faults and I love them very much.

Now I go on to prepare a special place in heaven for you. Why not read John, chapter 14, and be consoled by the beautiful words of Jesus, on the night before He died. I will love you and our God until my dying breath and then in heaven for all eternity.

Lovingly, Your Son,
Anthony

Fr. Tony signed the missive and addressed the envelope to his parents, licked it shut, stamped it and put his letter in a larger unsealed manila envelope and printed on the outside of the big beige folder: ***PLEASE RESPECT THESE DIRECTIONS: TO BE OPENED ONLY IN THE CASE OF MY DEATH. REV ANTHONY JOSEPH***. He walked over to the safe, turned the lock, opened it and deposited the manila envelope on the shelf inside. Then he shut and locked it and put back the books. Suddenly there was a rap on his door.

He was pleased to see Domitila Twabasabwa. She was a rather stout lady in her late thirties. Tony admired her wisdom, understanding and knowledge of life and her courage even more. She only had one leg and walked with one metal crutch that made her look clumsy and very heavy. As always she laid her crutch on the wall inside the door of Tony's office, and closing the door, hopped to the bench in front of his desk while leaning on the side wall until she reached the solid seat. Tony got up to help her but she said she could manage without his help. She had learned to be very independent and seldom asked for assistance. Tony walked over to her crutch that had a soiled towel wrapped around the top to protect her under arm. As he fingered the cloth she said:

"That metal really hurts under my arm. So I wrap a cloth around it and it is somewhat bearable."

Tony nodded to show he understood and asked her how long she had been disabled. Domitila told him that it was from the time she was a child. She had fallen down a rocky cliff and the doctor had to amputate her leg in the Vurura Hospital. It pained her a lot as she continued:

"*Pati*, you have always told us that we should accept suffering and that when we suffer, Christ suffers in us. I really meet the Lord quite a bit these days since I am called to suffer so much. Now there are added difficulties that come, not from my body, but from the political arena of our country. I cannot believe that so much evil has happened in the last few days and no one is capable of finding a solution. They tell us about 'the enemy' and call us to be on the alert, but there is total dissatisfaction with our leaders and a great deal of mistrust towards everyone else."

Then Domitila whispered to her pastor what was the purpose of her visit:

"My little girl in fine, but it is the boys that I am worrying about" she started to hesitate and slowly chose her words.

"What is the matter?" the priest asked, recalling she had three children, all miracles considering her state of health and that of her husband who was disabled and incapable of any physical work whatsoever. When all the killings on their hillside would come to an end in three weeks hence, he would be the only Muhutu adult male remaining there.

"Both my boys have worms and I am afraid if we don't get rid of them, they will both die. Can you help me?" Domitila went on, "Remember Petero Ruyigi who died last month? You buried him with your own hands? Remember his son worked for you here at the mission? Domitila asked the questions but they both knew the horrifying story of what had happened to Ruyigi.

Tony recalled Ruyigi's family fondly and how the young boy had come to work one day and told him his father was very ill. Tony had taken his bottle of pills and drove to the hut but when he arrived, Petero Ruyigi had just died, his body infested with worms. The worms had entered him as larvae and probably lived within him for a long time. They were probably ingested by drinking infected water. The larvae mate. Then the males die and the females travel throughout the body and grow. Sometimes they secrete a poison trying to penetrate through the skin. When they get free, they go back to a pond or water hole and await another victim. So Fr. Tony and the deceased man's own son put the cadaver in his volkswagen and the priest drove the corpse to the graveyard behind the church and proceeded with the burial. One's body didn't stay around very long when death occurred. People wanted a quick burial and, even though they were Christian, they were still afraid of vengeful spirits.

"Yes, I remember." Tony replied. "And do you think that your little boys are as ill as Ruyigi was?" he asked the mother. As Tony awaited her answer, a large heavy vehicle drove past his window and startled both of them. He got up, opened the door to see who had driven by and as he did, he saw a little boy beyond the road in a dirt area of the hallow fields. The little boy was Domitila's youngest son Alfonso. He was squatting in the field trying to defecate and there was a large white worm protruding from his rectum and already touching the ground. Tony wanted to throw up, realizing the horror of the little one's illness and the dire situation Domitila was experiencing. He briskly walked down the verandah, turned toward the backyard, looked out to the parking area and noticed a man getting out of a landrover. He was Arturo Shabaru, Minister of Defense and Head of the Armed Forces and Foreign Affairs Minister for the Batutsi government.

4. Shabaru: The Reprisals Begin

Fr. Tony had met Arturo Shabaru at the presidential palace during the farewell party for Mathias Becker a month earlier. He disliked this Mututsi immediately. Shabaru was loud and arrogant, discourteous and self-centered and never looked anyone in the eye when he spoke. He always exaggerated his stories, which he focused on himself. At the palace gathering, Tony wondered how vicious this man would be if ever he were confronted by anyone. As Minister of Defense, and Head of the Armed Forces, Shabaru would encounter many, many such situations in the weeks ahead. Stories had circulated throughout Burundi that Shabaru never wasted any time or effort in liquidating an enemy. Many called him "Sabimana's hit-man".

Jose had been in the dining room and came out to greet the public official. Tony walked to the landrover and welcomed him although he remained uncomfortable about the intrusion by this high-ranking Mututsi minister. He knew that the only *mukuru* that ever came to the mission as a friend was the president. All the others wanted something: to be driven somewhere, to have work done on their broken-down cars, to get some petrol that had run out or to build a house for their parents. He didn't think the Minister of Defence would come to talk about any political needs or about anything pertaining to the rebels. But he wondered if Shabaru would provide any extra security for the BanyaButova where the Batutsi reigned and Sabimana called home. Besides, that scene with Domitila's little boy still made him feel nausea. The pastor shook hands with Shabaru and Jose invited him into the living room for some refreshments. He accepted willingly and told his driver to stay with the landrover. They walked toward the verandah, up the steps to the common room. But Tony decided that the poor woman at his office was more important than this flake who drove around in a military truck. So he doubled back and went into his office with Domitila following him as she had exited his room when he had walked to the *kigo* (backyard). He handed her 21 pills telling her to give her little boy 6-5-4-3-2-1, a descending number each day for the next six days and the worms would all pass. Then he gave her a similar dosage for her other son. She smiled at the priest, her round face beaming and lighting up the whole room from wall to wall. She said:

"*Urakoze, Pati, Urakoze cane.*" (Thank you Father, Thank you very much. The word "urakoze" comes from the verb "to work" i.e. nice work, the Kirundi way to express thanks.) Tony locked his office door and proceeded to the common room where Jose and Shabaru were already talking seriously.

The Minister of Defense was telling the priest that the political situation was now under control even though they had lived a very difficult four days since Saturday. Tony joined them and asked if there was any part of the country that was still under siege. Shabaru reiterated:

"The defense corps of the Republic of Burundi now has the situation under control," he went on, "there is an enemy that is marching from the Lake to Muka and we had feared that they would come here. However the military is probably overtaking them at this very instant and so I have come to reassure you that your lives are in no danger whatsoever and that your people need not fear any attack," the highest ranking military person in Burundi lied to the priests while he sat drinking a large bottle of Primus Beer in their living room.

Tony smiled yet wondered why the Minister of Defense and Head of the Armed Forces and Foreign Affairs Minister had come to tell them all this when his troops were only a small distance away and in active combat! He had shared life with the Batutsi for the past three years and knew them and their outrageous behavior quite well. Why, he wondered, would Shabaru not be in the center of the action rather than sipping a drink with foreign missionaries? Mathias had taught him well. The first day Tony had been in the parish, Mathias told him never to trust anyone with any story whatsoever. "If you want the truth, go out, get two other men and bring all three into your office. Have the storyteller repeat his story. If he says the same thing and the two others confirm it, you can believe it as well! The only time we believe a story is when others can confirm it. If not, it's a lie!". So Tony always used this rule of three persons to come to objectivity. As he thought of what Shabaru had said, he also thought of the time when Bishop Moulin had come to the parish and preached one Sunday. He had said:

"You people are not strong at obeying the sixth commandment. You are even weaker at the seventh. But your greatest downfall is the eighth." Sad to say, Tony's parish in the Bututsi was filled with liars, even more liars than thieves or adulterers! Even though Shabaru was a *"Muproti"* (Protestant), he was a Mututsi through and through, and thus Tony was ready to question anything he might say. Lying and distorting the truth was as easy to Shabaru as breathing.

The Minister of Defense stood up and announced his departure. Both missionaries felt relieved, but they were both bewildered. Why had he come? It was considered politeness for a person of high rank to pass by the mission and greet the fathers when he was in the area. But Shabaru had never stopped before. He was not a polite Mututsi, nor was he given to graciousness. He was a mean son-of-a-bitch. What, then, would cause him to stop at the mission of Butova this day when his presence was certainly required elsewhere? As the landrover drove out from the mission and in front of the church, Jose and Tony walked back together to their offices which were side-by-side along the front verandah. Jose mentioned that before Tony had joined them, Shabaru had gone to extremes and in detail to explain how many of his friends and fellow-workers in the government had been killed. The Spanish missionary added that he noticed a vengeance in Shabaru that he had rarely detected before in any Muntu (noun for the collective name for all tribes of central-east Africa). When Tony mentioned that he always had seen him as arrogant and self-centered, Jose added that he felt the same way. But on this day he had even seen a more vengeful and egotistical side of the man.

As Jose turned to enter his office and Tony took out his key to unlock his door, an old man who had worked at the mission for many years, Eugenio Mugera, came up to the two priests and said how sad he felt. Eugenio had worked for the mission for many years and he was a simple, humble man who worked hard and was always respectful and quiet. Tony had surmised he was a Muhutu displaying these obvious characteristics of politeness and humility.

"I can't believe there is so much trouble in our dear country," Eugenio went on, "Shabaru's driver told me that all the Bahutu soldiers in the two military camps in Bujarundi and Gisumu have been killed. He said that Shabaru gave the order early that day and that they called all the Bahutu soldiers by name out to the courtyard of each military camp, stood them up against the wall and killed them all. He said there were over six hundred of them and that they had now taken their uniforms and were giving them to former Batutsi soldiers, conscripting them into the army in this time of war. Then the old man hung his head and mumbled that he had a son and two nephews who were in those two camps.

"Please say a mass for each of them, *Pati*," the old man said, taking three twenty franc notes from his vest pocket and handing them to the pastor. Tony realized that Eugenio would have to have cut trees and firewood for the fathers for two and a half days to earn this money. He folded the three bills and put them back into Eugenio's large right hand and said:

"I will offer tomorrow's mass for them and for all the soldiers who have suffered this plight. But I do not want this money. Keep it for their families. It is my privilege and honor as a priest to hasten their way to heaven by praying for the deceased. But, Eugenio, are you sure this is all true?" The old man nodded his head and said:

"I am sure they are all dead. The driver knew all the details and he had been with Shabaru in Gisumu and the capital when the killings took place. I am ashamed to be a Murundi today," he murmured softly as he walked away.

Jose and Tony looked at each other and their eyes met in that moment of total helplessness that came from complete bewilderment at anything that was happening. Tony looked at his confrere and said breathlessly:

"This situation is insane. We have just entertained a man who is responsible for killing six hundred healthy human beings and he didn't even dare mention it. I can almost taste the horrible slime that must be in his heart. That is, if he has one!"

"Maybe we should have asked him if he wanted confession," Jose said sarcastically.

"I'd like to have the privilege," Tony answered, "he'd get more from me than a rosary for penance. He'd be on his prayer knuckles for the rest of his existence! I'm sure he was only coming to see us to gather our support when the news breaks. Can you imagine? Lining up and shooting 600 soldiers who don't do anything.....no one makes a run for it. This goes along with the Bahutu way of being totally fatalistic. They probably believed that God would intervene and cause those who were shooting at them to die before the bullets were discharged! They hope and believe beyond all intelligence." Tony was totally disillusioned.

"I'm mystified," Jose responded. "I never trusted that creep and was polite to him only because he has an important job with the government." The two priests talked for a little while longer and parted ways shaking their heads and wondering what would come next.

They didn't have to wait very long! The following morning, May 4th, Tony performed the weddings in the church at 7am and said special prayers for Eugenio's son and nephews. There were three couples who married and the priest came back to the parish house jovial and walking at a brisk pace. He was happy so many people had appreciated the marriage ceremony. But it was the calm before the storm! After breakfast, he went out to his office and found many men were waiting for him. Tony had never heard so many people talking at the same time: "I need to see you, Father. *Akajambo, Pati* (a word, Father). He unlocked his office door, and heard Jose doing the same as other men were anxious to speak with him as well. Two men followed Tony into his office, right on his heels.

"Are both of you here for the same *palable (subject)*?" the pastor asked.

They both responded: "*Ego, Pati*" (Yes, Father) and followed him over to his desk. Both sat on the bench in front of his desk and told him a story he found difficult to believe. Immediately he thought of what Mathias had told him, the rule of three, and went to his door. He opened it and many men stood up and came towards him. Tony greeted them with these words:

"I want all of you, who have come to talk about what happened last evening at Ruhaha," he pointed with his chin to an undetermined area beyond the front mission yard to the hillside where the president had been born, "to come into my office right away." Tony used a method of direction that he had learned from the people as he marveled at how they could talk and point with their chins at the same time.

The pastor was astonished at the number of men who entered. In fact he had never had that many people before in his office at the same time. They sat on the floor, on the corner of his desk and many moved to the back of the room and remained standing. Some blocked the light from coming in the window, and there even was trouble closing the door. They were everywhere.

"Go ahead" he said to the man who had begun the horrible story before Tony had gone to invite other witnesses inside, "repeat what you were telling me a few minutes ago. After you speak, others can add what they have seen and heard."

The man, obviously a *mushingantahe* (elder), began by using the same words that he had already expressed to the priest when he had been with only one other witness in front of the pastor's desk:

"Late yesterday afternoon, I was walking near Ruhaha when I noticed a large group of people had gathered. There were two policemen and two soldiers that Arturo Shabaru had dropped off yesterday afternoon before he came here to greet the fathers. They had caught some young men and were examining their heads, yelling at them and beating them, saying they were traitors and rebels because they had scars in their hairlines that made them part of the plot that tried to overthrow the government last Saturday. They took them out two by two to the other side of the hill and shot them on the spot. I heard the bullets fly with my own ears. This scenario of bringing them to the place of trial, examining them and taking them off to be shot lasted until two or three o'clock in the evening (eight or nine pm) and I was told when I passed by earlier this morning that there were thirty-nine men and boys killed all together."

"I heard the number was forty-one!" said another short man sitting on the floor. They all began to discuss whether they had heard 39 or 41 and as they argued back and forth, Tony got up and went out to Jose's office. His Spanish dark-skinned confrere was white as a ghost as he too was listening to the unbelievable story that two other men were relating to him while they sat in his office.

"Jose, I have an office filled with *bashingantahe* who are recounting all the events of last night. Why not come with these two men and we can hear all the details together?

"I was afraid that madman Shabaru had done something evil since he wanted to be seen coming to our mission. He's a sly hypocrite!" Jose just shook his head in bewilderment.

They all squeezed into the pastor's office and the conversation went back and forth from one man to another as they gave all the gory details of the massacre the previous night at Ruhaha. Tony took out a piece of paper and a pen and began to make notes:

"Give us the names of those involved so that we know exactly those whom you are talking about," Tony insisted to no one in particular. So the men began shouting out names:

"Edwardi Mongu, son of Bumwe, Balatazaro Bizi, Natahaneli Poti….." said one man and then another: "Pascali Bucumi," and another: "Ruberto Sabi....." The names were coming so fast, Tony didn't have time to write them all down and asked the men to slow down for he didn't want to miss a name. They all agreed on each name as if passing each through a censorship board. When Tony asked who were doing the killing, all they could say in unison was "*Basoldat"* (Soldiers), mentioning no other names but indicating those that Shabaru had dropped off before visiting the fathers the previous afternoon. Tony wrote as fast as he could as the names continued to come. He counted all the names he had written and there were thirty-five.

"May God rest their souls in His divine peace," he said aloud and Jose suggested they all go to the church and recite the rosary for the deceased. Both priests ushered the informers out of Tony's office. Tony headed back to the dining room while Jose led the group over to the church. Tony could not pray, he was in shock and the anger of the situation and being taken advantage of by the so-called "Head" of the Defense and Army infuriated him. He went into the common room and threw a hard covered book at the chair where Shabaru had been seated less than eighteen hours previously.

He wanted to continue throwing objects all around the room but he knew that wouldn't solve anything. He fell to his knees, facing the wall where they had painted an abstract crucifix with the word "*Nkwirikire*" (Follow me) written beside it just above the organ that the president had given them. Tony wondered where the suffering Lord was in all this tragedy.

"If there really is a God in heaven," the pastor went on, "then come down and crush these murderers and this deranged Shabaru as soon as possible." Tony Joseph tried to pray as he fell to his knees but all he could feel was anger and hatred. The tears of sorrow and frustration kept running down his cheeks. He slowly got to his feet and realized he would probably never hate another human being with as much passion as he hated Arturo Shabaru at this very moment.

Jose and Tony didn't eat very much at table during the noon day meal. Both men had become totally introverted because of the wretched and horrible stories they had heard and now they were both convinced that this whole situation was racially and tribally rooted and that a lot of people had been killed because of prejudice. Never did they realize in their wildest imaginations that what they were calling "racially rooted" would become, in less than a week, "genocide".

During the meal, Jose and Tony told Luigi and Luc what the men had related to them earlier that morning. Tony noticed a crackling in Jose's voice and he sensed that he, like himself, had been crying. Their emotions were running wild because they felt so helpless and totally uncertain about the future. They knew soldiers were the cause of the murders at Ruhaha but they were not able to understand why all that carnage had taken place. Nor did any of the names resonate with people the fathers knew in the parish:

"I didn't recognize any of the names of the deceased that these *bagabo* have given us. Yet 65% of this area is catholic. So it stands to reason that if there were over thirty-five dead, then over twenty must be catholic and thus known in our parish," Tony reiterated.

The others seemed to agree with him but gave no reply nor acknowledgment that they had heard Tony or his math. The numbers didn't seem to matter nor the percentage of catholics! All that overwhelmed them was the horror of the acts themselves and the fear that they might be repeated.

Later in the afternoon, Jean-Bosco Musaba the parish secretary came to Tony's office. He was of average height, slender in build, with big round eyes, a small pointed nose and slender lips. He had a few small curls of facial hair growing from his chin. Bosco always wore a tweed colored shirt and a gray sports coat over it with dark brown pants. He knocked politely at the pastor's door. When he entered he told Tony that there was a special guest who had just driven up and parked outside the mission wall to the right of the office window. Tony mentioned that he had not heard the car, and Musaba explained that the car had not come into the yard but the guest was still beside the secretarial office, outside the mission The guest was Tomasi Muhwa, the Director of the Binka Experimental Farm and boyhood friend of President Sabimana.

Sabimana and Muhwa had often come to the mission together and the president never held back an opportunity, when he was with the fathers, of mentioning how much he liked Muhwa and that they had been friends since childhood. Once he even told them that during summer vacation one year, *"Pati Wati"* had given them the job of digging the outdoor toilets. Sabimana had laughed long and hard as he reiterated:

"Your jakes are both thirteen meters deep, *Pati*. That I can tell you first hand from digging them myself with Tomasi."

In the past, the fathers had noted that Muhwa was very much involved in politics. But they saw political allegiance as an expression of loyalty towards a friend who happened to be the President of the Republic of Burundi.

There were three families from Belgium living on the experimental farm as the husbands worked under Muhwa. The priests often stopped by to visit their fellow *Bazungu (Europeans).* They all disliked Muhwa for two reasons. He was too authoritarian with the Barundi workers, sometimes yelling at them or even hitting them when he believed that they had made mistakes. The other reason was that he never expressed himself much when there was a European in his presence. He would be very cold and unsociable. Even though he spoke impeccable French, he avoided discussing anything involving politics, giving the impression that this was his country and he would not tolerate any *Muzungu* making any comments whatsoever about domestic matters and policy. When it came to his work at the farm, he seldom talked about anything technical. The Belgians surmised that he felt very unqualified in his function as director of this big experimental farm and chose not to say very much when experts were around who were working in inferior positions to him.

Fr. Tony opened his office door and Bosco exited in front of him. They both saw Muhwa coming into the mission yard. To the priest's astonishment, he was carrying a rifle. Tony approached with some precaution and imagined Muhwa was taking stutter steps as he came up the stairway carrying the gun draped over his right shoulder. He greeted the pastor and then said:

"Could we go to a private room as I have a personal message for you."

Tony looked at him strangely and wondered if he were carrying the gun for his own personal protection, as Alberto Kizungu had brought the sword along the previous Monday night. He realized these Batutsi overlords, who had done so much evil in their lives, were now very frightened especially since so many *bakuru* had been killed in the attempted *coup* over the past weekend.

"Right this way. *Monsieur le Directeur.*" Tony spoke and motioned with his left hand at the same time. They went around the corner of the verandah, passed the refectory and turned left again in front of Tony's bedroom. Tony unlocked the door, and invited Muhwa into his private quarters. Seldom had anyone, even his confreres, ever been in his bedroom. It was his private area where he was not disturbed and where he normally found peace and quiet at night. Unlike the fathers' offices where so many people came and went throughout the day, they could leave valuables all over their bedrooms and not be afraid of them disappearing. The cost of such privacy though, was that they had to keep their rooms clean themselves and some missionaries were very untidy. Tony's room was not a model of cleanliness. He used to joke at the dust gathering and rolling around the room in a ball and said that the Lord had given him a natural rug. However this Friday his room wasn't too dirty, as he pulled out his desk chair for Muhwa. He, himself, sat on the bed.

Tomasi Muhwa was a tall and strongly built man obviously of the Batutsi tribe. He was rather handsome, with a long pointed nose and high cheekbones and medium sized lips. His forehead was round and shiny and his hair thick, curly and dark black. His skin, without any scars, was rather pale for a Muntu. He was wearing a grayish-blue African suit with short sleeves and open at the neck. Muhwa continued to hold the rifle between his knees as he sat and reached out to Tony, giving him a note: Tony read the note slowly, a bit uneasy that he was not paying attention to his guest. The note in French read:

"Mon Pere Antonio,

Je t'envoie ce fusil pour que te puisse proteger tes paroissiens. (I am sending you this rifle so that you may protect your parishioners.)

Bien a vous,

Monseigneur Luduvico Ruyaga, v.g."

Tony looked across the room staring at a blank white wall with a few family portraits breaking the monotony. He recognized the authenticity of the penmanship. It was definitely Ruyaga's writing. Luduvico always signed his name very formally and the *v.g.* for vicar general, seemed to make this gesture official. But the pastor couldn't understand the content of the note that accompanied the weapon. As the vicar general of the diocese of Vurura, why would he send this gun to the parish priest to protect his parishioners? Tony was mesmerized!

"When and where did you get this?"

"Did Ruyaga give it to you directly?"

"Does the bishop know that his assistant is sending guns to protect parishioners?" The pastor asked one question after another without allowing Muhwa to even try giving an answer or handing him the gun.

Tony thought of other questions he didn't dare express as he knew Muhwa was a terribly prejudiced racist: Does Ruyaga want me to take the Batutsi side? Is this another racial innuendo? Is this rifle to protect the Batutsi or can I also protect my Bahutu parishioners? Is Ruyaga supporting the Batutsi in general and the soldiers in particular?

Muhwa told Tony that he had received the rifle when he was at the diocesan store buying food. There he met Ruyaga who asked him to bring it to Butova. He had given him the gun directly, hand to hand. Muhwa scoffed a little at the third question, another sign of his racial prejudice. He wanted the Batutsi to always be in control and he admired Ruyaga, a fellow tribesman. The director always supported the vicar general especially in his decisions that went against those of the European Bishop Bernard Moulin.

"I didn't see the bishop and someone said he was away at another mission," was his curt reply.

Then Muhwa changed to Kirundi even though his French was excellent. Tony figured Muhwa was embarrassed to talk about something. When a Murundi felt uncomfortable about something, even if he spoke *Kifranza* (French) very well, he would revert back to Kirundi. It was a psychological way of saying: "I'm telling you this, but I hope you don't understand what I am saying!"

The director of the Binka Farm told the pastor that he had been at Vurura earlier in the day and before he had met Ruyaga at the mission, he had gone to the military camp. He related his story to Fr. Tony:

"When the governor of the military camp heard that I was coming to Butova, he called me into his office and told me I was to take twenty soldiers in my panel truck. I told him I could not take that many and the whole area of Butova was at peace and there was no need for soldiers. But he said: 'Then bring ten to the administrator of Puma'. Once again I told him it was not necessary. So he told me: 'Take seven, at least, to protect the birth place of President Sabimana. So I gave in, since he was the military authority of the area."

Tony wondered how he could invoke the rule of three! For Muhwa's sake he wanted to believe him. But that was making Tony look very stupid.

"Where are these soldiers you brought to this area, *Monsieur*?" Tony asked changing the conversation from Kirundi to French so that he would be perfectly understood.

"I left them at Puma before I came to see you," he responded in French as well.

There was so much frustration going through Tony as he realized the game this Mututsi was playing, barefacedly in his private quarters. He was one of the most despicable human beings Tony had ever met. Tomasi Muhwa would eventually turn out to be the master-organizer of all the genocide killings that would take place over the next three weeks in Butova and throughout Vurura Province. Tony figured Muhwa probably went to the camp and demanded seven soldiers and said he would deliver them himself. He then went to Ruyaga and told him the area was very dangerous and could be under attack very soon. So he got Ruyaga to write the note and Muhwa probably provided the rifle from the camp. Where would Ruyaga have obtained a gun? Now the director of the Binka Farm came trying to get the missionaries on his side. He had to make sure that the *Bazungu* would not interfere nor go against his super plan to kill as many of the Bahutu as possible. Tony was intrigued and curiously wondered why Muhwa was so involved:

"*M. le Directeur*," Tony began, "are they saying in the Vurura military camp that there could be an armed attack here in Butova?"

That seemed to be the question Muhwa was expecting and he responded quickly:

"Oh, yes, *Mon Pere*, that is the reason why they wanted to send troupes and protection here."

Tony Joseph felt upset at what he was hearing but relieved that Muhwa had started to put his cards on the table. He wanted to get soldiers and arms into the area and begin the killings and the major obstacle was the team of missionaries. That was why he had taken so much time and precaution with Tony. Tony now knew that there had never been an attack from the Congo and that was the way the *bakuru* like Muhwa were to keep people off balance, in their places and ripe for the slaughter.

Tony saw Muhwa to the door of his room and bid him good bye. However he refused to walk to the front steps with him for he didn't want his parishioners to see him with this dreadful menace to peace. This was the ultimate in rudeness towards an African visitor. To refuse *kuramutsa* (accompany a visitor part of the way home) was to send a signal that one did not appreciate the visit nor the person. Tony expressly wanted it to be clearly communicated to Muhwa that he was displeased with his lies and attempted cover-up. He realized that he had to carefully observe this rogue who had specific plans for the genocide that was to come over the next few weeks.

The four missionaries gathered around the supper table as a spirit of gloom permeated the dining room. Luc, who had many dealings with Tomasi Muhwa on different occasions at the Binka Experimental Farm, said he considered him to be a sneaky serpent. In fact he called him *inzoka (snake)* because as he had said:

"The man is slick and slimy and I would never trust him. I would prefer to deal with a greasy rattlesnake!" Luc was young and enthusiastic and had learned to love the Africans in their poverty and simplicity. It angered him tremendously that someone like Muhwa would try to extort money and goods from the poor people with whom Luc had developed a strong kinship.

"Tony," he asked sipping his soup, "was it not Muhwa that I saw coming out of your room this afternoon? What did 'ole inzoka face' want?"

Tony Joseph took a long breath and said simply:

"You'll never believe that he brought me a rifle from the vicar general to protect our parishioners!" Tony answered to the astonishment of them all.

"What?" Jose jumped into the conversation like an exclamation mark, "you better explain that one to us!"

Tony told his colleagues about his conversation with Muhwa and the astonishment and misgivings he himself had regarding the rifle.

"I could never shoot a rifle if someone were to pay me," Luigi Franco added, "well maybe if Muhwa had given it to me I would have made an exception..... and blown his brains out. What one could do with the right weapon and the right timing," he added sarcastically.

"I cannot understand the thinking of Ruyaga," Tony said to no one in particular. "Furthermore how can I believe that he is so dumb as to ask me to protect the *bakristu* (parishioners)? We all know that there are no rebels from the Congo who look like black Chinese people and who call out *Mi! Mi! Mulele!!* That was the rebels' battle cry in the Congo ten years ago. This is no more than a dim-witted plan by the government to keep the Bahutu in their homes and start the reprisals and blame it on some foreign enemy. They must think that we are as daft as the Bahutu." Jose continued in the same vain:

"They will never cease to put down the Bahutu as stupid and dumb. But I will tell you all something….." he reached a crescendo and waved his buttered knife through the air: "I always say: 'They may be crazy but they are not stupid' to quote a famous writer of Spanish literature."

They all burst into laughter, simple twitter that comes over grown men who are under tremendously emotional strain. Luc was the first to respond:

"I didn't know you ever read Spanish literature, Jose?

Luigi was next to reply jokingly:

"I never thought the Spanish had two different words for stupid and crazy. I though it was all the same to them!"

Tony had a final quirk as he added:

"Are you sure it was Spanish literature or were you reading a Basque novel?" he teased with a smile on his face knowing that Jose was very proud of his Catalan roots. Then he became more serious:

"I've compared the penmanship on Ruyaga's note to other letters he has sent me in the past, and the writing is authentically his. Maybe I should send a runner to Vurura tomorrow to ask him for further explanation. Then we would be absolutely sure what his intentions are."

"Good idea," Jose said, "but there are still barriers along all the main roads to Vurura and it will be hard for a messenger to get through," he added.

"The porter can go through the woods and there will be no problem with checkpoints. I'll choose a Mututsi so there should be no *matata* (problems in Kiswahili) with one of them out of our district or missing night watch. I'll write the note in English for Ruyaga spent his summers in London when he studied in Rome. So any imbecile who stops the porter at a barrier or elsewhere would never be able to understand it. I'll send greetings in French and add the important message in English." Tony had the exact plans in his head as he spoke to the others. Luc started to laugh:

"Yesterday I tried to go to Muka and was stopped twenty...(?).., thirty...(?)... times by barriers. One teenager at the barrier came to the car and said: *'Laissez-penser!'* (allow to think) instead of *"Laissez passer'* (allow to pass). Luc howled, thinking back to the error which for a Frenchman was colossal. He added: "I told him I would let him think from now 'til eternity. He never understood a word I said. *Zoot, Alors!!*"

The confreres finally got up from table, recited their evening prayer together, spending a long time mentioning the names of those murdered at Ruhaha the previous day. After chapel, Tony went to his room and could feel mental fatigue shooting through his head like a thunderbolt. He took two aspirin that he had in his small wooden medicine chest, washed them down with a glass of water, got into bed and switched off his flashlight . He slept soundly that night and woke, hoping for a better day on the first Friday of May. As he walked outside to wash, he was soon greeted by dreadful news.

Cypriano Kitwi came running towards Tony as he stepped to the common sink on the back verandah:

"*Pati, Pati*, there's lots of news!" the cook exclaimed. "Daudi Murore, the president's brother, just told me that the soldiers killed many people last night on the hillsides around Ruhaha. He said that there were more shot last night than the previous evening." Cypriano had come from opening the gate of the compound early that morning and there was a tad of *kitutsi* or smugness in his voice. He didn't have to say it but he surely was happy that revenge was being taken by the soldiers for the Batutsi leaders who had been killed on the weekend. Nor did he have to say that he felt the protection of the army at Puma that most people now knew was entirely Batutsi and out to kill every Muhutu that stepped out of line.

Tony stood on the verandah and looked out to the neighboring hills beyond Ruhaha to his right, to the region that lead to Vuvoga. Somewhere out there, he thought, men or boys have been killed again. Life that seems at times so precious to the Bantu people is extremely fragile. That life has been snuffed out. Why? Why? Why do these people hate each other so much? They speak the same language, they live in the same areas, they buy clothes and food at the same marketplace, they share the same religious values, they pray the same prayers, they worship the same God?

What is there in a Muhutu that is so despised by the Batutsi? What makes up a Mututsi that is hated by the Bahutu? Can christianity survive in this country? Is not all religion a coat of varnish? Is trying to christianize Batutsi and Bahutu, teaching them to love each other, is that not a mission that is impossible? But why is the grace of God not greater than any hatred or killing? And yet why do so many have to die because of tribalry?

For a brief moment, Fr. Tony Joseph thought back to the time when he was in the theologate in 1968 and the superiors had asked him to write an essay on the part of Africa he wanted to live in as a missionary. He wrote without any doubt whatsoever: "Burundi: the land where Christ is already alive and present in the people. I want to work hard all my life to deepen the presence of God in these people, the Barundi" He now believed this was all bullshit!

So many extraordinary missionaries had tried to build this vision for the past eight decades and now the Barundi were being killed at unbelievable rates by each other every day. It was a far cry from: "Greater love than this hath no man, that he lay down his life for his fellow man." All had failed miserably! All was lost, hopelessly destroyed by man's inhumanity to man! These savages were nothing more than pagans. Didn't the old missionaries who had given their lives to implant the gospel in Central Africa, ever teach the people the fifth commandment: 'Thou **Shalt Not Kill'**? Tony walked into his room, closed the door and heard himself utter something he never thought he would say nor did he ever expect anyone else to say: "Why, oh why, why did I ever ask to come to this god-forsaken country?" He threw himself on his bed as tears of despair flowed from his broken heart, through his eyes and into the pillow case. He tried to conjure up the courage to dress for the day ahead, but a strength greater than him paralyzed his muscles and did not allow movement. A long time afterwards, seeming like hours but only forty-five minutes later, he heard a knock on his door. It was Jose telling him that he had just heard of more killings and wondered if Tony had overslept. Tony wiped his face with a shirt he had picked up on the way to opening the door and felt the bitterness of the tears that had seeped into the side of his mouth. He did not want Jose to see him in such a state so he spoke through the door and told his associate he would be ready and in the dining room in five minutes.

On his way to the dining room he saw the gardener Barnabe Ntware, who had come to work early. He asked him if he would be willing to carry an important letter to the vicar general at Vurura and sleep overnight and come back the following day. The young Mututsi obliged and Tony wrote the note quickly and put it in an envelope. He asked Ntware to stay at Vurura until he could give it directly to Monseignor Ruyaga and await a reply.

Today, the first Friday of the month of May was the *mushaha wa bacobwa* (girls' retreat) so Jose was responsible for organizing the activities and the liturgy for the young girls. However Jose was the world's worst planner! From morning to evening there would be foul-ups and cancellations, mix-ups and hesitations throughout the whole compound. Many of the girls would be in the cinema while others would tour the garden when they were suppose to be at an instruction in the church building. Some were walking around the compound or leaving the mission to go to the market when a common visit to the garden was taking place. Women were ready to give a talk on hygiene in the old catechumenate but no one knew the talk was taking place. It was one blunder after another.

However Jose would never loose his enthusiasm for the young teenage girls. His colleagues would sit back and watch him in action, laughing, telling stories, showing cinema and running here and there to organize things that should have been set up days earlier. The Friday *Mushaha* normally drew five-hundred girls. They were asked to arrive for the 7am mass and stay until 3pm. But most were late in arriving and late in leaving. For a day each month, the mission was overrun with these girls, most of whom had never gone to school, but who took the *mushaha* as an opportunity to come to the mission and show off their clothes and latest fashions. The celibate priests were often overwhelmed at how beautiful the Barundi girls were, dressed in their colorful flowing *"impuzu"* (sari) with similar material wrapped around their hair, raising their heads sometimes to over one foot in height, making them seem majestically tall and extremely elegant.

So at table that morning, Jose mentioned that he was going to talk to the girls about the Blessed Mother and how she protects girls from evil. He would mention nothing about the political situation. The others smiled but no one said anything. There had always been a difference of pastoral perspective between the Latin thinking Jose and the Germanic-Anglo philosophy of Mathias passed on to Tony. They considered Jose's puritanical views as exaggerated fanaticism and regretted his impulsive attitude especially toward young ladies.

Later that afternoon, Tony and Luigi sat in the common room together relaxing after a tumultuous day. Many of the girls had gone to confession and then afterwards had come to the office for *majambo* ("words", meaning discussing personal problems). Often there were family issues usually pertaining to the dowry and promise of marriage. The girls found the priests' guidance helpful and encouraging. There were always cases of young ladies who had run off with young men without obtaining the blessings of the church. This was considered concubinage and the reparation was severe. They had to be reinstated into the good graces of the church which often meant thirty days in the catechumenate or a month's coming to daily mass. But they could not receive the sacraments until this public penance had been completed!

Finally Jose joined them and seemed disappointed with the attendance. He had counted only 283 *bakobwa* (girls) when he signed their "*mushaha*" cards before dismissing them. His two confreres thought the number was more than adequate to have filled their day with much work. But Jose's mind was wondering as he already was thinking of something else:

"I hear they are going to do judgments in public at Puma tomorrow. I think you should be there, Tony, to make sure they don't take advantage of those poor Bahutu who seem to be getting killed like flies." Jose said, rubbing his chin and frowning at the same time.

Tony assured him that he would take a trip to the local government offices the next day to see what was happening. Jose went on:

"These Batutsi are incredibly vicious and vengeful. Some girls told me that the soldiers round up some men and boys in their different areas and bring them down to a valley and shot them in front of witnesses. The soldiers were calling them *bamenja* (traitors) and justifying their killings because these had betrayed the country. But the girls say there is no proof that those now dead were guilty of any crime. Some have been killed simply because the local Batutsi did not like them and told lies or invented stories to condemn them. But there is no proof of guilt because they truly are innocent! *Zoot, alors!*" the Spanish missionary trained in France said with disdain in his voice.

"I will go to Puma later today and again a few times tomorrow to assure that everything will be done with justice to all," Tony responded, sternly.

The young pastor spent the rest of the day wondering what hideous situation was now upon him. He prayed imploring God to relieve him of this burden. Then the priest realized that God had always guided him and thus had His own particular reasons why He wanted him at the head of this parish when this situation looked so bleak. His prayer ended in hope and simple joy. He had a mission and God never promised it would be easy. But He did promise that He would always be with him as his strength. Tony knew, with God's help, that he could handle any situation that might arise. As he reflected, he felt filled with confidence. But still unknown to him were the countless situations that would arise over the next three weeks whereby he would totally question His God and what he would be compelled to do as this barbarous mayhem would play itself out in horrific calamity.

Late Saturday afternoon, Fr. Tony Joseph sauntered over to his volkswagen in the *kigo* of the mission and got behind the wheel. He said a short prayer, as was his habit, asking for protection and road safety. However he didn't spend any time thinking of the possibility of an accident! Rather he realized he wasn't going very far, just to Puma. But he feared the situation that was upon him. He had thought of inviting Jose but decided against it since the Spaniard, with his hot-blooded temperament could react emotionally and violently to the situation. And Luigi could not help much either, since he was still learning the language and was totally revolted by the savagery that he had seen over the past week. He had questioned his stay in Burundi and voiced a thought at table the previous day that when all this was settled, he would ask his superiors to send him to some other mission country. Luigi believed nothing could be as bad as what he had witnessed over the past few days. Who could blame him for wanting out?

So Tony drove alone, in front of the mission, out the gateway, in front of the church and then turned right, past the sisters residence and along the winding road to Puma. As he approached the *arrondissement*, he realized the number of people walking along the road on a Saturday afternoon was much more than usual. He stopped once he saw Sister Maragarita walking back from the common. She greeted him and then clicked her tongue against her teeth and lips, expressing to him that the soldiers were handling the prisoners very cruelly.

"I had to leave," she added, "it was terrible. You have to do something to stop the beatings, *Pati*."

Tony felt the burden on his shoulders getting heavier as he drove slowly onto the Puma compound. On his left was the courthouse and beside it was the prison. To the far right was the infirmary and directly on his right was Administrator Kizungu's residence. Since the road was filled with people, he had to stop many times before he finally found a place where he could park his car. As Fr. Tony got out of the car, he heard one voice over all others. In fact the large crowd, moving in all directions, was extremely quiet with most of the people looking down to the earth in useless abandon but listening to every word that was uttered. It was as if they didn't want to see what was transpiring but unwillingly listened.

As he walked in front of his car, the screams of a male voice overpowered the whole area. Then he heard a thundering sound, the thud of two heavy substances suddenly clashing. He looked over to a hut on the far end of the compound and saw a soldier with a large billy club in his right hand hitting a young man over and over and over again with the strap. It was, he quickly calculated, about ten inches long and was cone shaped with a diameter of two inches at the top narrowing off to one inch at the handle. It was obviously solid rubber and reminded him of a thick piece of wood that policemen throughout the world used as billy clubs to break up riots. As he heard the sounds the weapon made, he realized these weapons were thick reinforced rubber, probably taken from an old tire that had exploded into small bits of thick, heavy, synthetic rubber. The soldier was shouting at the top of his voice and beating the young man everywhere on his body. Since the youth had no shirt and only wore khaki shorts, most of his body was unprotected and bloodied. The soldier hit him continuously on the back of the head, on his neck, across his back and then, as he turned, on his exposed chest. As the man fell to the ground, the soldier lunged at him and hit him with the rubber hose over and over again on his thighs and legs and bare feet. From time to time the captive would let out a scream and beg for mercy. "*Kigongwe! Kigongwe! Kigongwe!*" (Mercy! Mercy! Mercy!) was heard all over Puma. The youth's arms were tied at his biceps by some thin cord and his limbs and hands hung limp, parallel to his hips as he continued to beg for compassion.

Fr. Tony Joseph went pale, his heart pumping nervously and his hands felt sweaty. At first he thought he had to intervene and then he realized that this would be impossible since both the soldier, his companions and the crowd were hysterical and totality uncontrollable. He turned quickly to God and asked for guidance to do the right thing and begged that this massacre stop. He prayed for the young man that his life might be spared.

Some people moved about in the general area where Tony was and then he saw Jean-Bosco Musaba, his secretary, walk by with Jacabo Karani, the local infirmarian. They both greeted the pastor and turned away half smirking but partly embarrassed to be seen in such a scenario. Tony filled with anger. These two pseudo-educated christians were more *kitutsi* bastards than followers of Jesus. Since Shabaru's passing, they were basking in the sunshine of a total domination, even annihilation, of the Bahutu. That some Bahutu were being beaten was sweet revenge for the *bakuru* who had been killed during the *coup* earlier in the week. Vengeance and violence would companion each other over the next three weeks.

Tony turned back to where the soldier now stood bellowing forth commands to the three other captives as the first now lay motionless on the ground. The three stood facing the crowd and the soldier screamed at them motioning to markings found in their hairlines. Because of these markings, they were considered supportive of the rebels that had killed the government officials the previous Saturday. They stood in front of the lead soldier, with their heads bent in submission to authority. Two policemen approached the men whose hands were tied tightly behind their backs with strong cords around their biceps. The policemen pushed back the heads of the first and third prisoner, bending their necks and pointing to their hairline as they shouted: *"Bamenja! Bamenja! Bamenja!"* Then the soldier was all over the three of them with his rubber club. He pounded their flesh relentlessly, and the sound of the weapon hitting their bare, fleshy bodies caused them to scream and beg for mercy. The setting continued for what seemed to be an endless amount of time and finally all the young men fell to the ground, obviously overwhelmed with exhaustion from the beatings.

Tony felt the urge to approach the area where the tragedy had taken place to make sure he had seen everything but his stomach felt so upset and churning that he decided to leave rather than prolong his agony. As he prepared to walk back to his car, he saw some policemen come forward, pick up the four accused and carry them by their arms and legs with heads hanging low and bobbing back and forth, to the hut that was directly behind them. They entered by a small door, carrying the young men one by one. Then everyone heard four loud thuds as the policemen let each prisoner fall to the hard ground floor obviously hitting the earth with their stomach and groin areas first.

Tony drove home realizing he had now experienced the passion of Jesus Christ. Never again on Good Friday would he have to imagine the beatings, torture, passion and death of His Lord and Savior. He had lived it that Saturday afternoon at Puma, Burundi.

The following day when Fr. Tony came into the sacristy to vest for the 7:15 Sunday Mass, Jean-Bosco came to him and told him that during the night, three of the four young prisoners had died! The priest felt his eyes well up with tears and could not control the words that he spoke to himself in the intimacy of his own heart: Killers, Killers, those Batutsi soldiers and policemen are all a bunch of murderous rogues.

5. From Reprisals To Genocide

The last thing Father Tony wanted to do on this Sunday morning was to say mass. But he had been taught in the seminary that sometimes, when a priest has settled into an apostolate, he can loose his desire and enthusiasm for the eucharist. Tony had always tried to fight this apathy. He loved the cliché: "Celebrate this Mass as if it were your first Mass, as if it were the only Mass you will ever celebrate, as if it were your last Mass". He wondered if the situation in Butova was so grave that maybe this would be his last mass. He consoled himself realizing that if he were to die, this horrendous situation would be over for him. He was starting to think fatalistically, like the Bahutu, almost inviting death.

Tony normally removed his watch when he celebrated. He believed that he was entering the timelessness of God and never wanted to hurry by looking at his timepiece and rushing. When he celebrated the Lord's Mysteries, time was non-existent. So, on this first day of the week, the only positive in his life was that the next hour or so he would be "alone with his God" in prayer. He gathered the servers together, along with the catechists, the readers and Sister Maragarita and they stood in a large circle in the middle of the sacristy as he prayed for God's blessings on the liturgical actions each was about to perform. Then he concluded his prayer by mentioning those who had been killed over the past week and especially the young men who had died the night before at Puma.

As they terminated the prayer, Tony noticed Jean-Bosco Musaba staring at Daudi Murore for a long moment and he read the message they communicated to each other: "This priest, our pastor, is praying for the Bahutu who are traitors!" They didn't have to translate their thoughts into words. The eye contact was enough for Tony to realize that they were more *kitutsi* than *kichristu*! (christian!) He knew that he had overstepped himself. This wasn't a prayer that would be acceptable to the Batutsi parishioners of Butova. But what the hell! He prayed it because he believed it to be the Holy Spirit who had put it in his heart and on his lips. His zeal for Christ and the coming of the Kingdom filled him with strength and he knew that he had a mission to accomplish. It wouldn't be easy, it wouldn't be safe, but he had to give witness to the justice of God and the life of Christ as handed down through the gospels. He took a deep breath after the prayer and prepared to march with Jesus to his personal Jerusalem.

During the mass on this, the fifth Sunday of Easter, he read the gospel from the fifteenth chapter of St. John. *"I am the true vine, and my Father is the vine grower,"* he expounded. "*He takes away every branch in me that does not bear fruit and every branch that does, he prunes so that it bear more fruit."* As he read the text, Tony realized that in God's plan there was absolutely no way of escaping the royal road of the cross.

"If you do not bear fruit," he told the people in his homily, "you are good for nothing and will be thrown into the fire and burned. If you do bear fruit, you will be pruned to bear even more. Pruning is surrendering to suffering." The pastor went on to tell his people that no matter who they were, and what the occasion of life might be, the royal road of cross, suffering, lay ahead for all of them. He analogized that sweet-smelling roses have thorns and vegetables grow best in manure-strengthened fields. So all suffering has a part in God's plan to bring about the kingdom. There was a drop of bitterness in every cup of life. Yet there was always much goodness and enormous beauty amid the suffering and pain.

Tony tried to avoid focusing on the political situation knowing that whatever he said would not bear any weight because the people considered him an outsider, a foreigner, a *Muzungu*, with absolutely no appreciation for their local affairs. However if he did say something, it could be detrimental to his position of authority since both sides would see him as interfering. He thought of the boys whom he had witnessed being beaten to death at Puma the preceding evening. If he opted to say nothing, who would come to their defense? He saw himself confronted by a similar analogy that Jesus presented in this Scripture. If you don't do anything, you are only good for the fire and if you do something, then you will be pruned for a more painful situation. But finally Fr. Tony realized that if he were truly connected to the Lord Jesus Christ and if he tried to do what Jesus would have done, everything would work out for the best. As he celebrated the eucharist, he imagined opportunities where he would be able to witness true Christ-like love and justice to all. It would not be easy, and like the Savior, it could lead to his untimely death, but if Father Tony Joseph had a mind to follow Jesus, he must learn to deny himself, take up the cross daily and walk in the Lord's footsteps.

'Christianity,' he thought, 'was a tremendous philosophy but a very difficult ideal to live.' He had often preached: "We must live as Christ lived! He lives in us!" Yet now he realized to live as Christ lived was the most difficult ideal to ever accomplish. Tony prayed that God's grace would strengthen him to meet the challenge.

There seemed to be a larger number of people at the Sunday mass this week. Certainly they far outnumbered those who had attended the previous Sunday. The Batutsi probably believed that peace had come back to the area while the Bahutu realized that the soldiers were extremely dangerous. They seemed to be more frightened and anxious than angry or frustrated.

Tony also celebrated the second mass that was attended by younger people and children, those who had stayed behind at their homesteads to guard their family's possessions. He always found this mass anticlimatical since there was such a large attendance at the first service and only a scattering of youth at the second. Many group gatherings would take place immediately after the first mass and he found the discussions both stimulating and practical. Sometimes he would have to leave these discussions, often before they had come to a consensus or common decision, to celebrate the second mass. At this service, he bit his lip once more and didn't mention anything about the political situation. But he did underline the teaching that had been the gist of his homily earlier: we are all called to suffer with the Lord and that no matter how often we try to avoid it, the Lord will be there to prune us if we are fruitful or allow us to be destroyed if we don't bear fruit.

After the church service, Tony watched the *Chiro* march outside and carry their flag all over the mission compound. Then he went to the youth center in the back of the mission where the *UGA* had gathered. This was Jose's special Sunday group and when he was there, he took great pains to animate them. However this Sunday, Jose had traveled to Ruhweza and only would return when the young people were in the process of finishing their meeting. This was one of the great disappointments of the missionaries' lives. Often there were activities taking place at the same time and, since their parish was so vast and the roads so bad, it was impossible for the same person to be at two or three simultaneous meetings. So they would substitute for one another, but then their own gatherings would suffer. Tony attended both the *Chiro* meeting and that of the *UGA*. But he would have preferred to have spent all his time with the *Chiro* and leave the *UGA* to Jose. Yet Jose was ministering to another community in the name of all of them. So mission life was very much teamwork. That had been the main reason why Tony had been attracted to the Missionaries of Africa: to work as a team with other committed men of God.

When the *Chiro* and *UGA* dispersed, Tony spent the rest of the afternoon preparing for the catechists' meeting the following day. This would be his first catechists' meeting as pastor and he felt a knot in his stomach as his nervousness started to show. He had admired Mathias and the way he handled the catechists. They had a nickname for him and it was *"Janja"* meaning "lion's paw". Mathias Becker was tall and strong, nearly two meters and 110 kilos. He dwarfed any African who would dare stand close to him. The Germanic ways often became apparent in Mathias especially when he had to make decisions. In a split second he would come to a conclusion and the Africans thought it reminded them of a lion prancing on its prey. You always knew where you stood with Mathias for his reactions followed his logic! But the Barundi appreciated him because everything was clear, direct and precise. He seemed to have mannerisms that would never exist among the Bantu people. For this reason they had held him in highest esteem and called him after the king of all the beasts.

Tony also had a nickname. When he had arrived at the parish two years earlier, Mathias and Jose had been alone, together. They laid down what was a very clear plan for the BanyaButova that was rather demanding. But they were fair. When Tony arrived, straight out of language school, a young man of 26 years of age, Mathias initiated him into the pastoral plan for the parish. Tony quickly learned not only the language but the demands put on the people so they named him *"Rudube"* which means "the difficulties are increasing". When Tony was appointed pastor to replace Mathias, the parishioners realized that the pastoral plan, already initiated, would continue and *Redube* would cause further problems! Tony never forgot his nickname and, although embarrassed about the negative connotation, used it when he needed the added force in what he was saying. Jose was frail and thin and when he walked his body seemed to curve in an arch. Thus the clever and observant Barundi called him "*Rubavu*" which means "rib".

The first Monday of the month was always the catechists' recollection and meeting day. However in May of this year, that day fell on the first of the month, which was the Feast of St. Joseph the Worker and a special day of celebration for the members of the Legion of Mary. So the catechists' day had been postponed to the following Monday. It was providential that the change had taken place, since the first of May had immediately followed the attempted *coup.* However life seemed somewhat normal on the second Monday and Tony was pleased that the postponement had given him some extra time to prepare his first catechists' meeting. He expected a full attendance of catechists who were forty-five in number all paid by the parish. They never missed a meeting, since that was the day that they received their salaries. So it was vital that each be there for they lived from one payday to the other. Most of the catechists were married men with children and received extra *francs* for their wives and each child.

The catechists started to arrive late Sunday afternoon. Those who lived farthest would leave home after the Sunday morning services at their own outstations. The earliest arrivals also included some who were old and could not walk three hours to Butova and three more hours back home in the same day. So they would arrive Sunday afternoon and some food would be prepared for them as they would sleep in the meeting room. The others, who lived closest, would come early Monday morning and be there for the meeting's start at 9 o'clock.

Tony hovered over the catechism book *Yaga Mukama* (Come to the Lord) and tried to pick out points that were relevant to the lessons the catechists would be teaching over the next month. Many of the head catechists had taught in their outstations for over thirty years. Before Tony had even been born! So he had the highest respect and admiration for most of them. Yohani Bora from Mundi who was a tall thin man, very serious in temperament and always concerned about people, would be there. Mundi was the largest outstation of Butova Parish with over 2,000 baptized catholics. Danieli Rutega from Vuvoga was another humble man that Tony liked very much. He always felt a surge of buoyancy when he was in Danieli's presence. The head catechist at Vuvogo had driven with Tony when they took Mathias to Bujarundi to fly back to Germany. Danieli had told Tony that it was the first time he had ever seen an airplane on the ground and was amazed at its size. The only airplanes he had ever seen were the few that had flown high over Vuvoga. Danieli had been a catechist there for thirty-three years.

Eusebio Bitega of Lusaga was first to arrive that afternoon. Eusebio was a short rather stocky man with a round face and pudgy nose. When he spoke he had a rasping sound in his voice and would often stop in the middle of a sentence to make sure Tony understood what he was saying. "*Urumva, Pati*?" (Do you understand, Father? literally: have you heard?). Tony loved the times he stayed over in Lusaga. He and Seb would get together often and the catechist would coach him in *Kirundi ciza* (good Kirundi). Eusebio was always cooperative and patient with the young missionary.

There were also some catechists that Tony didn't enjoy. They were mostly Batutsi who were very arrogant. The young pastor felt intimidated by them, as they seemed to judge him as incompetent because he was so young. They didn't give him a chance to lead the parish and find his own way. At the head of the list was Artimo Tanze of Bihovu. He was a tall, solemn man who never laughed nor smiled. Tony considered Tanze a real hypocrite. He didn't trust him and believed Tanze was only a catechist for the prestige and monthly pay day. At times, Tony questioned his judgment of Artimo since he had been a catechist for over twenty-six years. "There must be some good in the man," Tony tried to convince himself, "at least he's good at camouflage, for he tries to be seen as someone doing good. Yet he's a real charlatan!" Later that month, the assistant catechist of Bihovu would come to see the pastor in private. He would give him a letter signed by many BanyaBihovu. They wanted the church to discipline Tanze immediately. He had gone to the military and given them the names of many Bahutu who, because of the catechist's testimony, had been rounded up by the soldiers and killed. Many of the deceased were part of the catechumens that Tanze had prepared for baptism. Yet they had died without the sacraments, never seeing their baptism day that summer. Others he testified against were members of the outstation of Bihovu. The people now were calling Tanze *Judasi Isicarioti* referring to the apostle who has betrayed the Lord.

"They are angry, *Pati*, since they believe a catechist is a man-of-God and should not be the cause of others' dying," was the way the catechist worded it for Tony.

There was also Alberto Simba from Ruhweza. He was a short man with small features and a husky, sharp voice. Simba had short white hair. Alberto was his own man, oozing with self-confidence and had a *kitutsi* way that was very supercilious to the point of being overpowering. Alberto liked to make others work around the outstation of Ruhweza but never did very much himself. But Tony enjoyed his company because he spoke loudly and distinctly and thus was easy to understand. He laughed loud and often. Despite his good qualities none of the priests trusted Alberto with the BanyaRuhmeza and wondered how well they were being prepared for baptism. Tony knew he had to keep a special eye on Ruhweza to assure that all went well. Simba means "lion" and like the king of the forest, commands respect. In most instances, Alberto Simba got it. Most of the Batutsi catechists looked upon Alberto as their leader and spokesperson. However others, especially the Bahutu, respected Yohani Bora who also was a Mututsi but whom they trusted. By his judgments and actions, many could see that he was one person who had transcended race and tribalry through the power of Christ's love.

As Tony chatted with the catechists he realized that there were two who were missing. Stefano Muzoca his favorite catechist from Bucari was not there. He was a short rather stocky man with a receding hair line and small black mustache that ran in a thin straight line above his lips. Stef always had a ready smile and shared the problems of the BanyaBucari quite openly with the fathers. He talked about working in the fields with his wife and his chest would swell when he shared about his seven children. His eldest, Gerardo, had just been accepted into the high school-seminary. Tony sought out Eusebio Bitega since his outstation, Lusaga, was closest to Stefano's at Bucari. Eusebio replied casually dropping his voice to a whisper:

"People are saying that Stef was arrested for those things last week. A friend of mine came to the house yesterday and said the soldiers from Vurura took him with them to the military camp. This must have happened Thursday of Friday."

Tony churned inside. Why hadn't Eusebio shared this with him since a catechist missing was of tremendous importance to the missionaries?

The other missing catechist was the local secretary Deogratias Pungu. Along with Jean-Bosco Musaba, he worked in the parish office every day and helped with the catechetical teaching at Butova mission whenever there was need. Jean-Bosco, on the other hand, was a conceited Mututsi and the full time secretary. He considered the office his personal property and spoke enough French to communicate with the fathers when the situation warranted their talking about some particular item of business and not letting the Africans know what they were saying. He was valued by all the missioners because he was very intelligent and loyal to the causes of the church. He even considered himself part of the fathers' team and hoped someday to travel with them when they attended diocesan meetings in Vurura or the neighboring parishes of Lutana, Bumeza or Mutwe. However he was never invited to the catechists' meeting, but would come by to greet them all.

Deogratias, on the other hand, was just learning all the work in the secretariat and humbly did what he was told. He didn't speak or understand French and felt very inadequate compared to Bosco. It was similar to many Kitutsi-Kihutu situations throughout the southland. The Mututsi outshined the Muhutu in most instances! The Batutsi, more educated and overriding, took advantage of every situation to dominate and control the Bahutu with whom they worked. Deogratias never overstepped himself and Bosco always felt very much in control of the secretariat when the two men worked side-by-side. If Bosco were too busy with something, Deogratias cheerfully looked after the needs of the people who came to the office window.

So on this bright Monday morning, Fr. Tony moved around from one small gathering of catechists to another until he saw Jean Bosco who had come to visit:

"Where is Deo?" he asked his secretary.

"I haven't seen him since Saturday afternoon, when we closed the office," came his reply, "but I have heard that the soldiers have been arresting many who live on his hillside, Butano." This was all that Bosco would volunteer and Tony at once became very anxious about the whereabouts of Pungu and the danger that his secretary might be experiencing. Sad to say, Fr. Tony would soon be shocked when he would hear of the sort that awaited poor Deogratias Pungu.

Tony continued to greet the catechists and they came up to him shaking his hand and exchanging pleasantries. He kept asking each leader about news from his particular area and most were content with saying "*Amahoro*" (Peace) even if they knew that the events of the past week were far from peaceful.

At 9 o'clock, they all gathered in the classroom that Jose had remodeled to serve as a cinema. In the daytime there was little light when the curtains were closed. But this morning they were open and the bright light from the sunshine outside lit up the room. Tony welcomed them and handed out the fathers' schedule of visits to the outstations for the next month. Usually the priests spent the first week together in the mission and did the *"Mushaha"*. Then for the remaining three weeks, one father would stay in Butova and the other two would cover an outstation each from Tuesday until Sunday. This way they covered 50% of their parish each month, since there were eleven outstations large enough to warrant a priest visit for instructions, daily mass and singing classes, confessions, baptisms of the newborns and visits to the local school classes and the catechumenate. With all these activities, the fathers rarely had any spare time and relaxed by walking long distances to visit the sick and give them the sacraments. However with Luigi just learning the language and Tony being inexperienced as pastor, things had to be arranged at a slower pace over the next few months. Tony apologized for what he termed "youthful inadequacy" and asked them to be patient and compassionate. There were many snickers in the room! The Barundi could never understand how intelligent, learned men had so much difficulty speaking their language and understanding their way of life. In this case, it was not only Luigi's struggle with Kirundi but Tony's having to learn the intricacies of a Burundi parish: preparations for the Banyabatisimu to be baptized, first communions, marriages and all the processes dealing with school children. The catechumens had to be questioned in June (a two week process) and the baptisms of some 250 adults would be scheduled for sometime in mid-August with confirmation and baptism of their little children a few weeks later. Tony again asked for their indulgence with him as their new, inexperienced pastor.

Then Tony confessed to the spiritual leaders that the political situation was a great concern for him. He wondered if Burundi, a majority Roman Catholic country, would follow the principles of the gospel. Further he understood the responsibility of the teaching church to form the conscience of the people in accordance with christian morality. There was total silence in the room. One could hear a pin drop and no one dared show he was in favor or against what the pastor was saying. But Tony knew their fears were caused by their being more Batutsi or Bahutu than Bakristu! The events of the next two and one-half weeks would show where they stood as Christians and how they felt about their particular tribe and ethnicity. Many would betray their belonging to Christ's Kingdom and others would sacrifice their bodies for the principles of Christ's gospel.

After speaking about their common responsibility of witnessing to love and justice, Tony then reviewed different points in the catechism. There were not four parts to mass as they had been taught so long ago. Church catechetics, rooted in Vatican Council II, now asked that people understand that mass was an experience of the word and the eucharist, similar to the synagogue and temple encounter for the Jews in the time of the Savior. He corrected the misnomer: "Mass Without a Priest" and called their service: "Liturgy of the Word". Then he explained the content of the Sunday gospels over the next four weeks and gave them some ideas or homily hints on how to present the upcoming themes for their Sunday services at their particular outstations.

The morning seemed to fly by very quickly and soon it was time to pay the catechists and have lunch. Tony had taken two hours the previous evening getting each catechist's envelope ready. He thought that if he were an accountant, this would be a full time job! But it was only another chore in preparing for the catechists' meeting. Each received a base salary, according to the number of times, two or four, that he taught each week. Some taught Tuesdays and Thursdays, others taught Wednesdays and Fridays, and still others taught all four days. Then there were special bonuses: three francs for every year of service, and ten francs for a wife and five francs for every child at home. Some catechists made over 600 francs ($6.00 US). Others were between 550 and 600 francs but those who only worked part-time received 300 francs or less. It certainly didn't seem like very much but paying all the catechists totaled more than 20,000 frBu ($200.US) since they were forty-five in number. That was a lot of money to come up with every month when there was no source of income. Usually Bishop Moulin gave the missioners the catechists' salaries from the reserve he had received from the Propagation of the Faith in Rome.

The fathers always insisted on sharing the noon meal with all the catechists. One gospel theme that they were trying to instill into these leaders was that mass is a meal that calls everyone who receives the eucharist to be the first to serve others. It was hard to change their culture that men are masters in their own households. They had seen their fathers and grandfathers as the first persons to be served and waited on as their wives did everything for them. The missionaries felt challenged to remind the catechists that they were to take the initiative and lead by serving. So Tony, Jose and Luigi brought in the food and asked the catechists to sit down as the priests served them. Many of the catechists were embarrassed and Tony thought of a special gospel scene where Jesus washed his disciples' feet. "Yes," he thought, "it is sometimes easier for them to be served than to serve!" This was just one example of how the gospel challenges African cultural values and Tony believed the gospel was a calling to transform the Bantu practices that made men more important and more worthy than anyone else! "Inculturization of the gospel is a slow process and an extremely delicate one," he thought.

After lunch, some of the catechists came together to prepare the mass that would close their day. They practiced the hymns that they would sing and even learned a new one. Jose and Tony went to church and sat in their confessionals to give the catechists an opportunity to receive the sacrament of forgiveness. Since they lived so far away, they could not receive this sacrament regularly. This was a good opportunity to reconcile their souls with God. Tony always entered the confessional on catechists' retreat day with a sense of fear and trepidation. The only penitents coming to him over the next thirty or forty minutes would be these church leaders. Yet often they would be weighed down in spiritual darkness. He would cringe and shutter every time he heard adultery, or stealing, or drunkenness. He had once talked to Mathias about the sin of adultery. The strong man had laughed heartily and said:

"Adultery, for an Murundi, is turning the wrong way!"

What he had meant, Tony came to understand, is that in the Burundi hut, all the adults sleep on a mat on one side of the room. The children are all together on the other side. When there are guests, as can happen very often since there are no motels or guest houses in Burundi, they don't have special quarters, but sleep beside the hosts. In a semi-conscious state, a man could easily turn the "wrong way", or as Mathias laughed, "turn right but go wrong"! Tony knew most of the catechists by their voices. Even though the confessional was in darkness, he recognized Bora and Simba and Bitega and took much consolation in giving each leader absolution and new life in the Spirit.

The pastor stood up, left the confessional and went into the sacristy to vest for mass that would close the catechist's day and send them on their long walks home. They always tried to complete the retreat day by 3 o'clock so that all would be home when darkness fell at *inka zitache* (cows go home, literally six o'clock).

Since Tony had mentioned very little about the political situation that day, he felt a short hiatus from the carnage that was part of their daily life. He had felt like an asthmatic breathing pure oxygen for a short period of time. However he believed it would be important for them as leaders to pray for the situation that was becoming more and more mordant with each passing day. He also decided to say something to enlighten them on how the church should be witnessing to christian principles in this time of distress.

Fr. Anthony Joseph, the young pastor of Butova parish, knew what he had to say about the political situation of their beloved Burundi. He chose a gospel he liked very much, the one where Jesus says: "Render onto Caesar the things that are Caesar's and to God, God's". In his homily, he differentiated between church and state but then he told them that there are times when the church has to enlighten the political ideology as seen through the light of the christian gospel. He added that in this country, where the great majority of people were roman catholic, the gospel had to be their guideline and the state had to be reminded of certain principles.

As Tony looked at his audience, he wondered what they might be thinking. There was Daudi Murore the brother of President Sabimana who always looked so refreshingly alert and never disagreed with anyone in public. Tony wondered what happened when Daudi would meet someone with whom he differed. And the pastor wondered how Alberto Simba was relating to his message. Probably, in his sarcastic, mocking fashion, he would go back to Ruhweza and repeat the homily verbatim to his Batutsi cronies and include all the Kirundi mistakes in grammar and pronunciation Tony was making to mimic the *Muzungu.* But the person Tony worried about the most was Artimo Tanze. He seemed to shake his head back and forth in disagreement to what the pastor was saying during the homily. Tony had never met a more despicable, ignorant Murundi. There was no *kirundi* politeness and courtesy in him. He had still not come to see Tony, another sign of his arrogance. The catechists all came around the altar for the Liturgy of the Eucharist and reached out to each other after the Our Father, during the exchange of peace. As they extended their hands to receive Communion, Father Tony put the small, pure, white, wafer/host on their palms, saying: "Eusebio, Umubiri wa Kristu,.....Amina"; (Body of Christ.....Amen) "Alberto, Umubiri wa Kristu,.....Amina"; "Danieli, Umubiri wa Kristu,.....Amina".

He came to Samueli Samura one of his favorite catechists at the central parish of Butova. He often talked to Samueli in his office and loved the catechist's ready smile and jovial good humor. Samueli had six fingers on each hand and Tony had heard about that phenomenon in the language school just after he had arrived in Burundi. When the Kirundi teacher had told the class that some Africans have a sixth finger, a small finger with a nail looking normal and extending from the lower knuckle of the baby finger, Tony had grinned and then laughed out loud in disbelief! But many months later, in front of his office in Butova, Tony met Samueli Samura. He extended his hand to Samueli and had felt the extra finger. He took his hand away quickly, startled by the feeling. Then he looked down at the freak limb. Tony redressed himself quickly, not wanting to embarrass the catechist. The next time they met, Tony built up courage and asked Samueli to see his hand. He showed it to him with a bright smile on his loving face and said proudly: "I have six of them, twelve on the two hands!" He held his hands out, palms up, fingers spread so that Tony could count for himself.

Father Tony put the host on this hand with six figures outstretched. He knew it was Samueli Samura's and without moving his eyes from hand to face said: "Samueli, Umubiri wa Kristu". It would be the last time Samueli would ever hear these beautiful words or feel the outline imprint of the missionary's thumb on his left hand, leaving the presence of the Living Christ in his palm in the visible form of the weightless host. Samueli Samura would come face to face with his God in heaven later that week after being accused, arrested, maligned, beaten and murdered by the soldiers, a martyr for the cause of justice.

But at this eucharistic moment, Samueli had no awareness that what he was receiving, he would become later that week.

Before the evening meal, Tony sat in the living room and Luigi brought in his guitar to strum a song or two as they relaxed after the busy day.

Luigi was a very quiet man, slender in build with a long oval face, majestic nose, piercing green eyes and a black beard that made him look very distinguished. He loved to play chords quietly on his guitar and strum some unidentifiable song while the others talked quietly in the common room. So as it would happen, Luc and Jose came to join them and they talked about the busy day with the catechists. The conversation quickly moved to the political situation and Jose mentioned that people he met over the course of the day were very angry and exceedingly frightened. Every afternoon in May the people on the hillsides would come together at a designated place that they would mark with a cross and holy picture and say the rosary together. Jose would jump on his motorcycle and drive to one of these sites and pray with the people and after the prayer, he would get the latest news. Of course everyone's thoughts were about the political strife. Tony thought it was helpful for the missioners to be in contact with the common people but at the same time he considered it somewhat dangerous especially since Jose's judgment was so ramshackled.

"I hope you don't ask them any direct questions, Jose," he blurted out. "If they want to volunteer information or tell you how they are feeling, that is fine. But if you ask them impertinent questions, you could get us all in deep trouble."

"No, Tony," Jose responded, "I never ask any leading questions. I just let them talk and listen to all they have to say. It is funny, you know. They sometimes speak of their fears more than anything else. The Bahutu are extremely afraid of what they now are calling the 'reprisals'. They know a lot of damage was done during the *coup* and they are afraid that the Batutsi will exaggerate revenge and turn it into genocide."

The four men agreed that no one could really tell what would happen next. Tony suggested that they all meet in the chapel after recreation, to celebrate a common eucharist and pray for their people as well as for their own protection. He had celebrated mass with the catechists, but Jose and Luigi had not been there. So they went to dinner looking forward to their common prayer time later that evening.

Jose lead the celebration of mass. He said that he was tired but knew that he would draw strength and courage from their common time of prayer together. He had a special way of speaking to God that was simple, child-like and direct at the same time. His confreres always enjoyed his unique style of praying. When Jose lead their prayer, it was always from the heart, a sincere moment of honesty with the Creator. He prayed for the poor that lived throughout their parish. Also that this time of trial and difficulty would not lead the Barundi to despair and hopelessness but rather would give them an incentive to live their christian lives according to the gospel principles. Tony prayed for all those who had died. He mentioned many by name, those from the hills of Piga and Ruhaha opposite the mission, and added a prayer for the catechists who had been absent that day, Stephano Muzoca and Deogratias Pungu. Interrupting the prayer, Jose asked Tony about Deogratias. He had not missed him at the meeting and only now realized that the secretary-catechist must be in some difficulty. Tony told him what he had heard, the news from Jean Bosco and if the secretary knew any more, he didn't volunteer information for the *Bazungu.* Jose mumbled to himself what he thought about Bosco.

"He smiles at you to your face and then he kicks you in the ass when you turn around," he said as they all knew Jose didn't have much respect for Bosco.

They prayed for all the peoples of Burundi: Bahutu, Batutsi and the few Batwa. In a special way, they prayed for those who were preparing for baptism. They prayed for their families and friends, their benefactors and acquaintances and the deceased members of their White Father Society. Then they all gathered at the altar for the eucharistic prayer and words of consecration that would bring Jesus Christ into their midst and be their food, strength and sustenance, lifting their spirits and guiding their decisions over the next days. Each knew he needed the help and support of the others' prayers and the leadership of the Spirit, more that any other human force. But as yet they failed to realize how weak they really were and how the next two weeks would be like no other time in their entire lives as they would be filled with self-doubt, shock, horror, revulsion, disgust and sheer terror. Their people would show that christianity had no power over them and that human beings had the extraordinary ability to hate, crush, maim, torture, destroy and murder like no other creature God had ever endowed with the gift of life. As they headed for bed much later than usual, Tony suggested that they sleep in somewhat in the morning, get up for breakfast and pray the office afterwards when Jose will have finished the instruction.

Tony awoke early Tuesday morning and turned on the *Voix de la Revolution* coming from Bujarundi. A message was being played over and over again. The broadcaster spoke rather solemnly, saying that he was reading an official message from the Office of the President. He announced that the trial period was over and the rumor that there would be an attack by Chinese looking men from the Congo had been put to rest by the power of the Burundi army, headed by the honorable Arturo Shabaru. However all the men were still obliged to report to the local barriers every night, in case the enemy was not totally defeated. Tony caught himself whispering: "I knew it was only a rumor spread by the government and a plot to justify keeping the Bahutu all together. They are still contradicting themselves. If there is no enemy, why keep watch? To assure that all the Bahutu sheep will stay in the pen waiting to be lead to the slaughterhouse!" Then he heard the announcer conclude with unfathomable language: "Any person found outside his own *arrondissement* without proper identification and a *laissez-passer* is to be arrested. Since this is a time of war, the culprit is to be judged by the local military authority and possibly put to death before nightfall. This is how the eighty-seven *arrondissements* throughout Burundi will procede in this time of crisis."

Tuesday morning always brought with it the "beginning of the week syndrome". Normally on Monday, the confreres did something different from regular parish work. Often they traveled to another mission parish for a day off or went shopping at the general diocesan store at Vurura. So when Tuesday rolled around, it seemed like their weekly cycle was just beginning. If one or two of them were going to the outstations, they would leave during the day and only return on Sunday. So the three priests often worked separately for the rest of the week. But this week, because of the political problems, they canceled all trips outside the central mission. If they could go to the closest ones: Vuvoga, Ruhweza, Mundi and Lusaga over the next few Sundays, they believed they would be doing the best that was possible under the dire circumstances. So Luigi accepted to celebrate the morning masses that week and Tony asked Jose to give the instruction after each mass. Usually one priest handled both, but Luigi was just starting and preferred to put all his effort into reading the prayers of mass as best he could. Tony would alternate mass for the sisters and brothers Luigi, having the morning masses, would not have to prepare the couples for weddings this Thursday for it was a holyday and feast of the Ascension and they would be following the Sunday schedule.

As Luigi got ready to head over to the church to begin mass, Jose asked them for suggestions of a theme for the week's instructions. He asked this mischievously since he already knew what he wanted to talk about, but thought he would ask their advice in a spirit of collegiality. Still even if he invited suggestions, Jose didn't like others to tell him what to say as he had a great deal of confidence in his own ideas.

"It's the month of May. I think I'll speak to them about the Blessed Mother and the rosary," Jose opened the discussion.

"Suit yourself, Jose, but since the political situation is out of control, maybe it would be good to talk about justice, and love beyond culture and race. We don't want to interfere with the political situation but it is important that people live lives enlightened by the gospel values, not despite them. We are now witnessing a racial massacre. You speak Kirundi and make distinctions so well. Maybe you should stay away from that 'pialogy' (mixture of piety and theology) and give them the deep meaning of the truth!" Tony remarked.

Jose looked at him strangely and a bright smile lit up his whole face:

"I don't think I am brave enough," he seemed to kid Tony as he spoke. "Many gospel messages should be explained but I don't think I am the person that is brave enough to do that," Jose reaffirmed his position.

"If not you, then whom?" Tony joked a little with him as well.

"We'll leave that for Bishop Moulin. The last time he preached here he said our people were not so good at following the sixth commandment. They were even weaker at the seventh but their main downfall was the eighth. We could have the good bishop come to hear confessions and then preach again. He could add a *grande finale* to his pontifical discourse:

"Bakristu," Jose's tried to imitate the bishop's delivery, "you have failed three commandments in the past: sixth, seventh and eighth. You are adulterers, thieves and liars. But the last weeks have even seen you outdo yourselves. Your greatest accomplishment is that you have annihilated the fifth commandment: THOU SHALT NOT KILL!! Murderers, wretches, killers, rogues, assassins. You smell like the slaughterhouse. THOU SHALT NOT KILL!.....THOU SHALT NOT KILL!.....THOU SHALT NOT KILL!....." Jose concluded by mimicking the bishop who had the repugnant habit of repeating himself *ad infinitum* when he wanted to emphasize a particular point.

Jose concluded with a loud laugh and the others smiled right along with him. Sometimes he had such a peculiar laugh that it was infectious. There was no denying that they all thought the scene would be very amusing as they imagined Bishop Bernard Moulin banging on the altar and shouting about the fifth commandment.

Jose was intent on sidestepping the crucial issues and talking about some religious traditions. It was Mary's month and devotion to her was a wonderful practice but it certainly was camouflaging the real issues of the gospel that should have been confronted. On the other hand, the gospel message would totally condemn the people and their attitude. Once upon a time, a Missionary to this planet preached the gospel. In fact He and His disciples wrote the gospel as He dealt with the issues of His time. And He was killed for His witness and His principles! Wasn't it time for another, one of His followers, to lay down his life for CHRISTian values as stipulated in the bible?

Luc seemed to be getting more and more angry as the discussion continued. He was literally bursting from the insides out. Luc Grange was a tall man with curly blond hair that was seldom combed but sat like a little bird's nest on the top of his head. He had light blue eyes that sparkled when he spoke. His temperament was passionate and no matter what the subject of conversation might be, he spoke with strong convictions.

Being a Frenchman, Luc had his own ideas about the church and how, over the years, the church had dominated the poor people by creating guilt feelings when catholics did things that the church did not sanction. He saw the church leaders and clergy as very human, and after having lived with four missionaries for the past year, he saw many weakness and flaws in their humanity. Yet the three missionaries had learned much from Luc and respected youth so much more because of his witness and lifestyle. Thus Luc thought this was a time to speak his mind, and even if they were talking about the content of a religious instruction, he blurted forth;

"Jose," Luc began, "that is the trouble with the roman catholic church in general and you in particular! You skirt the issues and when you should be preaching the values of Jesus Christ, you replace them by traditions and stories. The rosary is a silly practice of little old ladies counting their beads, thinking that if they say as many as possible, they will save everyone from the wrath of God and all will have a comfortable place in heaven. Didn't Jesus Christ already do that for us? Stop preaching a religion of security and start preaching the values of the gospel that Jesus Christ lived and died for," Luc said with fury in his eyes.

Jose eyed the Frenchman as if he were a mad man and waited for him to stop. But Luc was uncontrollable and continued, looking the Spaniard right in the eye:

"People are killing each other by the thousands and you want to tell them that it is Mary's month and that they should gather to pray to her. What should they pray for? That their drinking water not be contaminated as they are now throwing bodies into the rivers and brooks all over this God forsaken country? Should they gather together on the hillsides to say the rosary and count prayer beads and also their heads to see how many have been cut off since the rosary of the preceding day? Should they say: 'Pray for us now and at the hour of our death' and realize that both moments, for many of them, will be the same instant in the next few days as the present moment will be their hour of death? Jose, I implore you to use your judgment and preach the gospel and not some useless devotion to Mary that has no sense in the lives of our people!" Luc shouted with burning rage.

Jose looked directly at Luc, their eyes focused on each other as if they were two wild beasts ready to annihilate each other. Finally Jose broke the silence as the echo of Luc's words 'now and at the hour of our death' seemed to penetrate the souls of all in the room. They had all been scarred by this confrontation.

"It is 'ok' for you to talk, Luc. People only see you as a grocery manager. But if I speak, they will condemn me and even put me in prison for I am their priest!" was the defense Jose managed to muster.

Luc cut in and screamed at the man who was fifteen years his senior:

"Wasn't St. Paul put in jail, didn't John the Baptist die in prison? They did so to proclaim, with their lives as well as with their voices, that the gospel message does not allow a christian to hurt, let alone kill, another person. They died for the gospel and for Christ. Isn't that why you became a priest as well? You should be ready to die for the gospel, die for the people, die for Christ!"

Jose's face was white, whiter than the White Father habit he wore, often shabby and dirty. His colleagues had never seen his bronze Mediterranean complexion that pale as he continued:

"Maybe, Luc, others will be able to do it. But frankly, I must confess that I don't have the courage. I came to Africa to live and help the people, not to be tortured and die at the age of thirty-four. Now if you will excuse me, I must go to give the instruction." Jose rose, and left the room, banging the door in frustration as he exited.

6. Deogratias Pungu Arrested, Rearrested

After breakfast, the missionaries came together in the chapel. They usually recited the Divine Office together. While Jose finished the instruction, the other three prayed the office and spent time in silent meditation. Tony and Luigi stayed a bit longer in the chapel as Luc went about his business. The chapel was a silent peaceful room with the walls whitewashed for brightness. There was an altar in the front, facing a person on entering the room. In the middle of the altar was the tabernacle and the missionaries felt happy about having the presence of the Savior with them physically for every minute of every day. There was a sanctuary lamp burning at all times, reflecting quietly, their faith in the living Lord. The altar had a white cloth draped over it and an old missal was closed, sitting on a wooden book-holder to the left. To the right of the altar was a make-shift closet with a curtain protecting its contents. It was there that they kept the mass vestments as well as altar wine, hosts, pyx and chalices. The altar area was one step above the rest of the room which only had enough space for four kneelers and chairs. The floor was painted maroon and a colorful rug, that had been given to them by the sisters, was placed in the center of the room and protected the painted floor. The chapel was a special area for all of them.

Many times in the past when one of the colleagues had a particular problem or needed spiritual strength, the others would come together and support their confrere in common prayer.

After prayer, Fr. Tony Joseph walked back to his bedroom to take off his sweater that he no longer needed as the bright morning cool air had been replaced with the warmth of a day sparked by the bright rays of the sun. He would walk to his office and begin to receive people who were already waiting for him before his door.

As Tony came out of his room, he saw a dark figure coming from his left. He stopped in his tracks and a smile came over his face as he recognized Deogratias Pungu coming toward him. Never was Tony more happy to see anyone! Deogratias was wearing a dark black windbreaker that Tony had given him from a box of clothing sent by his family. Underneath he wore a dark olive-colored shirt and light gray pants. He wore black sandals with beige socks and he was carrying a clip board in one hand and *bic* pen in the other.

"*Pati, Pati,*" he called out to Tony, "I need to see you…alone…as soon as you can see me. Could we go into your room?" his voice rang with anxiety.

Tony turned around and walked back toward his room. He unlocked the door and Deo quickly entered his room and closed the door. Father Tony was surprised that Deogratias asked to see him privately in his bedroom. He thought it rather strange that in the last week he had seen a Murundi alone in his bedroom on two occasions.

The private bedroom areas were off limits for all Africans since the fathers wanted to make completely sure that no scandal would ever be given. It was just not done. Sometimes when the confreres visited neighboring missions, they would go to confession to each other using their private rooms but that was among *Bazungu* and scandal was never given. Here in Butova, the missionaries never went into each others bedroom. They would gather in each others' office or in their common living room or dining room but through common accord, their bedrooms were off limits for everyone.

Tony motioned toward his chair so that Deo would be seated and he, himself, sat on the side of his bed:

"We missed you at the meeting yesterday, Deogratias. But I am sure it was impossible. Is that what you want to talk about?" Tony lead into the conversation.

The secretary-catechist began to speak in a low whispering voice half-imagining that someone was outside listening to every word he was saying. He was petrified that he might have been seen entering Tony's room by Barnabe Ntware, the gardener, or Cypriano Kitwi, the cook, both Batutsi. "*Pati,* when I went home last Saturday from work at seven o'clock (one in the afternoon), there were two soldiers waiting for me at my *rugo* (home). They claimed that I had gone to meetings before Easter and that these meetings were planning an uprising to kill the Batutsi in power and set up a government among the Bahutu. They said that they had many witnesses who gave testimony that I had gone to some meetings and had given money to buy machetes in Kijiji to help with the *coup d'etat* that has now taken place. They went through my clothes and produced a note that I had never seen before. But supposedly they said it was found in my pants. The soldiers believed that it was a receipt for five hundred francs that had been written in my name for money given to the rebel Bahutu.

They arrested me and hit me many times on my face and forehead in front of my wife and children."

Deogratias and his wife Clementia had eight children and were expecting their ninth in a few months time. Deo went on:

"They led me to Puma and threw me in prison and kept me there until early this morning. Today when they came in, they gave me the note back and told me I could leave. I came directly here to work and sent word to Clementia to come and see me here at the office," Deogratias said handing the note to the priest. Fr. Tony looked at the crinkled piece of paper. It had been torn from a bigger piece of paper and simply had the words: "Pungu 500 frBu".

"That could have been for anything," Tony commented to his catechist.

"Yes, *Pati*," Deo replied, "but you know I earn only 632 frBu per month. If I gave someone 500 frBu, my family would starve until the next pay day. I could not afford to give away 500 frBu to any cause. All my salary is used entirely to feed my children. In fact, if I were to have a little extra, I would give it to you toward the down payment of the house you are going to build for me. I have never seen this note before and I have never given 500 frBu to anyone. They were trying to falsely accuse me and for some unknown reason, they released me. I was really tortured in prison. Look at my arms and legs," Deo recounted as he stood up and tried to show the pastor his legs and arms at the same time.

Tony was completely dumbfounded as he examined the scarred body of his catechist with markings and blood caked all over his dark skin.

"It was terrible in prison. We were all thrown into one area. My wife and girls brought me food. Most of the time the guards took my food and ate it themselves so it was as if I had nothing to sustain me. In the night time they would bring us outside and make a fire and then they would sit us down on the ground close to the fire. Little by little parts of my body would heat up and then burn right through as if I were a chicken being roasted. Many times we would cry out with awful pain, but the Batutsi soldiers and police only laughed at us. I thought I was going out of my mind and I wanted you to know what was happening but they would not let me talk to Clementia so she could inform you." Deogratias Pungu recounted this extraordinary ordeal he had undergone over the past three days.

Tony's heart filled with admiration for this courageous man-of-God who, after the hideous ordeal ended, had come directly to work that morning.

All Fr. Tony could manage to say was a weak but sincere; "I'm sorry, please pardon me as I didn't know what was happening until you were absent from the meeting. Then no one except Jean- Bosco seemed to know your whereabouts. I went to Puma Saturday evening, but I never heard mention of your arrest."

"I was there, Pati," Deogratias went on "but I had no means of letting you know they had me in jail. They were questioning and torturing those four boys. What pain and suffering they went through, during the night until three died before sunrise. The other one they dumped in the common graves Sunday afternoon."

Tony suggested that they pray together to thank God for sparing him and returning him to his family. Deo was only too willing to pray with his pastor, but was unsure how all would end and if God would take special means to keep him alive and safe from his enemies. Deogratias now looked more like a withered and shrunken old man than the young, vibrant catechist Tony had known a few days before. The catechist-secretary went on:

"I am afraid that they will come back and arrest me again. No one told me why they were releasing me. Maybe they want to see where I will go and whom I will talk to and then arrest them as well. That is why I wanted to see you alone, where no one would know that we have talked. I am afraid for my life and for my brothers, my wife and children. They were accusing our whole household when they came to get me last Saturday. I fear that tonight, tomorrow, or some other time when I go home they will be waiting for me and arrest me again and bring me to prison in Puma. What shall I do, *Pati*?" Deogratias asked his priest serenely as he opened his mouth and indicated where the soldiers had put out their cigarette butts on his palate and on the sides of his gums.

Fr. Tony tried to remain calm and indicated that there was no answer to the dilemma. The soldiers and police did whatever they pleased and went from one area to the other and accused anyone they so desired of any crime they imagined. They used torture whenever it pleased them to see the Bahutu squirming like ugly worms along a footpath after a heavy rain. There was no way to defend oneself from that kind of menace. One just stayed alert and kept a low profile, hoping that the soldiers would set themselves on other targets. So that is what Tony told his secretary:

"Stay out of everyone's way and pray that they don't come back to get you. You cannot run away. They would arrest Clementia or your brothers and say that you were admitting guilt by fleeing. Besides, if you are caught outside of the Puma *arrondissement* without a *laissez-passer*, they will kill you on the very spot. Keep praying, Deo, that God will protect you and guide you over the next couple of weeks. Don't give up on God. He will see you through all this. He has already helped you get out of prison. So pray that he keeps protecting you and guiding you."

Tony then addressed a short prayer to God as he reached out and gathered the catechist's hand into his own. Deo's hands were callused and rough. He had worked long hours in the fields with his wife, cultivating vegetables for their children. He clutched the missionary's hand strongly and Tony felt him communicating his fear and anxiety to him. The priest offered all Deo's suffering to God through the merits, passion and death of Jesus Christ and praised God for allowing his suffering to contribute to saving the world.

"But, Lord, look kindly upon this man who loves you so much. Guide him, protect him, save him from the attacks of his enemies." The pastor prayed an oration that would fall on deaf ears, as Deogratias would be swallowed up by the Batutsi dragons in uniforms of Barundi soldiers.

Deogratias Pungu got up and prepared to walk out of the room. He took the note and handed it to the priest a second time:

"In case something happens, I want you to have this note. It will prove my innocence since they released me believing I already had had the note in my pocket. In fact, my having it proves they gave it back to me. So I want you, *Pati*, to have this proof."

Tony took the note, opened his wallet and put it behind a picture of his parents that he always carried with him. He said:

"I'll take good care of this and pray that I don't have to intervene. But I thank you, Deo, for trusting me. Oh, by the way, I have your envelope here with your salary as the others were paid yesterday." Deogratias Pungu took the envelope from the priest, thanked him and walked out the door looking to his right and left pretending he had been called by the pastor to be paid. The secretary-catechist had now been paid by his church for the very last time. Even though Tony had given him a brief moment of encouragement, he was almost certain that his trials were just beginning. The *bakuru* knew that he would tell the fathers about his release and hoped that it would create false belief that the government was trying to find a way to help the Bahutu.

Tony stayed in his room for about fifteen minutes trying to figure out a plan to protect Deogratias in whatever way he could. Yet he could not imagine what would be next on the government's agenda. No one really knew who was in charge. So many of the Batutsi *bakuru* like Tomasi Muhwa, the professors at the Teachers' Training College and others at the Boys' Elementary School, as well as other *bashingantahe* (those who plant the lance. In Bantu customs, the men plant the lance when they are going to speak. Thus they were elders of the community) gave the impression that they were in a position of decision-making, but they had no constitutional authority whatsoever. It seemed like the soldiers and police went out daily at their own whim and arrested anyone they pleased. Many innocent people would die for crimes they never committed. Already Tony had heard that Batutsi neighbors were taking Bahutu fellow citizens before the soldiers and accusing them of crimes that were fictitious. Then the soldiers sentenced the Bahutu and twice every day huge trucks would come fill up with bodies and drive them to common graves.

Tony was perplexed! Shouldn't he intervene? Should he remind the soldiers that the person had to be guilty of high crimes and misdemeanors before being sentenced to death? Should he not remind the civil authorities, Albert Kizungu and the newly appointed military governor of Vurura in particular, that they couldn't just dispose of people, blanketing their whole situation as guilty when there was no burden of proof? What about.... 'beyond the shadow of a doubt'? He walked up and down in his room, from one side to the other, and thought that he should talk with his colleagues to come up with a plan whereby the authorities could be approached to assure that no one would be killed who was not guilty. And then...guilty of what? Even though Tony considered himself a good friend of President Sabimana, deep down he knew that his government was a fruitless response to the true needs of the people. Sabimana held power because of a military *coup* but had no idea how to go about governing a country. And Burundi was a country in Central Africa where the problems of poverty and disease escalated daily.

He lay across his bed, clenched his fist and began hitting his pillow with all his might. If only he could use his brutal strength to turn this situation around! Where is God in all this? the missionary wondered. Shouldn't Almighty God, the *El Shaddai (God of Power)* save the *Anawim* (Poor)? Shouldn't *Adonai (Glorious God)*, intervene to reward the innocent and condemn the unjust? He realized he was asking the unanswerable question. Tony was uttering the unthinkable. How could he believe in a God of Power, Who was powerless? How could he trust in a God of Justice amid total anarchy and madness? He got up from the bed and prayed on his knees for a short while:

"Lord, keep me sane amidst all this insanity. Show forth your power by saving your people. Lord be our Rock of Refuge forever!" But the young priest could not help but wonder if there really was a God. If there really were a God .....of Love ..... of Justice ..... of Peace, then..... Why? ..... Why? ..... Why?

Tony left his room and walked down the verandah to his office as he had previously set out to do before he had met Deogratias. As he approached his door, he was pleased to see the *bafundi* (masons) waiting outside for him. The Barundi all knew that they needed improved housing. But there were many difficulties in having a new house built. Most Barundi had never been trained to be masons or carpenters. So even if they had the plans for a new house, there would be no way that they could do the work themselves. At the same time, they could never get the supplies: blocks of cement or bricks from the clay soil, iron frames for windows and doors, glass, cement for flooring, whitewash for the walls and corrugated tile called *mabati* for the roof. These supplies were just not available. However the fathers were always building and had all these materials stored away at the back of the compound. Every time they went to an outstation, they would bring along some bags of cement to improve the church, the catechumenate, the school or the office that also served as the priest's quarters when he stayed overnight.

Mathias had started a project whereby, when there were no big constructions underway, like a church, school, or catechumenate, he would engage his workers: masons, carpenters, brick makers and roofers, in building houses for different families of the parish. The husband would come to see him and make a tentative plan. He would have to raise one half of the money for all the construction: bricks, blocks, doors and windows, *mabati* and whitewash. Then Mathias would get the money from his benefactors in Germany. It was a victory for both sides: the Africans would have a new home, something they could never build themselves, and the *Bazungu* would be bettering the poor world. This was helping the needy, those ambitious enough to save money and invest it in their families.

When Tony arrived in the parish and Mathias had invited him to get involved in his own home-building project, the young missionary was rather reluctant. "Why don't the people and the workers just help themselves? Why do we have to be the middle-men?" Tony heard himself say. Mathias had laughed and told him he would soon learn. If the Barundi were left to manage house-building for other Barundi, they would take advantage of the situation and overcharge their brothers in every way. They would cheat and lie about the number of hours they worked or overcharge for all the materials and then not be able to transport them to the specific areas. Many people wanted houses built on the top of a hillside and it was very difficult to transport bags of cement and *mabati* up the mountain side. But if the fathers were in charge, they would arrange most of the transport. They would also assure that the work would be done honestly and justly. They would normally pay by project and the *bafundi* could take as much time as they liked. As the work came to completion, the fathers would inspect the house to assure that it was delivered as had been previously agreed upon.

Tony was now very proud of his team who already had built many houses throughout the parish area. He would rise early and go out to the area, climb a hill or descend to a valley and examine the work and give the *bafundi* directions for the next week's activity. It didn't interfere with his pastoral work and he, too, like Mathias, felt the consolation of knowing that he was helping the people improve their living condition.

Fr. Tony knew the *bafundi* had come for their pay checks but also for directions and plans for the next house. A bright smile came over his face when he realized that the next person on the list was Deogratias Pungu and his wife Clementia. In the solemnity of their conversation, Tony had forgotten to tell Deo that he should prepare himself for the workers would be ready to start his house very soon. So Tony walked right by his office, stopping only to greet the workers and shake hands with them. He said he would be back soon with someone whom they would make very happy. He continued down the corridor and turned the corner. Opening a door to his left, he entered the secretarial area. Jean-Bosco was talking to someone through the window and Deo was at the parish files at the far side of the room.

"Well, catechist, I have good news for you!" Tony stared at Pungu. "The workers have come to my office and I must pay them for the last house they have finished building. So, you, my friend, are next on the list. Come into my office with them and we will plan the house of your dreams. With any kind of luck, the house should be ready toward the middle of the dry season, maybe even before the end of July. Isn't that wonderful!" he exclaimed.

Tony looked at this faithful man-of-God who worked two jobs at the mission: he was a very capable secretary and whenever necessary he taught catechism to the adults and children. He even replaced Tony in the schools one time when the pastor had to go to the capital and couldn't get back for his classes. Tony continued to stare at Deogratias whose smile became wider and brighter with each passing moment. His face was beaming and his cheeks appeared almost rosy. His teeth shined through his open mouth and all he could muster to say was "*Urakoze, Pati, Urakoze*".

Tony led Deo from the secretariat back down the corridor to his office. The workers stood up outside and after allowing Deogratias to enter before them, they followed him into the office. The four of them, Deo and three *bafundi,* took their places on a bench in front of Tony's desk. There seemed to be no need for introductions. That was what Tony found extraordinary about the peoples of Burundi. They always knew each other even if they didn't live in the same area. Deo was known to many because he worked at the parish as secretary and catechist. He smiled brightly as Tony invited him to come to his side of the desk and then the pastor, as the chief contractor and architect, began talking about the plans for Deo's new home!

Deogratias Pungu and Clementia lived on the hillside of Butano, on the road to Bihovu. His land had been given to him by his father, so there was nowhere else on earth where Deo desired to live It was a good thirty-minute walk to the mission but Deogratias gladly travelled it each day. The hike to the mission was a simple happy daily commute. When he had married Clementia, thirteen years beforehand, she joined him at Butano where they were raising their family surrounded by his family members and some close boyhood friends.

Tony asked Deo to explain what he had in mind for a home. He spoke of three bedrooms, one for himself and Clementia and the youngest child, as well as one for the girls and one for the boys. Any visitors would sleep in the living room which would be the largest room. They would also build a dining room, a kitchen and food pantry and a toilet outside in the back courtyard. He also wanted protection from wild animals and robbers by building a fence around the compound with a large opening so that if he ever had the good fortune of getting some cows, they could find refuge in the *rugo* and be protected from outside dangers. They talked about two doors leading into the house, one in the front giving onto the living room and one on the other side of the house leading to the kitchen. They concluded by discussing about panes of glass and window frames and *mabati* for the roof. With each suggestion, Deo's smile grew bigger and brighter.

Finally Fr. Tony talked about the costs. He estimated the work to be two months and he said that he had most of the supplies. Later that week he would find time to drive the first supplies out in the van and do the measuring and calculations for each room of the house.. The *bafundi* would start working the following Monday. The workers then left but Tony asked Deo to stay behind. He talked loud and left the door ajar so that those waiting outside could hear the subject of conversation. He wanted Deo to feel secure and not allow anyone to think that they were talking about what had already been discussed in the privacy of the pastor's back bedroom.

"I calculate the building of the house at about 65,000 frBu. Deo, do you think you could pay half and I will get my benefactors to pay the other half? I calculate the materials costing about 50,000 frBu and the labor another 15,000 frBu. So you will be responsible for half of that, about 32,000 frBu." Tony spoke with generosity in his voice.

"I have very little money saved up, *Pati*, since we seem to run dry at the end of each month. We have to get what is needed for the children." Deogratias continue to play the pastor's game, "Three of the children now have to pay school fees and there are two others in bad health and Clementia always seems to have a baby at the breast," Deo responded with deep sincerity.

Tony smiled and said: "You know Deogratias, I would like to give you the whole house for nothing and get my benefactors to pay for everything. But word would get out and every catechist would demand the same favor. I don't have enough friends to permit that!" Tony chuckled and apologized at the same time.

Deo nodded his head that he understood and Tony added: "Why not calculate what you need in salary each month and take some out and give it to me on payday?"

Deo smiled again and took the envelope the priest had given him moments earlier in the back bedroom and took out a 100 franc note and gave it to the priest.

"This is my first payment!" he said as he gave the pastor the bright shiny bill with the picture of Prince Rwagasore in the middle and 100 frBu printed on the corners. Tony accepted the note, took out an envelope from his drawer and marked on it: *"INZU YA PUNGU"* (Pungu's house) as he put the bill in the envelope, stood up and placed it near his wall safe. He would open the safe and put it away later in the evening. Deo clapped his hands together, and had tears in his eyes. He shook hands warmly with Fr. Tony and thanked him sincerely and then bolted with joy from the office.

What he did not know was that he would never make another payment on his dream house. Nor would he ever see his new home built on the hillside where he spent his boyhood. But someday in the not-too-distant future, Fr. Tony would announce something special to Clementia. As a memorial to her wonderful husband and recalling his commitment to their family and the church, Tony would return the 100 frBu note and pay all the costs on a home for the whole family in memory of their father, the catechist-secretary of Butova. The home would be built and handed-over before Deogratias and Clemantia's last child would be born in the latter part of 1972!

Tony went to the sisters' residence about 5:45pm that afternoon to celebrate mass. The walk down to the sisters was always a pleasant one.

People were trotting hastily along the road, moving quickly to reach their destinations before darkness would blanket them quickly at nightfall. Two women with heavy sacks of beans and yams on their heads walked quickly past the priest, looking back over their shoulders and calling out: "*Nagasaga, Pati*" (Good bye, Father), recognizing his presence but unable to stop and talk because of the approaching darkness. Tony called back: *"Genda n'Amahoro"*! (Go in peace).

Tony entered the sisters' abode which was simple and small. The nuns had whitewashed walls and simple furniture. They seemed to all sleep in a common dormitory with curtains separating that area from the hallway. Six Beneterezia Sisters lived together in this house. Sr. Maragarita worked as catechist in the parish and as choir directress. Sr. Gloria, the Superior, taught grade one at the girls' school. Two other nuns were Sr. Anunciata, who helped Maragarita and Sr. Terezita, who looked after their house and did most of the gardening, cooking and housework. Finally two others, Sr. Domitila and Sr. Ana, also taught at the girls school. The Beneterezia Sisters were close to the soil and worked in parishes where they strongly influenced the women and girls.

Tony looked forward to celebrating this mass as he walked into the sisters' home. He longed for a liturgy where his every word would not be scrutinized and where he could relax and pray for the true needs of the parish and the country. He vested and heard Sister Maragarita announcing the first hymn and amid the blending of the six melodious voices of the nuns, the pastor entered the chapel for the celebration of holy mass. After the entrance song terminated, he allowed the peacefulness and silence penetrate every pore of his body. He knew the sisters appreciated the peace and quiet, the exact opposite to the events over the past ten days.

And so in the spirit of tranquility, they celebrated the eucharist. He prayed for the catechist Stefano Muzoca who had been absent from the meeting and for Deogratias Pungu, that he would be protected in this time of anxiety and turmoil. He prayed for Inocenti Gikobwa, the only female catechist in the parish besides the nuns. He had heard, just before leaving the parish office, that Inocenti had been abducted after the Monday meeting and he feared for her life and prayed for her protection especially from the soldiers, often drunk, at the end of the days' activities. And he prayed for Bishop Moulin and his vicar general Luduvico Ruyaga that they be inspired by the Holy Spirit to make the right decisions over the coming days, weeks and months. He also prayed for the president, Etienne Sabimana, and his ministers that they direct the country in justice and that a new frontier of peace, understanding and communion between the two tribes become a reality. Finally he prayed mentioning both tribes by their names, for Bahutu and Batutsi, that the presence of the Spirit of God eliminate all hostilities between them and that all the members, especially those who belonged to the catholic church, make every effort possible to build peace without hatred, hostility or bloodshed.

This was the first time the sisters ever heard Fr. Tony mention the names 'Bahutu-Batutsi'. The sisters seemed to gasp for air as he mentioned the tribal names and he looked at each one of them gazing into each pair of eyes wondering, as he moved from one person to the other, what tribe each belonged to. At this time, he didn't realize that things would become so tense a week later, that he would have to make another trip down to the sisters. This time it would be to ask each sister's tribal ethnicity and in that way he would know whom he would have to protect. Racism and tribalry were a deep source of conflict and the christian religion, preached by the missionaries for eighty years, had not succeeded in grazing the surface of these hard-core racists.

Once, Tony, optimistically and hopefully, had believed that catholicism was a living, moving force among the Barundi. These events of May '72 would now teach him that Batutsi-Bahutu blood was thicker than the waters of baptism and that any effort to christianize a people with so much tribal hatred would be an impossible task! Satan had seeded the only weapon he would ever need to overthrow the coming of the Kingdom. And he had prepared it hundreds of years before the missionaries ever set foot in Central Africa. These two tribes would always abhor each other because they were born and grew up with only one purpose; to despise, hate loathe, detest, abhor, torture, kill those of the opposing tribe. They were born to be racists and they had only one ambition in their hearts: to annihilate the other race.

Wednesday was a special day as Tony rose thinking of the many tasks he had to do on the day before Ascension Thursday. The following day was a holyday of obligation and so there would be confessions this Wednesday throughout the whole day and on Thursday they would follow the Sunday schedule both in the parish church and in the catechumenate. On the vigil, the priests would divide the day into six shifts of two hours each and each would be available in the church for the full two hours to hear confessions. The people knew that no matter when they arrived at church, there would always be someone there to hear their confession. The missioners had discussed the schedule the night before. Luigi had eight to ten and two to four and Jose had ten to twelve and four to six. Tony had six am until eight, and noon 'til two pm. Right away, Jose complained that he wanted to be free in late afternoon to say a rosary with the people in the *mihana* ("homes" from Kirundi word for banana trees which surrounded their living areas). So Luigi obliged, and traded his afternoon hours with him.

Over the past few days, it had been reported that Melechiori Nyabenda the teacher of grade five boys was gravely ill. But Tony had not followed up on his situation since there had been so many other upsetting events happening. Luigi had gone to Melechiori's home to give him the sacraments and hear his confession. During a meal back at the priests' house, he had told Jose and Tony that things did seem to be going well enough. Bernardo Minani, the sixth grade teacher, was standing outside Tony's office when he came back after confessions. Since it was a school day, the pastor was surprised to meet a teacher at the parish offices. Bernardo told him that Melechiori's situation was very grave and the resident infirmarian , Jacobo Karani from Puma, had come to examine him and said there was very little hope. Since Melechiori was a member of the *Equipes Enseignantes* (teachers' sharing groups), Bernardo asked the pastor to go quickly and prepare him for inevitable death.

"I know there are many people who are dying here every day. However Melechiori loved the church and taught in a catholic school and so we think you, as the pastor, should go to help him cross the threshold from life to death," was the way Minani put it.

Tony allowed the shocking words to penetrate his mind and then his heart and said 'yes,' he would go immediately. Bernardo said he would show him the way to Nyabenda's house and within three minutes they were in the van heading for Same, a small hillside just outside of Butova. As they arrived, Tony shook hands with the people gathered in the small little house that the teacher had built for his wife and six children. Tony found Melechiori lying on his side on a small cot. There seemed to be no life in his frail body. The priest approached him, turned him on his back but got little response. He took his pulse and it was beating ever so slowly. He grasped Melechiori's hand and asked him to squeeze in return to show he was seeking and receiving God's pardon. Tony felt the slight touch of a squeeze, like a feather brushing against his palm. Then the priest bequeathed the dying man's soul to God and asked the Blessed Mother and St. Melechiori to come and lead him back home to heaven. At that very moment, Melechiori gasped loudly and breathed his last. Tony experienced a peace in the room, a calm that he had often felt before, after someone had given up the spirit. It was the serenity of God's presence all around them. Then he walked outside, to Melechiori's wife and invited her to come into the room with him. She asked the priest if he were dead and he did not answer until she had closed the door.

"He has gone home to the Father," Fr. Tony whispered.

She approached the cot and touched her husband frantically all over looking for some sign of life. She placed her head close to his and cried quietly: "*Oya! Oyaye! Oya!* (No! NO! No!) Then she opened the door and began the horrifying screams of the *induru* (shrill cries of death) announcing to the whole household that her beloved had departed to the Lord. Within a few minutes, the room, where the body of the deceased lay, was filled with screaming women, and their high-pitched, hysterical bellows totally exasperated Tony. He left the room and invited the widow to come to the mission and make the funeral arrangements later that afternoon. He suggested they have a mass with all the school children in attendance. He got into his car and the shrilling screams of the *induru* left him bleak and cold as he drove back to Butova.

Later in the day, the widow came to Fr. Tony's office and they arranged the memorial mass for Friday at the normal time of the weekly school mass, ten o'clock. She wanted to have a full funeral mass with body and coffin. Tony thought it was an excellent idea since it would afford him an opportunity to teach the children about death and the afterlife.

"Melechiori was a good teacher and even in his death, he will teach the school children about the reality of life and death," his widow added.

Tony lead the widow one more time in prayer for the deceased and then walked her to the door and told her he would do all he could to make the funeral mass on Friday a truly beautiful tribute to Melechiori. In parting, she mentioned that her husband had a burial plot with his family in Lutana. It would be many hours on foot if they were to carry the body of the deceased. She asked if one of the fathers could drive the casket with some mourners in the van. As she was speaking, Luigi walked by the office and Tony asked him if he would consider driving the body to its last repose. Luigi was such a understanding and caring individual. He immediately said;

"Yes, count on me to be ready after the funeral."

Fr. Tony Joseph woke at 5:15am to the ringing of his faithful alarm clock on the morning of the Ascension. He peaked his head through his window blinds and noticed the weather was very hazy as the dawn prepared to come over the distant hills. He opened his door and could hardly believe how thick the fog really was. The rainy season was now over and the long dry season with cold damp nights was upon them.

Most of the conversation at table that morning was about the dense fog, They were all ready for a very dull day but no one realized the genocidal actions would make them forget the nuisance of the weather. The fathers voiced their concern for the people. So many dreaded going out along the roads, fearing being arrested by the police or soldiers. They didn't even know the reason why they could be arrested but they didn't want to take a chance either. So with the political climate and the dense foggy weather, the clergymen anticipated a much smaller congregational crowd for the feast of the Ascension, both in the church and the catechumenate. As they shared the morning meal, Jose mentioned that the feast of the Ascension was to commemorate Christ's return to heaven:

"And", he added "we must pray for the many Bahutu who have followed Christ through death to life this week." They all agreed that, deeply and silently in their own hearts, they would remember those brave Bahutu who were now united with God.

Tony rose from his chair and, as he walked from the room, made a final remark:

"I think there will be many more joining them over the next few weeks. This thing does not seem to have a foreseeable termination. Let's pray that the killings cease immediately and that we do all we can to bring about peace and non-violence." He opened the door and walked through the corridor across the yard to the church and vested for mass.

The missionaries had been right. The crowd at mass was hardly a handful of what it would have normally been. The fog continued throughout the morning and those who came tried to blame the small numbers on the weather. However they all knew that most Bahutu feared walking along the roads and suddenly being abducted and eventually killed. After mass, Fr. Tony came outside and talked to some of the people. This was one of his favorite times in Burundi when the priestly work had been completed and he could relax with 'his people' and show concern for the human aspects of their lives. He loved to ask them about their gardens, what they were cultivating and what had grown best during the rainy season now coming to an end. He would ask about their cows and sheep and goats and chickens. Over the years in Burundi, Tony had become aware of what was and was not important for these people who prospered or starved according to the success or failure of their gardens and animals. As the small talk continued, two teenage boys that he recognized as catechumens came running towards him.

"*Pati, Pati*," one cried out "they have come to the catechumenate while Deogratias Pungu was teaching us the lesson and they have taken him outside and are in the process of leading him away to the jail in Puma. Come quickly with us and stop them!"

Tony ran alongside the youngsters away from the small conglomerations of people gathered together in small circles still chatting after mass. On a couple of occasions, they had to slow down, as to not run into small children playing carelessly on the compound. They rounded the outside stone wall in front of the mission and quickly picked up speed along the trail beside the fence. Tony kept running and panting as his mind traveled faster than his feet. Soon they came to the back wall of the mission that turned left and they kept moving. Tony could see a large group of people in front of the old church that was now used as a place for the catechumens to celebrate their service on Sundays. Because they hadn't been baptized, the catechumens came to their own building and, while the believers were celebrating the eucharist in the church, they would have a para-liturgical service led by a catechist. Tony remembered that Deogratias Pungu had been scheduled for the catechumenal service this Ascension morning.

Some people directed the priest to the middle of the group where three policemen with billy clubs were holding Deogratias. One, who did not see the priest as Tony approached from his rear side, was pulling at Deo by the short hair on his head and shouting at him:

"Why did you give money to the traitors?"

Tony circled around him and came face to face with the policeman and, looking him right in the eye, roared at him:

"What are you doing to my catechist?"

The man, dressed in a beige shirt and pants and wearing black oxford shoes, released his grip on Deo's hair and responded to the pastor:

"We are arresting this man for treason. He is coming to Puma with us," was his blunt reply.

Tony looked at him with disgust and hoped the policeman would never forget his stare nor his anger:

"What proof do you have?" asked the priest.

"The soldiers have told us that some men have confessed receiving money to buy machetes. I know this man, Pungu, gave them 500 francs!"

"I wonder," the priest responded, "how you conclude that this man gave some money. I have the note that was found in his pocket and I believe it was planted by one like you who hates him and wants to see him dead. In any case, you have been sent here only to arrest him and not to conduct a public trial in front of his catechumens. I will speak to your superior about how you have conducted yourself today and the way you were torturing him in public." Tony spoke strongly and forcefully realizing it was time to step in and protest the horrible way the soldiers and policemen were treating the Bahutu that they presumed guilty.

Fr. Tony then bent down to minister to Deogratias who had fallen to the ground, blood flowing from the side of his lips and the top of his head. He asked the people to go to the mission kitchen to get help. Two women came back with a can of water and two rags to be used as cloths. Deo drank some of the water and when Tony had finished wiping the blood away from his mouth and head, the catechist said that he would be all right and wanted to stand up and walk. The policemen had spent the past few minutes away from the scene, conferring with one another. The one who had been holding and maltreating Deogratias came back to Tony:

"You cannot obstruct justice, *Pati,*" he said.

"I have no intention to do any such thing" the pastor responded. "I merely reminded you that your job was not to beat him or judge him publicly," the priest said in self-defense.

"We must take him to Puma" the policeman said.

"Do what you must but I assure you that if anyone touches this man unjustly, he will answer not only to me but to God on judgment day!"

After speaking these words, Tony turned on his heels and walked quickly away from the scene, wondering if he had not said too much in the public confrontation. He didn't turn to look back but walked briskly to the church courtyard. Most of the people had now dispersed. Tony couldn't stay and talk to the people about their goats and cows and beans when the life of a friend, catechist and secretary was at stake. He walked back to the mission compound and up the steps, down the verandah and into the living room. Luigi was strumming his guitar and Tony sat down in a chair, looked at his fellow priest and tears of despair, helplessness and fear started to roll down his cheeks. He had never remembered crying much as an adult, but when the tears began to flow, they were unquenchable. Luigi, aware of Tony's emotions, put down his guitar at once and came over to his brother-priest. He didn't say a word, probably because he didn't want to know what was the cause of these bitter tears and partly because he didn't have any tears left to empathize with Tony. He hugged his brother and held him tightly in his grasp showing sympathy, encouragement and support.

7. Butova's Teachers Doomed

Tony decided to relax in the early afternoon. He just couldn't face the people and the *palables*. Now the widows were coming to the mission to obtain some tangible expression of sympathy for their losses. Tony appreciated their visits but sometimes he needed time for himself to process what was going through his own psyche. He was already mourning the loss of Deogratias for he believed he had seen his friend for the very last time. When Tony had told Jose about the scenario at the catechumenate, the Spaniard didn't give him any hope that Deogratias would ever be released. In fact he said that it might go badly for Tony when he heard that the pastor had verbally accosted the policeman. Tony tried to show how insignificant he believed the incident to be since he didn't think that particular policeman had any real influence or authority. Jose responded: "If he had no influence, why did they send him? You better watch what you say, Tony, even if you're under duress."

It certainly troubled Fr. Tony that the soldiers might try to get back at the foreign missionaries by torturing any Muhutu that was a friend of the clergy. And the military knew that Pungu was an important worker at the mission and great friend of the *Bazungu*. So he decided to go and see the administrator, Alberto Kizungu after his *siesta*. Maybe the policemen or soldiers would see him entering the administrator's compound and fear that he might make a report protesting the way Pungu had been handled. Sleep would not come. Then he picked up a book and tried to concentrate but his mind moved back and forth to the events that had happened earlier in the day. He felt guilty for his outrage that might have repercussions on Pungu. Tony found himself staring blankly off into space and wondering what more he could have done to protect his friend. He heard himself voicing a prayer to his God:

"Oh Lord, I believe that you are the God of all justice and peace and love. Watch over and protect Deogratias Pungu in all that he is undergoing. Give him perseverance and strength and help him forgive all those who will be doing evil to him. And, Lord, free him so that he can go home to Clementia and their children. I love you Lord, and I trust you in these happenings that I do not understand."

Tony put down the book he was reading and fell into a comfortable siesta. He rose about 2:30 and was pleased to have had such a restful sleep.

He went to his office to console those widows who had patiently waited for him. Then he walked out to the back *kigo* and wandered through the garden, looking at how well the vegetables and strawberries were growing. Barnabe Ntware, the young gardener from Mundi, was a good worker and had planted a great deal of beans, tomatoes and strawberries. Tony liked walking through the garden and felt very relaxed. He noted how he could show the parishioners at the next *mushaha* how important it was to have a diversified and well kept garden. Tony was always encouraging them to plant lots of vegetables and fruit trees. He would have to get some orange trees when the rains would begin again in October and give them to the most motivated go-getters.

Barnabe was not working today because it was a religious holiday but Tony would have to inform him that he needed to weed most of the garden where he had planted the strawberries. Even though farming was not in his family roots, Tony enjoyed keeping an eye on the garden and trusted he could give some helpful hints because of what he had read about gardening over the years.

The pastor got into his car and drove to Puma. All was quiet there and seemingly peaceful. He turned a sharp right and stopped in front of Administrator Kizungu's house. As he disembarked, and proceeded up the walkway, a man came out of the house. Tony didn't recognize him but he asked if the priest wanted to see the administrator. When Tony replied in the affirmative, the man said that he was away for a few days on *safari* and added that he probably wouldn't be back until the following week. Tony showed some disappointment. What bothered him about this situation was that when the administrator was gone, which happened very often, there was no one else that could take his place. Jacobo Karani was his assistant in name only for he was incapable of handling a job like this. No one had any confidence in him and he was the laughing stock of the village because of his name. 'Karani' meant 'secretary' and thus the people laughed and said he held pencil and paper for Kizungu. So when the administrator was away, all came to a standstill. Actually when he was in Puma, business proceeded at a snail's pace anyway! So whatever the priest had to say would have to be kept for the time when Alberto Kizungu would be back at home. Kizungu was Tony's only recourse to justice, so waiting for the administrator's return was his only remedy. He drove back to the mission with a bitter heart because he worried about what the police and soldiers would do to Pungu and he had no way of intervening now that Alberto Kizungu was gone indefinitely. He felt frustrated and exhausted, the positive effect of the relaxing snooze he had earlier that afternoon was long gone.

As Tony drove back to the mission and turned left in front of the church, he noticed to his right a small group of teachers from the Teachers' Training College and the Boys' Elementary School gathered together and talking. He was surprised to see many teachers and wondered what specific reason would gather them together on the church compound. Maybe they had some specific ideas about the service for Nybenda, perhaps something that involved the school children. Or maybe there was some specific news about the political situation that he wasn't aware of that they were discussing. The non-verbal expressions of their hands and on their faces made him question why they were discussing so vehemently, seeming to be very upset. He decided to park his car in the *kigo* and go out to join the discussion.

Fr. Tony walked up to Bernardo Minani and his wife Pataricia who were chatting with Georgio Nabi, Lazaro Ndigi and two others. Looking quickly from one gathering to another, he noted that all those who were there were Batutsi teachers. He could not find a Muhutu among them. Tony approached Minani's group and greeted them:

"*Amakuru maki?* What's all the commotion?" he asked.

Bernardo, who was considered a special friend of the fathers, spoke up:

"*Amahoro* (Peace), *Pati*! We are talking about certain reports that have come to us this afternoon. The news is that some soldiers will be sent to our area tomorrow to investigate the racial situation at the teachers' training college, and the elementary schools," Minani said diplomatically.

Tony knew that Lazaro Ndigi was a professor at the college and he had always seen him as a racist-Mututsi. He had wondered why Brother Alex, had appointed him his Murundi teacher-in-charge. Tony doubted that Lazaro was even a good teacher, let alone given power over others! He had often heard reports from the students that Ndigi picked on the Bahutu and gave higher marks to the Batutsi. In one conversation about him that Tony had with Alex, the director defended his *protégé* as one of the best African teachers he had ever seen! The director had been very defensive about Ndigi, but Tony had concluded that this was merely Alex' unorthodox style. Tony tried to be non-judgmental and opened his heart as Ndigi spoke:

"We have been made aware, *mon cher Pere*, that soldiers are coming in the morning to arrest some of the students in the college. We were wondering if you could help us divert them?"

Tony tried to believe in the sincerity of the man but he did not allow himself to be gullible:

"Maybe we could go over to my office and discuss it in greater detail," Tony said in a warm, inviting manner. The teachers then formed a small caucus and decided that Bernardo and Pataricia go home since they hadn't seen their small children all day but that Georgio and Lazaro accompany the priest to the mission.

Once inside the office, they sat on the bench in front of Tony's large desk. Tony then asked them to tell the entire story and give him as many of the details as possible. They looked at each other and reluctantly shared how they had come to know about the military plans as a close trusted friend of Minani had come by Butova earlier in the day with the news. Tony believed them since it had come via Bernardo, his loyal friend. He certainly was one Mututsi who could be trusted to tell the truth. Tony reassured them that they were all in a very difficult situation and anything he would hear from them would be kept in entire confidentiality.

Georgio Nabi continued to speak. He was a tall man who taught one of the two grade six classes at the boys' school. Minani taught the other. When the principal, Gasipari Lubulu, was away, Nabi was the one who replaced him. He was also the one that Tony dealt with about the houses that the teachers shared behind the compound. Over the years, the mission had built seven small houses in back of the mission proper. Since these were so close to the boys' school, the fathers rented them to the teachers. There was never a vacancy as each house was full of teachers, spouses and children along with many other family members who often visited to pick up money for home from the teachers earning a good salary. It was Georgio's direct responsibility to see that the teachers had everything they needed in their homes and if they were tardy in paying their rent, the fathers would use him as their intermediary. Georgio was not married but shared a house with Salvatore Mizuri, another teacher, who taught grade five boys.

"The fact that we are called Batutsi and Bahutu is not from our culture or roots, *mon Pere*." Nabi, whose name meant 'bad' lectured the pastor whom he considered young and inexperienced. Tony looked right at him, wondering what would be next, astonished that he had called the tribes by name.

"We get along well with each other, both races, to the point where there is no difference between us. No one can tell whom the *Bazungu* delegated to be Mututsi or Muhutu. That is the *kizungu* way. Our way is that we are all the same. Both sides teach in the college, and both the boys' and the girls' schools. There are students of both tribes everywhere at the TTC."

Tony wanted to puke He thought of intervening and saying that the way he explained the tribes was far from the ratio of Bahutu to Batutsi in the country: 85% - 14%, or 5.5 to 1. He was also offended that Nabi would be so insulting and dumb as to blame the categorizing of the tribes on the *Bazungu* when every historian knew that five centuries beforehand both tribes had migrated to Burundi from very different parts of Africa. The Bahutu had come from what today is the Central African Republic, whereas the Batutsi were from Ethiopia, thousands of miles from each other. But Tony said nothing since Nabi was so comfortable, sharing his innermost thoughts!

Lazaro intervened with similar arguments just as ridiculous. Tony could not believe that these were teachers educating the Barundi men of the future both on the secondary and elementary school levels. Lazaro then continued:

"*Pati*, we have come to see you tonight because we need your help. If the soldiers attack tomorrow morning, as we are certain they will, there will be much bloodshed. No one wants that, neither Batutsi nor Bahutu. So I would like to ask you if you would drive us to Vurura tonight and we could meet with Monsignor Luduvico Ruyaga and the military and discourage them from coming to Butova tomorrow."

Fr. Tony sat back in his chair. Ndigi had played his cards carefully. He had mentioned the catholic vicar general first, to insinuate it was a mission of the church. In fact, he didn't even mention the name of the military authorities, figuring they were not familiar to the priest anyway. Also Ruyaga was the founder of the *Equipes Enseignantes* and Tony was the local chaplain of the Butova teachers' group. So the crafty Mututsi knew Tony had utmost respect for the vicar and vice-versa. He had made a very trustworthy offer to Tony who accepted to drive them as soon as possible. They decided that they would leave at 6:30 pm.

Tony grabbed a quick bite to eat and went to Luigi's room to tell him he was driving the two teachers to Vurura. Luigi was astonished for he knew Tony disliked driving the dangerous roads at night and asked if it really was that urgent. They both realized Luigi couldn't accompany them since the rule for the number of persons in the small VW was limited to three and four persons could not fit in the front cabin of the van.

"I think it is vital, for Nabi and Ndigi seem to be serious about the gravity of the situation. If the soldiers were to attack tomorrow, I would never forgive myself for not having tried everything possible to stop them. For once the Batutsi seem to be honest and helpful and want to save bloodshed," was his reply as he thanked Luigi for his concern.

Georgio and Lazaro were standing at the outside of the entrance to the mission compound as Tony drove his car in front of the offices. It was dark already and he had his headlights shinning brightly. Georgio got in first, and sat in the back seat. Tony noticed that he had a sword hanging from his belt. It was similar to the one Alberto Kizungu had brought into the same car ten days earlier. Lazaro sat in the front, beside Tony. The pastor looked at both men before starting to drive and felt so sorry for them. He didn't like Lazaro, didn't trust him, and found him so haughty about his self-importance. He considered himself better than the other teachers of the elementary school. Tony had observed how Nabi had entered the two door VW first, sitting in the back and leaving the preferential front seat to the more important professor, Ndigi, from the Teachers' Training College. Nor did he like Georgio any more than Lazaro. He was so suave and polished. But Tony knew that he was only that way to be well seen by all the people. Deep down, Tony knew he was a blood thirsty racist.

The men undertook the hour drive to Vurura with a minimal amount of conversation. From time to time a thought would be uttered about the different areas they were passing through. Even if it were pitch-black outside, both teachers knew every particular spot of land along the route. They talked for a time about the Binka Experimental Farm as they passed in front of it. Tony asked them if they knew Tomasi Muhwa well. He wanted to read their response. Nabi said that he knew him as someone to be admired. Ndigi agreed. Tony knew that they would never answer honestly but wanted them to know he was sizing up the "crime-monster". When they went by Lusaga, Tony asked about the school teachers since he knew there were four classes there and had remembered all the teachers being Bahutu. Nabi's response was:

"We don't know those teachers very well."

That was enough to tell Tony that his racial hypotheses were right! They considered the naughty Bazungu to have divided the tribes. Yet they, as Batutsi, would not admit they knew the other Bahutu teachers. And yet, Nabi, the assistant principal was their immediate superior! Within a few weeks, the four classes at Lusaga would be no more since the four teachers, that Nabi didn't know (!) would all be massacred by the soldiers.

Finally they started to descend the escarpment that would bring them to Vurura. Tony was pleased that they didn't ask to go to the military camp first. They had probably heard that every night the military authorities were to be found at the Bishop's House. Tony certainly had been scandalized when he had been informed of that fact earlier in the week. So anyone who wanted to meet the military or the religious authorities could go to the same location! It seemed bizarre and a scandal for the catholic church because externally it probably looked as if the church was organizing the reprisals. In the mind of most uneducated and uninformed Barundi, there was precious little difference in the two groups. They were all *"Bakuru"*, some Bazungu, some Batutsi!

It was 7:40 when Fr. Tony Joseph parked his VW in the courtyard beside the bishop's house entrance. He got out and asked the two teachers to stay while he went inside. Opening the door to the dining room, Tony was welcomed by the community still at table. Dismayed, he looked around and saw all the military personnel sitting at the bishop's table. Shouldn't this area be kept for the clergy as priests were bonded together by the table of the altar and the table of the church: spiritual food and physical food? Now it was obvious that this table had become a place for bargaining for catholic lives. He wondered if protestant or animist lives had any value around this chopping block.

Monsignor Ruyaga called out to Tony and invited him to join them at table. But Tony responded that he had some other guests who had stayed by his car. Ruyaga smiled at Tony and told him to go and invite them in. He did as he was told and when Nabi and Ndigi entered the refectory, all the soldiers seemed to recognize the two teachers and warmly welcomed them to table, even though it was not theirs anyway. Tony tried to understand the situation and realized that *kirundi* hospitality was an open invitation to everyone from everyone….especially to those who were on the correct side! They pursued the conversation for thirty minutes, small-talking about everything from planting gardens to acquiring cattle.

Little by little Bishop Moulin first and then the other missionaries got up and walked away from the table, without disturbing the others. Finally Ruyaga stood up and invited all to come into the recreation room across the hall. The soldiers preceded the clergy into the room that apparently, over the past ten days, the military had made their own. Tony noticed that all the Bazungu clerics including Bishop Moulin were not in the recreation room. They had parted company, probably going to their own rooms to get away from the lunacy.

Ruyaga brought out two bottles of Johnny Walker scotch whiskey and invited all to help themselves. There were shelled peanuts in bowls of water (a Bantu delicacy) on the table and large bars of imported Belgian chocolate. The soldiers, five in number, sat back, each with a Belga cigarette hanging from his mouth. They seemed to enjoy clerical life to the fullest! Ruyaga asked Nabi and Ndigi to tell the military leaders how things were going in Butova.

As most Batutsi did when they were asked a direct question, these teachers were no different. They beat around the bush and were as cautious as possible. They alternated back and forth talking about how well the soldiers were doing in bringing about peace in the area. Tony wanted to interrupt and tell them the truth, for he believed that the soldiers were the ones who were causing all the problems and getting the whole population antagonistic. But he thought better of saying anything since it was *kirundi* politeness to let the people speaking have their say, even if it were pure rubbish. He would have an opportunity of rebuttal by telling his side of the story. If he waited until invited to speak, there was more of a chance that they would listen to his story. The teachers went into great detail, mentioning each soldier by name and saying how well they all were defending the area. Tony wanted to throw up, but only showed his displeasure by staring off into space and not smiling or laughing when the others found something that would tickle their funny bone.

Then, without any special prompting, one of the soldiers said that the military were scheduled to go to Butova the following day because there had been reports of racial strife in the TTC. Tony perked up when he heard that and sat on the edge of his chair This was no time for a Muzungu to intervene and he felt Ruyaga's eyes on him, non-verbally telling him to keep quiet. Then the vicar general spoke up:

"I am sure there are no racial problems at the school. Ndigi, you teach there and are the second-in-command. Reassure the military that there's no problem."

Lazaro sat very straight in his armchair and admitted why they had come to Vurura that evening:

"We have come here, myself representing the Teachers' Training College and Mr. Nabi representing the elementary schools. There is absolutely no political trouble in Butova, at the TTC in particular and whole area in general. Even if there were, the seven soldiers there could handle any problems. We have teachers of both races in the three schools and the outstation schools and there are no problems, we assure you. *Messieurs les Militaires*," he stated taking a wet peanut, shelling it and putting the contents into his mouth.

One of the soldiers got up and said how much he liked alcohol and poured himself another drink. He emptied the bottle and placed it back on the table as if it were to fill itself up again! The empty bottle was what Tony called a 'dead soldier'. He laughed to himself thinking that the 'dead soldier' was proof that the military was alive, alcoholically speaking. Another soldier willingly grabbed the second bottle and went around the table filling everyone's glass. Tony, having to drive home later in the night, had already turned his glass upside down on the table.

"*Fanta, mon Pere?*" (soft-drink, Father?) a soldier asked the priest but Tony refused the hospitality saying he was full and did not need anything else. He was tired of being forced to say 'yes' to everything offered so as not to offend *kirundi* culture.

The man who was the military leader looked over at Ruyaga and assured him that they didn't see a need to go to Butova the following day. He added:

"It has come to my attention that there is more trouble at the secondary school of Kibembo than in Butova. That is where we will go tomorrow," he said with an assenting tone in his voice.

Tony was relieved and yet felt a crushing pain in his heart. Kibembo was a protestant foundation and he had often met the missionaries there who were from Sweden. But these soldiers were fed and nourished very well by the catholic cathedral! It would only be right, if they needed to terrorize anyone, that they would attack a protestant mission like Kibembo rather than ostracize the arm that was feeding them and pouring their drinks!

It was past ten-thirty when Tony stood up and said they must be going as tomorrow would be a difficult day, the funeral mass of Melechiori Nyabenda. Actually he did not know how tense and strenuous a day it would really be and that Nyabenda's funeral would provide some relief and tranquility amid the tension! The calamity of Friday, May 12th would be more than he could have ever imagined!

The three got into the car, Georgio getting in first, respecting the senior position of the secondary school teacher and allowing Ndigi to get into the front seat again. As they started to climb the escarpment going from Vurura to the interior, Tony thought that he was just imagining something: a light ahead in the distance along the road. But as he climbed more and more and zigzagged to maneuver the sharp curves and the potholes in the road, he realized that what he saw was not merely in his imagination! There was a vehicle on the road ahead close enough that he could even see the red taillights. He tried not to go too fast, allowing the truck to stay a long distance in front of him. At this time of year after the long rainy season, there was not much dust on the road to prevent one car from following another. It would have been impossible in August or September for he would have had to stop and let the vehicle get far enough ahead of him so as to have decent visibility. But in May there was no problem.

Nonetheless he couldn't stay back forever. He asked Nabi and Ndigi if they saw a car and when they responded affirmatively, he tried making a substantial effort to slow down but got closer to the vehicle that seemed to proceed slower and slower. It was bigger than he had first thought. In fact it was a dark-colored truck and was slowly meandering up the weaving road to the top of the hill. Finally Tony saw the red break lights illuminate and the truck slowly came to a stop on the incline.

Tony had dreaded this moment because of the impending danger in the dark Burundi night. The truck had not pulled over to the right side but had stopped right in the center of the road. Tony could not pass on either side.

As he stopped behind the colossal vehicle, Tony saw movement above the tailgate. Then he recognized the cause of his greatest suspicions. Three huge rifles came out from the top of the truck over the tailgate and they were pointed directly at the VW. Tony gasped for air, his breathing became irregular with sweat pouring from his body as the guns seemed overwhelming: huge cannons pointed directly at him. He instinctively put his arms in the air, touching the roof of the small volkswagen with his hands. In the darkness of the night, he couldn't see anyone, any faces behind the guns. The horrifying sight numbed every cell of his body. Then he heard shouts "Move over! Move over!" from inside the truck accompanying the irregular movements of the guns. They beckoned him to move from behind the lorry to the right side of the road. He turned on his motor and flipped on his indicator to let all know that he had heard the dictate and was following it. Then he turned off the motor, pulled the hand break on, shut off his car lights but turned on his roof light, praying that those in the truck were Batutsi and they would recognize him or his passengers. He could not bear to think of what would happen if the truck were filled with rebels. Finally the tailgate was unchained and thrown to the ground and three tall soldiers in full military gear jumped down and stood with their guns pointed at the volkswagen. Tony could not tell how many other soldiers were in the back of the truck but he heard a voice, yelling at him:

"Come out! Get out! Hands in the air!"

Fr. Tony Joseph opened his car door and got out. His back was tight and he felt a twinge of pain in his lower lumbars from the uncomfortable seat in the car. He stood by the car door with his hands above his head. He noticed that Lazaro also was disembarking from the passenger side and Georgio was fast on his heels. The soldiers with the pointed guns were in the center, now surrounded by a countless number of others who seemed to come from everywhere. Actually they all seemed to pounce on their prey in the same instant. Both Ndigi and Nabi were shouting *"Amahoro! Amahoro! Amahoro!"* (Peace! Peace! Peace!) for all the soldiers to hear. Then one of the soldiers, who had come from the right of the truck, recognized the two teachers!

"Nabi! Ndigi!" he cried out and threw his arms in the air, and approached the two teachers to embrace them, first Georgio who was closer to him and then Lazaro. Immediately the three gun-toting soldiers in the center withdrew their weapons, relaxing them by their sides. All the other soldiers approached Ndigi and Nabi and with extended right hands smacked each others' right palm making loud slapping sounds, a beautiful music of friendship amid the darkness of the quiet night. Tony approached the group and started to shake hands with all the military, as loud shouts of greetings and welcome came from everyone. Tony reflected how good it was that he hadn't transported any Bahutu, for the welcome would not had been as exhilarating!

The soldiers, looking very tall in their military uniforms, continued talking with the two teachers and the priest for almost twenty minutes. Lazaro and Georgio told them that peace had come to Butova and that the only problem there was the illness and unexpected death of their fellow teacher. When Nabi told them it was Melechiori Nyabenda who had passed away, many said that they knew him and were surprised and very sorry. Nyabenda had certainly been a Mututsi! The soldiers talked about the great losses of the previous fortnight when the Bahutu revolt had begun. But, of course, they failed to mention that they had been to all the villages in the Bututsi the past week liquidating as many Bahutu as possible. Tony recognized that the soldiers were now entirely Batutsi since the malicious deeds of Shabaru.

Then they bid each other *adieu* with handshakes and hugs. Lazaro and Georgio reassured them again that there was only *amahoro* in Butova. The three drove off very slowly into the night as they passed the truck cautiously, and headed for Butova where the nightmare would continue.

Arriving at the mission gate, Tony stopped the VW and the two teachers thanked him for the use of his car and time as they opened the gate, allowing him to drive in. They were always polite and courteous, these Batutsi, at least towards the priest whom they considered a person who, like tonight, could always be helpful. They closed the gate from the outside and walked home along the wall separating the mission compound from the surrounding *mihana*. Tony parked his VW in the *kigo* and climbed the steps slowly, unlocked his bedroom door and lit the petrol lamp he had on his night table. He quickly undressed and pulled down his bedcovers. He knelt on the side of the bed. His prayer was asking the Lord 'why?' Why had all this happened? Why had he been so mistrusting of Lazaro and Georgio? Why was everyone catholic so relieved that the soldiers were going to the protestant mission? Why did the catholic mission have to bribe the soldiers to avoid a slaughter in their schools and missions? Why was Deogratias being held in captivity? Why had the policeman made such a scene in front of the catechumenate? Why? Why?? Why???

The fear that Friday May 12th would be a horrible day inundated the subconscious mind of Fr. Tony as he tried to sleep. He tossed and turned and wondered if sleep would have been easier if he had said 'yes' to more Johnny Walker! His mind, imagining the future, was flooded with anxiety, anger and fear. Would soldiers come to attack the Teachers' Training College? Would Melechiori's funeral and burial be without incident? Would the Bahutu begin to stand up to what their dreadful enemies the Batutsi were doing to them? He yearned to be as far away as possible from all the strife. He dreaded being the one who had to speak in the name of the oppressed and words spoken for them could amount to treason. His path was a very narrow one and there was no room for error. He woke one particular time during the night and with bright eyes and clear mind asked the Lord to bless him with discernment and patience. He was so afraid that some small incident might cause him to get angry and speak insensitively to the soldiers and *bakuru*. Tony told himself that many lives were at stake, including his very own. He must keep calm and be cordial to all, lest the authorities misinterpret some word or gesture and take out their rage on the Bahutu. "Heaven knows, they have suffered enough," he heard himself say aloud as he fell back to sleep.

After breakfast, Tony found himself with a few moments to spare, so he went into his room to prepare himself for Melechiori's funeral. The fifth grade teacher had been a kind and gentle man and since the whole school would be at the eucharistic celebration, it would be an excellent opportunity for the pastor to speak of Melechiori's goodness, caring and simplicity, a true legacy for his family and his students. He would choose the scripture reading of the good and faithful servant and also include I Corinthians 13 on love. He would ask Bernardo Minani and his wife Pataricia to proclaim the word since they both read so well and were fellow teachers. He also wanted to honor this faithful husband and father. Tony would underline these values and say what an outstanding example and inspiration he had been for his children, family and the whole community. He jotted a few of these ideas down on a piece of paper, put the paper in his upper shirt pocket and went out to stand in front of the church.

As it neared 10 o'clock, the classes of schoolchildren came across the compound and entered the church. At first it was only the boys who arrived but soon the girls, in their light blue dresses, joined them, having a longer walk as their school was near the sisters' residence. Since there were no benches or kneelers in the huge church, the six classes on the girls and the twelve of boys moved up to the front of the building and sat on the floor. The grades were doubled in the boys' school and they had twelve teachers, with a new one who had substituted for Melechiori since he had become sick and now had permanently taken his place.

On seeing Minani, Fr. Tony called him aside and asked him to read from the Book of Wisdom. He also saw Salvatore Mizuri, the other fifth grade teacher, and asked him to read the prayer of the faithful that Tony had prepared on a separate sheet of paper. The pastor then found Pataricia with her fifth grade schoolgirls and invited her to do the second reading from I Corinthians 13. All seemed to be well organized so Fr. Tony went to the sacristy and started to vest for mass. There were six servers already dressed and ready to carry the candles and cross and attend to the priest during the service. As he finished vesting he thought of how much he enjoyed these school masses and had to remind himself that today was a very sad and emotional service. The casket, which few Africans would ever have the luxury to be buried in, was now in the back of the church. The procession, led by the servers with candles burning brightly, moved to the back of the church to join the corpse. Fr. Tony greeted the widow, children and close family members of the deceased teacher. Besides the many school children, the church was filled with family, friends and older people who held back tears during the melancholy service. At the end of the mass, Tony read the committal rite with the prayers for the deceased and asked the angels to receive the soul of Melechiori in heaven. Then all left the church and Luigi was waiting in the van to drive the body to Lutana. Six male teachers including Georgio, Bernardo and Salvatore lifted the coffin and placed it in the truck. Then they tied it with thick ropes that Luigi had brought along for security. Melechiori's wife and father climbed into the cabin as Luigi entered the driver's side. Some of the teachers and some relatives climbed up and sat in the back of the truck beside the coffin. Slowly the homemade hearse wended its way from Butova to Lutana. It would be close to an hour before they would get to their destination. On their arrival, they would take turns digging Melechiori's grave, lowering the coffin into it and covering it with earth and stones. After the final prayers, they all walked away sad and some were teary-eyed.

The family and friends decided to stay in Lutana with relatives of Melechiori and go home in a few days. So Luigi was now alone and headed for the mission to say hello to Walter De Winter and the two confreres who lived with him. But before driving to that part of town, he went by the hospital. Luigi remembered an old man that he had driven to the hospital a few days earlier. He wondered how he was doing and stopped the van to go in and inquire. Maybe the man would be well enough to return home to Butova with him.

As he entered the hospital, he walked down a small corridor. His eyes glanced into a room that he recognized as the recovery area after surgery. Luigi could hardly believe what his eyes were gazing upon. In the middle of the room stood a soldier in full military garb with a rifle held in both hands over his head. He thrust the huge weapon, banging the butt end down with all his force on the motionless body of a young man on the floor. The butt end hit the man again and again on the face and in the head and Luigi could see blood gushing from all parts of his skull as if it were caught between the weapon and the cement flood. Then the dreadful soldier turned the rifle around and bayoneted him in the heart. The soldier finally stopped, stood back and stared at his defeated prey. There were two other bodies not too far away from the one just murdered. Luigi took all the courage he could muster up and yelled at the top of his voice:

"Stop that, you murderer! Stop! Halt! Stop! Never do that again!"

The soldier looked over his shoulder at the Muzungu standing in the doorway and turned on his heels, retreating by a door on the other side of the room. Luigi ran over to the young man, lifted his head from the hard floor and blood was gushing from his nostrils and ears. There was no pulse, no heart beat. Luigi said a quick prayer and offered him to his Maker. He then went over to the two others, but it was also too late for any human intervention. One Mututsi soldier had killed three more Bahutu who had probably come to the hospital for healing. A place of curing had become an arena of violent death. An obnoxious hate-filled Mututsi soldier had lurked and pranced upon his Bahutu prey. There was no need whatsoever for the wretched soldier to have done what he did. No reason except racial hatred!

"When will this end?" Luigi thought and he went over to the corner of the big room and promptly threw up the badly-digested food that he had eaten earlier that day. Luigi walked around the hospital in a trance. He could not believe what he had just experienced. He had seen a human being unmercifully murder three others. He stopped by the doctors' station and reported what he had seen. One of the doctors was a Russian and in broken French he told Luigi how miserable he felt. He said that he had stayed up all night to care for a Muhutu doctor whom he had known while they studied together in Russia. The physician had been severely beaten by Batutsi soldiers. The Russian stayed with him all night nursing him as best he could with the few medical supplies he had at his disposal. Then early that morning while he was making his rounds seeing other patients, a soldier went into the room where his friend was and cut his throat with a surgical knife. The *musoldat (soldier)* called in the deceased physician's wife and told her to take the body to a burial ground as soon as possible. There would be no external manifestations of any kind, no funeral, no mourning, for the fact that this Muhutu was dead was proof that he was a traitor! The Russian physician accompanied his fallen comrade's wife and they dug the grave together. The doctor smirked sarcastically and said that he didn't believe in God but that every person deserved some prayers and a public funeral. Blurry eyed, Luigi headed for the Lutana mission and hoped that Walter De Winter would be there to listen and provide some healing.

All three fathers came out to greet him enthusiastically and invited him into the house for a cup of coffee. Luigi started to shake as he told the story of what he had seen at the hospital. Walter told him that sort of thing had been going on all week. The four priests stared at each other with tears flowing from their eyes as they told one horror story after another. Finally Luigi said that he was tired, got up and went to the van to drive back to Butova before darkness. Even though the sun was still shining brightly, he had never felt so dim and gloomy, so downcast, so totally depressed.

That same morning, shortly after Luigi had driven away with Melechiori's casket in the van, Tony crossed in front of the church to go down to the brother' residence. He wondered how they were handling the situation and wanted to tell them about his adventure with Lazaro Ndigi, the happenings at Vurura and the encounter with the soldiers along the escarpment. Tony wondered if they would ever stop trusting Ndigi. But before he had left the church compound, he noticed a light blue-gray Peugeot pickup parked along the main road. He thought it odd that a vehicle would be parked on the road in plain daylight so far away from any housing or buildings. Tony crossed over to investigate. There were school children gathered around the truck and some men there as well. Then, to his horror, he noticed that there were two men on their backs in the bed of the truck with their hands tied around their backs. He recognized them as Salvatore Mizuri who had just read at the funeral and the principal of the school, Gasipari Lubulu, who had also been at the service.

Tony could not believe his eyes for, less than thirty minutes earlier, these men were in church. Salvatore had even helped load the casket into the van. They had both received Holy Communion so recently that the Resurrected Christ was still physically in their bodies. Both men, humiliated, stared down at the floor of the pickup and there were two policemen guarding the truck but standing in the shade of a nearby tree. As Tony walked by, one of the policeman shouted at him in a despicable voice *"Bamenja! Bamenja!"* (Traitors, Traitors) as he spat on the ground to emphasize his disgust. Still Tony could not understand how this had all taken place so quickly and so quietly after the church service. This incident led him to believe that the whole country could be uprooted and most of the people would not even have a clue as to what was happening. He thought back six days previously to the public inquisition of the four boys also accused of being traitors. That had been so loud, so public, so thunderous. But this took place almost in private, with no display whatsoever, no raising of voices, no public accusations, nothing external. The *bakuru* had changed their strategy from an angry outburst of reprisals to a quiet, composed, well-organized genocide.

Then three soldiers came marching from the Teachers' Training compound. They walked quickly with rifles in hand and stopped in front of the truck and called the two policemen over. The five men talked quietly for a short time. So Tony seized the opportunity to go over to the back of the Peugeot.

"What are you accused of?" he asked the educators both at the same time, not looking at either one in particular. Salvatore Mizuri was a tall man, with a thin face and some curly hair on his chin. Tony had always thought of Salvatore as a Mututsi but now he realized he was terribly mistaken. The fifth-grade teacher had small piercing eyes that protruded back into his head. Since he lived with Georgio Nabi in one of the houses on the mission compound, Tony had surmised they both belonged to the same tribe. But now as Tony looked at Mizuri he realized, with him squatted down on the floor, hands tied behind his back and some blood running down from his forehead, that he was far from belonging to the menacing tribe. Salvatore was definitely not on the winning team!

Gasipari Lubulu was the other man being detained. He was a fine friend that Tony had always cherished. Gasipari was very short in stature, with a small curly mustache that brought a bright shine to his round face.

His smile was infectious and his eyes sparkled when he went about his duties as principal of Butova Boys' School. He was also in charge of all the schools in the outstations: Vuvoga, Bihovu, Ruhweza, Mundi and Lusaga. For this reason it was his duty to visit each outlying school every other week. He had purchased a motorcycle to travel from one school to the other. His *pikipiki* could often be heard from the mission as Gasipari prepared to make his rounds in mid-mornings. Lubulu had nothing of the pride and conceit of the Batutsi teachers and Tony had become very fond of his simple way of dealing with issues. Mostly they discussed and organized the weekly school children's mass or Tony's participation in teaching of religion. It had been easy to talk to Gasi probably because he was so self-effacing.

Lubulu was a true Muhutu, in whom there was no guile! He often had mechanical trouble with his *pikipiki* and although Tony could not help him in that area, he would seek advice from Jose, Luigi or Luc. The three had spent many hours with Gasi showing him how to change a tire, clean spark plugs or get the clay mud, that was the landfill throughout the country, out of his spokes. Lubulu was also a very professional man. One day, Tony was five minutes late for a class. Afterwards Lubulu waited for him outside and asked him to try to be on time in the future as he didn't want to impose an inconsistent timetable on his teachers. Tony, at first, was a little perturbed. But then he realized that the principal was right and had taken the utmost politeness to bringing the tardiness to Tony's attention.

But now, the principal sat in the back of the truck, a very dejected and humiliated soul. Some Batutsi school boys came by and covering their mouths with their hands in the Barundi tradition giggling and showing their shame and embarrassment. Many adults also snickered as they passed-by and one asked in mocked sarcasm: "Is this not the principal of our boys' school?" Another responded with a further question: "Is that not the teacher of grade five?" Another commented: *"Nta soni?"* (Are you not ashamed?) Other passers-by wondered why Lubulu and Mizuri were tied down as criminals in the back of the truck with an Arab in the driver's seat! But it was obvious this was the vehicle belonged to the Arabs and it had been commandeered by the soldiers.

The military finally finished their caucus with the policemen and Samueli Kufa, the chief of police, went to the back of the truck to make sure the tail gate was well locked and all was in place. Tony recognized Kufa as the soldier who had treated the young men so badly the previous Saturday. As he passed in front of the pastor he gave a short, abbreviated, almost mock salute but Tony ignored him, looking off, far into the distance.

Even though this looked like official business, Tony certainly didn't give his approval. Kufa then spoke to the driver:

"*Tugende kwa Puma!*" (Let's go to Puma!)

The other soldiers and both policemen got into the back of the truck and Kufa went around the front of the vehicle getting into the passenger's side. The Arab turned his truck around in front of the church, and as they passed the House of God both detained teachers were seen bowing their heads profoundly in respect to the presence of God in the sacred building. It was a simple gesture that spoke volumes as they bid *adieu* to their meeting place with their God. As they drove back toward the main road, Mizuri shouted to the crowds lining the sides of the truck:

"Nagasaga, Bagenzi! Tuzobonana Mw'ijuru!" (Good-bye, Friends! We will meet in heaven!)

Certainly there were many who believed Salvatore and Gasipari were innocent. However the Batutsi plot would eventually eliminate tens of thousands of Bahutu tribesmen, who were innocent, accused of crimes they were incapable of committing and carried to their deaths. But for now the slaughter was just in its initial stages, as the soldiers arrested either the educated or the prominent, the successful or the well-known, the sophisticated or the financially-stable Bahutu. It seemed they were being arrested, accused and murdered methodically and the Batutsi wouldn't finish until they killed every Muhutu in Burundi.

Since Friday was a market day in Ruhweza, there were thousands of Barundi coming and going on the road in front of the mission. Tony was so traumatized by the arrests that he decided to go back to the mission house rather than spend time chatting with those who were passing-by. As he turned the handle to open the living-room door, he heard someone calling his name. It was Brother Louis who came running up the outside steps motioning to him. He looked pale and anxious and asked for a word with Tony who invited him into the living room. Even before Louis was seated, he told Tony that there was trouble at the TTC. The police had come to the school during class that morning looking for a Muhutu professor, Gregori Sumve, who taught Kirundi literature and culture at the school. Sumve was short in stature and very intelligent, especially in Kirundi classics. He had read everything that had been written since the arrival of the missionaries some eighty years before and was known as one of the foremost authorities in his field.

The soldiers had planned to arrest Sumve along with Lubulu and Mizuri but they had failed to find him. The military went to Brother Alex Labine to protest, believing that someone was hiding Gregori. Labine then called all the brothers together for a private meeting and gave them thirty seconds in silence to confess who was hiding the professor. No one admitted anything and Alex became furious while the other brothers looked at each other in bewilderment and dismay. Labine accused three of the brothers in particular but none of them admitted any knowledge of Sumve's disappearance. Since Louis had now become the local superior, chosen by the whole community, he stood up and confronted Alex for he was quite sure that it was not one of the brothers who was hiding Gregori.

Alex stormed out of the room, his authority undermined in the eyes of his confreres. He retreated to his office where he felt totally in charge. Immediately he called an emergency meeting of all the professors. They all attended except, of course, Sumve, who was one of the few non-Mututsi on the Barundi staff. The seven brothers who were on the staff also were obliged to attend. Once again Labine spoke to all about the soldiers accusing someone of hiding Sumve but none of the professors showed any signs of being an accomplice. The soldiers were circulating in the corridor outside the office and could hear much that was being said especially from Alex who got more enraged, shouting louder and louder as the meeting progressed. Lazaro Ndigi sat beside him and affirmed everything that the brother director was saying.

When the meeting ended with Alex no further enlightened than before, the director went outside, found Kufa, and told him that the meeting had been an exercise in futility. There had been no admissions of any sort, no clues as to who was helping Gregorio. If they wanted to search the school, they were welcome to do so. However he asked them not to ransack or destroy anything. The soldier told him that it was not their responsibility to look in every corner of the school but that if anyone was withholding information concerning important data, he, the director, would be responsible and the first to be arrested. Alex shrugged his shoulders and said that he had done everything to co-operate and was sorry they could not accomplish their mission. Tony realized that it was then that the soldiers had left the school and walked to the truck to tell the police about their lack of success in finding Sumve. So the soldiers had driven away very angry at the *Bazungu*, believing they had interfered with military orders.

Tony listened to the entire story as Brother Louis told it, one incident after another. He was surprised that so much had happened during and since the funeral celebration. He asked the brother:

"Well, *Frere*, I want you to be honest with me. You have come here to talk openly. So tell me: who is hiding Gregori and where is he right now?" Louis was a very sharp individual and knew the personal lives of everyone on the staff and more facts than he needed to know regarding the teachers of the TTC.

"I think the one who did it was Gerard Proulx!" the brother spouted out, with all his words seemingly linked together in the same syllable. Gerard Proulx was not a brother but rather a layman whom Alex had recruited in Canada to teach along with the brothers. He had never married and, having no family, was free to live independently in Africa. At the TTC, Proulx taught French grammar and literature. He was in the second year of his contract with the brothers and was making a very good salary that was paid directly to his bank in Quebec. He was radical about the problems in his native Quebec and didn't hesitate to say that he lived for the day when *La Belle Province* would be freed from Canada. That had created tension with Tony, who saw Canadian politics very differently. When he had heard Proulx' divisive ideology on his arrival the previous year, Tony soured in the relationship.

"But are you sure?" Tony asked Louis hoping for a sign of Proulx' innocence.

"As sure as I can be!" was the reply, as Louis smiled for the first time since their greeting.

"I watched him when Alex was talking to all the teachers and he seemed very aloof and disinterested. That convinced me that he knows where Gregori is and probably has helped him 'disappear' when the police and soldiers arrived. If it is Proulx, he lives in such a fantasy world that he has no idea what dangers could come to the school and what would be done to him and Sumve when the truth would be discovered," Brother Louis blurted out to Tony.

"The way that the soldiers have of persuading people to tell the truth by their torture, I wouldn't want to be in Proulx' shoes. Do you think it would help if I spoke to him individually?" the pastor asked.

"Probably. It can't make the situation any worse. But I would like to be with you to observe his reactions when you point the finger at him," Louis added as he got up and both men walked out the door and over to the school to find Proulx.

As they got near the school compound, they recognized Brother Alex coming their way.

"Where were you, Louis?" Alex demanded as the brothers came face to face. "I needed your support!"

"I went over to see Tony to find out how things were going in the parish." Louis lied.

"Well that fool Proulx has now admitted that he has been hiding Gregori Sumve. He hid him between the ceiling and the roof of his own bedroom! I might have figured that out for myself." Alex responded, belittling Proulx' senselessness. It is now his responsibility to bring Sumve to justice."

"What have you done since he confessed? The pastor asked.

"I haven't done anything. I have told everyone to remain calm and stay in the school. The brothers are all in our house. I really don't know what I should do next!"

"That is the first mistake you are making, Alex. It is not for you to do anything! It is for Proulx to drive Gregori to the soldiers if the Muhutu wants to give himself up. If he doesn't, then let him flee as fast as he can. Either way it is not your problem. Where is Proulx now, in your house?" Tony asked the brother.

Alex nodded "Yes".

"Louis, let's go over and see him right away," Tony said.

"But what should I do?" Alex asked, oblivious to what was being said around him.

"You go back to the house, go into your room, pick up a good book, put on some relaxing music and stay there for the rest of the weekend! I have already told you it is not your decision or problem and I will make Proulx very aware of his responsibilities. And maybe someday when all this is over you can bring a bottle of *Primus* (kirundi beer) to Kufa and laugh about old times. If you whet his whistle, he will forgive you for something you didn't do and your guilt will vanish!" Tony responded sarcastically.

As Louis and Tony strode to the brothers' residence with Alex following close at hand, the three missionaries saw a car leaving on the other side of the compound. They approached the brothers who were all watching the car drive into the distance. Brother Jean-Guy Tranchemontagne came over to Alex, Louis and Tony and told them that it was Proulx who was driving the brothers' car taking Gregori down to Puma to give himself up to the authorities. He went on to say that when the brothers were all together at the first meeting with Alex, Proulx had decided against speaking out because he still had thought he could free Gregori. Then when the whole professorial staff was called to Labine's office, he had questioned his reasoning but was then afraid to admit that he had hidden Gregori. He had gone to his room and shaved as a way of relaxing and being alone to reflect. While he was shaving, he realized that it was an impossible situation and he could not continue to hide the professor. By himself, he couldn't provide food for him and Sumve would have many other needs as well. As he finished shaving, Proulx washed his face with cold water and dried it. Immediately he went up to see Sumve and told him he had no other choice but to surrender. The professor reluctantly came down from the make-shift shelter and spoke to his mate for a few minutes in Proulx' room. Then they walked out together and Gregori Sumve shook hands as a "good bye" to all the brothers who were in the recreation room. Brother Jean-Guy then saw them to a car as they drove to Puma. They hoped that if he went alone in their car, the authorities would not see Proulx as an accomplice, but as someone who was bringing a wanted man to justice and let the ex-patriot go free.

"I now fear for Proulx," Alex said, "I consider myself responsible for his safety." The director only seemed to care about his own responsibilies.

"I fear for Proulx as well. When they see him they will accuse him of hiding a wanted man, obstructing justice." Louis added.

"*Bonjour, les freres!*" (Good-bye, brothers) Tony saluted the brothers and turned on his heals and walked away. "Keep relaxed and cool!" he shouted back to Alex and smiled at Louis.

Later that afternoon, Fr. Tony Joseph drove down to Puma. There were many people still on the roads visiting, purchasing, walking and talking to their fellow Barundi. Women walked to and fro with large, heavy baskets on their heads, balancing their loads with stick in hand as they traveled some to, and others back from, the marketplace. But when Tony arrived at Puma, the area was almost deserted. He turned right and parked in front of the administrator's house. Walking up the sidewalk. Tony met Jacabo Karani, the infirmarian who worked across the square in Puma's twelve-bed infirmary. They talked for awhile, and the *muganga* told him he had almost no medical supplies and was worried about the lack of penicillin. He had only two small vials for the entire population in his jurisdiction, 47,000 people! Karani told Tony that it was very difficult to get medicine into the southland. Usually it was stolen before it left the capital or somewhere along the way. Karani threw his hands in the air and said it was impossible to do his job when he was not given the right medications. He often thought of leaving Burundi and going back to his native Rwanda. Tony understood Karani's dilemma. He was a Mututsi from Rwanda who had to flee when the Bahutu took power in the mid 60's. Moving to the Bututsi southland, he felt superior to the Bahutu in Burundi. He made his living and supported his family in Puma. The possibility of his ever being happy and successful in Rwanda, now under Bahutu rule, was very remote.

Tony continued to listen but said nothing. He really didn't trust the *muganga* and if he had only a small amount of medicine, it was because he was keeping stock for his family and close friends or selling it to make a profit himself! Certainly he complained enough about being underpaid as the local infirmarian. But Jacobo Karani was certainly increasing his income on the pharmaceutical black market!

Finally Tony asked Karani if Kizungu was home for that was the reason why he had come to Puma. He responded that the administrator had gone to Vurura earlier in the day and he wasn't expected back until Sunday. Then he added that in the absence of the administrator, he, the *muganga,* was in charge of all the civil matters.

"Will there be anything I can do for you?" he volunteered.

"I've come down to inquire about the three teachers that the soldiers arrested in Butova this afternoon. Do you know where they might be and what charges have been brought against them? And while I am asking you, I have not heard anything about my catechist and secretary Deogratias Pungu who was taken into custody yesterday."

Karani cleared his throat and kept the priest waiting for an answer:

"*Mon Pere*," the *muganga* always spoke to the priest in French, "I don't know anything about these arrests or holdings. I have replaced the administrator, but they were arrested by the military. So you better deal with them directly," the acting-administrator said exonerating himself from all responsibilities. Never had Karani been more polite to the pastor nor more direct in what he had to say. These Batutsi could ignore the Bahutu protests but they feared the Europeans, especially the missionaries who had a captive audience from the pulpit every Sunday. Karani was very concerned that the fathers could upset the genocidal reprisals that seemed to be succeeding so well. He and Tony bid each other 'Good Night' and the priest wondering if Karani, like Pontius Pilate, was going to the kitchen to wash his hands of his part of the guilty crimes!

Tony got into his car, backed up around the corner and then drove straight ahead to the hut where the soldiers were sure to be. They often had prisoners with them, doing the cooking or clean-up. Tony *hodied* (the kiswahili word '*hodi*': clearing throat or coughing near the door to let those inside know there is an awaiting guest.....no doorbells in Africa) and a soldier came out. He said that they were all busy and had no time to speak to him right now. He, like Karani, was very polite. Tony turned and walked toward his car, hearing loud laughter from inside the hut and knew that they were not busy or doing any work. He remembered how Africans will never insult you by saying they don't want to talk to you.

They merely say they are not available. You can figure it out for yourself. Hearing the laughter of the 'busy' soldiers, Tony wondered if he stayed at the *arrondissement* long enough, would he not see and hear Kizungu as well?

It was a lonely drive from Puma back to the parish house. Tony felt very discouraged. What amplified his feelings of inadequacy and uselessness was the frustration that the three teachers were being physically abused and the realization that he would never see them again. When someone 'disappeared' in Burundi, it was not as if they had died. Rather it was as if they had never lived! No use asking about them. No one would ever admit to having known them or so the authorities assumed. How difficult that seemed to be for Tony since those who had been taken today were all special personalities and friends at the mission. Gasipari Lubulu was the symbol of stability in the school system. Gregori Sumwe stood in highest respect for Kirundi academic studies. Salvatore Mizuri was one of the most respected male teachers. All of them were now gone, and surely they would never return Even back in the USA when a man was put to death, all newspapers and radio-television programs wrote and talked about nothing else for days and days before the execution. Here in Burundi, they were taken away and people who dared inform as to their whereabouts were told they had 'disappeared'! Those who asked when their trial would be were told that they had 'vanished'! When a wife or daughter came with food, she was told that they had 'departed!'

As Tony drove into the mission courtyard, he saw a small group of people waiting before his office door. He parked his volkswagen around the house in the *kigo* and walked quickly towards his office. It was now after five o'clock and those awaiting a word with him would soon panic if they were not on the road for their homes.

Tony was pleasantly surprised to see Antonia, the wife of Gasipari Lubulu, waiting for him. He ushered her into his office and she sat on the bench in front of his desk. She was a small featured woman who was not educated as had been her husband. She had a baby on her back and Tony had remembered baptizing little Adriano a few months earlier. They had four other children, the two eldest now going to school. Antonia was overcome with grief. She put the corner of her *impuzu* (woman's garment wrapped around her upper body) up to her face to dry the tears from her eyes and asked in a low whispering voice:

"*Pati*, what are we going to do? They are out to kill us all."

Tony could not deviate from the subject. He knew she had come because they had arrested her beloved husband. Also to ask useless questions about his whereabouts, for she obviously knew the answers, too painful to imagine. So he asked her what he could do for her. The woman sat before his big desk and said in all simplicity:

"*Pati*, just stay with us in our sorrow and pray with us that God send us peace."

Tony wanted to take the opportunity to pray for Gasipari as he believed that the only sensible thing left to do was to hope and trust in God. He had seen Mariya the wife of his sacristan Bernardo Inzu also in front of his office as he approached. He had stopped to ask her how she was and she had told him that the previous night, the policemen had come and taken her Bernardo away. So Tony now went to the door and beckoned Mariya into his office. She sat on the bench beside Antonia and Tony sat in front of them, behind his desk. The two women, who were in the process of becoming widows, faced the priest and Tony began a prayer for their husbands. He spoke to God first about Gasipari and how he was such a great instrument in the hands of the Father. Then he said prayers for Bernardo and spoke about how much he had loved his family, how each week he traveled forty, fifty, sixty miles on his bicycle to find vegetables or trinkets he could then resell at the marketplace for an honest profit. He was known as one of the hardest working merchants in the area and Fr. Tony wasted no words in thanking God for the goodness He had invested in this man. He thanked God for the work that Bernardo had done around the sacristy and for the sacredness of his faith, as daily he went about preparing the holy vessels for the services. Bernardo never missed morning mass. Fr. Tony's conclusion was that through these injustices, God had to be inviting both of these great men into the heavenly home and that through their love for their families and their commitment to society, God would give the men eternal life and their families blessings and peace. The two women got up to leave. They had come to the *Pati* for prayer and intercession. Now their husbands had been prayed for by the pastor and it was time to return home and attend to their fatherless children.

After dinner, when the quiet of night had descended upon Butova, Tony sat at recreation with Jose, Luigi and Luc. He had told them about the events of his day and now Jose asked about Gasipari's motorcycle:

"Antonia told me," Tony replied. "that as soon as she had heard that her husband had been arrested and driven away by the soldiers, people had come to her house to take the motorcycle. However Gasipari had driven it away from the house that morning and she now had no idea who had it, be it those who hated her husband or the authorities."

He went on: "Mariya's story about Bernardo was basically the same. Some vultures had come as soon as they had heard that he was taken away and had confiscated his bicycle and all the supplies he had planned to sell at the marketplace. Further the wretches took his radio and 27,000 frBu that he had in cash at home. However she had recognized these brigands as neighbors, people living around their house. They had said that Bernardo was a traitor and thus they had the right to confiscate anything that had belonged to him. Mariya said that she was now penniless and Antonia said her lot was the same."

Jose wondered out loud:

"Have people taken all these possessions because they believed the arrested were guilty or did they testify that they were guilty in order to be able to take their possessions?" It was a good observation and a question that would never be answered. The truth was that many people were being killed and it just could not be that they all were part of the planned revolution. Much foul play was happening and many petty feuds between neighbors were being settled by accusing and subsequently liquidating the Bahutu.

Luigi was no fun either at the meal or recreation. He could not keep any food down for he was still nauseated from the scene at the hospital. He had hardly spoken since he had seen that soldier club the man to death before his very eyes. Luigi wanted only one thing: to get the hell out of Burundi and to go either to Zaire or back home to Italy. He had seen enough violence from the Barundi to ruin both a vocation as a missionary and a lifetime as a priest.

When Tony arose Saturday morning, he felt delirious and would have preferred to stay in bed. He had that feeling: 'if I pull the covers up over my head, life, people and disastrous events will disappear from the face of the earth.' But duty called and he realized that part of his role now was to be a sign of hope and encouragement for those around him. Jose was very discouraged. Luigi was angry and physically sick to his stomach. Luc, who had always been vivacious and enthusiastic, had become very sarcastic. He still tried to do as much as possible for the poor and those who belonged to his co-operative, but he, too, had lost the excitement his companions had always seen in him.

Then there were the sisters! They were a mixed community, Batutsi as well as Bahutu. He had to encourage the Bahutu to remain calm and quiet and the Batutsi to protest quietly but strongly. And the brothers! They were all Canadians and they were basically unaware of anything that was happening in the villages. Their only interest was their students and they favored those who were most open and friendly towards them, usually the Batutsi. The students took advantage of the special gifts and other favors they could obtain by being friendly to the brothers. When Tony saw the professors organizing a softball game one day in Butova, he really had to step back and laugh. The students would try to stop a baseball with their legs and feet. They had no understanding of a North American game and the brothers thought it inconceivable that they couldn't play softball! They always had problems accepting the Barundi as they were with their particular interests and values. Not having been properly prepared for Burundi, they tried to transform their interests and values from Quebec to Burundi. That wasn't working out, even though academically they were performing miracles with the students. If they were not trained missionaries, they certainly were well-formed teaching professionals. They still had six more weeks of school remaining before the summer vacation when some of them would return to Quebec. The brothers feared the day when a truck of armed soldiers would roll up to the school, jump out and start shooting all the students. That was what was happening in the predominately Bahutu schools in the north and center of Burundi and, Tony surmised, that is probably what happened the previous day in Kibembo. He wondered how many bottles of Johnny Walker it would cost Ruyaga to keep the soldiers away from Butova. So when he recalled the many times in the seminary when he had been taught that the priest is a man for others and he lives and sacrifices for others, Tony Joseph, the priest, realized the challenges of his calling and the depth of Christ's goodness that had to accompany his every gesture. He had to live for others and be a priest for all.

On this early morning, Fr. Tony felt grateful as he walked into the chapel, thankful that he would have the next forty-five minutes to be lost in prayer before the Lord. Tony had always loved the quiet time of prayer in the morning and it never ceased to give direction to his day. He prayed this morning in a very special way for Deogratias Pungu and then his mind settled on Gasipari Lubulu, Salvatore Mizuri, Gregori Sumve and even Melechiori Nyabenda. He felt great pain when he realized that the schools of Butova had lost three teachers and a principal in the very same day. In an era when the teachers and school administration was all very young, this was an abysmal tragedy. How will they be replaced? What do we say to their students who saw them dragged away right after the funeral mass? If

8. Hopelessly Helpless Or Helplessly Hopeless?

After breakfast, Fr. Tony went to his office, as Saturday was always the day for baby baptisms at Butova; the mothers would come with babies on their backs. Sometimes there would be between ten and fifteen christenings. The priests always waited beyond the scheduled time as habitually the people were late. They didn't want anyone who walked long miles for the baptism to be denied because of tardiness. Nor did they want to repeat baptisms throughout the course of the day. Strangely in Burundi where there was so much importance attributed to the family, christening was seldom a family affair. The mother would come to the mission Saturday morning and she would be accompanied by the godparent who was the same gender as the child. Afterwards no one hastened home as they did when weddings were over. Maybe they saw baptism for its spiritual significance and not an occasion for a party. In any case, this was Saturday and Tony was responsible for the baptisms. He would get them written up in the parish register by Jean-Bosco, who would also prepare the church ceremony since Bernardo Inzu had 'disappeared'.

As he went through the different events of his day, Fr. Tony Joseph allowed his mind to meander back to his days in college when he had been taught theology and spirituality. His thoughts drifted to the time he had studied the Pascal Mystery: the Passion, Death and Resurrection of Christ. He remembered a Jesuit professor at Loyola College who referred to this experience so often that he called it by its initials.

"The PDR is the central event of our faith," he recalled Fr. Dave Asselin SJ saying so often. When the PDR was taught, one of the important attitudes that was studied was that of the Blessed Mother, the woman who saw her Son, Jesus Christ, murdered and die on the cross on the first Good Friday. Mary lived the first Holy Saturday in recovering hope. She had been present at the crucifixion of Christ and now she lived for the Resurrection. Mary knew in Whom she had placed her faith and she awaited, with anxious anticipation, the total victory of her Son who was God. Every time Fr. Tony gave a retreat, he reminded his retreatants how Saturday was Mary's Day because this was the time that her sorrows and sufferings were transformed into hope and then victory. Simple Ignatian Spirituality!

Tony recalled how the previous day, Friday the 12th of May, had been a day of excruciating pain and suffering for Gasipari, Salvatore, Gregori and their families. As well, it had been one of the most difficult days of his life. Tony could only think that the teachers were taken away and probably killed on the same day of the week, even at the same time, as the Lord and Savior had been beaten, judged a criminal and obliged to walk the royal road of the cross to his shameful death on Calvary. Fr. Tony was amazed at the close similarity to the death of the Savior and what these three men had suffered. He wondered if Bernardo had been murdered at the same time and taken to his burial with the three teachers.

But now it was Saturday, time to move on toward the ultimate victory of the Resurrection: Sunday. Hadn't Jesus said: "Unless the grain of wheat fall into the ground and die it remains merely a seed; but if it die, it produces much fruit?" This Sunday would be the day of transformation and change, from death to life, from defeat to victory, from mourning to celebration and Mary was the model of hope for the priest. If only he had the faith and hope of the Blessed Mother! If he trusted in the Lord that all this had happened for a reason and that, as Christ died to give us life, so too Gasipari, Salvatore, Bernardo and Gregori died to transform our tears and sadness into dancing.

Tony prayed as he went about his Saturday tasks, but stopped from time to time wondering why his hope was not as radiant and animated as he had imagined the Blessed Mother's to be. Then he realized why he could not draw consolation from these events whereas Mary had lived the ultimate hope on that first Holy Saturday. For her, all was over! Christ had died and the event of His Resurrection was breaking through as the spectacular rising of the sun transcends the horizon every morning. However the situation here in Butova was continuing with no end in sight. They had taken away Inzu and Sumve and Lubulu and Mizuri but how many more would they come, arrest and carry off before their ethnic cleansing was over, before their war of genocide would be completed? Christ had died once for all. But the Suffering Christ, in these poor people, was still struggling against the forces of evil all around them. This was the nightmare that he was living even if he believed in his heart that victory would be theirs. Nevertheless in the depth of his being, he could only feel helplessly and hopelessly useless. He kept telling himself that hopelessness was a negative characteristic in his soul when he completely abandoned God and His power to change a situation. Helplessness, he thought, was realizing that he was incapable of doing anything on his own. He believed he had no control over either of these alternatives but if he had more faith, even if he would be helpless, his faith would prevent hopelessness. He tried to think of other thoughts but felt the anxiety and emptiness of God's abandon. "Lord, give me some semblance of hope even when I don't trust you anymore," Tony prayed.

There were only three children for baptism. After Jean Bosco had done all the annotations in the parish register, Tony went over to the church with the three mothers and two godfathers and one godmother to perform the baptismal rite. His mind continued to wander as he thought of how silly it seemed to baptize these infants. The people believed that if the babies were to die without baptism , and there were so many infant moralities in Burundi (one out of five children died before five-years-of age) they would go to limbo! Tony could not believe that anymore. He knew that these little babies, admitting the horrible possibility of their deaths, baptized or not, would go directly to God in heaven. God was not programmed or mathematical, nor did He depend on a priest pouring water on a baby's forehead! What had baptism done for the people of Burundi? The missionaries had poured millions of gallons of water on the people as a sign of cleansing and conversion and yet now they were falsely accusing their neighbors, having them arrested, telling lies to have them carted off to their makeshift graves and then going to their homes and stealing all their material possessions they had left to their poor wives and children! What kind of conversion was that? Their sinful attitude contradicted their baptism charisma and showed that they were not christians in any stretch of the imagination! Christianity was not a matter of baptism but rather living a Christ-minded and Christ-hearted way of life. Tony believed that, over the last weeks, Christ had vanished from their hearts and from the church of Burundi and all that remained was the devil himself. He went about the ritual believing he was wasting his time and resenting the hypocrisy of the people and the church that demanded these meaningless religious rituals.

Often when Fr. Tony did baptisms he recalled two years previously when he was still very new in the parish doing his first baptisms in the outstation of Lusaga. There were over twenty baptisms that day and after they had all been registered by Eusebio Bitega the head catechist, Tony started to do the baptisms in the church. He was so nervous reading all the prayers in Kirundi and trying to get the pronunciations correct, that he reached out to pour water on a baby's round head with his eyes still glued to every syllable in the ritual. When he finally looked up he was pouring water on the mother's left breast, as, in his peripheral vision, he had confused the round outline of her bosom with the head of the youngster whom she was breast-feeding to keep quiet. Tony had learned his lesson and from then on he always looked up before starting to pour the water of baptism and anoint the baby's forehead with oil!

When the baptisms were over he headed for the dining room to join his colleagues for lunch and then spent the rest of the afternoon preparing his homily and mass kit. Early Sunday morning he would be off to Mundi to celebrate two masses at the largest outstation of the parish. There were over two thousand catholics registered in Mundi.

The usual situation for most Sundays at Mundi was that there was no priest to celebrate mass. The catechists were in charge of the church service. Yohani Bora (Bora means 'good' in Kiswhili) was the head catechist of Mundi and a very capable leader of the catholic church in that area. Yohani was the only catechist at Mundi that the fathers would allow to preach. He always did an outstanding job. Yohani was well respected by all the people of Mundi. Whenever the fathers did not understand the mentality of the people, they would undoubtedly say: "The next time I go to Mundi, I will ask Bora. He will explain the true kirundi meaning!" Yohani and his wife Teresia had ten children who all still lived at home with them. Their hut was about one mile from the chapel and, rain or shine, Yohani was always on time. He was a tall, slim man in his late forties and Tony knew, from previous conversations with him, that he had been a catechist since he was very young. His longevity was similar to that of Alberto Simba of Ruhweza and Danieli Rutega of Vuvoga. Yohani had been a catechist for over twenty-five years, probably starting just a few years after the mission had been founded in 1940.

But Yohani Bora was in a class of his own. When the catechists would gather together each month for their day of renewal and recollection, all the other catechists would look up to this humble man for leadership and direction. When Mathias Becker had found some teaching difficult to explain at the catechists' meeting, he would speak to Yohani beforehand who never failed to give Mathias the right direction. Becker would present it to all the catechists and sometimes ask Bora to make his comments. Yohani had a way about him that built confidence and created reassurance and yet did not impose his own ideas on anyone.. He could always be counted on to give an objective opinion and one that was in-line with the principles of the gospel. Tony knew this gentle man loved the Lord and would do anything to follow Christ. The only thing that prevented Bora from being a priest was his wife and ten children! The fathers thought celibacy was an odd way of preventing true pastors from celebrating the sacraments in the roman catholic church. Tony wondered why the church would starve her members of the eucharist when witnessing celibacy to Africans had no meaning or value in their culture. Everyone was married for that was where God called and lived with all His people. So Tony really looked forward to his Sunday, being in Mundi and celebrating the two services in the presence of a large group of people including Yohani Bora.

So on Sunday May 14th, Fr. Tony rose with great anticipation and had breakfast with Jose, Luigi and Luc after the morning office. Jose was to say the first mass at the parish church and he would also preach for Luigi at the second mass. Tony quickly got up from the breakfast table and bid his confreres a happy day of ministry. He said he would see them when he got back, probably in mid-afternoon. He told them not to wait lunch for him, that he would eat when he arrived.

The drive to Mundi was a short one, about thirty minutes. Mundi was in the heart of the Bututsi and most of the christians there were Batutsi although there were also many Bahutu and a few Batwa (pygmies) who lived in the densely populated forest area. But the Batwa never came to church except when the missionaries were giving out food or clothing. Driving in the middle of the crowds to the church building, Tony had to slow down because there were so many people along the sides of the road. He was very happy to see so many people and most would stand and wave to him as he went by. What joy was theirs that they would have mass and be able to receive the Lord in the sacrament of eucharist! Many of the women and girls carried kneelers on their heads, shoulders or in their hands. This was a small, home-made three piece wood-ensemble that was joined together and used for both sitting and kneeling during mass. One always knew that people were going to church when they saw them carrying their kneelers.

When Tony arrived, the entire area surrounding the church was overflowing with women, men and children. Outside the church, many people had gathered together, blocking the usual back entrance to the church. The chapel was long and narrow. One of the construction problems in Burundi was that there was never wood long enough to stretch from one lateral wall to the other. So most churches were built very long and very narrow, with the width depending on the wood length that could be obtained in that particular area. In Mundi, there were three walls standing but the back wall of the church had not been built. After the service would begin, there was no possible way to get through the crowd since they blocked the area completely. Both side walls were ten feet high made from mud bricks with little windows high over the heads of the people. Outside, on the right hand side, the ground was slightly inclined so that when the church was filled and there was no visibility from the back, late-comers could stand on the hill, look through the windows and follow mass. The priest would celebrate facing the people. There was a step up to the altar area so that he could be easily seen. The altar was made of cement with big flat stones adorning the outside. To one side, on a podium but braced to the wall, stood the tabernacle. Actually the tabernacle was a large wooden box that had been sent from Europe containing a dozen bottles of Johnny Walker Red Whiskey! But now this box held the Divine Presence between masses and when the priest stayed permanently. Many years before, whiskey had been the drink of preference among the Belgian diplomats and the missionaries. Now it was almost impossible to obtain. So the wooden box was a precious relic both for what it had contained and especially for what it now contained..

Tony had brought along two loud speakers that he set on the roof of his volkswagen, plugged them into the lighter and started to play some religious music that had been recorded on mini-cassette in one of the parish churches in Gisumu. The people were always amazed at how the music would be projected from this tiny leather covered machine that seemed so small. The people started to sing along as soon as they heard the music. *"Mukama, Mukama, tugir' ikigongwe"* (Lord, have mercy) and all joined in the chant that was adapted from a wedding song that was sung as the bride left her home and parents to go to the church for her marriage. Since everyone knew the music, it was easy to sing along with the recording of the Gisumu Church Choir.

Fr. Tony headed up the main aisle of the church and two boys followed carrying his green-metal *caisse-chapelle* (mass kit) wherein all that was needed for mass: hosts, wine, water, books, vestments, crucifix, candles and linens were contained. They placed the case on the altar and Fr. Tony opened it. Yohani Bora's first assistant catechist, Nestori Mwiza (Mwiza means 'nice'), came forward to set up the altar. Tony thanked him and told him to make sure there were lots of hosts since the number of people at the church today was very great. Nestori, like Yohani, was a very humble man. He was much smaller in size than Yohani, probably only 1.7 meters but had a ready smile on his thin face. Little did Tony realize, as this faithful catechist set up the bread and wine, that this would be the last mass he would attend in this world, the last time he would prepare the water and wine and unfold the linens and ready the vestments It would also be the last time Nestori would read the word of God in the scriptures and receive the presence of his Lord until he would come face-to-face with his God in heaven.

Tony began the celebration of mass. Nestori proclaimed the first reading and Yohani the second. Then Fr. Tony rose to read the gospel. The reading was from the beginning of the seventeenth chapter of St. John where Jesus asks the Father to glorify Him for He has spent His whole life glorifying the Father. The pastor thought of all the men who had died so bravely over the past week His mind danced from Gasipari to Salvatore to Gregorio to Bernardo to Deo: hundreds of faceless, nameless men and boys who had been subjected to the most gruesome of crimes. These past two weeks the gift of life, endowed on each by God, had been snuffed out by the soldiers, policemen and Batutsi authorities. A spirit of profound anguish came upon him as he realized that he would never see these men again. The pain grew even greater when he reflected that their deaths would never be officially recognized. No one would ever be certain about their demise. He was perplexed by the thought that no one would ever know about the certainty of their deaths. What each was accused of. What each man's last words were. What evidence condemned each. How each was tortured. Where and when each had died. How each met death. How each courageously went to greet his Maker.

In the presence of so many Batutsi and in the heart of the Bututsi, Fr. Tony prayed that the Bahutu would glorify the Lord by the way they were being put to death by their adversaries. He whispered to himself: "It all seems so absurd, so anti-Christ, so damned deceitful; this 'ethnic cleansing' whereby his best friends and companions, in building up the Body of Christ, were falling like flies in a battle that had absolutely no sense whatsoever." However he welcomed the opportunity to pray and he felt closer to all his friends as he prayed the Father of heaven to glorify them in their new home.

Pastor Tony thought of how Gasipari gave glory to God by building a spirit of christianity in the school that he principaled. His mind wandered to Deogratias who gave glory to the Father by teaching about the Kingdom and now was probably readying himself to take possession of the Reign of God. He thought of Gregori and Salvatore who recognized Jesus in the injustices done to other members of their race and how their deaths would someday bring peace to their *Burundi Bwacu* that they loved so much. And he thought of Bernardo who lived every morning so close to the Body of Christ in the tabernacle and who would clean and dust the altar so that the house of the Lord would give glory to the Father. Fr. Tony found himself speaking their names gently on his lips and brought the memory of each of these brave men to the sacrifice of the mass that Sunday morning.

Tony normally relaxed by talking to the people between the two masses. Usually there was an hour before the drum sounded to begin the second service and he would stand outside, chatting and bantering with the parishioners. Often he would also attend a meeting, usually organized by the Legion of Mary, where the people would say what they had done over the course of the last week in order to be apostles of the Lord.

However this Sunday was very different. Tony felt the depths of depression as he remembered his friends that had now probably met the pangs of horrible and terrifying deaths. He was dealing with a great deal of inner anger and anxiety as he though of the teachers and catechists who were forced to die without the last rites and the sacrament of pardon since the authorities did not want any of the church *bakuru* to know when and where they would kill those who had been arrested. He reflected on his reason for becoming a priest. He had dreamed of accompanying so many people to their final resting place with the Lord. Yet now he was cut off from giving any gesture of forgiveness since the soldiers and policemen considered those arrested to be traitors and would not allow a priest to talk to them. So Tony decided to stay in the church when the first mass was over and since there were consecrated hosts in the tabernacle, he looked forward to praying and adoring Christ in the sacrament of His Body and Blood. He would then celebrate the second service and get into his car and drive quickly back to the mission of Butova. However all that was not to be!

Yohani Bora approached the pastor who had turned his chair around to pray facing the tabernacle. He sat about ten feet in front of the stand, which held the Prince of Peace. All of a sudden Yohani appeared, standing tall over him. He bent down to get Tony's attention and begged his pardon for interrupting his prayer. The catechist asked to sit down on the only chair in the church. He squeezed into the left side of the chair and Tony moved to his right to give him room. Tony had always been amazed at how the Barundi would share chairs, sometimes trying to sit three on the same chair. He jokingly called it sitting 'cheek to cheek'! However even though he had seen others share chairs very often, Tony never had anyone do this with him. He felt rather uncomfortable yet happy that Yohani would take the initiative. So he considered this a special time of closeness. Even though Yohani had great respect for the *Bapati,* he was insightful enough to realized the priests wanted to be close to the people and share everything with them. So he felt no inhibition about sharing the pastor's chair. And besides, what he had to say was painful and he wanted no one else but the pastor to hear his story.

Yohani began by whispering apologetically to Tony and indirectly to God for having interrupted the prayer. He mentioned that he had waited for Tony to come out and relax with the people and maybe go to the small room that served as office up the hill. However because Tony did not come out, Yohani felt compelled to tell him immediately what had happened during the night.

9. Mundi, Sunday, May 14, 1972.

"A soldier came here last night, just a bit before dusk," Yohani Bora whispered to the priest, "and he went right to where some men were gathered for night watch. For some unknown reason, he shot all seven of them as they all were Bahutu" As Yohani continued with his story, Tony's eyes opened larger and larger until he felt them as huge as saucers.

"No one came to bury them since they are all afraid to come out of their houses at night. So this morning at dawn I buried them with the help of my brother who shares the same *rugo* with me. The soldier came to my house last night and asked me to name the Bahutu who had been at a meeting about three weeks ago here in Mundi." Tony had never heard the even-tempered Bora more animated.

"And did you give any names?" Tony interrupted.

"*Okayed!* (No) I don't know their business," Bora replied. "They are Bahutu and I am a Mututsi! If they had meetings, they would surely not invite me!" Bora replied in a rather cynical way.

"And what are you going to tell the soldier if he returns?"

"He said he would return, today at five o'clock in the evening and if I don't have names for him, he will kill me as well!"

"You can't give names, especially if you don't know any," Tony remarked logically.

"He also asked me about Nestori Mwize, but I don't know his business either. I couldn't even say that he was or wasn't in a meeting because I was never told anything about his affairs. The soldier then asked me about twenty-two other men who attended the meeting and of course again I pleaded innocence.

"You did right," the pastor reassured him, "since you don't know anything about all this, you have to remain silent."

"Pray for us, *Pati*." Yohani added and got up and slowly walked away from the chair.

Fr. Tony turned back to the Lord, made himself comfortable having regained the entire chair, and prayed in the depth of his soul for the seven men who were murdered in that area the previous night. It felt strange to sit there in this quiet chapel and realize that a mad man, a soldier who was called to defend the people of his country, would set about to murder those who were at night watch. They, too, were protecting the people from the enemy! And from a foe who never existed! He heard himself groan and smirk and whimper to the Lord: "I cannot believe what is happening in this dreadful country!"

At this time, the only remedy that made sense to the priest was to remain before the Blessed Sacrament and pray to God. He talked to the Lord and decided not to ask 'why' but rather to seek the grace of pardon and forgiveness and reconciliation between the Bahutu and the Batutsi. But the more he prayed, the more uncomfortable he felt. He wanted to ask for peace but every time he imagined the soldier killing those seven innocent men, he became more furious. How could he ever ask the Bahutu to reconcile with the Batutsi when they were being destroyed by hatred and murder? He thought of Jesus saying: "Turn the other cheek" and he heard himself say out loud: "This is crazy! stupid! ridiculous! Only God could forgive such animalistic and diabolical behavior." Tony was so overcome with rage that it was pointless for him to remain in prayer. He got up and walked to the back of the church.

People were just arriving and were entering the church to ready themselves for morning prayer before the second service. So he went out, climbed the small hill beside the church and entered the tiny house that was a combination of office, bedroom and dining area when the priests would stay overnight at Mundi. Once inside, Tony fell to his knees, feeling pain and stress throughout his whole body. And he prayed: "Lord, only You can change my heart. Take away my hatred for the soldier and these killers and replace it with the same attitude as You had when You were dying upon the cross of Calvary."

Little by little, Father Tony heard himself say ever so gently:

"Father, forgive them, they do not know what they are doing!" And for the first time in the past hour, or maybe the past day or week, or maybe the past two weeks, Tony received the peace of Christ in his heart.

Soon it was time for the second service. So Fr. Tony returned to the church, turned his chair around to face the people, placing it beside the altar, to the left of the tabernacle. Then he vested while a member of the parish council came forth and prepared the water, wine and hosts and lit the candles. Fr. Tony Joseph wondered how he would even get through this mass. It certainly would not be easy, since he was so depressed on hearing the news of the slaughter of the seven Bahutu watchmen. He wondered if he should announce that he was offering the mass for the repose of their souls but thought better of any official announcement that might provoke the

Bahutu who must have felt repressed and overwhelmed by the murderous gesture. Besides he wanted to avoid any triumphant responses from the Batutsi. He really didn't know how such an announcement would be received. Furthermore, if anyone had not heard the news, it would distract their prayer and cause an uproar. He decided that from now on, when he celebrated the eucharist, he would offer it without any announcement for those who had been murdered over the past weeks. Little did he understand now that this would be his mission as a consecrated priest of God for the rest of his life.

As the congregation began the entrance hymn, the church filled again to capacity. He looked outside and it was clear and sunny with a bright blue sky. It was now 10:15 and the brightness of the day filled the prayer chapel of Mundi. Fr. Tony paused in silence so that all might ready themselves for the opening prayer. In a mildly distracted way, he happened to look outside, through the windows on the top of the wall. There he saw what he had been dreading since Bora had given him the news.

A man in a soldier's uniform was walking along the pathway, from the back part of the church to the front, on the incline. He had a rifle in his right hand and was nodding to the people around him, distracting them in their prayer and reflection. Even though the moment was solemn and spiritual, Tony cursed the wretch in his mind but no words came forth from his lips. So much for the passing peace he had felt earlier in the small house! He was totally disgusted with this assassin and wondered how he had the nerve to show his face in church after the debauchery done the previous evening. He hoped the soldier would not approach to receive Holy Communion. For the first time in his priesthood, Fr. Tony knew that he would refuse the sacrament of the Body and Blood of Jesus, since this man had committed an abominable crime and certainly was far from repenting.

Tony wondered if the presence of this sinful creature would effect his thoughts and preaching at mass and he tried to focus on the people and their need for hope. As he reflected on the first two readings of mass, he concentrated all his attention on the spiritual message. Why should this hypocrite distract him from God? He praised the grandeur of Christ and God's triumphant glory, even if part of his creation, humankind, was a killer and the most wretched of all creation. He thought how ironic it was that he had been given a rifle by the vicar general to protect his parishioners and when this would have been the ideal time to use it, he had left it back in his bedroom in Butova!

As Tony began his homily, he tried to rid his mind of the deceitful charlatan and, since he had already preached at the earlier service, it was easy to stay on track and not deviate into the situation that had made him so angry and vengeful. The rest of the mass continued without incident. From time to time, as the pastor celebrated and read and sung the prayers, he looked about the congregation and then focused his regard on the place outside where the soldier was still standing. At communion time, the people came to the Lord in large numbers but the soldier did not budge, remaining outside the church walls smiling scornfully in his arrogance.

When mass was finished, most of the people left quickly to go back to their homes. But as was the custom, some stayed outside the church and chatted with their fellow parishioners. Tony packed his mass supplies and had two boys carry them to the car as he exited by the back of the church. He wanted to assure the killer that he had seen him and also bid Yohani Bora and the other catechists good-bye and pledge his protection and support to them. He walked up the hill and felt the soldier's eyes staring at his back. He ignored his presence, a specific insult to a person in authority. Since the military man considered himself important yet was ignored in public by the clergy, the moment was rather embarrassing for him. Tony wondered if he would seek revenge: "I don't get angry. I get even!" was how he imagined the soldier's thinking.

Tony continued walking to the little office and before entering, called out over his shoulder to some boys who were following him. He made sure his voice echoed loud enough for the soldier to hear every word:

"Tell Yohani Bora that I would like to say good bye to him!"

The chief catechist came walking quickly, half-running since he didn't want to keep the pastor waiting when he was getting ready to drive home. He knocked on the door and Tony welcomed him. The two men sat down and Tony began to speak:

"That soldier has stayed in the area so he will probably be here as he said at five o'clock. When I leave, I will go directly to the administrator Albert Kizungu or if he is away to the *mugging* Jacobo Karani and tell them what has happened here last night. I will also tell them how the soldier has threatened you. I will definitely come back at 4:30 and will stay until it gets dark. I'll invite the administrator to accompany me. But how about you, Yohani, how are you coping? Would you want me to give you the sacrament of penance?

"Okayed, Pati!" (No, Father) was this brave man's reply. " I'm ready!"

Yohani went on to say how close he felt to God and had received Communion at the morning service. Thus he had received the Body of Christ in His glory and didn't need to receive Him in reconciliation. Besides there was no need for pardon as he didn't have any sins on his conscience. He added that if God was calling him to die, because of the hatred between the Batutsi and the Bahutu, he would gladly offer his life as a ransom for the Batutsi-Bahutu abhorrence. How wonderful it would have been if Mathias Becker had been here to hear the words that this catechist had just uttered, Tony thought. Mathias, more than anyone else, had trained Yohani in the gospel values and very often had spent his evenings at the outstation talking to Bora and explaining the spiritual commitment to Christ that called for sacrifice and reconciliation. Now Tony realized he was cultivating the harvest of Mathias' planted seeds. He was so proud of Yohani and told him that he admired his faith. He was an enormous sign of hope for Tony.

"You have made the right decision, Yohani, and God will reward you for it through all eternity. What are you going to do between now and nightfall? You are welcome to come back to Butova with me and there you will be protected."

"Oya, Pati," (No, Father) Yohani answered, "thank you but that would leave my wife and family in danger and I am the catechist. I must use all the influence I have to prevent other killings. Besides, I am going to go home and spend the rest of the day with my family!"

Tony could hardly believe what he had just heard from a Murundi male. Normally men didn't pay any attention to their children and never spent any time with them. That was the wife's duty and responsibility! But here was this man-of-God, man of the gospel, giving what might be his last day and his final hours to his family. Tony thought of the scripture text where Jesus had said: "Never have I found such faith in all Israel!" He realized that he would never find such faith, such authentic love and such self-sacrifice in all Burundi. Tony grew in admiration of this fine person. He thought: "Maybe the extraordinary generosity of one man is worth all the wretched behavior of so many others."

As Yohani got up and prepared to leave, Tony hugged his catechist, believing that they were probably parting for the last time. He reassured Bora once again that he would alert the authorities at Puma of the volatile situation in Mundi. He then shook hands with the people who were waiting to bid him *adieu* at his car and noticed the soldier had left. Many of the people, being polite in the *kirundi* fashion and customs, would not leave before the priest drove away. Tony disconnected the speakers that had been playing music from his car and put them on the back seat and then was off.

He decided to go directly to Puma passing by the mission along the way.

About six miles from the turn off from the main road leading to Butova, there was a place called Luconi where the roads from Vurura and Mundi become one, leading to Butova. As Tony approached the main road, he was surprised to hear and then see a truck coming along the road from Vurura. They both came to the meeting of the two roads at the same time and as Fr. Tony looked over his shoulder at the truck on his right he saw an Arab driving the big vehicle. He was wearing a round white cap that sat on his full head of hair and had a dark round face with a long gray beard. Through round, piercing eyes, he looked down across the road at Tony. His face was stern and his dark skin, contrasted with the funny white cap, made Tony smile. He could also see soldiers in the front of the lorry with the driver and counted three others in the back. He stopped, as the truck had the right-of-way to precede along the major road. After a mile or so, Tony was bored driving behind the lorry at such a snail's pace. Since it was only the start of the dry season, there was no dust on the road and so passing would be safe. But Tony was determined to get some news of the teachers taken away Friday. Hopefully if he played his cards correctly he might catch the soldiers with their guard down. He would confront them and ask about Gasipari Lubulu, Gregori Sumve, Salvatore Mizuri and Bernardo Inzu and try to read their reactions.

Tony motioned to the Arab as he passed the truck that he needed him to stop. He then drove directly in front of the truck. slowing his vehicle and finally stopping. He got out, and not to frighten the soldiers into doing something foolish, put his hands in the air and shouted:

"Ni jewe, Padri Mukuru wa Butova! (It is I, the pastor of Butova!)

Unlike the frightening encounter with the truck of soldiers Thursday night, these greetings were cordial and without weapons. Tony went right to the passenger side of the truck and extended his hand to the soldiers sitting in the front of the lorry. They all were men he did not recognize. Kufa was not among them nor were any of the soldiers he had previously seen at Puma. Tony keep telling himself to smile and act casual and try to keep a step ahead of these jovial but very nasty killers. Finally he told them his reason for stopping was to ask them a very important question:

"Tell me, Honorable Sirs," he slowed his speech so that every word of his Kirundi would be heard and understood. "My friend….. Do you know where he is now?"

Of course, this begged the obviously reply: "Who is your friend?" two of them asked at the same time.

"Well, the principal of the boys' grade school, Gasipari Lubulu, of course!" Tony stated trying to look casual but inside felt extremely nervous. He hoped the churning and butterflies in his stomach didn't show on his face!

The soldier, who was obviously the leader, sat closest to the door of the lorry. He answered rather sternly:

"We don't know. All we know is that he has disappeared!"

Tony looked right at him, their eyes meeting, eyeball to eyeball. Then immediately the soldier turned away. Tony took this as a sign of guilt. He concluded:

"We were such good friends. If you hear any news about Gasi Lubulu, would you please come by the mission and let me know how he is doing?" Tony added uselessly. He understood the *kirundi* mentality so very well. When you want to show friendship to someone, ask him to do you a favor. He will feel flattered and might even tell the truth. However Tony never expected the truth. His mission was to let the soldiers know that Lubulu was a friend of his and an important person. He somehow delighted in seeing the killers squirm. Maybe they even felt guilty since their hands were dripping with Bahutu blood.

"I must be going," Tony added, shaking hands with the killers and sauntering back to his car. As he drove away, he spoke loudly to God:

"Lord, who am I to judge my brother? However if these men have done wrong with the liberties you have given them. please, I beg you, have them stop the slaughters immediately." He was praying to a God Who would, it seemed, never answer his prayer.

Tony arrived at Puma about ten minutes before the lorry rambled in carrying the soldiers. All the people who were at the *arrondissement* rushed over to see the huge truck. Tony sought out the *muganga*, who told him that Kizungu was still away and he didn't expect him back for a few more days. He, of course, added, being a proud Mututsi from Rwanda where the Bahutu had expelled the Batutsi many years before, that he had been left in charge of the *arrondissement* and asked what he could do to help the priest.

"There is something dreadful that had happened at Mundi, *M l'Administrateur*." Tony began, flattering Karani with the official title. Karani nodded and allowed him to go on without interruption:

"A soldier went there, possibly from the military camp of Vurura. He came upon seven Ba-hu-tu at the beginning of night-watch," Tony spoke slowly and accented the three syllables of the word Europeans were not suppose to know or use. "And he shot and killed all seven Ba-hu-tu! Have you heard this news, *M. l'Administrateur*?" Tony asked.

Jacobo Karani cleared his throat as if he were going to give a wordy discourse and simply said "Yes, I have heard…." And the silence between the two men was disturbing.

Tony finally broke the long silence to ask another question:

"As acting administrator, can you allow such amoral behavior to take place in your jurisdiction? What, may I ask, are you planning to do about all this?"

"Your question is well founded, *mon Pere*," Karani continued. "We need a car or better your van to transport soldiers, police, the secretary and myself to Mundi where we can conduct an investigation. Please bring us there this afternoon, *mon pere?* Karani asked and demanded in the same words.

The last thing Fr. Tony Joseph felt like doing that afternoon was to turn around and go back to Mundi. But if they were going to get an investigation underway, he would gladly take them. Since it was a two-hour-walk each way, the earliest they would set out would be the following morning. Maybe they would never go. And furthermore with the threat that the damn soldier had made to Bora, there could possibly be more killings, even Yohani himself, that very evening. Tony continued:

"The soldier has used seven bullets to kill and he still has more ammunition in his rifle." Tony tried to say in a kirundi way that a person who starts a bad deed will continue in the same way.

"I'll go back to the mission and get the pick-up." Tony replied.

"I will get everyone ready here," Karani went on, "I need a policeman, a soldier, a secretary…..so all together we will be four or five." Tony almost laughed out loud at the insinuation that this chubby, well-fed and well-portioned, healthy *muganga* would venture too far away without protection and bodyguards. He hadn't mentioned this need when he asked for the van a few minutes previously. It was then that Tony realized that the *muganga* was more cunning than smart!

Tony drove back to the mission, passed through the dining room and ate some bread and fruit. Then he sought out Luigi and Luc to inform them of the events that had happened at Mundi. Jose was out there somewhere, enjoying his time with the *UGA*. Luigi, characteristically, offered to drive in his place but Tony considered this to be his personal battle. Furthermore, he understood how very upset Luigi still was at what had happened Friday at

Lutana. Luigi was in no mental state to undergo any further manifestations of violence. And there were surely many more still to be encountered beyond the mission gates.

Tony thanked Luigi for his offer but asked him to stay back and say some prayers that things might work out and that no more lives would be lost in Mundi. They walked out to the van together and Tony drove away, returning reluctantly to Puma. He parked the vehicle in front of the administrator's house and Karani came out along with a man carrying a clip board. Beside them walked a tall heavy-set man who looked rather mean. He had two scars down both sides of his cheeks and he accompanied Karani to the van where the priest was standing. There were no introductions. Neither extended a hand of friendship. Finally Tony addressed Karani:

"Is this man also coming with us? And if so, who is he?"

Jacobo Karani looked a little embarrassed and mentioned that the man was a close friend and that he would accompany them to Mundi. It was *kirundi* culture at its best. Those in authority would work their plans out for themselves but seldom tell others who had direct concerns. In Burundi, when the *bakuru* decided, everyone else found out only after the fact.

A policeman and soldier fully armed came over from the prison across the square. Karani and his personal bodyguard got into the front with Tony and the soldier, policeman and secretary climbed into the back. They were joined by two other men whom Tony recognized as people who often worked around the administrator's house. He wondered if they, too, were Karani's other bouncers! This time he didn't ask for an explanation since he knew the *muganga* would not give him a direct answer anyway. So why bother? Off all eight went to Mundi!

There was not much small-talk in the front cabin of the van. Tony didn't even know, nor did he care to know, the name of the big thug sitting beside him. He felt surrounded by stinky bodies as both the *muganga* and the bodyguard were robust people. There wasn't much extra space in the front cabin! Tony was feeling the fatigue of the day as the hot air came through the rolled-down windows. He felt the warm sun on his left arm. He didn't want to say much to Karani especially in front of the bodyguard, since he did not know whether he understood French or not. Furthermore he wanted Karani to realize that what he had to say to him was for his ears only and if, as administrator, he invited another person, even the bodyguard, into the cabin, it meant Karani didn't want to hear anything further from the priest.

"At the same time," Tony mused, "maybe that was the reason why Karani told him to come up to the front." There was little love lost between the pastor and the *muganga* because Karani resented the priests' position of authority and the influence the missioners had over the people. Karani considered the foreign missionaries as obstacles and troublemakers for the *kitutsi* cause! Tony's attitude was simple: he didn't trust the porky slob nor any other pigheaded Batutsi *bakuru.*

Tony drove directly to the church of Mundi and stopped the van. There were only a few children playing *mupira* (ball) with a rolled up piece of clothing that had been tied with home made string, more oval than circular. Most of the times it didn't roll very well! The youngsters ran to the van when they recognized the mission pickup and shouted:

"*Pati, Pati, mupira!, mupira!*" (Father, Father, a ball, a ball.)

Tony smiled broadly in hearing the children but had to tell them that he had come only for a short while. So, alas, he had not brought his rubber ball with him. "It has stayed behind and other children are playing with it in Butova." Tony informed them. You never told an African that you didn't have something. They had so very little that they could never believe the Bazungu were lacking in anything. But if they realized that others were playing with the ball, then they were more than pleased to share it.

As Tony talked to the children, he expected his passengers to disembark. However, to his amazement, no one moved! And to his further surprise, Karani motioned for him to get back in and drive on. Tony began to wonder if Karani knew more about the situation than he had let on. The missioner felt the awkwardness of being a foreigner in the mist of Africans.

So Tony drove back onto the main road and up an embankment that zigzagged along the side of the hill. He drove on for about one mile, but there was no one on the sides of the road. Then he recognized Yohani Bora's house on the hillside, near the road. When they arrived at the top of the hill, Tony stopped the pick-up. There were only a few people there but Tony could see that this was the area where the nightwatch had taken place. There were many logs, some burned in half with rocks around them to prevent the fire from spreading. He could see some tree stumps that had been used for chairs as the sentinel watched and waited for the enemy that would never come! He took the keys out of the ignition and started to get out of the van but Karani said:

"No wait.....we must go on....." Tony started up the vehicle again and drove about fifty meters more along the road that came to a sharp incline. He drove to the top and started to descend the other side of the hill. All of a sudden, Tony couldn't believe his eyes.... the bodyguard and Karani seemed astonished and frightened.

Straddling both sides of the road were large groups of people who had come out of the trenches on the roadside. They were mostly men but also there were some women. No children were to be seen anywhere. The people had clubs or spears or machetes in their hands and all looked very angry. They were all Bahutu, as Tony read their tribe by the roundness of their faces, the short stockiness of their bodies and the poor clothing they were wearing. Many had only blankets around themselves. Others wore light khaki shorts and all were barefoot. The *muganga* and bodyguard got out and Tony disembarked from his side of the van. The soldier, policeman, secretary and two others jumped down from the back of the van. But, once down, they stayed together like rats for support and mutual encouragement.

Karani spoke loud and clear, introducing himself as the acting-administrator and said that he had come to the area to investigate. One of the Muhutu said that a soldier had come the previous night and had killed the nightwatch. Then Fr. Tony couldn't believe what Karani said next:

"We, the *bakuru* of Puma, have not come for you to denounce one who has been sent here to protect all countrymen! I have heard that there were twenty-three men in this area who organized secret meetings to try overthrowing the government. We have come to bring them back, those who have attempted such an evil deed of treason!"

Fr. Tony Joseph was flabbergasted! He had rarely been more angry in his entire life! He wanted to scream at Karani for the way he was controlling the Bahutu. Further he also wished he could yell at the Bahutu that they were ludicrous to allow themselves to be dominated in such a fashion. Then he remembered what Mathias Becker had told him: where there are three Barundi to discuss truth, all lies cease because there is total objectivity. He made an act of confidence in this principle and decided to trust rather than to interfere. Maybe he would finally see the goodness of God unfold in these people. But the more he thought of it, the more absurd it sounded. He, the pastor and priest who had celebrated the Body and Blood of Christ twice in that area that morning, now had returned, accompanied by the local government officials, who were about to arrest people whom the despicable soldier would accuse! It was the greatest farce of his life! The most ridiculous thing he had ever heard! But sadly it was Burundi and these Batutsi had the authority to dominate the Bahutu who seemed too terrified and foolish to defend themselves. He looked around and saw over sixty angry people who seemed determined to hold their ground. They were infuriated because their own fellow tribesmen had been savagely murdered. Under his breath Tony heard himself slangly say:

"Go! Go, get'em boys! Kill every last one of them!" He was not anxious about his own life. Being white and a priest-missioner was ample protection. And he recognized many of the catholics from the outstation of Mundi, including the catchiest Nestori Mwiza who would defend his good name. After a few minutes, Fr. Tony became factious. He couldn't believe that these sixty people, most of them well-bodied men with weapons of various sorts, would not attack together, pounce on the seven officials and kill each one of them. He kept waiting and waiting for some reaction. In a skirmish, probably one or two of the locals would have been killed by the soldier. But the officials would have been outnumbered and would have fallen like leaves off a tree. But alas, it was not to be. Fatalism would overshadow the Bahutu to the very end.

After the *muganga* made his speech, the local Bahutu started to disperse: strolling in all directions, finding their own pathways home. Tony was bewildered by the whole experience and spoke in a rather loud voice to the remaining Bahutu who had stayed out of respect for him:

"Please excuse me for bringing these people to you," he kept repeating over and over again.

"They deceived me, telling me that they were coming here to investigate the soldier who did the killings. When we arrived, they were not even interested in hearing what the soldier had done but rather were trying to seek out the twenty-three whom they want to arrest!" Tony shouted to no one in particular.

"I can't believe they have deceived me so!" Tony kept rehashing over and over again as he walked from group to group until finally he came to the *muganga* who stood together with the six others, mutually supporting each another.

"I am leaving for Butova immediately. I refuse to take any of you hypocrites back with me. You can find your way back yourselves!" Tony said hoping he would give a public sign of dissociation from the sneaky bastards to the people around him. But then he turned around at the sound of a familiar voice saying:

"*Amakuru maki, Pati?*" (What's the news, Father?) It was Yohani Bora who had just come up to the top of the hill from his house. Tony turned to greet him and once again told the story of how he had been deceived. He asked Bora to let as many people as possible know that he had been tricked by the *bakuru* and had not driven them there for any reason except to investigate the malicious actions of the soldier.

Tony knew his words and gestures would hinder further relations with Puma especially since he might need them to save lives in the future. But he just couldn't control his anger. He couldn't remember being taken advantage of in this way before and he was furious beyond all telling. He said goodbye to Bora mentioning that he would come back at four-thirty to assure that all was peaceful. Tony got into the van and started to drive away. He heard a loud call: "*Pati! Pati!*" and stopped as fast as he had started. It was Karani! Tony readied himself for the worse kind of scenario, maybe he would be threatened, maybe he would be attacked, maybe he would be kidnapped at gun point and made to drive them back to Puma. But he was not ready for the stupidity that was to come from Karani's mouth. Certainly this village infirmarian had no brains whatsoever:

"*Mon Pere*, could you render us a further service? We have a heavy case of beer and wonder if you could bring it to the *calabu* in Mundi?"

Tony glared at the moron who was the acting civil leader and sole medical authority for 47,000 people. He stared angrily at the selfish fool and said:

"*M. l'Administrateur*, carry it yourself!" and drove away as quickly as he could find the gas pedal.

As he drove down the hill, he stopped at the chapel of Mundi and got out of the pickup to greet the people who had gathered there. Many of them had already been up the mountain at the place where the murders had taken place. They had gathered at the church to talk things over. Tony approached them. They were about thirty. Once again he told his story of how he had been deceived by Karani and asked them for pardon as he sought reconciliation. He was so affirmed and encouraged when one of the men started to speak in the name of all in that area. He was a *mushingantahe*:

"We know you, *Pati Antoni*, and we know you love us as we love you. You are our father and we are your children. Just as a father would never do anything to harm his children, we know that you will never do anything to hurt us. You have been tricked by those whom you trusted. We are sorry for you but know you have now learned a good lesson. Pray for us, *Pati*."

Tony thanked the elder, bid the people *adieu* and told them he would be back at four-thirty for a meeting with Bora and invited all of them to attend. He wanted as many people as possible to be present if the soldier were to return. He wondered if there would be further confrontation with the soldier and the other seven authorities he had brought into the area. It was a two and a half hour walk to Puma so if they didn't leave within the hour, they would have to wait the night in the area and seek out *indaro* (an overnighter in someone's house, providing food and sleep mat). So he knew that if they were not on the road by three-thirty, they would surely remain. And thirsty as they might be, they couldn't possibly finish the case of beer within the hour, or could they? However if they knew Tony was coming back by pick-up they might count on a ride from him. At that very moment, he decided to change cars and come back in his Volkswagen beetle. That way he could refuse them all. Tony envied his freedom to choose!

The drive back to Butova was rather tiring for Tony when he realized he would still have to return to Mundi one more time, later in the afternoon. Actually he wondered why he was returning home at all and then realized that under normal circumstances he would have stayed. But for two reasons he had left. First of all, Tony just had to get away from that ugly environment. And secondly, he wanted to change cars so that he could not be talked into driving any of the bastards back with him. He laughed to himself when he thought of driving to the same outstation three times in the same day. Normally only one of the fathers went there every five or six weeks. Three trips in one day! He had set a record! Certainly the only reason for such zeal was to save lives.

When Fr. Tony arrived at the mission no one was at home. Sunday mid-afternoon was always a good time to go visit the people living in the mihana close to Butova. So Tony was somewhat disappointed because he had wanted to share the story with Jose and get his reading on the situation. He wondered why Jose was never there when there seemed to be something important to discuss! But that was Jose Suarez! The confreres often said that the African mentality extended as far north as Spain. Jose never seemed to put anything into the perspective of time! Yet Tony knew many Spaniards in the White Fathers who were always punctual. So it was not a Hispanic defect but more of a personal deformation. He then realized he was very upset and emotional and was unfair in his rash judgment of Jose.

Tony entered the chapel, shut the door and knelt before the Blessed Sacrament. His prayer begged God to bring him inner peace. He prayed for his friends, presuming that they had now met their demise. He asked God that the blood of Gasipari, Salvatore, Gregori, Deo, Bernardo and thousands of others bring love and healing to the area. But somehow he lacked belief that God Almighty could possibly answer such a prayer. There were no signs that the people were willing to forgive or be forgiven for all that had happened over the past ten days. It would be a long road to reconciliation and he feared the worst was still to come! He prayed for Yohani Bora smiling as he recalled the wonderful man with whom he had spent part of his morning and afternoon. He asked God to watch over him. And, astonishingly, he was able to ask for the grace to forgive the soldier who had done such evil acts the previous night. The Spirit moved him to realize that the greatest reconciliation of all time was the forgiving words of Jesus on the cross. So his prayer ended by his focusing on the soldier and allowing the Holy Spirit to place these powerful words on his lips: "Father forgive him. He knows not what he has done."

The young priest thought of all the killings that had gone on before his very eyes over the past while and heard his voice repeat over and over again: "Father, forgive them.....they know not what they do." It was past three-thirty. Time to leave once again for Mundi!

Fr. Tony Joseph found himself driving slowly on the road that led to Mundi. Usually he was pressing to get there on time. However it was Sunday afternoon and most of the people he saw along the way were heading home after the heat and activities of the holiday. He felt relaxed and, since his prayer of reconciliation, somewhat peaceful inside. But there were deep feelings of anxiety as well. What if the soldier came back as he had threatened? What if he would use his gun again? What if the Batutsi in the area supported his nonsense? What if, on arriving, Tony would discover that the soldier had killed Yohani Bora? As he thought of each of these scenarios, he felt his right foot putting a little more pressure on the gas pedal and he had to tell himself that these imaginings were just his mind playing tricks on him. He wanted to believe that there would be no danger ahead.

Amid Tony's search for peace, he also felt tremendous resentment. He had been on the road all day. This was his third trip back to Mundi because of that pompous soldier. Tony wondered why he, a Muzungu, had to go out of his way to protect the people from their soldiers. But then he thought of that tall, wiry, man they called the spirit-filled *mukuru*, Yohani Bora. Tony knew that he was driving back to do all he could to protect his friend, his catechist, this magnificent man-of-God.

As Tony turned the final curve in the road and went down a small valley to the outstation, he saw a barrier that had been set up on the road. It had not been there earlier. There were barriers all over Burundi to prevent the Bahutu from fleeing to different parts of the country. The government said that the barriers would intercept the enemy from Zaire. But most people now knew that they merely had been an invention by the *bakuru* to keep the Bahutu at home! The barriers, also, were there to prevent the Bahutu from being driven by the Bazungu missioners to some other part of the country where they would be less known and more able to survive the wrath that had come upon them.

Tony stopped at the barrier and two young men, still in their teens, came over to his car. The older one, whom he did not recognize, asked him who he was and where he was going. Tony answered that he was the *Padri Mukuru wa Butova* and that he had a meeting at the outstation church with the head catechist, Yohani Bora. The other was a young man who often came to mass when Tony visited Mundi. The youth walked over to the barrier which was a long tree trunk straddling the road, supported by two posts. He took one end and dragged it to the other side of the road to allow Tony to drive through. When the car had passed completely, Tony stopped for a second and shouted:

"*Urakozi cane, bagenzi, nagasaga!*" (Thank you very much, friends, good-bye!)

Arriving at the chapel, Fr. Tony got out of his car. He looked at his watch. It was 4:25 and there were only a few people gathered at the outstation. He reasoned that those who were there lived in the immediate area and had seen or heard his car and came to greet the visitor. He asked them if they had seen Bora and they answered that he had left hours earlier. Obviously they were referring to his departure after the service. Since the head catechist was the only person who had the key to the office area, Tony stood outside talking to the people and then went into the church to spend some time in prayer. He felt lonely and ostracized from everything and everyone, even though many children had followed him into church and prayed on their knees beside him.. He had prayed very deeply in the morning and also at Butova in the afternoon. So he just couldn't get his mind on prayer this time. He wanted to be a million miles from this God-forsaken-place and wondered if the trigger-happy soldier would surprise him and come into the church. Then, once again, he told himself that there would be no danger. The soldier would not return. He probably had gotten drunk as most soldiers did on Sunday afternoons or he could have found a young lady and would stay with her over night as was common for these roving military. He decided that if Bora did not show up by 4:50 he would drive to his house. Thus he would get there by 5 o'clock.

As Tony came outside, many more people had gathered. There were some he recognized as having been there earlier when he had made his speech and asked their pardon. Many of the adults seemed to show surprise that the pastor had returned for a third time that day. As they gathered around him, he told them that he was going on to Yohani's house and that if the soldier were to come back, they were to send someone to tell him immediately. That way, he could cover both areas at the same time. He got into his car and a man walked over to greet him and volunteered to be the scout. Tony told him he was counting on him and the man gave his word of honor.

After thanking the scout, Tony drove away from the chapel and back along the road that would take him to Bora's. The road was filled with pot holes and large cracks that shook and bounced his VW in every possible way. Finally he recognized the area where Bora lived and parked on the side of the road and meandered his way down the hillside to the *rugo.*

Yohani Bora lived with his wife and ten children in a mud hut that was painted with whitewash. There was a corral to protect the animals at night. Now they were out grazing somewhere. On the sides of the house, there were African drawings in green, red and brown paint on the whitewashed walls. Yohani came out the door of the hut as Fr. Tony came through the main gate of the *rugo.* He greeted the pastor. Then Teresia came out of the hut. She was carrying their youngest in her arms. Finally all the children seemed to come from all directions at once. Some came through the gate as they must have been playing in the neighboring *mihana.* Others were hiding around the back of the house and a few toddlers came out from the house itself. Yohani brought a folding chair for Fr. Tony. Teresia, having extended her hand of welcome to the priest, went back into the house and then returned with a bowl containing banana beer. She handed the priest a bamboo straw and gave one to her husband and the two men drank together to reaffirm their friendship and dedication to each other. Finally Fr. Tony asked Yohani:

"Have you seen the soldier?" He was relieved when Bora replied in the negative. The two men sat, Tony on the only chair that the family owned and Bora on the ground beside him. This time he didn't attempt to share the furniture. They chatted until dusk. Their conversation turned mostly around the authorities and what had transpired after Tony had left the so-called investigation that afternoon. Bora reassured the pastor that the people understood that he had been tricked. The fact that Tony did not drive anyone home to Puma was the determining factor that proved to all that Tony had made a mistake in trusting the muganga and that he regretted his miscue. Finally when it was inka zitache (six o'clock in the evening when the "cows come home"), it was so dark that Tony could hardly see his outstretched hand indicating to Bora that he was leaving. They both were content that the soldier must have stopped somewhere along the road for some comfort! Bora walked the priest back to his car and the two men said a short prayer asking God's help and strength in the days to come. Yohani mentioned Nestori Mwiza's name as he prayed. Tony felt at peace that this great christian was praying for an official foe, a Muhutu. But he also knew that Bora was praying for him because his life was in peril and he was a brother and fellow catechist. Tony had also thought that Mwiza was a suspect and Bora's prayer sadly confirmed his suspicions.

The drive back to Butova seemed slower than the one to Mundi had been. It was dark and the road was difficult to see at times so Tony drove slowly. He arrived around 7:15 and found the others at table. He washed up and went in and told them of the alarming events of his Sunday at Mundi.

Even though Tony's story was frightening, Jose looked for the silver lining and considered it a small victory since Yohani Bora was protected and safe. He, too, had the utmost admiration for the head catechist of Mundi. Further, Jose mentioned to the others at table that he was happy because he had received a note, via a porter, from Pedro Sanchez, a White Father living at the neighboring mission of Mutwe. The note said Pedro would come to Butova for a visit the following day, Monday.

Sanchez was kind and very intelligent. He always had time for the other confreres to listen to them and advise them with their problems. Pedro had already been seen as the successor of Mathias Becker, the person responsible for the White Fathers in the Southland. He was in an excellent position to give this responsibility his full concern since he had so little work in Mutwe. The pastor was Angelo Bertuzzi who, in temperament, was the total opposite to Pedro: controlling, impulsive, arrogant, manipulative and a loud bragger.

Bertuzzi had been in the area of Bumeza-Mutwe for over twenty-five years and his way of talking to the people was to embarrass them and make fun of their downfalls. He could be an utter humiliation for his colleagues. Pedro had mentioned to some how horrified he was one Sunday when, at the end of the mass, Bertuzzi stood in the pulpit at the time of the announcements and read the names of parishioners, most of them teenage girls, who had been late for mass. The arrogant padri mukuru (pastor) had been in the area so long he knew everyone by name. He had the habit on belittling people when he climbed into the pulpit and opened his big mouth!

He prided himself on being a very close friend of President Sabimana, who often came to visit him in his parish house. For any favors, such as special permissions or supplies the he needed, he went directly to the president and therefore did what he pleased in Mutwe. He had the habit of name-dropping anytime he thought it would benefit his cause! Bishop Moulin had not appointed anyone to Mutwe to live with Bertuzzi because, as the ordinary often said: "That would be condemning a priest to hell".

However when the strong, personable Sanchez returned from home leave the previous year and there was not a parish in need of a pastor, Moulin talked him into spending some time with Bertuzzi. As the bishop put it: "Stay with the nuisance until you cannot stand it anymore!" The bishop promised to reward Pedro with one of the nicest parishes in the diocese the next time there was an opening. Moulin wanted someone to live with Bertuzzi to try and talk some common sense into him and suggest that he retire and return to Italy. The bishop was pleased that Bertuzzi had raised all the money and built the church, catechumenate and parish house at Mutwe. But Bertuzzi did everything his own way and relied on his presidential contacts to get what he needed. Moulin felt intimidated for Bertuzzi criticized him and challenged his authority whenever he could.

Fr. Jose was delighted that Sanchez would come over the following day since they had studied in the seminary together and traveled together throughout Europe during their vacations when they were at the Missionaries of Africa theologate in Belgium. Pedro was a year older than Jose and had as positive an influence on him as Mathias did. Just as Jose was so inconsistent and made bad decisions, Pedro was the total opposite: level-headed, intelligent, calm and cautious. Jose continued to say how delighted he was about Pedro's visit and Tony wondered if it would have a positive effect on his confrere. Maybe Tony could get Pedro aside and ask him to speak to Jose one-on-one and try to talk some common sense into him, especially about his traveling out to the people every day to pray the rosary with them in the afternoon. Normally that would have been a commendable thing. However the people were starting to talk. Some of the Batutsi were saying that Jose had been a leader in the Bahutu uprising earlier in the month and was still commanding their forces! They came to this conclusion because he would go to the Bahutu areas for prayer and pray publicly for those who had been killed. The people believed that he was praying only for the Bahutu. Tony had talked to Jose and asked him to stay home, but, of course, he refused preferring to do his own thing and trust his own weak judgment. Tony hoped that Sanchez was being sent their way as an angel of light, so that Suarez would escape the darkness.

10. Mutwe Visits Butova

Usually the missionaries of Butova kept Monday as a free day. They tried not to schedule any activities on that day so that they could take some time off together. Oftentimes they went to a neighboring parish for some relaxation. The deanery meetings, where they came together with two other parishes in their area, were always on Mondays, as well as the catechists' meetings. So these activities, impossible to organize on another day, gave them a change from normal parish work. If they needed to go shopping in the capital, Monday was the only favorable day for that as well.

There were absolutely no activities on the Butova priests' agenda for Monday May 15th. After breakfast, Tony went into his office and was not surprised to see that there was no one in front of his door. The people understood that Monday was a day of rest and other activities for the missionaries and normally they would not risk a long walk from home to find the mission closed. Tony took out the folder containing the names of the *banyabatisimu* (those of the baptism class i.e. last year of catechumenate) who were scheduled to be baptized in August. He counted the names folding back one page over the other. There were over four hundred to question before they were called to receive the sacrament. He flipped through the other names of the *banyasacramentu* (those who were studying the sacraments and would prepare for baptism the following year). Then there were the names of the *banyamedali* who had received the medal the previous year and who were over two years away from baptism. All together, these were roughly 2,000 adults and children preparing to be baptized in the roman catholic church of Butova over the next few years.

Judging by all that Fr. Tony had seen in the people "living" the message of the Good News, he thought it a big mistake to give others the sacrament of baptism when so many, already baptized were not living their baptismal promises of loving one another. The church, he thought, had made a tremendous mistake! Even though the missionaries were very demanding that the catechumens attend all their classes and that they know all their prayers and catechetical answers, yet the big error was that they taught them catholic answers. They taught the people "religion", catechetical questions and answers about the catholic doctrine when they should have been teaching them the essence of christianity: "Love your neighbor as I have loved you!"

The *Bakristu* (Christians or those of Christ) knew the laws, but not the lawgiver, Christ, Who was unconditional forgiveness and selfless love. True christianity had now disappeared in Burundi during the time of the *coup* and reprisals! And the people felt abandoned by God, since they had forsaken Him! They had their *kirundi* ways and even if they called themselves *Bakristu,* most of them did not belong to Christ, the church or christianity. Their blood was thicker than the waters of the sacrament and they were out to even any scores that had festered between the two tribes over the years. They were certainly more *kitutsi* or *kihutu* than *kikristu.*

Tony firmly believed, after having seen so many examples over the past fortnight, that the Batutsi justified killing or torturing the Bahutu, since the latter were all considered traitors to Burundi. It didn't matter what the Bible said or what the church taught. These were the practices of the Bazungu missionaries, the ways of the Europeans. But they saw some kind of heroism in taking the law into their own hands and witnessing against their Bahutu neighbors even if they knew, in their hearts, that what they were saying was criminally fraudulent. This was an invention of a people totally traumatized into believing that the Bahutu were their enemies and all of them were out to kill the Batutsi. They, in turn, protected themselves from being killed by accusing their enemies who would then 'disappear'. They thought that the condemned had attended meetings that were political, or that they had given money to buy machetes and other arms. But there was absolutely no proof. The way the Batutsi overcame their fear and anxiety was to accuse the Bahutu first, and then justify the situation later. They presumed all the Bahutu were suspicious of overthrowing the government and thus guilty and condemned to death. And they would make a citizen's arrest, tie the Muhutu's hands behind his back and march him off to Puma where he would be beaten, 'tried' more or less by the soldiers and driven to a common grave the very same day.

A truck load full of men and boys left Puma every afternoon between 4 and 5 o'clock. They had been arrested by some Batutsi, usually policemen from Puma who had heard certain accusations against them. The fact that they 'disappeared' meant that they were guilty! Everyone who had died gave proof that he was guilty because he was dead!. What insane, illogical bull. Tony wondered how many innocent people had been killed by the soldiers. He had heard that this was going on throughout the country, in all eighty-seven *arrondissements.* If the soldiers conducted themselves elsewhere as they were doing at Puma, the country would be bathed in blood! But this was only the first two weeks! When it would all be over, the final figure of the dead would be three times Tony's present calculation.

"My God," thought Tony, "there is no end in sight. These savage Batutsi will kill every last Muhutu in the country!" He didn't know how well he had perceived the evil in the Batutsi! When the bloodshed would be over, the count would be in the hundreds of thousands. May of 1972 would turn out to be the darkest, most horrible month in the history of Burundi. Fr. Tony continued doing some calculations and then was distracted by the sound of a car coming in front of the church and into the mission compound.

The car flashed by his office and Tony saw a slight beige blur and recognized Fr. Pedro Sanchez' light-colored volkswagen. He put his papers away, locked his office door and went around to the back of the mission where he found Pedro parking his car. He was pleasantly surprised that Pedro had come with another White Father confrere, also a Spaniard, Fr. Raphael Saturnino. Raphael had been living at Mutwe for the last two months to support Pedro. Tony had thought how silly had been this appointment. Because of one arrogant priest who would not be kind, loving or understanding to any colleague and who lived for himself and to feed his own ego, the bishop had to send the most capable White Father in the diocese to be his 'assistant' and then had to waste another priest to keep Pedro sane. Life was truly strange! Another confrere, the pastor of Muka, Fr. Kees Van Riel, a Belgian who was also Bishop Moulin's other vicar general, had said that he would gladly go to Mutwe and would place only one condition on the appointment: that Bertuzzi be gone five minutes before he would arrive! Obviously Bertuzzi's colleagues truly didn't appreciate him and considered him a brainless, arrogant individual.

Before going to Mutwe, Saturnino had spent some months with the missionaries in Butova. Tony came to like him a great deal. They had once gone on a long safiri together to Tanzania, Uganda and Rwanda. Raph knew the Kirundi language very well and could make all kinds of puns and plays-on-words when he spoke to the people or preached in the church. Tony learned many new words and expressions by listening to him. He was a born artist and had painted many biblical scenes on the walls of the churches, in priests' houses and in many different outstations. When Raphael was relaxed, flourishing and fulfilled in his new environment at Butova, along came Bishop Moulin, who said he had come to get Saturnino for he wanted him to 'accompany' Sanchez in Mutwe! The price they all had to pay because of the idiosyncrasies of Bertuzzi!

Tony greeted both confreres with warm handshakes and a big bear hug. The Belgian and German confreres usually shook hands. But the warm-blooded Spaniards liked to hug when they knew each other. They were aware of the traumas each had lived over the past two weeks and were very supportive of each other. The brother-priests had many things to tell each other and would try to build each other up amid the tragedy that was happening throughout all areas of Burundi.

Tony welcomed them into the common room and Luigi heard the loud voices and came in to greet his fellow missionaries. Tony left to find Jose but, after looking everywhere, he finally gave up, exasperated. He came back and told them that Jose was really looking forward to their visit and the four men smiled when Pedro asked: "Why, if he was so anxious to see us, was he not here to greet us?" Luigi responded out of the side of his broad Italian mouth:

"Only Suarez knows where Suarez is. Only Jose knows why Jose is like he is!" And they all laughed loudly once more as it sounded more that Jose was lost in his mind rather than in his body.

Cypriano arrived with a hot thermos of fresh coffee and some cookies he had baked that morning when he heard that Fr. Pedro was coming to visit. When Pedro had been assigned to Butova many years back, Cypriano had instantly taken a liking to this calm man with the broad, full-faced smile. And when someone was a favorite of Cypi, he went all out to prepare special food to make him happy. They all realized by the smile on Cypriano's face that the food would be outstanding for their noon meal. But for now, they all sat back and enjoyed each other's company. This was the moment they all appreciated in celibate community life. They felt a common love for Africa and especially for Africans and since all of them had only worked in one African country, they shared a common dedication to these people who were struggling with such a catastrophe.

Out of a clear blue sky, Pedro said:

"When this is all over I'm going back to Spain and find myself a loving and kind woman and raise a family and forget about Burundi and the awful scenes we are witnessing. They all knew that he was only joking sarcastically but the idea was very appealing to all of them.

"Pedro. here's a thought! After all we have seen, after all we will hear in the confessional over the next few months, the government will have but one desire for all us. They will have only one requirement: that we pack up and leave as soon as possible! They will seek any and every means to expel us. Maybe they will even pay our transportation back to Europe and have some pretty women lined up for us to marry! We have all seen too much of the arrogant, blood-thirsty Batutsi and the ignorant, fatalistic

Bahutu! Seriously, we won't be very welcome when this is all over." Tony didn't know that within seven years all the missioners would be expelled from Vurura diocese.

The four men continued their bantering and bartering until it was close to lunch time. Then Raphael mentioned that he had a witnessing plan for all the parishes that he was willing to initiate himself. Tony and Luigi thought he was only trying to amuse them. But soon they understood that he was dead serious!

"You know that the Arab or Greek trucks pass in front of our mission every day at about 4 or 5 o'clock with a driver and two armed soldiers. Sometimes they are burying so many, that they have to use another truck, this one in the morning. I presume they do the same here in Butova?" Luigi and Tony nodded wondering where he was going with his strategic game plan.

Saturnino continued: "They are filled with Bahutu who have been tortured and beaten to the point where they are semi-conscious, as they are driven to their common graves in Vurura. I, in Mutwe, am planning to put on the black mass vestments and stole, alb and black chasuble, and stand in the middle of the road. It is really not very large in Mutwe and thus the driver, with all those bodies beaten and half-rotten with open cuts and broken bones, will have to stop suddenly or run over me. It might be my demise but at least I'll die in solidarity with the Bahutu cause and openly witnessing to the Batutsi brutality. I'll witness or maybe I'll die witnessing the values of the gospel and the unconditional love of the Savior for all." Raphael stared right at Tony who looked pale and petrified with what he was hearing. Tony wondered if the artist had given in to his emotions or his mind was gone!

"And you, the pastor of Butova," Raphael went on, "would you be willing to die for your people? You have preached the gospel of Christ to them. Aren't you ready to live the message of Christ, by literally laying down your life for your people?" A deafening silence descended on the room!

Tony was overwhelmed by the challenge put to him as Raphael and Pedro looked at him wondering if he would ever reply. Luigi sat back and remained totally taciturn. Tony felt his face flushed and realized that this artist, this deeply-reflective Spaniard, was more pensive and Christ-like than he had ever imagined him to be.

Tony finally was able to mutter a few words:

"Well, Raph, I have never thought of this position in exactly the way you are phrasing it. When I entered the seminary ten years ago, I gave my life to Christ, and for Christ. However I never thought of dying before my twenty-ninth birthday! I will have to give that question some more time and reflection."

Raphael went on: "We have been talking about this, Pedro and I, for the past twenty-four hours and I have come to the realization that it would be one way of handling the present crisis: to die giving Christian witness. The people are not listening to what we are preaching in church. In fact if they had been listening, since the advent of christianity in Burundi seventy some years ago, we would not be in this horrid mess. Actions speak louder than words! So I am ready to vest and stand on the road in front of the church when the truck passes. I want to re-write my will and a few letters to my mother and family and then I'll be ready. I have invited Pedro to join me. If both of us are on that narrow road, they can't help but get one or maybe even both of us!" Raphael added this with a contemptuous regard on his face. There was a long silence that enveloped all of them as they considered the circumstances and weighed their options.

"What do you think?" Tony asked, looking in Pedro's direction. The intonation in his voice indicated that he was asking Pedro his thoughts and reflections.

Pedro answered with a smile referring to something he had shared earlier: "If I were to vest and be run over by a truck, I wouldn't be very good for that little woman that I hope to marry some day back home in Spain!" The whole group broke into laughter. But then Pedro continued on a more serious note:

"I haven't had any clear indication that God wants me to sacrifice my life and my future as a missionary for this cause. But I was talking to Bishop Moulin the other day when we met along the road. I asked him an even more realistic question. Here's how I phrased it:

" 'What is our role as priests and missionaries in this situation right now, here in Burundi?' Well, you all know Bishop Moulin. He is always so straight forward when he speaks, the personification of '*Natura Prima*'. He said: 'Your role is to let them see you seeing them. Let them carry this to their graves: that they were responsible before God for killing so many of their brothers. Yes, your role is to make them drown in the deep ugly oceans of their misdeeds!'"

"So the last two days," Pedro went on, "I have parked my car just inside our courtyard with the gates wide open. When the lorry comes by, taking a truck load of 40 or 50 Bahutu to their common graves in Vurura, I wait until it has passed our gate by about fifty meters. Then I drive after it. I honk my horn many times, presumably to let the driver know I am passing.

However in this way the soldiers in the front with the driver and the two others in the back with the live *cadavers*, look out and see me. I make sure that I have my white habit on, so that they will know I am a missionary. As I pass the truck carrying all those bodies, I reach out with my right hand and make a big sign of the cross so that the military will know that I am giving the *cadavres* general absolution for their sins. Last Rites in the fast lane! Then when I go by the cabin of the truck, I stare at the occupants so that they can see me seeing them. I then drive on ahead and about a kilometer up the road, I stop, turn my car around and go back and pass them again so that they realize the only reason for my adventure was to give forgiveness and blessings to those poor, beaten, *bagabo* and *bahungu*. Yet I have accomplished my mission: their consciences will reek forever with the guilt of having been seen doing their hideous evil acts."

Tony's face brightened when he understood what Pedro Sanchez was suggesting. He thought how easily it could be done in Butova as well, for the truck requisitioned from the Greek or Arab merchants, passed right beside the mission, going from Puma to the same grave site as those from Mutwe.

"A great idea, Pedro. Does the bishop know you are doing this?" Tony inquired.

"When he told me our role was to have 'them see us seeing them', I told him my idea. And he said that if I didn't get arrested, it would be great witness. However he told me to make perfectly sure that there would be as little danger as possible. The bishop told me that one Italian priest, Guiseppe Agusto from Ruziga, has been confronted by the Batutsi after he had locked many Bahutu in his church. They demanded, with a sharp sword at his throat, that he open the church. It was locked and he had deposited the key in the safe at the mission house. Padre Agusto responded by saying: *'Haninahazwe! Yesu-Kristu!'*" (Praise be to You, Jesus-Christ!)

Pedro Sanchez continued his story:

"And the Batutsi *bakuru* walked away leaving Agusto alone, for deep down they had catholic consciences: afraid of a God of Vengeance, and intimidated by their own evil. But the bishop said we should not take any extraordinary risks. He said that what he was telling me was a wonderful act of bravery by Agusto, but he wants alive priests not dead martyrs."

"You both give us a great deal to think about, Pedro and Raph! Let's continue the conversation at table," Tony motioned toward the dining room and the four men walked through the doors that joined the living room to the refectory.

Raphael Saturnino was a small-featured man with dark rimmed glasses. His frail build contrasted with his voice that was deep and majestic, even at times booming. He commanded attention when he spoke both in French and Kirundi that he knew very well. He was an artist and brought his aesthetic temperament to everything he did. The previous year, Bishop Moulin accepted him from the diocese of Gisumu where he was having trouble finding a community to live with since he was so outspoken and temperamental. After quickly consulting Jose and Tony, Mathias accepted him since he believed that if one missionary could be rehabilitated in a life-giving community, there would be another priest to work with the thousands and thousands of people who needed his ministry.

However Raphael had only spent three months in Butova when Bishop Moulin appointed him to Mutwe with Bertuzzi and Sanchez. Mathias had objected but the kindly old bishop told him to stay out of it. He had made the decision that he knew was good for meeting the needs of the *Bakristu.* But Mathias had pointed out that his decision would not fulfill the needs of this priest who would fall back into his own depression when he would not be respected by Bertuzzi. The bishop scoffed at him saying he was too seeped in 'psychological idealism' and as the ordinary of the diocese, he had to look at the pastoral needs first. Mathias responded by saying he believed Moulin was ruining the life of a brother to both of them in giving a fellow White Father such a death sentence. Moulin merely laughed at him and said his decision was final and had to be made for the 'good' of the church of Vurura.

Mathias told Tony the day after Saturnino's departure that he believed Raphael would not last two months with Bertuzzi. He said:

"The bishop looked at our parish and counted four. Then he looked at Mutwe and counted two. Then he looked at his hands and counted his fingers. Four on one hand and two on the other. Now he took away one finger from the hand that had four and added it to the hand that had two and that made three on each hand! *Base*! (Kiswahili: that's it!) 'Even-Stephen!' Everybody was happy! Everybody was happy? The bishop had evened up the score, three to three, and in the process destroyed a colleague who had had some semblance of fulfillment for a while and had been happy again!" Mathias snarled with sarcasm, resenting *"Natura Prima"* for committing 'suicide' on his own White Father identity.

Meanwhile Raphael took his time, packed his artistic equipment very slowly and Mathias and Tony had driven him into the lion's den and gave him over to Bertuzzi. The two greeted each other in a friendly manner, but Saturnino would eventually mention that that was the first and last time he had seen Bertuzzi smile at him! He considered life in Mutwe a living hell and became extremely depressed and introverted. Having another fellow countryman, Pedro Sanchez, with him simply meant that Raphael had another person to whom he could complain and voice his resentments. Slowly but surely Bertuzzi wore both of these fine missionaries down. They had the potential, being three in number, for the work of a large Barundi parish of over 20,000 baptized catholics. However the community life was terrible as Bertuzzi dictated the polity to the two men as if they were children and continued to do everything his own way. There was never a community meeting nor did he even ask Raphael or Pedro for their opinions about anything, whether it concerned pastoral policy or their common life together. Since Bertuzzi kept most of the work at the central parish for himself, they sat around their rooms all day, reading books and articles or working on their hobbies. From time to time, Bertuzzi would ask one of them to spend a few days in an outstation. But they had to do the apostolate in the way he wanted it done. They both evaluated his ideas as archaic and seldom did what he had directed them to do in the ways he expected them to do it. After a while he stopped asking them to go to the outstations since they were not doing things according to his expectations. Life became burdensome and the tragic end for Raphael Saturnino was on the horizon. He soon would become the 'sacrificial lamb' symbolic of the sort the Bahutu were subjected to in every *arrondissement* of the country.

Pedro enjoyed reading and caught up on his theological books and Raphael painted everything that didn't move. He painted the house with beautiful frescoes on the walls of the dining room and sitting room and a beautiful painting on the outside wall where Bertuzzi received guests on the patio. All Bertuzzi could say when he saw it was that he hoped the president would like it when he would come to visit! Bertuzzi always received the president with pomp and ceremony and overflowing wine and his confreres, like Tony and Pedro, were not even invited to come out of their rooms. Once Raphael had wondered out loud:

"When Sabimana will be overthrown (and that was inevitable in a country like Burundi, in the decade after independence) will the rebels not also come to Mutwe and cut off Bertuzzi's head as well?" Such fraternal charity!

During the early uprisings the first weekend of the *coup*, the Bahutu rebels, attacking one area on the road from Bujarundi to Ruziga, were quoted as saying: "They were going to climb the mountains to Mutwe (the word means 'head') and cut off Bertuzzi's head and carry it around on a spear". Raphael bragged that his prediction would someday come true!

Bertuzzi was considered the Muzungu most derogatory to the Bahutu as he heaped continuous praise on the Batutsi. Mathias had often said that Bertuzzi's work was over, gone, accomplished, completed. The time of the missionary as a paternalistic philanthropist was long gone! He should be thanked for his accomplishments and given a gold watch and a one-way plane ticket back to Italy.

But for Bishop Moulin, Bertuzzi was another warm body and he would keep him as pastor of Mutwe for as long as he wanted to stay. Moulin was an ecclesiastic puppet only concerned that the work was done, the people were being catechized and fed with the sacraments. All that seemed to influence him was that the numbers were growing. Rome would be impressed! Angelo Bertuzzi looked good when the statistics were submitted and converted into financial subsidies for Moulin. How the priests were living with one another had little interest to him, to Rome or to the organizational church. Most of the colleagues from the rest of the diocese believed that the stats were inflated and invented by Bertuzzi and that his picture, seemingly very rosy, was a sham. Since Saturnino was so free, he often drove to the neighboring parishes and soon he would be into the most negative of conversations about Bertuzzi. Everyone seemed to take Saturnino's side in the struggle and Bertuzzi was even more unpopular now that the word got out how he was running Mutwe and destroying his curates.

Most of the times when Saturnino came by for a visit he talked so disapprovingly about Bertuzzi that everyone was demoralized after he left. He had the bad habit of dumping manure all over his confrere! Consequentially the missionaries of Butova had decided to never ask him about the situation and quality-of-life with Bertuzzi. But most of the time he did not need to be prompted. Raph was very loquacious and spontaneous!

As they passed from the living room to the refectory, the door from the inside corridor opened and in came Jose and Luc. They both apologized for being late, Jose saying that he had to go talk to a girl whom he had heard was planning to leave home on concubinage with a soldier. The others ignored what he said and both Pedro and Raphael hugged their fellow countryman tightly. Then they all sat at table.

This Monday at the noon meal, they all tried to introduce many other various subjects to discuss at table. The conversation went from the latest appointments of the White Fathers and new bishops throughout the world to talking about football results and weather patterns in Europe. They deliberately went into detail to prevent the conversation from falling into a lapse that would allow Saturnino to bring up the latest episodes of the Bertuzzi saga. Cypriano outdid himself knowing that the charismatic Raphael would compliment him as the best cook in the diocese. They ate fried chicken, Belgian *pomme frites* (fried potatoes) and cauliflower with a cheese topping. Cypi had baked a Japanese-prune pie for desert and the men were all in good spirits as they ate heartily. All except Luigi Franco. He was starting to look very frail for he still had no appetite and had been losing weight. He who could ill-afford to be any thinner! Luigi was now having more nightmares and had trouble getting a good night's sleep. But he did sit at table with the community and managed to drink a glass of water in small sips. Tony was worried about him and how this situation would effect him psychologically. None of them could imagine that the worst was still to come!

Saturnino, Sanchez and the local missioners relaxed again in the living room enjoying an after-dinner coffee. Eventually the *BanyaMutwe* got up and headed for the door as the four local missionaries walked them to their car. Tony mentioned how much he appreciated the visit and that Pedro had given him inspiration and a game plan that he would begin as soon as possible. But he still had to reflect more on Raphael Saturnino's gem of an idea!

As the two Spaniards drove away, the pastor went back to his office in the front of the mission. There were two people he recognized waiting for him in front of the office door. One was Clementia, the wife of Deogratias Pungu, the catechist who also doubled as parish secretary. The other was a *karani* (secretary) from Puma. He looked at them and realized that they were at opposite ends of the spectrum: one the wife of the man arrested by the local authorities and the other representing the local *bakuru*! He welcomed Clementia into his office and realized that the *karani* would be somewhat insulted that this 'lowly woman' whose husband was being held at Puma as a traitor was being welcomed first by the Muzungu priest. Tony certainly had not lost his sanity nor sense of humor!

Clementia looked very tired and drawn. Her face was haggard and strained. She didn't sit down but rather went right up to Tony and in a loud whisper told him that her husband had now been brought to the dispensary at Puma, across the square from the prison.

"They have beaten him all over! They have burned his mouth with cigarettes and his entire body is scarred by embers of firewood. He's very weak, so weak that they thought he would die in prison. So they have placed him in the infirmary and my daughter has gone there to prepare his food. Maybe if he eats he will not die. Please pray for him, *Pati*, and if you can do anything, please try to intervene on his behalf. He is such a good and religious man, *Pati*." As she headed for the door to leave, Tony tried to reassure her that he would do all he could to have Deogratias freed.

The karani then entered the office and greeted him although in his mind Tony imagined, 'Here comes more trouble and bull from Puma!' The Mututsi office clerk handed him a letter and he read it reflectively behind his desk. It was written in bad French, in the most authoritarian of tones, by the administrator, Alberto Kizungu:

Most Reverend Father Pastor,

By this letter, I hereby place an act of requisition on all the vehicles of the mission compound. We will need your co-operation, without further notice at any time, to assure that justice and peace be re-established in this arrondissement. We will also require your services and that of your colleagues as drivers of the vehicles and also as mechanics whenever necessary. Please make sure that the two vehicles in your possession, a Volkswagen pick-up and the Volkswagen 1300 will always be available for our use. Further there are also three vehicles on the brothers' compound: A Peugeot truck and two Volkswagen 1300 cars. Make known to these foreigners that their vehicles are requisitioned as well.

Thanking you kindly for your cooperation in this matter, I reassure you, Reverend Father, of my most dignified and gracious respects.

Ni jewe, (It's I)
Mr. Alberto Kizungu
Administrator of Puma.
May 15, 1972.

Tony opened the door and asked the *karani* to wait outside as he prepared a reply.

Alone now, he crushed the letter in the palm of his right hand. It was written on 'onion paper' and didn't resist the obvious angry, gripping palm that destroyed it. As he went over to his typewriter, he heard a voice inside him saying: 'be nice for when you write and sign something it can fall awkwardly into the hands of your enemies and be read by those who desire your demise.' He promised himself to write a stern, direct reply but with no judgments on the situation he was facing. Above all he was angered at the thought of the Batutsi *bakuru* taking his only real possession, his VW, and demanding that he drive them around the countryside in it while they went about their witch hunt and debauchery. He heard himself say, 'Never, never, never in a hundred years!' Furthermore since the only word that could describe what the Batutsi were doing was 'genocide', how could he co-operate in the most evil of inexcusable crimes? Fr. Tony Joseph sat in front of his typewriter and the ideas seemed to flow faster than his fingers could move along the keyboard.

As he began the letter, he realized what a great opportunity had been given him. The administrator would surely receive him, if not in person then through this letter. If Tony played his cards cautiously, he could place Kizungu in a very arduous position of accountability. In fact Kizungu had told the *karani* to await the reply. So what a grand opportunity to discuss with the chief, who would owe Tony a personal favor for driving Karani to Mundi. He would inquire about the whereabouts of Deogratias Pungu and what had happened to the teachers Gregori and Salvatore, the principal Gasipari and the sacristan, Bernardo. So as he began to write Kizungu, he realized that the ball was in his court and that the more vague he would be the better to get an interview with the administrator.

le 15 mai, 1972
M. l'Administrateur:

I have just received your letter in requisition of our vehicles. There are some important issues that must be discussed, such as insurance, number of personnel carried in vehicles, petrol, oil change, drivers etc. before I can give permission to use these vehicles since they are the property of the mission complex and thus that of the Roman Catholic Diocese of Vurura. I would be willing to come to Puma, at your convenience, to discuss these issues with you. Thanking you kindly.

Ni jewe,
Rev. Anthony Joseph, pb,
Pastor, Butova Mission.

Tony smirked as he folded the onion-papered response and sealed the envelope. He had thrown in 'oil change' simply to confuse Kizungu and wondered why he had not added changing air in the tires! Alberto would not know the difference! Furthermore, his car was his own personal possession. But it was the property of the church for it was to establish the church that his family and friends had made this purchase possible. Again Kizungu could never understand what belonged to the individuals and what was property of the church. Above all Tony wanted a private moment 'off the record' with Kizungu to let him know that there wasn't a chance in hell that he would lend him or any government killer a vehicle. In fact if he had a bicycle he would not let any of them sit on it! However he thought he could go a long way in getting some inside information if he let this situation give the impression he was co-operating with the *bakuru.*

He handed the letter to Kizungu's messenger and walked into Jose's office and told him about the request. They both laughed at the irony and audacity of these Batutsi leaders. They were all imbeciles to think that after deceiving Tony one day, he would allow them to requisition the vehicles the next day! Jose surmised that Kizungu must have been away somewhere on the weekend and had heard about the requisition idea in another district and thought it would be something he could try at Puma. Tony was bound and determined to make sure Kizungu's ingenuity and cunningness would fail miserably.

"The gas gauge is broken on my motorcycle and always shows full. I should lend it to them and tell them there is lots of petrol in it and then when they get 15-20 kilometers away from home, the *pikipiki* will die and they will have to push it all the way back here!" Jose added with a smirk.

Tony smiled as well:

"They would not push it themselves. They would get some poor Muhutu who would be going to his grave and they would have him push it along if he still had stamina enough." Both men showed their displeasure, thinking of the sad sort of the Bahutu.

Later in the afternoon, Tony drove to Puma. He entered the square and passed in front of Kizungu's house. He kept driving until he reached the infirmary, turning left around the square. He stopped the car and walked briskly to the entrance of the dispensary, a very gloomy place where so many people passed from life to death daily. As Tony entered the small quarters that served 47,000 people, he saw twelve beds, in two rows of six, lining both sides of the rectangular room. Each had a simple spring, but mattresses, sheets and blankets were no where to be seen. If the room had once been furnished with the essentials, these were now all stolen. The walls were painted with whitewash on the top and dark green from the bottom to about five feet above the flooring. This way, the dirt, blood or spit would be less visible than if they were all white. But still there were huge blood stains and dirt all over the whitewash. In fact the room looked so depressing, Tony wondered how anyone would not feel sicker because of these conditions. Looking down the rows of beds, he saw that most were empty, for in the daytime the patients would go outside to lie in the sun. However half way down, in the third bed to the left, he saw his friend Deogratias Pungu. Deo lay on a mat that surpassed the springs on all sides. There was a dark gray flannelette blanket covering his body. He saw Fr. Tony and sighed as Tony came over to stand beside his bed:.

"*Barampiga..... cane..... Pati...... umubili wote..... misi menge.....*"

("They have beaten me…...so much …...all over my body…… for many days…...") Deo said almost out of breath. "At night…... they would drag my body…... close to the fire. My skin smelled…. an awful odor. They put lighted cigarettes…... in my mouth. My whole body…...is burned or broken…...from beatings with sticks."

Tony lifted the blanket from Deo's mutilated body. His wounds made him look dehumanized, like a cadavre prepared for burial. He wore only a small dark-blue pair of underpants and his whole body seemed to be afire with wounds and pain.

Beneath his breath, Tony cursed those who had done this repulsive deed and wondered what the good man lying in excruciating pain could ever have done to merit such treatment. How could he have acquired such spiteful enemies? 'He is a Muhutu that is his only crime!' he thought. Tony regretted that he had not brought his camera along since there was no one else in the room and he could have taken as many photos as he so desired. He promised himself to sneak it in the next time.

Deogratias Pungu seemed embarrassed that the pastor would see his nakedness and agonizing wounds. He seemed to want the blanket pulled back over his body, but he could not move his arms. He asked Tony for a blessing. The pastor prayed over him and gave him absolution and pardon for any sins. Then he told Deogratias that he would return the following day with the host so that he could receive holy communion as a comfort in his distressful state. Deo asked that Tony do whatever he could to assure that the authorities would not return him to prison:

"I prefer to die…... than go through that again," was the way he put it. Little did they know that he would have his wish fulfilled very soon.

Tony drove back to the mission slowly, struggling to prevent the scene of Deo's mutilated body from penetrating deeper into his heart and mind. Then an hour before sundown the same *karani* came to his office again. This time he brought another letter. Once more it was from the administrator saying that he would come to Butova the following day to speak about the request for requisition. Tony understood that this would give Kizungu a chance to see the vehicles up close. Furthermore it showed also that he was willing to bend a bit as he would come to visit the pastor and not require Tony's displacement. He thought of flattening some of the tires on both vehicles but then thought better of it. He would certainly be needing the vehicles himself especially since he had planned to follow Pedro's idea of 'being seen, seeing'. But Tony relished the opportunity of getting the administrator alone for a short while. This discussion on the requisition of the vehicles presented a great occasion for his speaking the truth.

Tony went to his room after a short recreation with his confreres and thought about his day. He was so thankful for the visit of the colleagues from Mutwe and especially for the new-found energy that they had generated within him. The following day's game plan was ready. Whenever he would hear the Arab's truck going down the main road and heading for the *arrondissement,* he would have his VW ready and would wait along the road for the truck to come back loaded with corpses, some dead, others only half alive and still some alive and petrified with their arms and hands tied up and heading for their common grave. He thought of where he should position his car for the best run at the truck and decided to park it either at the sisters' house in the girls' school playground or over at the boys' school beyond the mission. At either place he would have to move quickly.

Then he thought it might be better if he followed the truck when it came by Butova going to Puma and see them loading it up. It sounded very risky and dangerous but the more Tony thought about it, the more he was challenged to do so. Yes, the next morning he would drive to Puma and see how the soldiers and police were loading up the Arab's truck with poor Bahutu semi-conscious corpses.

Then Tony thought how his White Father community had always reassured him that he would never be alone. Raphael and Pedro had certainly affirmed that principle. And now that he was in the worst scenario possible for a young missioner, he felt the reassurance that he wasn't alone, that there were others who were supporting him and challenging him. He could count on them just as they were counting on him. He knelt beside his bed and thanked his God for religious community and for the strength that he had drawn from the *BanyaMutwe.* He then gave his life to God for the Batutsi-Bahutu cause and asked the Good Lord to be with him the next day and to support and protect him in this dangerous mission that he knew he had to do. His optimism would carry him through the night but would quickly disappear the following day.

11. "Death - Encounters" At Puma

Tony was having a second cup of coffee with Luigi when Cypriano opened the dining room door and announced that Administrator Kizungu was waiting for *Pati Mukuru* in front of his office. Tony quickly finished his coffee, got up from table and backed to the door in one huge gesture.

"I can't wait to see the twit," he said to Luigi over his shoulder as he opened the door.

Kizungu was standing in front of his office, the tall man with a long narrow face that looked even longer and narrower as he stared at Tony. It seemed as if all the problems of the world rested on his shoulders. True they might, Tony thought as he greeted the administrator:

"*Bwakeye neza, bwana,*" (Good morning, sir,) Tony mixing Kiswahili with Kirundi as if he were searching for a word that would be worthy of Kizungu's austere presence!

The administrator returned the greeting:

"*Bwakeye, Pati!*"

Tony unlocked his office door and invited his guest to enter. The meeting was cordial and friendly, which surprised Tony. He was ready for a conversation that would act out the harshness of the letter of the previous afternoon. But as Alberto talked to him, Tony heard the administrator's need to share more than the pleasantries of life.

Kizungu thanked Tony for offering his car the first night of the turmoil and for driving him from checkpoint to checkpoint. And he also thanked him for driving the *muganga* and the soldier, policeman and *karani* to Mundi on Sunday. He further mentioned how necessary it was for the government to depend on the mission for transportation! Tony allowed him to finish because he knew that as a polite Mututsi, the administrator would also listen attentively when Tony would speak. He welcomed an equal opportunity.

Finally his turn came. He began by mentioning how difficult it must be for an administrator these days, being dominated by the military. But he also added that as a priest and missionary, he represented justice for the Bahutu as well as the Batutsi. As Fr. Tony spoke these words, he knew he was risking his whole life. What if he would be perceived as someone interfering with governmental and *kitutsi* justice? In fact he never said: 'Batutsi-Bahutu' to reassure Kizungu of his politeness.

The words opened Kizungu's heart and he started to pour out his frustrations to Tony. He mentioned that he never wanted the job of administrator but his brother, Bonaventuro Ruha, had talked him into it and had spoken to President Sabimana, who had appointed him to the important office.

"When all the trouble started in mid-April, the Ministry of the Interior sent me a message that I was to organize checkpoints throughout the *arrondissement.* I had no money to pay anyone so I did the best I could with some of our boys as volunteers. Then after the trouble in Vurura, Arturo Shabaru, the Foreign Affairs Minister and the Head of the Army, came by. He spoke to me in private and I have yet to share these words with anyone. He said that they were going to kill as many Bahutu as they could and that I had better go along with what the soldiers would do. If not, they would have a hole to bury my head in as well."

Tears seemed to well up in Kizungu's eyes and Tony could hardly believe what he was hearing. This was the local mayor who was telling a foreigner that the head of the army said he would kill him if he didn't go along with all the carnage! Parts of the puzzle were finally falling into place. The Minister of Foreign Affairs had master-minded the whole genocide on the home front!

Tony, his anger dissipated, wanted to reach out and hug this poor man who sat bent over in front of his desk. But he realized that such an expression of empathy might alarm Alberto and could hold back further sincerity. So he gave the reassurance that he had surmised this all along. And so he had! He promised Kizungu his support and to his delight he also saw a way of refusing the two mission vehicles that had been requisitioned. Tony realized this would also be an excellent opportunity to bring up the subject of Deogratias and his whereabouts.

"Alberto," he began, "we have only two vehicles here at the mission. We need them at all times for our work of bringing God and the sacraments to your people. We can not allow these vehicles to be used for anything that would deprive them of being at the service of the spiritual needs of your people. The money that purchased these two Volkswagens was given by poor Europeans, and we cannot allow these vehicles to be damaged by non-church activity. I must inform you that I cannot grant your request under any circumstances. However I want it to be known by Shabaru or the president or anyone else who might be involved with this request, that you asked me and I had to refuse for the reasons I have just outlined. I take full responsibility. I will address a letter to you that you can show to the authorities to prove that you tried to obtain the vehicles and I refused. If they expel me, then so be it. They cannot expel you, but they can put you in prison or kill you. So you must protect yourself," Tony said responding as if the initiative for the request was from others rather than Alberto himself. Besides, if the administrator was being haughty, then this would pull him down a peg or two. There was nothing more humiliating than telling a person that you were dealing with his superiors. It made him feel inferior and incapable.

"Now there is one other thing I would like to discuss with you, *M. l'Administrateur*: my catechist and secretary, Deogratias Pungu. He was arrested by your policemen last Thursday after the Ascension service in the catechumenate. Do you think that you could permit me to see him in prison, for he has been there five days already?" Tony never showed that he was aware that Deo had been so mutilated by the soldiers' torturing that he had been placed in the infirmary. He wanted to try Kizungu to see what response he would receive.

Kizungu stood up but made no response. There wasn't anything that Tony could read in his body language that showed he had heard the request. He merely grunted which Tony seemed to think was his way of trying to avoid the question. So Tony, too, stood up and decided to take all the stops out. He said directly to the administrator:

"I would like to have written permission to visit Pungu, *M. l'Administrateur*. In that way, when I have your permission, I will present you with the letter of response to your request for the vehicles that you can keep in your files!" Tony bargained. Kizungu replied evasively, not wanting to be committed to a position:

"Tell those who are guarding the prison door that I have given you permission to visit your catechist," Kizungu said without any sign that he knew Pungu had been taken from jail to the infirmary.

Tony realized he was getting shafted. He also knew that unless he himself said that Deo was in the dispensary, Kizungu would not disclose anything he knew. It certainly was an embarrassment to the *bakuru* that Deo had been beaten so much that he had to be hospitalized. Kizungu had little defense. Further he did not want a European to see the filthy, slimy conditions the prisoners were subjected to in the Puma jail. Tony still had more ammunition. He thanked Alberto for coming to visit and reiterated that he could await the official letter, after he, himself, received the administrator's permission to visit Deogratias Pungu. Both men went outside and Tony extended his hand to the administrator as a gesture of friendship. Lately he had refused to shake hands with any government official in public because that could be seen by the people as a sign of affirmation of government policy. However he felt so sorry for the bind that Kizungu was in, that he believed he needed to affirm him. He watched as Alberto walked away, crossed in front of the church, made the sign of the cross and then drifted out of sight along the road that would take him home to Puma.

Tony then walked out into the front yard by himself and spoke to a young man, Stefano, asking him if he would do some work for him. The teenager accompanied the pastor back to his office and Tony asked him to stand in front of his office and watch for the Arab's truck coming up the road on its way to Puma. Then when he would see the truck, he was to find Tony wherever he would be: at meetings, in his office, in the church, in the fathers' house, and interrupt what he was doing to let him know immediately. He would pay him the following day. Stefano sat proudly in front of Tony's office with his eyes glued to the road. Tony trusted that the young man would inform him the second he heard and saw the truck.

But Tony found it strange that he hadn't heard from Stefano before lunch time. On the other hand he reasoned: "If there be no news about the hearse, then that would be even better! Maybe the killings have stopped at Puma and Butova through divine intervention!" Oh, God, he wished he could believe that.

Walking outside after lunch he saw Clementia coming toward his office door. Tony greeted her and welcomed her into his office. Her face looked bleak and dreary;

"I thank you, Pati, for visiting my husband and giving him some hope. I have sent my eldest daughter to stay with him and soothe his wounds. But he won't eat anything. They have beaten my poor man so much. His body is wounded, all over. He would surely have died if he had been kept in prison"

As she continued speaking, Tony heard a hard knock on his window. Then there were noisy steps that came to his door. The door burst open and Stefano shouted:

"*Hariya*" (Way over there).

Being a typical Murundi, Stefano pointed the distance using his chin, uplifted, to physically show Tony the direction where he believed the truck to be.

"*Hariya! Hariya!* (over there!) *Ni.....motocari!* (It's a motor car) *Ha-ri-ri-ya!*" Stefano elongated his words to signify it was still very far away but coming up the road going to Puma for the pickup.

Tony thanked him and ran to the chapel where the fathers prayed in the morning. They also kept the Blessed Sacrament in the form of consecrated hosts in the tabernacle. He took out some hosts, placed them in his pyx that had been ready and waiting on the altar. And now carrying the Creator of the universe in his left upper pocket, the place closest to his heart, Fr. Tony talked to Jesus, as he always did when he was carrying the Blessed Sacrament, seeking solace, asking for protection and sharing his intimate thoughts with the Living Lord. This was one of the most meaningful parts of his ministry, to be able to carry the presence of the Lord to people and to have this moment of intimacy with the Savior. He would go to see Deogratias in the hospital at Puma and bring him the presence of Jesus Christ. That was reason enough to go to the *arrondissement*. But above all, Tony wanted the soldiers to 'see him seeing them' loading up the 'hearse'. Someday maybe, just maybe, they would blush with shame because of their horrible crimes!

As the priest drove the few miles to Puma, he continued to talk openly to the Jesus whose existence as Lord and Master of the universe was now imprisoned in a small golden pyx held preciously close to his heart. He marveled at how God, whose presence could not be contained in all the oceans of the world and whose grandeur was greater, higher and larger that all the mountains in the universe, allowed Himself to be embodied within the simplicity of a wafer host. He asked Jesus to be with him and to strengthen Deogratias Pungu and all the other poor Bahutu who were being so badly treated by the authorities, soldiers and policemen throughout the country. So rather than await the truck, he decided to go directly to Puma.

As he approached Puma, he saw the truck that was driven by an Arab. It was parked on the far corner of the square, directly in front of a hut where the soldiers had beaten the young men ten days earlier. The truck had been turned around, backed in to the hut. The back of the lorry was close to the mud shelter. Tony drove his car straight ahead toward the hut. Then he turned right and stopped directly in front of the hut, parking on the left side of the road. He was about fifteen meters from the mud building. His regard focused on the grass enclosure built of dried mud that had been painted with whitewash. The roof was thatched with straw and cone-shaped, reaching to the center which was about three-and-one-half meters off the ground.. The side walls were about two meters above the turf. There was only an open space for the door and since the walls were rather high, most people did not have to bend their head as they entered or exited as often was the case in normal Burundi dwellings.

The priest got out of his car and closed the door behind him. Then he leaned against the back left fender of the car and looked all around at what was in front of him, wondering if someone would notice the motor shut-off. He expected someone to come out and see who had arrived.

Then he saw some men he recognized as policemen, carrying out a young man or maybe a teenage boy. He was only wearing khaki shorts and they hauled him awkwardly, lifting his upper body and dragging him with their hands around his shoulders and biceps. His feet dangled behind in the dirt. They lifted him up to two others who were in the truck who took him and threw him down with a thud. The men then went back for another body. Two more men carried out another young person and went through the same process of tossing him up to the others who were waiting in the truck. All the Bahutu seemed unconscious and half-dead as a result of the beatings that they had received. Tony became terribly depressed and almost nauseated as the repulsive operation continued over and over again. As he looked around in back of his car he saw that there were only a few people in the whole square who had stopped to look at what was happening. Many people were walking back and forth, by the dispensary, in from of the administrator's house, at the court house, on the road leading to the house of the *muganga*. But few noticed what was happening as the policemen continued to fill the Arab's truck with human, half-naked corpuses Tony could only wonder why no one seemed to care. Were their other preoccupations more important? Or were they afraid to stop and look, in case they might be arrested as well. Or had they grown accustomed to the scene? There wouldn't be a Mututsi strong enough to ask what was happening. Most Bahutu were far from Puma, not daring to be seen and fearing to be arrested.

As Tony turned back, gathering courage to look again at what was happening, he saw two very tall soldiers who were coming directly toward him. They stopped about ten meters from the priest, who was still leaning against the hood of his car with the Blessed Sacrament in his pocket. The *basoldat (soldiers)* both dropped to one knee. They pointed their rifles directly at Fr. Tony and cocked their triggers, one after the other. Then one of them shouted from behind his weapon:

"*Genda! Genda!*" (Go! Go!)

Fr. Tony Joseph responded rapidly. He stood erect, turned his back to them, opened his car door and got into the volkswagen. He whispered to the Lord who was hidden in his pocket: "You died because people hated you, what you said and what you stood for. I would like to think that I could die in the same way…..but Lord, no! no! no! I am not ready to die for this absurd cause or any cause. Forgive me Lord for not having the courage and faith that you had to stand up and die for your brothers. Come with me Lord, and stay with me as the day is drawing on." He started the car and drove down the dirt road and turned the corner, He stopped in front of the dispensary and thought:

"I will go in and take solace that Deogratias Pungu is not going through what I have just witnessed." Tony got out of the car and some men, who were there to obviously visit others in the hospital, came over to him. From afar they had seen his encounter with the soldiers and tried to console Tony. Finally one of them suggested he visit with those in the dispensary. Tony agreed and added that he had come especially to see Pungu and give him last rites. Their silence accompanied the priest as he went around the back of the small building to enter by the only door, which strangely was at the rear As he entered, he saw a few men and women in different beds. But when he looked over for Deogratias, there was someone else in his bed!

Tony panicked and turned around to the men who accompanied him and asked where Deogratias was.

"They took him out by truck last night," was the only response Tony got from one of the men who seemed to have been there when this tragedy had happened.

Tony reached into his pocket and grasped the pyx. "May God judge every one of these ruthless villains! O that they receive God's eternal justice," he heard himself muse in his native English as he angrily stomped from the room still holding the precious vessel.

Tony went to his car a defeated and dejected man and drove away from the dispensary. Driving up the road to the mission, he felt some tears roll from his eyes, onto his cheeks and down the side of his jaw and onto his shirt. He had loved Deogratias Pungu so much and now he would look after his widow Clementia and their eight children. He would make sure she had a comfortable home and enough room to bring up these children to be good christians like their father. At home, he parked his car in the *kigo* and stayed in his seat for a long time. He wondered when this murderous genocide would end….. or even if it ever would end.

Tony's stupefaction caused his mind to wonder how he could ever tell Jose and Luigi and Luc and the other catechists, all the people working in the office, the sisters like Maragarita, Gloria and Anunciata or the brothers. Finally he got out of the car. The day was slowly twilighting into evening and he walked back to the house, opened the chapel door and, genuflecting, stood in front of the tabernacle. He opened the small door and took out the ciborium containing the consecrated hosts. Then he returned the hosts in the pyx to their habitual vessel. It was a gesture, he thought, of returning the scarred body of Deogratias, that had been lent to the world, back to his Creator. Deo's mission was completed even though his life and energies had been sadly interrupted. The hosts had traveled a long and difficult journey that afternoon and now they were returned to their Source. Tony reflected on the analogy as he placed the hosts in the larger ciborium:

"Jesus, Deo doesn't need your sacramental presence any longer. He gazes on your glorious countenance directly from his place in heaven. He is contained in your grandeur now. Lord, have mercy on Deo's killers. They do not know what they have done."

As the priest concluded the prayer, he realized that the power of God, maybe through the intercession of Deogratias Pungu, was surely upon him. For of his own feeble humanity, he could never have uttered anything but curses on these outlandish killers.

Now all he could feel was pity, grief, misery and sadness for them.

Tuesday night, May 16th, was one of the most disheartening times in Fr. Tony's young life. At table, he told the story of what had happened to Deogratias to Jose, Luigi and Luc and when it was time for recreation after the meal, he felt the need to be alone. He excused himself, explaining that he needed to work out the events of the day in quiet reflection.

He left the room and walked back and forth along the veranda that lined the back courtyard. The two big watch dogs had been released at dusk and came running to him. They walked back and forth with him a couple of times and then, hearing a noise in the garden, ran away to that part of the property. Tony remained in a pensive mood. Inside, his heart was broken. He was very restless, thinking that in the past week he had lost so many of his close collaborators. Even though he took some consolation in imagining Deo and the others in heaven in the presence of the Lord, nevertheless he felt depressed, discouraged and downtrodden, at what had happened to these men whom he had believed were leaders of the church and would have been influential in the church of tomorrow.

His reflection drifted to his own personal vocation:

"Of what use is the life of a missionary who leaves his family and friends, who commits himself to a life of celibacy without a wife and children, in order to build a living community of faith, the catholic church, here in Butova? Because tribalry and genocide predominate reason and faith, what difference does it make if they have been baptized and washed in the Blood of Christ or not? What difference does it make if they receive the eucharist, the Body of Christ, at Sunday mass? Does it really matter if they receive the sacrament of God's pardon and forgiveness when they sin? What difference does it make if they follow all the rules the missionaries have preached to them for the past eighty years? They do not KNOW God, nor KNOW Jesus Christ, nor LIVE under the influence of the Holy Spirit! Chaos has overcome this country, hatred and murder now reign! The devil has now had victory in Burundi! They have mutilated the Body of Christ, destroyed the gift of salvation. Better for them to have been left in their paganism. Now their sin is even greater since they have rejected the message preached to them! Satan reigns!!"

The more Tony reflected on the ways of his people, the more he realized that his life until now had been totally wasted, one grandiose mistake! Oh, he had helped certain individuals to be better persons and come to know, love and serve God in a more perfect manner. However, concerning the christianization of the Barundi, nothing had really been accomplished. They were still as much savages and barbarians as they had been when the first missioners set foot in their country just before the turn of the century. What a waste of lives, money and effort. Tony thought back to the time he and his *confreres* had spent over the past years questioning the thousands of catechumens and encouraging them to become baptized. Just to do the questioning took over five complete weeks each year for the three priests and two sisters who helped them in the pastoral work. And the catechist meetings, and the outreach to the youth groups especially the *UGA* and the *Chiro* and the hundreds of children who had no place in the public schools and who were trained in catechism, hygiene, and agriculture at the mission. He thought of his trips to the outstations, the many times in the rainy season when his volkswagen slid into mud and he had to dig the wheels out before he could go on his way. He recalled the times he crossed over bridges, driving as fast as he could in case the thin branches cracked and his vehicle end up in the water. Then on the other side of the bridge, he would disembark again and go back to reassure himself that the bridge was strong enough to support the next vehicle. Tony thought of the hours and hours he had spent in the confessional, days that seemed never-ending, hearing confessions from after mass in the morning to a few minutes before dusk in the evening... or the masses that he had celebrated for the school children every week ...

The more Fr. Tony reflected on all this, the faster he walked. His pace became more rapid and he realized that, psychologically, he was trying to run away from the whole painful situation. As he soured about his vocation, he felt bitter about his superiors who had sent him to Burundi. He wondered why his parents had encouraged his vocation and he questioned his own sanity in embarking on such a foolish endeavor. It certainly was the road to nowhere! Rather it was leading him… into total oblivion… into the deepest, darkest depression he could ever have imagined! He wanted to pray, but words and even thoughts of God would not come. He realized that he scorned all Africans: the Batutsi as well as the Bahutu. He despised the Batutsi for being liars and killers, in such a barbaric way. He resented the stupidity of the Bahutu, who did absolutely nothing to try to fight back, to defend themselves. He recalled the scene two days earlier at the hillside overlooking Mundi when there were more than 60 Bahutu armed and ready to attack and yet they feared the consequences and remained cowardly and gutless. No! Prayer would not come. He had been reduced to emptiness, a void, a mere vacuum. His world had come to a sorrowful finale.

Deep within himself, all that Tony could feel was fury and malice as he realized that over the past three weeks he had become a total skeptic. He still believed in God but he had lost complete trust in humankind. He still wanted to believe in humankind but had lost complete trust in God. He fell to his knees and heard a cry come from the uttermost depths of his heart:

"Oh Christ, God Almighty, you cannot be real. You cannot be a God of love, peace and justice and still be alive in this country. You have abandoned us and sent the seven most powerful devils from the bowels of hell to destroy what merits your act of salvation and death on the cross could possibly have obtained for these wretched people. When did you abandon us, O God? When did you depart, O Christ? We now live without you and these have been the worst hours in the history of this possessed country. Hear my prayer. Stir up Your power and proclaim your grandeur. Come back, once again, and bring peace. Lucifer, be gone to everlasting hell that was prepared for you and your kind from all eternity and allow these people to be free."

Tony, still on his knees, was directly outside Jose's room. The window was open and he could smell the foul odor from the small narrow room. Jose always smelled offensively, but his room, being so small and having very little circulating air, was of unbelievably bad stench. When Tony inhaled, he breathed in the odor and felt so sick to his stomach he almost threw up. He got up from his knees quickly and went into the chapel but prayer there was not any better. Then it dawned on him! Rev. Fr. Anthony Joseph, young pastor of Butova, man of God, trained in prayer and spirituality, was on the verge of scorning God for all that had happened.

He wanted to puke on everything and everyone in his life in Butova. All he could manage to say was:

"Cursed, cursed, god damn it, cursed be everything and everyone. To hell with all of them!!! May they all rot in the fires of everlasting Hades!!!"

Once again that night Tony tried to sleep and once again he just tossed and turned in his bed that had been too warmed by the fire Cypriano had lit in his fireplace. He wanted to get up and read for awhile but that would mean lighting the petrol lamp. So he decided just to lie in bed and dream with his eyes wide open. He realized that he had already made a life-giving decision… to leave Burundi as soon as things calmed down… and get a new, fresh start somewhere else. He realized, that although as a twenty-four-year-old, four years previously, he had given his life to serve the missions of Africa, he now became very angry when he thought of the people he had been called to serve. He recalled the dogma of 'Grace' in the seminary, studying how God's gift of grace is grafted on human nature and that one can't give what one doesn't have. He now was void of passion and ambition. There was absolutely no zeal in his human nature. How could the evangelical virtues come to dwell in the hearts of these Batutsi when their whole character, temperament and nature was vested in destroying the Bahutu. How could these poor Bahutu now receive the message of unconditional love and perfect forgiveness? Their whole life was to despise the Batutsi. Was Tony ready to devote his whole life to preaching the gospel of reconciliation? He heard a strong voice within him saying 'No! N0! Never! NEVER!'

Throughout the whole night, Tony kept going over his options. Would he leave Burundi immediately or stick it out until the end of all this? Would he leave in a month or two if the killings didn't end? Certainly he had lost all his interest in staying until his regular leave which would be due in two years time. He thought about living in these conditions for the next two years and he couldn't stomach it for a second. Although he wouldn't abandon these people at the present moment, he certainly couldn't imagine himself staying there for a prolonged period of time preaching a pointless gospel that they had failed to understand. He remembered having begged his superiors in Canada to send him to Burundi. Now that he had experienced the most disillusioning experience of his lifetime, he wanted to run away, put his head in the sand like an ostrich and forget about this nightmare for the rest of his life. He heard himself continuing to curse the events of the past weeks, the people who had failed the gospel test and all the other missionaries who had wasted their time and effort preaching a unity that was incapable of being achieved.

Tony rose with the rising of the sun. He washed quickly and dressed but avoided going to the chapel at prayer time. He knew that the others were probably deep into their prayer already and they needed his presence, but he just couldn't respond. Never before had he felt so paralyzed, so dry, so bitter and so despondent. He realized that what he needed to do was to go into the chapel and kneel in the presence of God and ask pardon for his lack of faith and hope but there was absolutely no movement of this spirit within him.

He returned to his room and straightened up his desk and started to plan his day. First he wanted to go to Mundi to see for himself how things were going. Then he would come back to his office and try to get in touch with his team of builders to start on the house for Clementia. If he would be leaving the mission soon, he wanted to be sure that her house would be completed. He thought of the other constructions that had not been started yet: four classrooms for the primary school at Vuvoga, a church for the new out-station of Borogoro, a church and school for Cibikenke, a school of four classrooms for Ruhweza. As he thought about the constructions, he reflected on the nuisance all these would be for him. He realized that he had never thought in this way before. He had learned from Mathias never to count the cost on himself. But now he recognized that his enthusiasm for the mission had evaporated and his courage had waned. Tony wrote 'Vuvoga' and 'Cibikenke' on a piece of paper. He still felt somewhat sympathetic to their needs. These would be buildings that would benefit the children that he loved so much. But also they were in predominately Bahutu areas and he realized that the bias he always had in favor of this tribe now permeated his thoughts. He thought of both Ruhweza and Burogoro that were in the heart of the Bututsi and he saw himself drawing a big 'X' across both names on his paper. He just couldn't think of helping these people anymore. He realized that this was confirmation of what he had been reflecting about all night long. If he decided to do or not to do things for people because of tribal preference, it was time to pack his bags, ring down the curtain, shut off the lights and egress this god-forsaken hell-hole.

After breakfast, Tony walked out to his car, got in and set out for Mundi. He was still in a very reflective mood and was astonished that he had caught himself having decided to never again do anything for the Batutsi. He was bewildered at his ability to reject a race especially since so many of them were catholics and thus his spiritual children. He wanted to say that their fatalistic attitude lead them to become orphans and although the situation demanded his full attention in Burundi right now, he pleasured in the day-dream about what he would do after leaving Burundi. He loved being a priest and wondered if he should not go back to Canada and do priestly work in his home diocese of Montreal. Being able to speak French as well as English would give him a great advantage in working in that cosmopolitan city.

As Fr. Tony drove on a road that skirted the hillside, he noticed that there were many people coming toward him along the road. Taking precautions, he slowed down almost to a stop and then realized that they were a group of men led by a soldier who was armed. They were walking or staggering along the road, one after another, tied together at their wrists. A few slowed down to almost a stop and stared at his car. In the middle of the group was another armed soldier and then Tony's eyes grew as big as saucers as he recognized Nestori Mwiza, the assistant catechist to Yohani Bora at Mundi. Nestori was wearing a long plaid overcoat and waved at Tony as he recognized the pastor's vehicle. Tony understood the gesture. Nestori wanted him to know that he was being taken to Puma for judgment. They were all being led to their trial as Tony saw another soldier also armed at the back of the group. Driving by, he quickly counted them: there were twenty-three! That was the exact number mentioned by the *muganga* the previous Sunday. That was the same number the soldier had mentioned to Bora. It had taken three days to round up these twenty-three Bahutu and Tony wondered if they had been arrested because they were guilty of any crime whatsoever or had they been in the wrong place at the wrong time and the soldiers had volunteered them for trial. Furthermore he wondered why they didn't try to run away. What fatalism! These grown men, over twenty of them, allowed themselves to be captured by three soldiers. If they had attacked the military, some might have been killed but most would have escaped. Now they were close to Puma and, after a short trial or no trial at all, after some beatings, they would be thrown on the truck later that afternoon and kicked off in the common graves near the military camp of Vurura. How could they be so fatalistic? How could they be so stupid? How could they saunter to their deaths without thinking for a moment about trying to escape? Did they overestimate the power of the military? If they were caught leading an insurrection, would their penalty be any greater? They were doomed to die and they walked to their death trusting that if God wanted them saved, God alone would intervene! Was this what the missionaries had taught them about faith? about God's will? about hope? Surely someone, somewhere had misinformed them on this one! Was this a valid gospel attitude? They would never have a chance of turning the other cheek again. They had presented their final cheek! As the hideous human caravan moved on toward its demise, Tony looked back at the twenty-three sheep being led to the slaughterhouse. Nestori Mwiza and his companions would all die before the sun set on that horrible Wednesday!

Tony drove on to Mundi and found Yohani Bora in the church, teaching a class of children. The catechist walked to the opening in the back of the mud brick building and shook hands with Tony. Then he said:

"The soldiers came yesterday and had a short questioning period and then they arrested 23 Bahutu. Nestori Mwiza was one of those taken. They led them away to Puma this morning."

Tony responded by saying that he had seen them along the road and wondered why they were so submissive. Bora shrugged and walked back to the children. He was the finest African Tony had ever met, a man-of-God living close to his Savior. Moreover Tony surmised that if Bora had been in the same situation as the twenty-three Bahutu along the road, he certainly would have done something to try to escape. Tony turned, walked towards his car and said out loud in English:

"I guess the Bahutu are so stupid they don't deserve to live!"

Realizing that peace had now come to this area, Tony turned his car around to head back over the road to Butova. Ahead of him, as he drew near the mission, he once again saw the armed soldiers with the twenty-three prisoners being led to their Calvary. This time he drove by them and when he got a short distance ahead, stopped the volkswagen by the side of the road. He wanted to make sure the soldiers, in particular, saw him. So he disembarked and walked over to meet them. He noticed that their steps toward him were very slow. They seemed to be intimidated and afraid of the white skinned missionary. Tony tried to relieve any suspicion:

"Don't be afraid. It is I, *Pati Antonio*, *Padri Mukuru* of Butova. Two of the soldiers came up to him and laid their guns on the ground and, to his displeasure, shook hands with him. The other soldier, who was in the rear, spread out to cover all the 'captives' who were now crowding around their pastor. The soldiers told him that they were headed for Puma as they had captured these *bamenja* in Mundi.

Tony responded: "Do you really think that these are bad people who deserve to die for acts of treachery towards their country?" He continued, "I know one of them very well. He is employed by me as the assistant catechist of Mundi. His name is Nestori Mwiza. Do you even know who he is? Do you think this man-of-God has been disloyal to Caesar?" Tony's voice descended on the soldiers like a shrill whistle. He saw Nestori take a step closer to him when he heard his name, a look of hope glimmered from his countenance as he thought this might be his ticket to freedom. But like all the others, fatalists as they were, they did absolutely nothing to save themselves.

Tony looked over this small group of men, a sector of humanity that he knew would soon be eliminated. For the second day in a row he turned away from soldiers with loaded guns, although today they weren't directly pointed at him. He got into his car, rolled down the window, looked at the group one last time and prayed God for their readiness to accept eternal salvation. As he drove ahead of them to Butova, he realized that he had been so caught up in the human realities of their arrests and immanent deaths that it hadn't occurred to him to give them general absolution and forgiveness of all their sins. However he knew that these prisoners would be a convenient excuse for him to exert his importance as spiritual shepherd of those convicted to die. He would go to Kizungu and ask him for permission to see the prisoners before they were placed on the truck that would carry them to their deaths. He would make a case of being the priest responsible for the sacraments and thus held accountable for giving them the last rites, confession, holy communion or viaticum.

Rather than stopping in Butova, Tony drove directly to Puma and found Kizungu outside his house talking to some men who were policemen in the area. At the arrival of the car, the administrator came over to Tony who decided not to get out of his vehicle. After some salutations and greetings. he voiced his query directly at the chief:

"There are so many people being arrested and taken to different places of execution, Mr. Administrator. Most of these men are roman catholics, people like yourself who belong to my jurisdiction. As their pastor, I have a favor to ask of you."

Tony felt the tension grow on the face of the man who stood tall outside the window of his car. He could see his neck muscles bulge and his face become ash in color.

"Ask, *mon pere*," Alberto Kizungu intervened politely, "and I will see what I can do for you."

Fr. Tony recognized the *kitutsi* courtesies and believed that his query was already given a negative response. He remembered how Jose used to say:

"These people are the only ones on the face of the earth who can smile warmly at you and yet politely kick you at the same time.

"Well," Tony went on, "I ask you to grant me permission to spend some time with the prisoners, those who are taken out from here every morning and afternoon to go to their deaths. I would like to give them an opportunity of reconciling with God for their misdeeds before their fate on earth comes to an end. I would like to go among them and spend some time with them before they are placed on the truck. It is only right that as catholics, they have access to the sacraments, especially before their deaths. I ask you for this indulgence, *M. l'Administrateur,* counting on your spirit of justice, fair play and your catholic background and conscience."

Kizungu straightened to his full stature. Tony could not see his face any longer and realized that if their positions stayed that way, refusal would be relatively easy. So quickly he got out of his car and Kizungu had to back up quickly as the door opened. The two men stood with eyes glaring at each other, Kizungu a good head and shoulders taller than the priest. The mayor finally looked away, glancing toward his house and said:

"*Mon pere*, you do not know what you are asking me. I must cooperate with these soldiers as they have indicated that they have a hole for my head if I don't go along with all that they are doing. So I am not in a position to grant you this favor. However if you addressed your query to the soldiers and they would grant you permission, then I would certainly agree," the administrator added in a dirge.

Tony realized, once again, Kizungu was being polite toward a *Muzungu* since he knew the soldiers would never give any such permission. They were both bantering in circles. He turned on his heels, shook Kizungu's outstretched hand to return the administrator's courtesy, got into his car and drove back to Butova.

At lunch time, the discouraged pastor talked to the others about how desperate the situation was. They were all appalled at the arrests of the twenty-three Bahutu from Mundi and especially the detention of Nestori Mwiza. Furthermore they were stymied at the administrator's refusal of Tony's request. Jose suggested that since priestly work was now denied them, then he and Luigi should stand on the side of the road and give general absolution and final blessings to those in the truck as it came up the road from Puma on its way to the common graves. At the same time he suggested that Tony continue to follow the truck down the road, pass the ambulatory morgue and then turn around at Luconi and come back again.

"If only we could stop the truck for a moment or two so that all these men will know that they have been forgiven," Jose said.

Tony responded saying that it would be a true gift to each Muhutu but it probably would be impossible to do. They could not interfere directly with the operations of the military:

"I fear that if we disrupt them directly, they won't hesitate to shoot. And our role here is not to die for the cause, but to remind them of the wrong they are doing. We have to preach the gospel of Christ and stay alive in our preaching. Again, I believe the Lord cannot use dead missionaries but alive prophets. Maybe it is more important to preach Christ's love to these wretched soldiers than to the suffering Bahutu." Tony concluded almost in a whisper.

The missionaries continued to talk in such a discouraging way about the situation that they each decided to pray personally that afternoon and come together later to decide some practical steps of action to accelerate their witness. Tony asked each one of them to come up with one particular gesture that would be a witness. Then he put his cards on the table:

"I really believe that as long as we stay here doing nothing we are giving silent consent to these murderers. If we cannot do anything to stop them, then maybe it would be time for us to show our protests by walking out or at least stopping all church activities. Let's think and pray about all that is at stake and then come together at 5 o'clock and make some practical decisions."

They all seemed to agree, at least about the meeting and got up and walked out of the dining room. That afternoon, there was a greater silence at the mission house than usual. Tony lay on his bed for awhile and when it was time to go to his office to do some paper work, he felt completely confused. "What is the use?" he asked himself. "No matter what we do today, the killings with still continue tomorrow. The people that the missionaries have prepared over decades to carry on the work of the church will continue to go to their deaths. This situation is totally absurd and I don't see any use in staying here any longer. It is time for action, time to witness, time to stand up and be counted," he mused.

Soon he heard Stefano's wrap again on his door telling him that the truck was coming up the road from Luconi to go down to Puma and load up with bodies. He brushed by the messenger and hurried to Jose's office. He wrapped on the door but there was no answer. Then he went around to the back and wrapped on his bedroom door. Again nothing! As he walked away, Barnabe Ntware, the gardener working on the flowers in the courtyard, called out to Tony that he had heard Jose leaving on his motorcycle. "Damned," thought Tony, "we decided to do this common gesture of solitary and the truck is loading up and Jose can't be found."

Tony knocked on Luigi's door and told him the truck would soon be up from Puma and that he was on his own as Jose was not to be found. They both voiced their disappointment that Jose was not there and how important it was for them to look and feel united in the common witness of their apostolic community. But Luigi agreed to give forgiveness alone:

"Jose is a bamboozler. He promises the world but when it is time, he's out riding his *pikipiki*. I believe in the sacrament I will be giving and that God's pardon will be with me. This might be the most important gesture of my whole priestly life!" Luigi commented as he prepared to cross over to the church.

He went right to the sacristy, vested in a white alb that hung down to his sandaled feet. His long, dark black, curly hair made a striking contrast with the white colored robe. He put on a black stole, symbolic of death, and took out the bucket with holy water that had been blessed by Mathias during the Easter Vigil. Luigi had often said that he didn't understand the meaning of blessed water but today, anticipating the gesture of pardon and forgiveness he was about to perform, the the holy water symbolism seemed rich with meaning. He would sprinkle the moving vehicle with holy water reminding everyone that these martyrs, who were going to their common deaths, were washed in the waters of baptism and saved by the Risen Christ. So many of them would have been baptized in this particular church, in God the Father, Son and Holy Spirit and washed free of their sins. The sprinkling would not only recall for many others their former baptism but the fact that they at present were washed from all stain by the power of forgiveness. Luigi then read over the formula for general absolution that he found in the ritual:

"By the power entrusted to me by the Lord Jesus Christ and the Catholic Church, I absolve you of all your sins, faults and failures in the name of the Father and of the Son and of the Holy Spirit." Luigi read over the Kirundi text a few times and thought it would even look better if he were to take the ritual with him and read the words of forgiveness out loud, concluding with the blessing. He walked out of the sacristy, down the side of the huge church and out into the hot May sun. A few people came up to him when they saw Luigi garbed in alb and stole and asked for "akasacramentu?" ("a little sacrament": referring to confession). Luigi looked for his best Kirundi expression and told them he was to give those being taken to their deaths general absolution and that they would also be permitted to share in the common sacramental pardon, if they stood by the

side of the road and prepared themselves. He then walked to the road with the penitents following him and waited for the truck. He saw Tony's car about 50 feet ahead of him on the same road also waiting for the truck.

As Luigi looked the other way, down the road from whence had come the truck, sure enough he saw Jose coming along on his moto and heading for the mission. As he prepared to turn toward their house, Jose noticed Tony's car and then he saw Luigi vested, with a crowd of people around him. When he realized Tony was in his car, Jose drove across the pathway to greet him. Tony mentioned that he and Luigi were awaiting the truck that had gone down to Puma about fifteen minutes earlier and added that they expected Jose to be there with them. Jose apologized saying:

"Sorry, Tony, I forgot."

Tony was a bit apprehensive that the truck would come by when they were talking so he reminded Jose of their meeting at 5pm and asked him to host the gathering in his office. Jose agreed and again apologized and drove back to the mission.

As he left, Tony could hear the vibrations through the ground and the rumblings of the lorry coming up the hill from Puma. He looked back at Luigi who was getting ready with his ritual and holy water in his hands. Soon the big dark blue truck was very close to the vested cleric as it passed beside the long church. Luigi stepped out and stood about two feet from the gulf in the road that had been made by thousands of trucks and cars over the years. When the truck was about twenty feet from him he started sprinkling the water all over the road, the place of the approaching vehicle. He prayed in his native Italian and followed with a blessing in Kirundi:

"*By this blessed water*,' he held his right hand high above his head, "*may you recall that you have been baptized in Christ Jesus and washed from your sins by the power of His death. May the Lord purify you until the end of time when He will come and carry you away to the place that has been prepared for you for everlasting life."*

Then Father Luigi made the blessing, the truck rumbled by him as he stood on the side of the road and forgave the men their sins:

"I absolve you from all sins, interdictions and forms of excommunication, in the name of the Father and of the Son and of the Holy Spirit." And all the people around him, mostly Batutsi, shouted out: *Amen!*"

As the words rolled off Fr. Luigi's lips. he felt a tremendous wave of fulfillment. This was the reason why he became a priest, why he was a missionary, why God had sent him to Burundi. His *raison d'etre* had been to be present to these people in this area, at this particular moment of history, and to be the pardoning Christ for them. He had been God's chosen instrument to have these people receive the Lord's pardon and forgiveness of all their sins. Luigi believed with all his heart that the forgiveness he had granted was in the name of the Lord, Jesus Christ, Savior of the universe. They were on their way to a common human grave but he was also certain that they souls soon would rejoice in the sight of the Beatific Vision in heaven.

Fr. Tony allowed the lorry to ramble along and then, when the truck had traveled for some time, cut out and followed the Bahutu hearse. He looked up at the back of the big vehicle as he prepared to pass and could see absolutely nothing as the truck's tailgate was shut very tightly. He pulled his volkswagen to the left and accelerated as he passed the truck. He slowed to look up at the driver and saw a soldier in the passenger seat. Tony smiled in salutation. Having passed the lorry, he then turned back, before coming to the fork in the road at Luconi, and drove back up the road toward Butova. Soon the truck was coming down a hill and almost upon him. He pulled over to the right side of the road to allow the truck to pass on his left. As he looked back, he saw a soldier on the very top of the back part of the truck. Tony surmised that he had to be standing on his human cargo. So he prayed for the many half-dead bodies that were in the lorry. He wondered if the catechist Nestori Mwiza was among them. Or had he already died? Or was he there in pain and suffering? Or was he unconscious in the bottom of the pile? Or maybe he was still awaiting judgment at Puma? Tony hoped and prayed that those from Mundi had not been judged already for if they were, they were now on their way to burial.

Tony started his car and drove back to the mission very slowly. He could not have believed that anyone could have become more depressed that he had been earlier in the day. Now, he thought that his depression was even deeper. He realized what a sad state his emotions were in! His mind and heart were so saturated with depressive feelings. He wanted to throw up but his stomach had nothing to regurgitate. He decided to stop his car on the side of the road just before arriving at the last turn before the mission. There was no one on the road, no people walking toward his car or ahead of it. Fr. Tony Joseph, 28 year old Missionary of Africa, put his head in both his hands and he cried and cried and cried. After a lengthy period of time, Tony took his hands away from his face and looked down at them. He could see the stain of the tears on his palms. He was a grown man, weeping like a baby. He had reached the bottomless pit!

12. Decision To Witness Together

On arriving back in the courtyard, Tony saw Luigi come out of his room. He hadn't realized that it was almost five o'clock and they should be starting the meeting soon. Luigi came over and Tony hardly recognized his upbeat colleague. His voice sounded so enthusiastic. His appearance reflected his joy of dispensing the sacrament of reconciliation. Luigi felt pleased and proud that God had used him to give absolution to the dying men who were presently getting closer to their burial spot somewhere along the road near Vurura. He said that it was a mixture of sadness and peacefulness. The men had been forgiven, yet they were now at death's door. Tony quickly walked to his room, got some paper and a pen for the gathering and joined his colleagues at the meeting in Jose's office.

Somewhat unnecessary, Jose began the meeting by asking Luigi and Tony for pardon for fouling up the plans. Tony didn't take the apology seriously simply because he didn't believe in Jose's sincerity. If Jose had truly wanted to, he would have been there. He'd taken the easy way out, apologizing to regain their trust. The pastor did not want to get into a discussion for more than once, in Mathias' time, they had spent entire meetings arguing about Jose's forgetfulness and tardiness. He could be excused for being late but what did that matter? His problem had to deal with unwillingness to consider others rather than forgetfulness. So Tony dismissed it by saying that in the future, they all had to join together in mutual support and that when they made a common decision, everyone was obliged to be on time and carry out the resolution. They then proceeded with the meeting saying a prayer to the Holy Spirit to guide them in the decision-making process.

Luigi was the first to speak after the meeting was officially opened and his morose tone surprised his colleagues since they thought he had briefly regained his enthusiasm. He said that he was totally discouraged, had not eaten for five days and had decided that as soon as he could, he would leave Butova and Burundi and never come back again. He called the people 'wild apes' and 'killers' and said that the missioners were mad to try to preach the gospel of Christ to those who were a band of 'savages'. Although the missionaries had worked so hard to make God present, the country seemed to be devoid of any divine presence.

"What are we doing here?" he asked no one in particular. "We have not even touched the surface of having them realize their guilt and wrongdoing. Yet they are killing by the tens-of-thousands! The best thing that can happen to Burundi would be that all the priests and missionary sisters and brothers leave and let the people kill and kill and kill until there would be only a few left. Maybe a new church would emerge from this '*diaspora*' (small groups of committed people who gathered together and built the larger church). Then they could invite the missionaries to return and to re-introduce the gospel."

Jose reacted negatively to what the Italian had said. First he made a joke: "I certainly would not want to work with the diaspora, for the populace that would be left would be those who are doing all the killings!"

Of course he had been in Burundi for the past nine years and his life was much more invested in the country than that of Luigi who had been there for the six-month language course and from March to May in the parish of Butova. It was nine months opposed to nine years as Jose mentioned how many good people he knew:

"We should not judge the situation too severely for the people will soon come to their senses and there will be peace and reconciliation," he counseled.

Tony brought them back to the initial subject, saying they were not reflecting on the character of the people or the problems of preaching the gospel. What needed to be addressed was their own value as missionaries in the parish of Butova at this present time. How could they give meaningful witness? Should they continue here, even though their presence seemed to affirm the repulsive actions of the Batutsi killing the Bahutu. Or should they not take special measures to protest their opposition to what had developed in their area.

" 'Silence gives consent!' summarizes how I feel," he said.

Jose was the first to address this question as well. He said, vehemently, that he wanted to stay in Butova as it was important to stand behind the people and support their actions towards reconciliation:

"I want to stay for those who are painfully experiencing this genocide," was the way he explained his position.

Luc then cut in. He agreed with Jose that making the decision to withdraw at this time might be too drastic. He talked about his work in the cooperative and said that it had taken him many months to encourage the people to become members and if the missionaries were to withdraw, that would mean the end of this effort to invoke their trust. However, he did add that he saw absolutely no value in the others doing "priestly work". He had come from France where there was strong criticism toward the catholic church in general, and the clergy, in particular. Even though Luc went to mass and joined the fathers in prayer, and had mentioned that he was thinking of a priestly vocation, he now stated that he thought the people were completely devoid of christianity. To give them the sacraments was utterly ridiculous. Like Luigi, Luc considered this situation to be a lost cause for the church!

"At least stop all the hypocrisy that these sacramental signs connote."

Tony smiled at Luc:

"You seem to be saying that you, yourself, should stay to look after the material needs but that we, the spiritual overseers, should leave?" he asked frivolously.

"Or should we stay in the house and support you or even work along with you in the cooperative and just close down the church?" Jose asked whimsically.

Luigi added, also in partial jest:

"Maybe we could move the cooperative over to the church and then, Luc, you could buy all the *ibiharage* (beans) and *imiwi* (bananas) in the area!" They all had a laugh at Luc's expense and then they started to become serious again.

"I would like to build on this idea that Luc has given us." Tony went on: "He has said that our work as priests here in Butova is very close to useless. Our presence here has not stopped the Batutsi from killing the poor Bahutu by the hundreds, if not thousands. Further we cannot practice our ministry as the *bakuru* forbid us to give the sacraments and prepare those arrested who will die. What kind of witness could and should we give to show the government and the Batutsi that we totally object to their policies of killing in this area?"

Jose added to everyone's surprise:

"Then the only solution would be to leave. If we left, then the people would see that we are protesting against what the polity of killing has been. We could write a letter and I could photocopy it and leave copies everywhere in the area. The message would spread like wildfire."

Luigi rehashed the same idea: "We could take a day and ready ourselves to leave and then make hundreds of photocopies of a letter to the people explaining to them why we are leaving. When a Muhutu got a letter he would understand that we were supporting his race in a drastic but camouflaged way. When a Mututsi read the letter, he would understand that we were condemning his tribe's actions. I like that idea and think it is what we should do."

Tony surmised: "If I hear what we are saying, we all agree that we should leave....."

Jose cut him off: "I am not sure, Tony, that I want to leave. And Luc sounded as if he wanted to stay. So 'leaving' is only one option." he concluded abruptly.

Tony looked at Jose directly, eye-to-eye, and asked him, accentuating each syllable of his sentence:

"Jose…are…you...say...ing...that...we…should....or…should…not... leave...the…mission?"

Jose shrugged his shoulders: "Don't quote me either way, Tony. I am not sure yet what I would suggest that we do..."

There was silence throughout the room as they considered the contradictions that Jose brought forth. The three colleagues realized that they were once again in the middle of a "Suarezism" better known as a dichotomy. No matter what you would say, Jose would disagree with you. But in fact, as he disagreed, he would try to find a valid argument to change his position and then give reasoning why he supported you. He had said that he wanted to stay. Then he had said it would be good if they evacuated. Then he was trying again to give an analysis why they should all stay. But now he wasn't sure at all! But he was not the only one who was dealing with all the contradictions. They all seemed confused, disorientated and baffled. The whole situation was impossible to deal with in theory. But beyond the hypothesis was the reality

Tony asked them to think about leaving and what repercussions such a decision would have on those in the parish who depended on them. For example the brothers, sisters, catechists and parish employees would not survive much longer if the clergy shut down the mission and departed. And if they were to go, would they not take all the money with them? What about the material part of the mission, or their own possessions in their rooms and offices? What about church valuables: tabernacles, chalices, vestments, cases of altar wine? Or what about the buildings, classes, teachers' homes and all the property that made up the Roman Catholic Parish of Butova? If they were to leave, the soldiers would certainly come and occupy the mission and then people would be really confused saying that it was the catholic mission that was persecuting them.

Luigi wondered if the fathers abandoned the mission, would the brothers do the same in their school.

Tony responded, saying that the religious could not leave since they had signed a contract with the bishop to direct the school and to be present throughout the whole school year. And their school was still functioning, since all the students were on the site.

Jose added: "We have to stay for the brothers and for the sisters as well. Do we know what tribe each sister belongs to?"

Tony answered that he had gone over to the sisters the other day and had taken the superior, Sister Gloria, aside and asked her the ethnicity of each religious.

"And what did she say?" Jose asked quizzically.

"Sisters Terezita, Anunciata and she are Bahutu. The other three: Ana, Domitila and Maragarita are Batutsi. So at the sisters there are three Bahutu and three Batutsi." Tony responded logically.

"It would be a shame to see those nice women taken away, as we saw the teachers arrested," Jose said. "The easiest sisters for me to get along with are the three Bahutu. If staying would save their lives, I would suggest that we stay!" The other three admired his courage in wanting to remain behind to help the religious, but also understood that their decision had to be based on helping all the Butova population and not simply one small community of six sisters who happened to be their friends.

Tony then gave his point of view:

"There is no doubt that we would be helping the whole population in general and these sisters in particular by staying. However we have to weigh our actions. If staying means that we all are being puppets for these god-forsaken soldiers, I think we should take a radical position, and pack, leave a letter and quit the area. But on the other hand, if we think that the Batutsi would pulverize the Bahutu because we, the missionaries, would not see them, then we have more influence than I had thought. It will never be easy to decide. God help us. Maybe we should take a few moments privately, try to think clearly and logically by ourselves and then come back into the room, finish the discussion and make a final decision. I suggest that we vote at that time, either to stay or to leave."

After a break of twenty minutes, the men came back to Jose's office and continued their meeting. Luigi said that his mind was clear: they were wasting their time in Butova and his decision was a strong affirmation for the plan to evacuate. Jose spoke up and said he was undecided and that he would go along with the majority. That shocked Tony, not that Jose would officially straddle the fence, but that he would leave the hard decision-making to Luc and Tony. If Luc disagreed with Luigi then the deciding vote could obviously be cast by Tony. It would be his decision entirely for them to stay or leave. If Luc agreed with Luigi, then Tony's vote was superfluous. So in another sense all depended on Luc and if his vote nullified Luigi's, then all would depend on Tony. Yet how ridiculous this whole scenario was since Luc was only nineteen and not a member of their religious community. Despite Tony being the pastor and superior of the mission yet he didn't feel comfortable in making the ultimate decision himself.

"Darn you, Jose," he shouted as he surmised what had happened, "are you not intelligent enough to realize that you are placing both Luc and myself in a terrible bind? If Luc cancels Luigi's vote then I am forced to make the final decision. So I suggest that we all take a piece of paper and vote 'yes' for leaving or 'no' for staying and then we'll count the ballots."

The men passed around bits of paper and the votes were placed in front of Tony. He opened them and three votes said "yes" and the other, to no one's surprise, had a large question mark written on it. They all sat back in their chairs, somewhat relieved that there was partial unanimity and talked about when and how they should evacuate. But Jose only joined in the conversation when they talked about writing a letter that was to be photocopied and left behind for all the people to read. He offered to draft the letter. Tony finally said:

"Well, men, only one thing remains: to bring the decision to the bishop. If you all agree, I'll leave for Vurura early tomorrow morning. If he is not there, I'll stay until he returns. When I get back if he gives his permission, we can decide how and when to leave then. I'm sure the bishop will have his own directives to give us as well!" Tony added sounding relieved that the decision had given them the semblance of unity, Jose added that he thought the bishop would never approve:

"Bishop Moulin has but one interest: to make sure that the mission parish of Butova is serving the catholic population of this area. Imagine when you will go to him! If you tell him that we are all leaving the mission, abandoning the parish as priests, he will fly off the handle and start screaming and yelling and jumping around like a kangaroo all over the place. His blood pressure will go so high, you'll think he is having a stroke! I can hear him now: "*Tu es imbecile! Tu es imbecile, mon pere!!*" (You're an imbecile, Father). The others couldn't help but laugh as they recalled so many instances in the past when the bishop disagreed with someone and would start yelling at the top of his voice: "You're an imbecile! You are an imbecile!"

Tony, calming his laughter, trying to be serious:

"I must tell him that it is a unanimous decision with one abstention. Maybe he will trust us." he added, his voice filled with hope.

The men left their meeting, went to the dining room for supper and spent some time relaxing in recreation after the meal. The evening was filled with old stories, jokes and smiles on the faces of the four colleagues. Tony felt great support from his confreres and for the first time he believed that they were about to give a common witness to their people.

But when he entered his room for the night, he stopped in his tracks after closing the door. He scrutinized his mind and his heart as the questions came at a furious rate. Was he not unjust in not listening to Jose? They were not in agreement in any stretch of the imagination. Was not part of his reason for abandoning the mission, his personal fear and unwillingness to lay down his life for his flock? Had they moved too fast, trying to solve the problems without being willing to suffer personally because of the disunity? What right did they have of preaching unity and love to the people when there was disunity and contradictions between them. He begged God for pardon and asked Him to intervene through the bishop or some other means so that the right decision be made and the divine plan be followed. He had mentioned to Luigi how pleased he was that they finally seemed to be of common mind and heart. But were they? He told the Italian that for the first time in Africa, it felt like they were living as the first christians in the time after Jesus had lived. But were they? The first christian community, depicted in the early chapters of the Acts of the Apostles, was being reenacted in Butova. He had quoted Acts, saying: "The community was of one heart and one mind." Was he serious or the world's biggest dreamer?

They had mapped out a common plan of action. All that remained would be to carry it out! With the difference of personalities, divergence in nationalities, estrangeness of characters and opposition of points of view, this had been a monumental challenge! There was a horrible misunderstanding between these two tribes that differed so much from each other. But dichotomy would not only be among the African tribes. The *Bazungu* would fail to be united, nor would they give common witness to the church or to Christ! 'Love' and 'Unity' were words far easier to say and preach. To live them out would be unachievable.

13. Bishop Bernard Moulin

The next morning, after a fast cup of coffee, Tony left for Vurura. Bishop Moulin was an early riser and Tony hoped to catch him before he would have the chance to leave on safari for a mission station. He arrived at Vurura around 7:45 and met the bishop as he was coming out of the refectory after having breakfast.

"What a surprise to see you so early, Tony!" the bishop exclaimed. Bishop Moulin had aged considerably over the past few weeks. He had turned 69 the day the revolution started in Vurura on April 29th. But he looked more like a man over 80. His face was drawn and he walked with a slower pace than Tony had ever remembered him. Long thin crimson-red blood vessels were visibly showing on his cheeks. It was a known fact that Bishop Moulin had a dreadful case of high-blood pressure and had to be checked quite often by the missionary sisters who had come from Northern Italy. The patriarch was a tall man, with white hair that he kept combed with a part along the right side of his head. He had a small white goatee reminiscent of former days when all missionaries were required to have a beard. He often tugged his facial hair with his fingertips and thumb when he was in a pensive mood. His eyes were sunken into his head but as he smiled they seemed to twinkle, his whole face lighting up in joy. The sisters spent their time telling the stubborn bishop to relax, get lots of exercise and not worry about the many complex problems of his diocese. But if there was one group that the bishop would never take advice from, it was these Italian sisters who spent so much time warning him about his failing health.

The bishop led Tony into his office and they sat down with a small coffee table between them. The table was decorated with a maroon cloth covering it and had an opened Bible on a stand in the middle. But the book was not there for creative beauty! It was hard-covered and had dog-eared pages-corners showing it had been read over and over again. Bishop Moulin gave Tony a welcoming smile before they started chatting as he sensed that it was something important that had brought the priest from Butova so early in the morning. When the bishop had appointed the young missionary as the pastor of such a large parish, he had mentioned that if there were any problems he, the bishop, lived only a one-hour drive away. Furthermore, the bishop had become a man of incredible pastoral experience over the forty-five years he had spent in Burundi. He had been appointed Bishop of Zugozi in 1949, the year Tony started grade school back in Canada! After twelve years in the north, Bishop Moulin was asked to found this new diocese of Vurura. Zugozi was 95% Bahutu, whereas Vurura was in the heart of the Bututsi, probably having a majority Batutsi. Moulin had come to appreciate the Bahutu more than the Batutsi, for their simple ways and loud laughter made them more appealing to his simple tastes. Furthermore he didn't keep it a secret that he loathed the *kitutsi* in the Batutsi.

Vurura diocese had made great progress under the leadership of Moulin over the past eleven years. Parishes had been founded, schools built and African vocations, both clergy and religious, were increasing. But the events of the past weeks were a traumatic experience for the old man who, more than once, had mentioned that he wanted to retire in 1974 on his twenty-fifth anniversary as a bishop. Everyone knew his fondness for his vicar general, Luduvico Ruyaga, and if the bishop had known for certain that his diocese would have been turned over to Ruyaga, he would already have passed on his miter to him. Moulin had been a strong voice at the Ecumenical Council in Rome from 1962-1965 and had applied the teachings and directives of the extraordinary meetings with all the world's bishops to his diocese. He considered the first steps of renewal completed and believed that now was the time for total africanization of the church. The culmination of his work would be to see Monsignor Ruyaga installed as his successor at Vurura.

Before asking Tony the purpose of his visit, Bishop Moulin mentioned that many of the priests in the diocese were rather original in pastoral solutions to fit particular problems and situations that had come up in their areas. He mentioned two parishes on Lake Tanganyika whose pastors had decided to shut down the parish dispensary indefinitely because the soldiers had killed unarmed people in the hospital.

Tony protested somewhat when the bishop told him the story: "That will not help the poor Bahutu since they are probably the ones who will be needing the medical help," he interjected wondering about their own decision for Butova.

"No!" agreed the bishop, "but at the very least it is a sign and witness that we, of the church, are protesting these atrocities."

The ordinary went on to tell Tony another story of how the rector of his cathedral at Vurura, had locked so many Bahutu in the church that they had to cancel mass on Sunday! The bishop sat back in his chair with a large grin on his face as he added:

"That is probably the first time in the history of the church that Sunday mass had to be canceled because there were too many people in church!" he laughed "Or maybe there was too much human feces!" he added making a vulgar joke as he always was prone to do.

Tony saw a way to open the conversation in his favor so he seized the opportunity. He told the bishop how disheartened they all were in Butova. But before he could go any further, Bishop Moulin interrupted to ask about Luc in particular.

"He's probably the strongest of us all," Tony answered with some embarrassment on his face. "He's young and very enthusiastic and doesn't seem overwhelmed by the atrocities. He hasn't been present yet when people are being killed. So he doesn't have any nightmares as Luigi does. The four of us had a meeting yesterday and I have come to present the results of the meeting to you, Bishop" Moulin raised his eyebrows as he often did when surprised at some ideas different from what he had expected:

"And what conclusions have you come to, Tony?" the bishop asked with a tone of sarcasm in his voice. Tony wanted to tell Moulin how difficult it was to speak to him about this and how he wasn't making it any easier by the way he seemed to treat their meeting and decision-making so lightly.

"Bishop Moulin," Tony sat up in his chair and continued rather forcefully, "we have decided that the best pastoral plan for Butova at the present time would be for all of us to address a letter strongly condemning the murders by the government soldiers and then leave the mission, driving away, closing and locking all the doors as a sign of protesting government brutality. We, of course, are not intimidated nor afraid of remaining there but when you have lived among the savagery that we have observed over the past weeks, we believe that something must be done as a clear sign to witness peace and justice and the gospel message of love and respect. So I have come to ask your permission that we abandon the mission as soon as possible."

Bishop Moulin looked up when the silence indicated that Tony had made his point and that he was awaiting a reply. Since the chairs were side-by-side, straddling the table, it was difficult for the two men to look straight at each other. Many times before, Tony had realized that you don't ever speak face-to-face to Bishop Moulin! He looked sideways toward Tony and said:

"I thank you for coming and openly stating your decision. I do hope that you are all in agreement. Was the decision unanimous?" the prelate asked.

Tony turned his body to his right to come as close to Bishop Moulin as the space would permit:

"Yes, Bishop, we all agree but there was one undecided vote."

Moulin interjected showing how well he knew his priests:

"I guess that was Suarez!" Moulin said rather harshly. Tony recalled once hearing the bishop say of his confrere: "You can change a man's heart but you can't change his head." Moulin could never appreciate anyone whose attitude was stubborn.

"Bishop," Tony continued, "he said he would go along with whatever we decided," Tony replied defending his colleague.

"Yes," said Moulin, "but that means that you, Luigi and Luc have decided. You only have three years, plus one, plus one… five years of total experience in Burundi and you are deciding to abandon the mission of 47,000 people?"

Put that way, compared to the bishop's forty-five years of experience in Burundi, Tony felt totally outclassed, defeated, annihilated, abused… dead in the water!

A sense of betrayal overwhelmed Tony as he continued:

"You appointed me knowing my age," Tony went on, "and that I had very little experience in Burundi. You said then that the gift of youth helps all to see the mission through new and virginal eyes: to perceive the work of the spirit without the baggage of the traditions and culture of the past. You mentioned that the new frontier of mission was communities like we have in Butova. But now, you are condemning us for not having experience! You can't have both, Bishop, you can't have it both ways! We, your young missioners, have lived a horrifying two weeks in Butova and now we have decided that we want to be a sign, a witnessing value for the church of Burundi. We want to leave in order to proclaim the gospel of justice and peace."

Moulin seemed, however, to be uncertain if this would be a good decision or not:

"I admire you and the other two young men. However it is not my decision to make, whether you should stay or leave. The governmental authorities won't listen to me when I speak to them. Thus I have decided to turn all diocesan operations over to Monsignor Ruyaga. He is away for the day at Muka. So please stay until he returns and I will see to it that he meets with you as soon as he arrives. I will not stand in the way of his decision, no matter what he decides."

Tony knew his bishop well. The confreres often joked about him, using a French expression: "*Moulin n'a jamais la langue dans la poche!*" (Moulin never has his tongue in his pocket!) He always gave his opinion whether you asked for it or not. Tony had heard the story of how in 1958 Moulin had been in Europe and visiting the Vatican when he mentioned to a Curia member that he didn't allow youngsters who were catechumens to be baptized if they did not know how to read Kirundi. Moulin's argument was that unless they could read in their own African tongue, they would never be able to deepen or keep up their faith and would digress from the practice of catholicism.

The Vatican spy system instantly broke into action. When this 'abuse of power' was reported to the Curia Office for Missions, Bishop Moulin was called on the red carpet (but not given the cardinal's berretta!). He was forcefully told to change his policy immediately and sign a paper to prove he had given his word (what childishness, Moulin once said). Only in this way was Bishop Bernard Moulin allowed to regain his diocese. The whole process kept him, the ordinary, away from his diocese for another eighteen months since he spent much time trying to avoid the signing of a paper that he believed to be a contradiction to his authority, since he was the bishop of Zugozi. It took all that time for the two sides to come to an agreement. The Vatican opposed his logical policy, fearing people not baptized would not go to heaven. The Barundi were without their bishop and no new catechumens for almost two years. Moulin finally re-entered his diocese when the discussion was over and took due pleasure at the Vatican Council telling many of the progressive bishops about what had happened and how the Vatican had in his words 'birth controlled his catechumenate' for eighteen months. "When they finally came to their senses, I re-entered my diocese and set up my own birth control so that no babies, who could not read, were conceived. I finally took off my protection but only allowed my wife to have children who could read!!" The bishop would raise his knee and slap his thigh accompanying the gesture with a huge bellowing laugh coming from the depth of his expanded chest. Moulin had no trouble insisting that the decision to allow the priests to abandon the mission of Butova was to be Ruyaga's. No one else had the right to make such a decision except the African vicar general who had been appointed by the bishop!

Tony stayed at Vurura the whole day which gave him time to pray and visit the different offices of the diocese: the garage, the furniture-making shop and the general store where the diocesan workers were able to buy supplies from Europe at excellent prices. In the afternoon, as he was walking outside following lunch, Bishop Moulin came to join him. The two men walked up and down the path that was behind the cathedral. From time to time the bishop would stop in his tracks and look right at Tony making one point or other. As they walked past the back of the cathedral, Moulin stopped and pointed up to the cathedral that hovered many meters over both of them.

"We were so triumphant, the church of Burundi! We, the missionaries, we thought we had conquered this whole country and won all these savages over for God. Now we realize that all we have done was given them a coat of varnish, constructing buildings and making monuments to ourselves! The church has not been planted in *kirundi* soil. It certainly is not implanted in the hearts of these ungodly people!"

Tony wanted to reach up to his tall bishop and cover his mouth with his hand, to stop him from saying things he would regret in his old age. Certainly Tony felt devastated in hearing this man, who had been a giant in seeding christianity into the loam of Burundi, talk this way. Here was a bishop, a man who had spent his lifetime in Burundi. He had once said, half-jokingly: "And when I come back from the dead, I want to rise in the center of Burundi!" Now he seemed to be regretting his life, almost cursing his vocation and the works of the catholic church. He continued to repeat the words: "We were so triumphant! We were so triumphant! We were so triumphant!"

Later that afternoon, Ruyaga came back to the Bishop's House in Vurura and he, Moulin and Tony sat down in the bishop's office. Tony was very surprised that Moulin, as they entered, offered his chair behind his desk to Ruyaga who gladly sat in a position of power. Both the bishop and Tony sat in the same seats as they had earlier in the morning. Then Tony presented the pastoral team's ideas to Ruyaga to get his approval. He was aware that the vicar general acted in total control and he had to admit to himself that this was certainly the best idea Moulin could have had. Ruyaga was a Mututsi and accepted by the soldiers and the authorities. He was in a position to decide what would be the best for the church and the country at this point. Tony also believed that if there was a Mututsi that respected and loved the Bahutu it was Ruyaga. So, as he spoke, he formed his mind-set. He would accept whatever direction Ruyaga would take!

As Tony presented the details, he could read the Monseignor's decision written all over his face. He, a Mututsi, a brother-priest, the unofficial African leader of the church of Vurura, would never allow the catholic church to become a laughing-stock of southern Burundi by allowing her priests to abandon Butova, the mission in the heart of the Bututsi.

When it was time for the conversation to conclude and a decision to be taken, the answer came from behind the bishop's desk. Monsignor Luduvico Ruyaga didn't hesitate in responding! In fact as Tony concluded his presentation, it seemed like Ruyaga's head was already shaking "NO! NO ! NO !"

"I thank you, Reverend Pere, for coming here to share your concern with me and waiting for me all day. However the answer is a firm: 'No,' which the bishop could have told you earlier, since he knew, like me, that this would leave us in an embarrassing situation in Butova. Do you not realize the problems we have had there in the past? Once, about seven years ago, the three fathers who were there decided to leave, since they were having difficulties and almost fist fights with the people. One of them, the pastor, locked the church doors at the start of mass one Sunday, since the BanyaButova were notorious for being late. The bashingantahe (elders) were so angry at the clergy that the bishop had to go there, correct the situation and appoint three new priests. If you leave now, they will believe that you have done something wrong and we will not be able to appoint another team when this is all over.

Further, there are the sisters and brothers to consider. You must stay there and support them and their efforts. We will give you all the help and support you need, but please don't abandon the mission. In fact, I order you to stay there under any and all circumstances. Failure to comply will result in all Church sanctions including suspension even excommunication!" the vicar general concluded with an inflection in his voice that reflected pomposity.

Tony was mystified! He had not expected such a dictatorial response and Bishop Moulin, always a person to speak at the right moment, said:

"Tony, you have said to me that what you want is to be a sign, a witness to the community, Well, I believe that you can be more a witness by staying, as the vicar says, than by leaving. What I mean is this: if you stay you have the opportunity of saying things exactly as they are and witnessing to their savagery."

Tony immediately understood what the bishop was getting at. "Bishop Moulin, I believe you are right. I told you this morning that I feel sick to my stomach when I have to say mass for them. What do you and Luduvico think if we at Butova would not say mass for them on Sunday? I would love to get up in the pulpit and tell then why we are not celebrating the eucharist. Would you give me permission to not give the sacraments if I promise to explain the situation to the people?" the pastor asked staring from one prelate to the other.

But no response was forthcoming, neither positive nor negative, from either of the authorities. Tony was pleased, thinking: 'silence gives consent' and presumed that permission was granted. He was sure that if either of them had particular reservations, they would soon come forth.

So for the last fifteen minutes of the meeting, the three men discussed what Tony and the other priests should do this coming Sunday. Tony was very pleased and was now seeing the gathering in a positive light. He was glad that he had stayed the whole day in Vurura and that Ruyaga was present for the final decision.

Since the following Sunday, May 21st, was Pentecost, the bishop encouraged him to allow the fire of the Holy Spirit to burn new life into the BanyaButova. He sat back in his seat and started to give directions, as if Tony were taking notes:

"I would write a short homily to explain to the people why you are doing this. Make sure they are all there. The BanyaButova are infamous for being late. Maybe you should have the choir sing a few hymns before and come in rather late so that all will hear what you have to say." As the ordinary spoke, Tony wrote down some points since he always considered the *mukuru* full of wisdom.

Then Monsignor Ruyaga added that he hoped President Sabimana would happen to come to the area and be present at his home parish of Butova on Pentecost Sunday. Ruyaga was sure Sabimana would feel the flames of the Holy Spirit descend on all the catholics in Butova and maybe even be touched himself. Then the vicar general continued with some advice. He mentioned, as Bishop Moulin had a few minutes earlier, that it would be good to start such an important teaching-moment late to be sure that all would hear the message. He added that this might be an opportune time to invite all the catechumens to the church for the service. And he concluded by mentioning that he would consult a few of the African priests he trusted in Vurura and if Tony had not heard from him by sundown Saturday, it was understood that permission had been granted by the Office of the Bishop. Luduvico made this all sound very official. He had not voiced one syllable of contradiction to the Butova community's requests and suggestions to expanding their witnessing.

Tony stood up shook hands with both his bishop and the man who would someday be bishop and drove back to Butova. Night had fallen and it was dark along the road. There were countless barriers and checkpoints but Tony felt peaceful and renewed. He didn't let such trivial things disturb him. His thoughts turned to community witness and he looked forward to getting back to the mission and telling the others about his day at the diocesan offices. As he went by the buildings at the experimental farm of Binka, he wondered what gruesome stories awaited him when he would get back to Butova in the next half-hour. Obviously there would have been more killings and arrests that day. The others would be happy to see him, but their faces would look drawn and pale as they would tell him of the events of the day. He feared what decisions Jose might have made since his judgment was always so flawed. Without someone there to hold him back and force him to think twice about situations, he could easily have made decisions that would have very serious repercussions.

Tony talked to God wondering why such a situation had developed during his first week as Butova's pastor. Further he had questioned why God permitted Jose Suarez to be under his jurisdiction. Once again he pleaded with God to somehow make Jose disappear before the situation got out of control. If, as he now would have to present it to the others, they were forbidden by the religious *bakuru* to leave the mission of Butova, it would be very difficult continuing to live with Suarez. Both Luigi and Luc respected him and they would follow all the directives that they decided together in community meetings. But Jose just made the whole situation unbearable. He always pulled his own way, distancing himself from the others. He was very disappointed that Tony, his junior by six years, had been appointed pastor by the bishop when Mathias left and seemed to continually undermine Tony, especially with his knowledge of Kirundi. But every time Tony asked him to help with something in the native language, he refused. Tony then thought that one way to involve Jose in the decision about not celebrating mass on Sunday was to propose that they write a common homily that Tony would deliver. He would try to get Jose involved directly.

Coming to Luconi and turning right onto the road leading to the Butova mission, the pastor wondered how much blood had spilled that day into the clay earth below his wheels. He said a prayer for the people: fifty? seventy? one hundred?, who had been driven by lorry along this same road and then buried near Vurura. He placed a hand on his brow and could hardly contain himself from thinking of the slaughter that had happened a few hours earlier. Then Tony saw the lights of the Teachers' Training College and drove past the buildings and turned right to enter the mission gate. Luc and Luigi came out to greet him and said that Jose had also just got back. The three went into the living room and Tony started to tell them about the happenings and events of his long encounter with the bishop and Ruyaga.

Jose came into the living room and they continued their conversation about Vurura. Then they decided to have supper allowing only light conversation at the meal. They quickly establishing a particular policy: to keep all further conversation about the decisions they were to make, later for the meeting in the evening. Now was time to relax and try to eat and drink and talk about other more pleasant subjects.

The four men had a pleasant meal and afterwards they took ten minutes to put personal things in order before beginning their serious meeting. They came back into the living room and prayed vespers together. They said special prayers for unity, asking the Father to bind them together in a common decision and give them all the courage to carry out what they were to decide as a team of presbyters for the area.

As the prayer concluded and they put down their breviaries, Tony began by telling them what had transgressed over the course of the day with the bishop and then the vicar general. He mentioned that he now realized that Bishop Moulin was totally out of the picture as the ordinary and could only listen, although he would always be more than willing to give his opinion on any subject! Maybe he was still the bishop in charge of the spirituality of the diocese but everything that pertained to the political circumstances had been turned over to Monsignor Ruyaga. He explained how the bishop had understood their dilemma and had been ready to make Butova an experiment, allowing them to abandon the mission. But then he would not give him permission. He insisted that Tony wait for Ruyaga and when he arrived, he shot down the idea. It had been like a cold shower on a very warm and humid day. He said that he agreed with Ruyaga's second argument that the brothers and sisters needed protection and support. He added that he really didn't appreciate Ruyaga's first point: that he would never be able to appoint another team of priests. Sarcastically, out of the side of his mouth, he said that he didn't know another priest who would want to come to Butova anyway. He further added that the BanyaButova should be left priestless after all these horrible events. As he was concluding his expose, Jose cut in:

"I am having second thoughts myself," he said. "I don't think we should make any major decisions. To abandon the mission would be a mistake. And it would also be wrong to denounce the government policy in writing or condemn it verbally from the pulpit!"

Tony felt red-flame anger rise to his neck and face. His cheeks were flushed. But he controlled himself and simply said that it was not what he heard the bishop say at Vurura and Monsignor Ruyaga agreed with him. They had strongly suggested that the priests of Butova give particular witness through the pulpit.

Tony then raised his voice:

"The bishop and Ruyaga said to make as many strong witnessing-decisions as you can, but don't abandon the mission. Put as much pressure as possible on all the people, the police, the soldiers and the *bakuru*, but do not leave."

Jose turned towards Tony. As eyes met, Tony was pleased that they were able to have eye-to-eye contact. Oftentimes at important conversations, Jose would not look at Tony when he disagreed with him. But the two men were now eyeball-to-eyeball:

"The bishop agreed that we not celebrate Eucharist for the people on Sunday but rather wait until they are all in church, have a Liturgy of the Word and then explain why we can not celebrate mass."

Jose's face became flushed and he responded directly:

"Ah zoot! How can we have a Sunday without the Eucharist? That is the catholic peoples' right. There are some who come to mass and communion every day. Are you going to tell them that they cannot receive communion on Pentecost Sunday?" Jose snarled in an agitated voice.

"Yes, I am!" replied Tony. "I presented an idea to the bishop and Ruyaga and they encouraged it and gave me many creative ideas. What more can I say but that is what the diocesan *bakuru* expect us to do."

"Well, I will have to think about that one," responded Jose. "I can't remember a Sunday when I didn't celebrate mass," he scoffed.

"Maybe you could make a sacrifice and offer up your disappointment for the people. I think it is a good idea." said Luigi looking at Tony with strong affirmation.

Tony thought of the many evenings when Jose would return late for supper. He would be so tired that he could hardly move and his body ached for his bed. But Jose would ask him and Mathias to come to chapel so that he would have the courage to celebrate 'his mass'. The three would drag their tired bones into the chapel so that Jose wouldn't 'miss mass' that day and with all three almost falling asleep, they would long for the mass to be over. Suarez certainly had a warped understanding of mass and so much guilt about missing one. Tony realized that there was an enormous problem there that they couldn't discuss at the present moment.

They then asked Luc to give his opinion. He said that whatever they decided as a community, he would support. He also added that he thought it a novel idea to have a Liturgy of the Word on Sunday and tell the people that they were unworthy to celebrate the sacrament of love and unity and peace. He added;

"I was wondering how the people would give the sign of peace to each other during the mass last Sunday. But they did. Another meaningless ritual of the catholic church that is totally void of sincerity. Everyone reached out to everyone else, even though they had witnessed against each other during the past week to the extent where people had been killed because of it. Or they accused each other and then on Sunday went about smiling and pretending to love one another. '*M. Untel* (Mr. Someone) went to church on Sunday but he went to hell for the things he did on Monday!' Hypocrites all of them, '*Maudits Hypocrites*'!" he concluded.

Tony reached out to Jose asking him to pray and open his heart to what the Spirit was indicating through the bishop, vicar general and the three others in this room. Jose sat back and said he would think it over but could not promise to collaborate with them. The pastor responded by saying that the problem between the Batutsi and the Bahutu was disunity which had led to jealousy, mistrust, hoarding, envy and finally hatred and murder. And it was time for the fathers to come together and show how strong they could be when they were united. He added that sometimes pride can stand in the way of the right decision:

"This is not the time for you to make a decision to show balanced divergent opinions," Tony accosted, "but we must be united when we go to church together on Sunday morning." Yet deep in his heart he wondered if Jose could ever be united in thought and ideas with anyone over anything.

They concluded the meeting by praying compline together and as they prayed, Tony asked His God for a spirit of unity between Jose and himself. But he recognized that he was asking God for something these traumatized mortals would never receive.

14. Father Mikieli Kayoya Is Dead!

Friday May 19th was already overcast as Fr. Tony walked from his room to the wash station down the corridor and outside the prayer chapel. He dreaded the dawning of a new day and feared events beyond anyone's control that might come *a l'improvist* from all directions. As he washed his face, he heard a person approach, heels dragging on the cement floor. He turned and, to his surprise, saw Fr. Jose sauntering to the chapel. He was pleased that Jose had risen early. It was unusual for him to be a half-hour early for anything, especially morning prayer. He normally was overtired and had trouble waking-up. The seminary had trained both men to be comfortable in absolute silence before breakfast. Normally they only communicated via gestures or signs. To get into a conversation, no matter how important the subject might be, was hardly thinkable for either man. It was their "alone-time" with God and a constant reminder of how celibacy led to being introverted. They had both been trained in the era of *magnum silentium* (Great Silence) when it was forbidden to talk for any reason from night prayer until breakfast.

Going back to his room, Tony dressed quickly, and soon found his way back to the chapel. Luigi Franco had also come into the prayer room so the three priests knelt before the Blessed Sacrament, praying for their beloved Barundi and probably for each other as well. It was two days before the feast of Pentecost and their common prayer was to ask enlightenment from the Holy Spirit. Tony reflected on the marvelous story: how the Holy Spirit descended on the Apostles in tongues of fire and the Disciples spoke and praised God, each in his own language. He prayed that at this Pentecost '72, his people would hear the Holy Spirit speak to them in Kirundi and descend on them in a powerful manner. He wondered if this fire would burn with passion within every person of the parish renewing the face of the earth in a modern-day Pentecost. But he also worried that the absence of mass would cause consternation and anxiety, and justify their already hardened positions in tribal hatred? It was difficult to predict which way the people would go after they learned of the canceled Pentecost Eucharist. It was a gesture Tony believed had to be posed. Yet it could also end in disaster.

The confreres prayed Lauds together and concluded the prayer of the Church slightly before seven o'clock. Tony got up and left to celebrate mass in the church and Jose and Luigi were joined by Luc at the breakfast table.

Later in the morning, after having a quick breakfast, Tony walked down the corridor to go to his office. An old woman named Clara who came to mass every morning was waiting for him outside the door of his office. As the pastor approached, she stood up and greeted him. He always had trouble understanding what Clara was saying, since she talked into her *impuzu* out of shyness and humble respect for the priest. It seemed, as Clara spoke to him mouthing into her *sari* that was thrown over her left shoulder, that she rebuked Fr. Tony for not having prayed for the deceased priests earlier at mass. Tony, mystified, asked her what she was talking about, what priests were dead? She proceeded to tell him the horrendous story of what had taken place to the north of Gisumu. The horrible murders continued in this sad country and now they were even killing their priests. Three priests! Professors at the middle-seminary of Bugera, killed by soldiers who had invaded the privacy of this school of formation for future priests. Clara had a tear in her eye as she continued:

"One of them was Pati Mikieli Kayoya!" Tony was as flabbergasted as Clara was tearful and they both reached out to console each other realizing the uselessness and tragedy of what had happened. Tony, with deep feelings of despondency, finally prayed a short prayer for the deceased priests with Clara and then bid the old lady *adieu*. Alone in his office, he went over to his desk and pounded on the wooden table and wanted to curse and swear and damn a god who seemingly did not care.

Mikieli Kayoya was, thought Tony, the leading cleric in the Church of Burundi. He was a poet, a writer, a story-teller, a teacher, a holy priest and an intelligent theologian. Word had already leaked out that he was next in line to receive a bishop's miter and would do honor to that office as well as to his ethnic or tribal origin, for he was a Muhutu. But now he was dead! Clara had told Tony that the soldiers had come to the seminary looking for three Bahutu priests who, they believed, had preached racial-over toned homilies against the government. They found the three priests in the dining room singing hymns from their religious song books and prepared for the worst. The soldiers put the three clerics up against the wall of the refectory and riddled their bodies with bullets. With this scene had died much of the hope of the Bahutu tribe as well as the whole Roman Catholic Church of Burundi!

"What, for God's sake" Tony heard himself ask out loud, "is left of Bahutu leadership when the whole *intelligentsia* is being eliminated

Tony let the sheet drop to his desk, put his palms to his face and felt the tears trickle down his cheeks. Right now he had absolutely no thirst for Jesus Christ. God must be the father of all ironies to have allowed the vile Batutsi soldiers, the majority of whom were roman catholic, to kill this man who could have continued to lead thousands to Christ. What a deception! What irony! What a dichotomy. What rubbish! As he reread the poem, Tony realized that the author had been a contemplative. He knew Jesus Christ in the spiritual sense and thus he also knew the frustration of possessing the greatest truth in the world yet being unable to communicate it to those who needed it the most. Kayoya was executed with two other priests by a firing squad that was sent to the seminary where he taught. Tony wondered what must have gone through the priest's mind as he looked out at the soldiers, pointing guns that would bring eternal silence to his prophetical tongue. Did he not see them as persons of little worth who will never know Jesus Christ? But what consolation must have been his when he realized that his time on earth was completed since he had the only necessary baggage for his journey: he knew Jesus Christ! As Fr. Mikieli Kayoya looked out at his assassins standing behind dining room tables, he saw the irony of these hostile soldiers in a refectory with nothing but emptiness, hunger and thirst within themselves. They yearned to be filled but would be famished forever because they did not know Jesus Christ!

Tony took his hands away from his face and looked down at the sheet of poetry staring back at him from the desk top. Yes, Mikieli loved nobly to the very end. He knew Jesus Christ in this world and now he was contemplating His glory and grandeur for all eternity in heaven. He tried to console himself with the thought that Mikieli Kayoya, like Jesus Christ, must have given up his life rather than have it snatched away from him. He died in the arms of the Lord and even though he died, humanly and politically a defeated and ostracized man, nevertheless, he was the victor. "By loosing your life," Christ had said, "you gain it!"

Tony reflected on how Kayoya, whose name meant "little child", might have lost some human years but he gained an everlasting reward for all eternity. Kayoya, the priest with the child-like faith, was silenced a few days previously, but now his message will be proclaimed to every corner of the globe: This man knew Jesus Christ and laid down his life for Him!

Tony felt his lips quiver and heard these words from his own mouth:

"Good Mikieli in heaven, pray for us, pray for your people who are suffering so much here in Butova and throughout your beloved Burundi, *Burundi Bwacu*." He slumped to his knees with his hands joined in prayer still resting on his desk.

Hearing a rap on his door, Tony was surprised to find Jose turning the handle and entering. He had just heard the news about Kayoya and was taking it very badly as well. Jose had gone to a retreat two years earlier lead by Fr. Mikieli and had developed a fondness as well as a deep appreciation and respect for this strong Muhutu. He, too, could not believe that Kayoya was dead, and wanted to trust against hopelessness that there had been a mistake about the whole episode. But the only mistake was that the soldiers had eliminated a marvelous Murundi leader. Tony took advantage of the situation to tell Jose that they must remain more united than ever before. They were fighting a common enemy, for Satan was truly alive and preying on everyone. Perfect honesty and the gospel values would be the only way to witness to Christ and handle this horrific situation. Jose was so overcome with sadness and sorrow that Tony wondered if his colleague had even heard his words.

Later that morning, Tony received a visit from three women. They were Gaudentia Bucumi, Marita Minani and Superanca Gikobwa. He knew the three women from having seen them often at mass and around the parish common. They entered his office together and sat on the bench in front of his desk. Each woman reported that her husband had been killed over the past few days by the Batutsi soldiers. They asked Tony for spiritual support to ease their pain and financial help to feed their children. They said that they had not spent much time in their gardens over the past weeks because they had to scrounge around for food to bring to their husbands who had been detained.

Tony took out a note pad and drew some vertical lines on his horizontally etched paper. He asked the widows pertinent questions about how their husbands were arrested, where they were taken, who brought witness against them, how they were finally taken away and what methods or devices were used to snuff them out. Fr. Tony was somewhat uneasy about asking these young widows and mothers to describe the horrendous crimes that had been committed against their husbands. But with great determination, the pastor continued. Never for a moment had he dreamt that over the next six weeks he would continue such interrogations until he would have recorded over eleven hundred deaths, every one leaving behind widows and orphans, parents and siblings, everywhere in his parish! His heart swelled in admiration for the courage of these three women whose poor husbands had been snatched away and murdered at the hands of ruthless rogues.

Gaudentia told the story of how they had come for her husband two hours after they had arrested his brother. They accused him of going over the border into Tanzania and buying machete knives that the rebels used when attacking the military camps during the first and only night of the revolution, April 29th. Tony asked her if he was ever away from the house and she said;

"Never, never did he ever go near the Tanzanian border and hadn't slept outside our family home since we were married!" she recounted with bewilderment on her face.

When Tony asked her why they had killed her husband, Gaudentia replied with strong disdain:

"Ni Muhutu! Ni Muhutu!" (He was a Muhutu! He was a Muhutu!)

Then Superanca (name derived from the French: "*Esperance*" meaning "hope") told the most horrible of all stories:

"*Pati*, they arrested my husband and took him to a dry part of the terrain. There they threw him to the ground and took large nails and hammered them into his hands and feet against the hardened earth. He died in the same way as Our Lord and Savior, Jesus Christ died, nailed to the cross!"

Tony's face grew white with horror. He took some money from his bill fold and divided it among the three women. He asked them how many children each had to feed at home. Gaudentia said "benchi" (many) and Marita and Superanca expressed their needs as well. He gave them some cooking oil and powdered milk and told them to pass the word around among the other widows that they could seek help at the mission. The three young women expressed their appreciation and left quickly, each with a young baby on her back As they left, Tony reflected that these three mothers and babies represented so many women and children who had become widows and orphans at the hands of barbarous murderers. Would any other situation in life be worse than what these Barundi had done to each other? As Tony went through his day he wondered how the situation could become any worse. He thought of a saying he often used in a comical fashion: "Cheer up, things could get worse! And I cheered up and sure enough, things got worse!" Tony Joseph truly believed that he would never smile again. Yet little did he know that there were still six days of killings in Butova that would reach preposterous proportions before it all was over.

The mission had become idle, even quiescent, over the past three weeks. When Mathias had been pastor, Butova Mission had been a thriving center from early morning to dusk. Tony had looked forward to continuing

Mathias' vision of receiving all the Barundi with courtesy and warm friendship. However since the soldiers and police had been roaming about the area over the past weeks, people had feared coming to the mission. In the afternoon, the area, that had once thrived with the buzzing of activity around the parish offices, was now barren and strikingly deserted.

After lunch, Fr. Tony went to his office to prepare his Sunday homily. He thought the best place to start would be to write down the reasoning for not celebrating mass as precisely and concisely as possible and ask people to go home and pray that peace be restored to their area and throughout the whole country. He opened his missal at the Sunday readings and said a prayer to the Holy Spirit to give him the gift of wisdom and enlightenment. The truth had to be said. The decision had to be explained to the people. Yet it had to be done, not to incur rage, anger or frustration. The gospel of love had to be proclaimed but not in a way that people would mistrust the message, disregard the overall ideals, or see the gospel values as interfering with them politically. He continued to ask for God's help, as he did before preparing each and every homily. But this time, his communication skills would be challenged! The future of the mission depended on the way that the pastor could speak to his people and invite them to turn inwardly, seeking pardon and reconciliation and not outwardly, coldly rejecting his homily as a judgment of white *Bazungu* (Non-Africans) on black Africans. It would be tricky! He felt as if he were walking on egg shells: inviting the people to true contrition as well as opposing their fears and arrogance. He realized that his Kirundi would not be good enough to make clear distinctions but he counted on Jose to put the homily into *Kirundi ciza* (good Kirundi). Jose did speak the language like a native and had a way of turning expressions to make people smile at the truthfulness of a statement. Tony prayed, asking God to help Jose participate in the homily and realize how much he could contribute. He hoped that Jose's heart be changed and that he use his gifts to witness to the gospel and not try to draw attention to himself by rejecting their common witness.

Fr. Tony opened his Bible and read the different texts that explained the mystery of Pentecost. The Acts of the Apostles described in colorful detail how the hearts of the apostles were changed through the gift of the Holy Spirit. The first chapter of Acts had been read in the church nine days before on the feast of the Ascension. Now was the time to move on to the second chapter, the story of how the Holy Spirit descended on the apostles and disciples and filled them all with the presence of God. Tony wondered how he could retell the story in the context of what was happening in Butova and throughout Burundi. How he yearned that the people would invite the Spirit of God to lead them from sin and oppression to grace and freedom. He flipped to the front of his bible and read the story of the tower of Babel in chapter 11 of Genesis. He then turned to the prophet Ezekiel, chapter 37, and read about the dead men's bones coming to life and manifesting the power of God's Spirit. So many men had died in Burundi. Hopefully they would not die in vain but the power of God's Spirit would overwhelm the whole tragedy. He read the story of Acts, chapter two, once again and felt the power of the Spirit coming upon him and gifting him with wisdom and peace... "a strong divine wind, and tongues of fire resting on everyone!" He imagined people at Sunday Mass being inundated by the power of God and recreating the Church anew. But then Tony started to doubt... not so much his strength as a preacher of the gospel or the fact that he still was a neophyte in the native language. He doubted the power of God to change the situation, the power of the Holy Spirit to transform men into believers and doers of the word! He had seen too much killing, heard too many words of hatred, listened to too many threats of revenge and too many screams of horror....that he now realized, in this unforgettable nightmare, that literally God had abandoned the country. God wasn't to be found in the hatred and the murders and the false charges and the torture and the anger and the lying. God had vanished, fled the country and no matter what Fr. Anthony Joseph, pastor and 28-year-old missionary could and would do, God was not in the country, the mission, the church, the province, the people, the sacraments! It was all pious verbiage, a figment of a person's imagination. It had been a nice dream, but now the little boy had to grow up and put away the fantasies of the seminary. He doubted that Christ was even in the host that dwelt so passively and helplessly in the tabernacle of the church and the little chapel down the hall. God had left! He was gone! It fact, God had never been there. Heartless country, God-less people, abandoned by love and now disemboweled by brothers Tony felt so cynical, so downtrodden. He felt a tear flow from his eye down his cheek and fall onto the white stationery on his desk where he had been unable to write a word. He took up his pen and printed very largely on the paper: "Help Me! Help Me!!". He stood up and threw his pen across the room, crushed the soiled paper in his massive hands and proceeded to rip it to shreds. He then threw the mess into his wastebasket and stormed from his office. He dared not present the ugly thoughts he had in his mind to his parishioners on Sunday. He wanted to dig a big hole in the garden outside and jump into it and bury himself and his dismal feelings forever.

Tony walked into the dining room to get a cup of coffee and, to his pleasant surprise, Luigi was there also pouring himself some imagined cappuccino from the flask on the table. The pastor needed to talk, so the two men sat down and Tony expressed his frustrations. Luigi agreed with him and said that he, too, was totally despondent. Coffee over, the two men decided to go for a walk and visit the African sisters at their house down the roadway. Luigi grabbed his guitar and said he could only relax by singing and needed an audience. Tony laughed at him jokingly saying it would give the sisters an opportunity to practice charity! Actually Luigi had a lovely deep baritone voice and everyone enjoyed his fine music and singing. How many wonderful evenings they had spent together singing and playing and enjoying the fraternal life God had blessed them with at Butova Mission.

The Beneterezia Sisters greeted the two fathers with great excitement that was their way of showing appreciation for a visit from the local clergy. The sisters led them into their common room and set some *inzoga* (banana beer) in front of their guests. Even though the fathers had just finished a cup of coffee, one never refused the sign of hospitality in Burundi! So they willingly accepted the bamboo straws and drank from a large pitcher along with the superior, Sister Gloria. Then after the fathers drank freely three times, the other sisters approached the large pitcher and sipped three times, also in groups of threes. As was the custom throughout Burundi, the sisters would put the straw in three times and take it out thrice, all in unison. Thus was the ritual for drinking *inzoga* together and no one ever ventured from the customs or traditions.

Luigi crossed the room, picked up his guitar and started singing and playing. The thoughts of being a butterfly filled Tony's mind as the words sung by Luigi, with his strong Italian accent mispronouncing simple English words, made Tony smile. They all hummed along as Luigi played for an hour or so, and then Tony mentioned to him that it would be good to visit the Canadian brothers across the compound. The sisters accompanied them, although the brothers did not speak Kirundi very well and the sisters spoke little French. But this would be a time of relaxation and trying to find strength to go on believing against disbelief that God was somehow with them and guiding them through this tragedy.

The two priests and six sisters arrived at the Brothers' Residence and began singing outside, on the compound steps. Brother Jean-Guy Tranchemontagne came to the door and had a smile on his face, a grin from ear to ear, as he invited them all to come in. He led them into the living room and one-by-one the rest of the community joined them, having heard the song and music. Brother Alex Labine always seemed a little out- of-place and stiff-necked in social gatherings. He entered, followed closely by some of the others who were already singing. It was hard to believe that these religious were dealing with life and death situations every moment of each day and yet took time to gather together with others who were consecrated to the church of Burundi. Jubilation permeated the whole room. They were able to put their problems on hold for a little while and enjoy the music and songs and each other's company. Tony realized that they should have more of these moments when they could all come together and have fun singing and laughing and joking. They all sat back and every face was smiling and laughing and filled with joy. What a delightful spontaneous gesture of fraternity and friendship they expressed to each other. Suddenly, God did not seem so distant from Tony's life anymore!

Tony realized the marvelous response he had now received from God! God was not dead! God lived on the face and in the heart of each and every person that graced this room. If God were in this room, then He had not left Burundi. Despite the ugliness and sinfulness of the situation, God was here in every tragic and bleak moment, supporting them all! God could not leave. The only despair was believing that He had gone and that He would dare turn His Holy Face away from His people. As Tony and Luigi walked the sisters home and then doubled back to the mission, they felt relieved and inwardly freed. Tony had not written his homily, but he now had the strength of the Spirit to write and say what he must as God's chosen prophet to the BanyaButova. (those of Burundi).

As night fell, the missionaries gathered in the dining room for the evening meal. Luigi led the prayer-before-meals and asked for strength that they continue to witness to the gospel values of Jesus Christ. Jose wasn't there so they started the meal without him. He could be anywhere and they dared not think of what mischief he could be creating. As they were finishing their soup, Jose burst into the dining room, exasperated and seemingly very angry:

"I went over to Piga for the rosary and all the people are saying that they will arrest Petero Tumba very soon. It seems that his name has come up quite often at the public trials. "Many of the Batutsi I talked to are happy that he is being accused and want him arrested as soon as possible," Jose said with his voice dripping with disdain for the accusers.

At that moment, Cypriano Kitwi entered with some warm soup for Jose. The confreres lowered their voices to make sure that Cypriano, who didn't understand French, would not get the drift of what they were saying if they mentioned names, hillsides or used other Kirundi expressions. When Cypriano went back outside to the kitchen, Tony asked Jose to elaborate on what he had heard and who was accusing Petero. Everyday they all heard rumors, mentioning many different Bahutu by name. But the pastor realized that in several instances, the Batutsi made up stories and accusations of certain Bahutu whom they wanted to see put to death. So he wondered who the culprits were that were trying to get Petero Tumba liquidated. Jose mentioned a few names but Tony didn't know them.

The discussion then turned to Petero Tumba. He was a good looking young man in his early twenties who had been raised in the strong Kihutu traditions of Muka. His family was well known to Mathias when he served the BanyaMuka as a young priest. When Mathias was appointed to Butova, he saw to it that Petero was enrolled at the catechists' school near Bujurundi. It was a three-year course and Petero applied himself diligently. He possessed a beautiful tenor voice and after he graduated from the catechists' school, Mathias offered him a job in Butova. Catechist Tumba became enthusiastically involved with the ministry at the central mission and taught the Banyabatisimu (those preparing for baptism) in their final year of catechumenate. He often sang solos and directed the choir when Sister Maragarita was absent or involved in other activities. At choir practice, when Petero directed, Tony had noticed that the *banyachoir* (choir members) were quite jealous of the catechist from Muka. Actually Tony realized that with someone like Petero, the sisters became obsolete because he could teach with more imagination, sing more beautifully and speak French better than any of the religious. Petero would converse with the fathers on their level and attend parish meetings with the clergy that were normally held in French. Tony had a special affection for Tumba because he seemed like such a nice, clean-cut young man. He often teased him about the girls being attracted to him because he had an important position in the parish. He was very good looking and had a gorgeous smile. Petero had a thin mustache above his top lip that made his good looks stand out even more. Tony thought that he looked like a black Clark Gable.

Tumba lived at the mission. This was another thing that set him off from the other run-in-the-mill catechists and even created some jealousy among the school teachers and other intellectuals living at Butova. In the evenings, they normally gathered in the recreational hall. Most of them were Batutsi. So they had developed a hatred for Tumba since he was a Muhutu, and a successful one. They considered him different, and attributed the incongruity to his coming from Muka which was considered a poorer area. However the sophisticated catechist held his own and weathered many storms, keeping good relationships with everyone. But his charm didn't prevent him from being loathed by the Batutsi intellectuals.

Petero Tumba lived in a small room in the back of the mission with the back door opening onto the big courtyard of the fathers and the front door opening onto the roadway beyond the back walls of the mission. In the evenings when the gates were locked and the dogs were released to protect the missionaries from thieves, Tumba could come out his back door and into the mission compound. However since his room ran along the protective wall of the mission, his front door led outside the compound. People walked back and forth in front of his door allowing him to be in the center of life at Butova, both in the daytime as well as in the evening. It was here, beside the catechumenate, that Deogratias Pungu had been arrested on that fatal Ascension Thursday.

Petero Tumba lived with another trained catechist who had also graduated from the catechists' school near Bujarundi. His name was Saverino Imbwa, a Mututsi from Mutwe and a favorite of Father Angelo Bertuzzi. He had sent Imbwa to the catechists' school but when he graduated, Bertuzzi didn't seem to want him in his home parish and talked Mathias into taking him at Butova. Imbwa was rather lazy and slow moving and seldom worked hard preparing his catechetical classes. Anytime he could get out of work, he managed to do so. Tony didn't like Imbwa very much and after Mathias left, he sought an opportunity of getting rid of him. He once mentioned to Luigi that with the money paid Imbwa, five other part-time catechists could be hired who had families to support.

Petero Tumba, the Muhutu, and Saverino Imbwa, the Mututsi, lived together, cooked for each other and slept in the same quarters. They shared the same debts, pooled their money for purchases and were often seen together. The missionaries sometimes wondered how well the two got along since tribalry was so critical an issue in Burundi. But Mathias had often bragged that they had two catechists trained at the catechetical school who lived together and ate at the same table, sharing the same dishes, food, and debts. He used them as an example of unity and harmony between the two tribes. "Was it not the love of Christ that gathered these two men of the gospel together in one home and made them witnesses to all the Barundi?" Tony had thought. The answer was yet to come.

Still at table, Jose, Luigi, Luc and Tony broached the situation that involved Tumba. Since he was a Muhutu, it was extremely dangerous for him in this area around Butova. Jose volunteered to go back to the catechists' room after supper and tell Tumba to beware of the immanent dangers. He would ask Petero to stay in his room over the next few days since he needed to keep a low-profile and not provoke any Mututsi enemy into a regretful situation. He'd get the two catechists together, and tell Imbwa that he was the one to go out for the food and teach all the classes, both Tumba's as well as his own. Jose would even forbid Petero to put his head outside his front door.

As the others spent some time in the common room after the meal, Jose concluded his task of talking to the two catechists. He didn't get back to the mission until after nine o'clock. So on his way back, he turned off the motor since the others were in their rooms already getting ready for a quite night's sleep.

Tony lighted his oil lamp and attempted to finish his homily for Sunday. He realized that until it was finished, he would not rest peacefully. So he went to his office, picked up his notes and Bible and brought them back to his bedroom and hoped he could complete it quickly and then get to sleep. Once again he prayed to the Holy Spirit asking help and guidance to deliver the message that God wanted the people to hear. His gathering with Luigi at the sisters' and then with everyone at the brothers' had brought him some inner peace and satisfaction. He felt enlightened, energized and ready for the homily, the most important one of his life. Above all, he felt calm and peaceful and psychologically ready to convey a special message. If his heart were unsettled, how could he ever talk about peace? If there was hatred in his soul, how could he ever talk about love? He remembered what he had been taught in homily class years ago in the seminary: "One cannot give what one doesn't have!" Now filled with peace and harmony, he readied himself to proclaim the gospel message. His attitude seemed to change from one of total pessimism to a semblance of optimism, as the joy of preaching the message of the gospel filled his heart. Surely this was the worst of times but maybe it was also the best of times to hear the evangelical message. He longed to deliver a prophetical statement based on the gospel principles of Jesus Christ. In any case, Tony knew that he would have a captive congregation on Sunday and he remembered the passage of St. Paul: "Cursed be I, if I do not preach the Gospel of Christ". He had no choice but to deliver this gospel message and to speak his words clearly, precisely and emphatically. It would be a "K.I.S.S. homily". Keep It Short & Sweet!

Since many of the BanyaButova came late to Mass every Sunday and often arrived after the gospel and homily, Tony decided to wait and start the church service thirty minutes late. That would keep the people anticipating what was being prepared and would give the latecomers a chance to be there for the message. He would also close the catechumenate and invite all the catechumens to join the baptized at the church service. Many were preparing for baptism into the catholic church. Was there a better place to hear the official teaching on social justice and condemnation of this genocide but in the church building itself? Since such a large number of parishioners came to Sunday Mass and filled the church from the altar to outside, Tony realized he would have a captive congregation. To create a special effect, there would be no choir. He would tell Sister Maragarita that she had the day off and the *banyachoir* would sit outside the sanctuary with the rest of the people. No one would be asked to read. The fathers themselves would do all: readings, prayers, preaching. He didn't want anyone to participate in any way whatsoever. This was the missionaries time to witness and take total responsibility for proclaiming God's Word.

Fr. Tony realized that if he tried to combine the two themes: praying for peace as well as the coming of the Holy Spirit, there would be great confusion in the minds of all the people. He had to be extremely precise and deal with the immediate situation and that alone. Any thoughts of the gifts and fruits of the Holy Spirit would have to wait for another occasion. Tony needed to be guided by the Holy Spirit to proclaim the gospel values of forgiveness and reconciliation. Tony decided to change the readings he had already chosen. He took a piece of paper and turned to the story of Cain and Able in Genesis. Since all who would be attending this Sunday liturgy were brothers and sisters in Christ and yet were murdering and killing each other by the hundreds, it would be a timely message: "Don't be like Cain who killed his brother Able unjustly."

The second reading would be from the Apostle Saint John where, in his first Epistle, he says: "Anyone who says he loves God and hates his brother is a liar." Strong language! But didn't Bishop Moulin accuse all the BanyaButova of being liars? They were weak in obeying the sixth commandment and even weaker to the seventh. But their greatest fault was the eighth! "Liars, liars, all of them are liars," Tony thought. "They lie in not speaking the truth. They lie in inventing stories to accuse one another. Then they lie in not accepting their sisters and brothers whom God has given to them to live with in peace and work side-by-side with for the fulfillment of God's promise: a Burundi that should resemble the Risen Body of Christ. They are liars, liars all of them liars!" Fr. Tony felt nauseated, overcome by anxiety and grief but put his mind to the task at hand: preparing the Sunday liturgy.

Once the pastor decided not to use the usual Gospel of Pentecost, it was easy for him to choose the text of the main Scripture: the story of the Good Samaritan. He turned to Luke's Gospel, chapter ten, and read the verses starting with the twenty-fifth. Tony decided to end the gospel reading before coming to the precise parable of the Samaritan, since he didn't want the people to be caught up with the idea of ministering to the sick or needy. The gospel asked the question: "and who is my neighbor?" This would be an excellent way of presenting the gospel message: the Batutsi should reflect on their acceptance of the Bahutu and the latter were called to love the former, despite their cruelty. But it struck Tony as extremely difficult, a demand that a normal Murundi was incapable of accepting. His heart filled with cynicism again as he realized that the gospel message was far beyond the human capabilities of his people. In fact he had even abandoned the idea that God's grace could make a difference. Burundi was beyond salvation!

Tony decided that after the gospel reading he would leave time for silent reflection allowing the message to stand for itself. He would invoke silence after the other two readings as well. Then, in a homily, he would go back to the pulpit and simply tell the people that there would be no mass this day because mass is the celebration of our unity and peace in Christ as children of God and there is absolutely no peace nor unity among the BanyaButova. So there can be no mass! He wondered how they would accept the message. The BanyaButova were a proud people and had strongly shown displeasure with the missionaries tactics a few years earlier when they accused the people of being slothful and lazy. The people demanded a change of all clergy immediately and Bishop Moulin had obliged. Tony put his head down on his table and wished he were a million miles from Butova. When he had accepted the pastorship a few weeks earlier, he never thought such an albatross would be placed around his neck. But he was the pastor. The bishop had chosen him and had approved of his idea of telling the people why, in conscience, he believed he could not celebrate mass. He would accept his responsibilities.

Fr. Tony finally raised his head from his desk and felt numbness in his forehead from leaning against the wooden table. But now he knew where he was to go with the homily. He put the ideas on paper, first in outline form in English and then developed the equivalent ideas in Kirundi. He had hoped that Jose would help but now the idea had to be abandoned. What the hell! His Kirundi was good enough to explain the message loud and clear. He finished writing on both sides of a lined piece of paper, blew out the lamp and got into bed. Fr. Tony slept soundly hoping the strategy of his contrivance had now been mapped out and believed God was pleased with his work. The Lord was the builder and Tony prayed for the strength to build according to the plans of the Master Craftsman. He would not succumb to the temptation of deviating from the Lord's blueprint.

15. Preparing For Pentecost

Tony awoke on Saturday May 20th well rested and filled with a spirit of hope. He was a man entrusted with a mission, and nothing or nobody would deny him fulfilling his obligations and responsibilities. He felt guided by God and heard himself whistling and singing a song from time to time that morning as he went about his business in the parish office.

At about eleven o'clock Tony heard a car approach and when he went to the window of his office, he saw a beige volkswagen go by at a fairly high speed as he caught sight of the driver's dark blue beret on top of his head. Tony jumped and yelled at the same time 'Lambert!'. He had recognized the driver as his regional superior, Father Jean Lambert, a Frenchman who lived in Bujarundi. Obviously Lambert had been permitted to travel in the interior of Burundi to visit over 200 Missionaries of Africa for whom he was responsible. Three years ago, Lambert had come to the airport to welcome Tony, who had been edgy in beginning his missionary life. Right away a fine friendship was formed and Tony's fears dissipated. Tony respected Lambert for his knowledge and spiritual values. The fact that he had come to visit at such a crucial time was like a breath of fresh air, a gift coming straight from heaven.

Tony closed and locked his office door and moved around to the back courtyard where Lambert had just parked his car and was walking towards the house. Tony ran to meet him and shook his hand enthusiastically as Lambert asked him how things were going. The pastor made a special effort to smile and said that things had been better in the past but that the confreres were managing despite the frightful atmosphere. He invited Lambert into the common room for a coffee and pointed to the sink and running water outside the chapel and mentioned he could wash up if he so desired. Living with the Barundi had taught most missionaries that they should wash their hands before eating and drinking. And Lambert was coming from a long safari on the dirty roads. So he gladly accepted Tony's invitation. As he waited, Tony called out to Kitwi for fresh coffee and Lambert soon joined him in the common room.

Within a few minutes, Luigi joined Tony and Lambert. Jose was soon heard in the distance coming back on his motorcycle. He recognized Lambert's car and came into the common room with his safety helmet on and his rubber boots dangling below his khaki *gandurah*. (soutane of the

White Fathers imitating the Arab gandurah, robe). Few White Fathers still wore the religious habit. But Jose often wore it when he traveled a distance from Butova so that people would recognize him as a priest.

Tony went over to the co-operative to find Luc and invite him to come visit with Lambert, his fellow countryman. As they walked to the mission house from the co-operative, Luc mentioned that he was very worried about the safety of Petero Tumba. He had heard in the store that many people were saying Petero was part of the Bahutu meetings before the attempted *coup* and that he should be arrested and tried. Tony realized that if this had been so clearly expressed to Luc who was just being initiated into Kirundi, then the people were sending a clear message to the missionaries through him. He told him that Jose had spoken to Petero and told him to stay in his room and not go out for any reason whatsoever. Even when he was to go to church for a service, he was to go and come back accompanied by one of the priests. He added that he was pleased that Petero lived so close to them that they could protect him. Both men mentioned how much they admired Tumba and that they would do anything to protect him from the savage Batutsi who were envious of his good manners and suave personality. Little did they realize that Petero's popularity would be the cause of his death within the next week.

Back in the common room, the four missionaries listened as Lambert told story after story about the different missions he had recently visited. There were so many heroic gestures performed by so many good christian people who wanted only one thing: harmony between these two estranged tribes. Lambert went back over his *safari* that had taken him down the east coast of Lake Tanganyika. He had stopped at Bumonge, Vurura, Muka, Bumeza, and Mutwe. The morale was good among all the missionaries although most of them were horrified by the number of Bahutu that had been killed by the government soldiers. Bumonge had been under siege for a few days during the beginnings of the Bahutu uprisings but peace had been restored after some fighting between the rebels and the soldiers. But the missionaries in Bumonge were very young and extremely discouraged. They had thought of a plan that they were determined to initiate after all this was over. They believed that the church of Burundi should go back to the pre-evangelization days, stop all the sacramentalization (baptisms, mass, confessions, marriages) and spend all their time proclaiming the gospel teachings. Their understanding of the situation was that these catholics did not understand the commitment of the gospel and made a farce of the sacraments. The priests of Bumonge believed that the church of Burundi had to begin again, this time with more fervor than ever before.

They believed that the only way the church could progress was if they initiated a conversion that would lead the people to following the Christian message in a totally radical way rather than give lip service to the church. Tony remembered that Mathias had often quoted the Prophet Isaiah: "These people offer me lip-service, but their hearts are far from me."

Tony scratched his head and was the first to respond to Lambert's expose. He said that he understood where they were coming from and they were certainly onto something important. Jose rejected the whole idea and mumbled something that since they were Italian, they always wanting to do things in their own particular way: "Fifty-three million Italians and fifth-three million Italian political parties!" he ranted, "Each man has his own ideology as long as it is different from everyone else's!'"

Jean Lambert was a very dynamic person who had been a missionary in Burundi for many years. Most of this time had been spent teaching in one of the seminaries. But then he was freed from academics and enjoyed working with the simple people in parishes. However, since he was a man of such outstanding quality, he didn't stay in a parish very long. The Missionaries of Africa made Lambert their assistant regional and after a few years, he had taken over as regional superior. Lambert was accountable for all the Missionaries of Africa who worked in parishes and schools throughout the five dioceses of Burundi. He loved his job since it afforded him travel time from one mission to another. When he came to visit the missionaries, most of the confreres had little difficulty opening up to him, accepting his wise advice and following his directives.

Lambert dressed like a missionary who had lived in Burundi for many decades. He wore dark blue trousers with a similar colored shirt and brown sneakers. His blue beret and rimless glasses gave away his French heritage. Above all, Jean Lambert loved the church and the people of Burundi. He had suffered greatly over the past three weeks, hearing the stories of so many Batutsi, whom he had taught in the seminary, being killed in the first week of the *coup* or then taking the initiative to put to death their fellow Bahutu countrymen during the genocide. When Lambert now spoke of certain situations, mistrust of individuals filled his thoughts and he spoke with a great deal of irony and sarcasm. He had mentioned often that when this was all over, he would go back to France on leave and rethink his responsibilities and obligations for the future. He was bewildered, questioning what form of witness the White Fathers should give as a particular missionary community. His vision for Burundi and spreading the gospel in this country was being cast in a dark and lackluster shadow. Lambert said that he planned to stay in Butova until mid-afternoon and that if any of the community wanted to see him privately, he would be very happy to meet with them. He planned to leave for Lutana and stay overnight at that mission. Then he motioned to Tony that he would like to talk to him privately, so the two men went out the door to Tony's room.

Jean Lambert relaxed behind the closed door in the privacy of Tony's room and the two men really opened up to each other. The young priest told the regional what had transpired over the past two weeks and that they had gone to the bishop and finally decided to boycott the Sunday mass the following day: "Pentecost will be the ideal time to deliver a strong message to the whole catholic population," Tony said summarizing for the regional what their plans were.

Lambert was pleased with the initiative they had already taken and supported the decisions that had already been made. He continued to tell Tony how important it was that they had the support of Bishop Moulin and Monsignor Ruyaga. In fact he added: "I have known Bishop Moulin for the past twenty-five years and we have worked together in two different dioceses. I have all the respect in the world for the bishop's decisions, and so I'm certain he will always back you up with total support," the regional stated.

Tony told Lambert what he planned on saying in his homily and through the Scriptures the next day. Lambert seemed to be very supportive of the idea and told him that he should not only say that to celebrate mass in these circumstances would be wrong. It would be a sacrilege! Tony was taken by surprise. He thought of the harsh sound this word, especially in Kirundi. And Jean Lambert was suggesting this to him! 'Sacrilege! *Isacirilego! Isacirilego!*' It left a ring in both men's ears. Yet Tony agreed with Lambert that is was the most appropriate word the church could use in these dire circumstances.

Lambert continued to encourage Tony. He knew he was still young, the youngest pastor in the country. Why did one man, with such a bright future, have to face so much adversity? However, this wasn't the time for a change, so Lambert did all he could to build up Tony's optimism. Tony said finally: "You know, Jean, this is the darkest hole I have ever been in! Yet I can handle the situation, even though every day brings it's own particular problems. I have support from the surrounding White Fathers: De Winter from Lutana, Saturnino, Sanchez from Mutwe, Kees Van Riel, Leo Calcutta and Franz Noker from Muka. They are there for me and I try to be there for them." As Tony said this he remembered many wonderful times he had spent with Noker and Calcutta in Muka or entertaining them when they visited Butova. Franz had been really close to Mathias since they were both German and had so much in common. They were both giants of men and loved to race their BMW motorcycles along the roads of southern Burundi. Tony continued:

"And of course, we still pray together every day in the morning even though the more we ask God for help the farther away He seems to be! Somehow after all I have seen over the past two weeks, I believe that at this time God has abandoned this dreadful country. I, myself, will stay until peace comes back to the area, but then I have decided I will pack my bags and leave. These people are animals and I don't think God is calling me to give my life for their cause. They don't deserve to hear the gospel message preached to them! If they cannot live love on the human level, then it is useless to try to talk to them about supernatural love. All the Batutsi want to do is kill every Muhutu that has ever breathed! And all the Bahutu are going to do over the next fifty or one hundred years is to seek revenge. If I had an extra lifetime, I would think of spending time here in this landlocked, God-forsaken country. But since I only have one life, I'm going to get it together after this is all over, kiss the Burundi soil good bye and walk away from this hell-hole of an existence!"

Lambert sat back in his chair, saddened by every word the young missionary was speaking. He realized that Tony was coming from an enormous hurt. He, too, had spent a lifetime giving to the Barundi and what was the result? He envied the younger missionary who could pick up his life and move on.

"Don't give up. now, Tony, we really need you and your energy here in Butova," Lambert interjected.

"No, I won't abandon now, Jean. I made that promise to Bishop Moulin and I will be faithful to the bitter end. But every day presents new situations and new deceptions and a realization that there are very few good people among the christians that we have baptized. 'Strike the shepherd and the sheep all flee!' So I'm trying not to be struck. Amid all the pain, I understand that God has His hand in here somewhere and I can help to save many many lives by being present and keeping a cool demeanor at all times. It is not easy but I am trying to be prudent as well as an encouragement to all." This was how the missioner described his role in the midst of the genocide. "So you can count on me. I will stay no matter what tomorrow brings. However I do have something that I need to talk to you about."

"Speak, frankly, Tony!" Lambert encouraged him.

"Jose Suarez has been depressed ever since Bishop Moulin appointed me pastor. He thought that he was capable of doing the job. Isn't that a serious lack of judgment? That, in itself, shows his poor insight in not knowing and accepting his limitations. He could never handle the job. But now he is so depressed that I believe he is taking it out on me. No matter what I say or do, Suarez takes an opposite position. Sometime soon it will be tragic because when people see us divided, there will be no way whatsoever of speaking to them about unity and harmony and peace. The blind cannot lead the blind. They will all fall into the ditch." Tony reminded Lambert of the gospel teaching as he went on:

"I have tried to explain to Jose that we cannot afford to be divided but he always brushes it off, trying to find justification in any position different from ours." Tony explained that the dispute was not entirely between him and Jose but between Jose and the all the community:

"I listen to Luigi and Luc and I try to make decisions based on a common consensus. But Jose always opposes any stated position. Actually, Jean, I must tell you that dealing with him is even more stressful than dealing with the Batutsi *bakuru* and *basoldat*. At lease I can speak to them and they hear the message. But Jose simply chooses to rise above us by taking an alternate route. I keep telling him that we must show the people a common front and not let them see us divided. Jose went to Kees Van Riel in Muta for spiritual direction. Van Riel is such a direct man. Jose thought he would mollycoddle him to feel sorry for him. Kees told him to pack his bags, go directly to Bujarundi, get the first plane ticket available and fly back to Spain and stay there. Jose was flabbergasted and came back here more depressed than ever. He even told me what his director had told him! I had the audacity to tell him I thought that Van Riel's advice was very wise and I would be willing to drive him to the capital! He spent a couple of really bad days after that but he is so stubborn that now he won't even think of leaving but wants to stick it out to the very end. A further reason for his obstinacy now is to show Van Riel that his counsel was incorrect. I'm dumbfounded about the whole thing and remain very stressed because of what he might do since his judgment is always so erroneous. He follows his heart when he should be thinking. But at other times he tries to think out a decision with his mind and he should be following his gut feeling. Jean, please speak to Suarez because I'm at my wit's end !"

Tony went on: "Wednesday we made a common decision. At least the three of us were in favor of abandoning the mission to draw attention to the atrocities. But Jose wouldn't commit himself and we hoped he would go along with us. When the bishop and Ruyaga agreed that it would be better that we stay and protest by not saying mass tomorrow, Jose started to criticize the whole idea since we all seem so favorable. Luc and Luigi are supporting everything one hundred percent, but I think Jose will find a way to stab the whole situation in the back if we give him the chance. If you talk to him, I am sure it will not have any effect. He will contradict everything you say. But, Jean, you are the regional superior. You must get across to him before a tragedy breaks out. What if you were to stay here until after the morning mass tomorrow and talk to him continuously and tell him he has to support us and the common decision that has been made by this team along with the diocesan leaders. Then maybe things will go all right. Then what would be the possibilities of you taking him along with you and having him stay in another mission for sometime or even bringing him to Bujarundi for a couple of weeks? Maybe you can suggest he go home to Europe on vacation for a while?" Fr Tony, exhausted after expounding all the possibilities, shook his head and looked at Lambert waiting for his reply.

Jean Lambert had his legs crossed as he listened to Tony. He uncrossed them and then crossed them back the other way to show his tension. He said that there was an urgent reason to get to Lutana as he thought a decision had to be made about Walter De Winter's health. He had put on a great deal of weight in the past four months and the doctor had reported that he had quite a bit of fat around his heart. Over the past week, he had been confined to bed and the regional needed to go there so that a decision could be made as soon as possible. He had announced the visit for late that afternoon and a confrere's health was never compromised. So Lambert promised to speak to Jose and insist that he follow the common decisions. Tony started to get red in the face and told Lambert that he understood the situation but that one night would not make much difference. A runner could be dispatched to the mission of Lutana and they would await the regional the next day. He could be there after the mass, maybe around 10:30. Jean Lambert didn't want to discourage the insistent confrere so he said he would think about it over noon time and give him an answer after lunch. The two men stood up and shook hands and Lambert said that he would ask for a council meeting of all after the siesta at around 2pm.

"Unless you need a nap?" Tony emphasized, "none of us takes a rest. We prefer to use the time for other things."

As they left the refectory after lunch, Lambert approached Jose and asked him for some time together. The two men walked off and the other three went directly for coffee in the common room. A good forty minutes went by before Lambert and Suarez came into the common room together. They both looked solemn and Tony made a wish beyond his

wildest imagination. He thought: 'What if they announced that Jose was going to pack his bags and leave with the regional for Bujarundi and take the plane back to Spain?' He realized he was allowing his mind to play games with him. Life was not that easy nor was he that blessed!
But alas, fantasies aside, there was no such conversation, no such dream come true! The reality of life would continue in Butova. Lambert led them in prayer and asked for the guidance of the Holy Spirit. Then he mentioned that he had two good conversations both with Jose and Tony and he congratulated them all on the efforts they were making. He went to great lengths to describe the many talents and qualities he saw in the young pastor and asked all to give him total support . He mentioned that those who were White Fathers had taken an oath of obedience to the Superior General. Ironically only Tony and Jose were White Fathers so his words were obviously directed to them, specifically Jose. Since the mission had a superior and he, a Regional Superior, then that meant that obedience, pertaining to their exact life-situation in Butova, was directed towards Suarez. Tony wanted to laugh out loud if Lambert thought that Jose would be obedient to him and his decisions. That was the joke of the decade. Nice try, Jean. Obviously he didn't understand how mixed-up Jose's mind really was. Lambert had just wasted forty minutes of regional time! And life would go on in Butova!

Jean Lambert then turned to Tony and asked him to share what he planned to say and do at the mass the following morning. Tony was relieved and pleased that they would have a final detailed meeting concerning the Pentecost Mass in the presence of the regional. Furthermore he hoped that this would force Jose to finally support the decision not to celebrate eucharist and to tell the people why. He went into great detail to let the others know that he had thought out every detail and now he was putting all on the table so that every part of the plan could be discussed, questioned, scrutinized and then hopefully supported by all.

"First of all," Tony said in a strong voice, "we are going to start thirty minutes late so that the many, many people who are always late will have a chance to be inside the church and hear every word. Also we will go over to the catechumenate service and invite all the catechumens to come over to the church. This will take some time for them to get organized and arrive at the church building. We three priests will conduct the whole service. We will vest in the sacristy in albs and red stoles. The red is for Pentecost but it can also remind us of the hundreds of people who have shed their blood in our parish over the past two weeks. He turned to Jose:

'Could you see the Banyachoir before the service and tell them that there will be no singing during mass?'

Jose stared awkwardly into space and gave no sign of acknowledgment. Had he heard what was asked of him? He certainly did not give any sign that he would do it. Did this attitude mean that he didn't agree with the choir not singing? …or that he did not want to be the one to tell them? … or that he didn't agree with the idea of not celebrating the mass? Amused by Jose's childish attitude, Tony wondered what Lambert had really said to Suarez.

"Let's plan to start the entrance procession about 7:45? There'll just be the three of us without servers?" Tony alleged with his voice elevating, to allow them to question the idea if they so desired. "Luigi you go first and carry the Bible and we will follow you, bow to the altar and go to the presidential chair. I will then begin the penitential rite and pray for pardon for the acts of hatred in the hearts of so many over the past weeks. I will try to give as much silence as I can so that each word will sink in and will be as solemn as possible."

Tony lifted his head and looked toward Jose:

"There are many things I would like to say at the service," Tony went on staring at Jose, "but I need to make special nuances in Kirundi. Jose, later today, would you be kind enough to help me to come up with the right expressions?" There was no response from Jose and Tony became perturbed. He realized that this was the ideal time, in the presence of Lambent, to confront Suarez:

"Jose, did you hear what I am asking you? Are you with us in this? … Are you willing to help by using your talents to aid this mission?" Jose was now pleased to have an invitation to express himself and so he startled them by saying what they all had realized was inevitable:

"Tony, the more I hear you talk about 'your plan' for mass tomorrow, the more I don't want to give you my support by helping you. I believe that we should say mass for these people and leave the politics alone. Giving them mass and communion will give them grace to change their ways." Jose spiritualized as he rose from his chair and told the others that he had promised to visit some homes and believed the people were waiting for him. It was a lame duck excuse as Jose was always late and no one ever counted on his arrival until he appeared! So no one would be waiting for him at a particular time.

And low and behold, Luc stood up, went right to the door and blocked it with his tall, large frame. His structure, not far from two meters, covered most of the door and his blue eyes were filled with rage. He pointed to the chair that Jose had just evacuated and told him to go back and sit down and be a man and learn to discuss, give all his opinions and then work hand in hand for the common good. Luc barked:

"Jose, you do not have the right to walk out because you don't agree with our policy. We have discussed this for the last three days. Tony had it approved by the bishop and vicar general and now we must execute together. And yet you decide that you are going to oppose us by walking away as we discuss the final plans. Probably the only reason why you are not in agreement with us is that you always want to take a stand contrary to what the group holds in common. Please sit there, listen to what is being said and if you don't agree, say so. But when the meeting is over, I want you to walk out with us, agreeing with the common decision that we all will be making together. This is not a time to have a childish and selfish attitude and go your own way. I personally will not allow this to happen! We will all stay together in this room talking about what has to be and then we will all carry out the mission together. Do you understand what I am saying, Jose?"

All that could be heard was the loud echo of Luc's voice and then Jose mumbled something about not getting any respect. And Tony could only think of Rodney Dangerfield and the comical saying he always used: "I don't get any respect nomore!"

Luc took up the conversation again as he came back from the door and sat down in his chair. "Respect is not something I give because someone wears a cassock. It is something that is earned. And right now, Jose, you have the opportunity of earning it or acting like a child. Please participate in the meeting and support our common decision. We want to respect you as well!"

Tony had been looking around at the others as Luc spoke. His eyes had met those of Lambert and both men could feel pride in Luc and what this nineteen-year-old, doing his military service in such an awkward setting, was teaching the priest. Luigi's head was bobbing up and down as he was in complete agreement with what Luc was saying. And so, Tony thought, 'Let's proceed, believing that Jose will be in this with us 100% and he will participate totally with everything we decide. If he doesn't, we will deal with the each problem as it arrives.' He tried to keep his thoughts positive.

"After the opening prayer for Pentecost Sunday, we will invite the people to be seated and then ask for silence to prepare for the scripture readings." Tony heard himself saying: "Jose," Tony asked, "could I ask you to introduce the first reading? The theme is love of God and love of neighbor and Luigi will proclaim the word from Deuteronomy on the ten commandments." Jose looked up at Tony and without saying anything, nodded a placid approval even though he realized the pastor had once again changed the reading.

"Don't make any particular reference to our situation, but make it clear enough that we are inviting the judgment to come upon us if we do not live by the gospel values. During the reading, Luigi, could you stop a bit before the fifth commandment: **'Thou shalt not kill'** and without putting any overstated accent on it, pause briefly so that all can spend some time reflecting on their christian responsibility not to kill. "Maybe they will get the impression that they are murderers and will line up after mass for confession," Luigi laughed sarcastically.

Then they all came to a hush and Tony continued:

"After the reading, we will leave some time for personal reflection so let's not be hasty, Luigi. We truly want the message to sink in to every person in church."

"Now let's prepare the second reading from John's first letter. I propose we do a long reading for the second lesson because it repeats the same message over and over again and I think that the more people hear these words, the more they will welcome them into their hearts and realize that all these killings are totally unchristian. The reading is from chapter 3 verses 11-24," as Tony took up his Bible, opened it at I John and began to read:

> *"For this is the message that you have heard from the beginning: we should love one another, unlike Cain who belonged to the evil one and slaughtered his brother. Why did he slaughter him? Because his own works were evil, and those of his brother righteous. Do not be amazed, brother, if the world hates you. We know that we have passed from death to life because we love our brother. Whoever does not love remains in death. Everyone who hates his brother is a murderer, and you know that no murderer has eternal life remaining in him. The way that we came to know love was that he laid down his life for us; so we ought to lay down our lives for our brother. If someone who has worldly means sees a brother in need and refuses him compassion, how can the love of God remain in him? Children, let us love not in word or speech but in deed and truth. This is how we shall know that we belong to the truth and reassure our hearts before him in whatever our hearts condemn, for God is greater than our hearts and knows*

everything. Beloved, if our hearts do not condemn us, we have confidence in God and receive from him whatever we ask, because we keep his commandments and do whatever pleases him. And his commandment is this: we should believe in the name of his Son, Jesus Christ, and love one another just as he commanded us. Those who keep his commandments remain in him, and he in them, and the way we know that he remains in us is from the Spirit that he gave us."

Tony closed his Bible and a reflective silence penetrated the whole room. One after another, Lambert, Luigi, and Luc said the reading was exactly what should be said. It was condemning for all who were involved in the killings and encouraging for those who were trying to be just. Tony added that he liked this reading because it always spoke of 'a brother'. "When they realize that they are taking a life away from a particular human being, then, I hope, they will come to their senses."

Luc asked who would do the reading and Tony suggested that Luigi could introduce it in a few words and then Jose would 'do a great job in proclaiming it'. Just the reverse roles from the first reading. We now come to the Gospel.

Jose broke his silence: "I guess that will be Tony's part, as we will have done our duty." he said in a tone of self-degradation.

Tony felt hurt and embarrassed in front of his regional as well as Luigi and Luc. But he decided to respond to the painful remark:

"Yes, Jose" he went on, "I believe that as pastor I am the first person responsible for the potential shock of this witness and I am willing to proclaim the most important part of the liturgy of the word and suffer whatever consequences that might arise. You know, of course, the local soldiers and administrator could come and put us in prison for what we are going to do and say. And I am ready to suffer the consequences if needs be. So, yes, I will proclaim the gospel and read a short homily that I would love you to help me prepare." There was no anger in his calm voice.

"For the gospel reading," Tony went on, "I have chosen the text from John's Gospel, chapter 15, where Jesus speaks about loving one's brother. Jesus parting word at the Last Supper is to command us to love one another. 'No one has greater love for his friend than to lay down his own life.' What I hope might happen to many of the Batutsi when they hear this reading is that they will understand that God is calling them to love their brothers and sisters, the Bahutu. I pray that they might be more Christian than Mututsi and that in their hearts they will oppose the present policy."

Tony looked at Jose and then said that he planned to have only two short pages as a homily because he wanted the scripture readings to predominate. However he added that he would like to give the community a brief outline of what he intended to say for their suggestions. First that what has happened in and around Butova over the past seventeen days has been a sad tragedy since so many people had been killed. Furthermore it was totally uncalled for because it was racial. There was no love or justice in the community and thus on that Sunday, with the bishop's permission, they would not celebrate mass which would be a sacrilege for it would be inviting God's presence into a situation where there was no brotherly love. "No love, no God!" he said as a cliché. Lambert interrupted to support the word 'sacrilege' which, of course, he had given to Tony earlier that morning. He insisted that the word in Kirundi was just as strong, if not stronger, than it was in French or English.

"So," Tony concluded, "I will invite the people to leave the church and go home and pray that peace comes to the area. Only if peace returns in the forthcoming week, will there be mass next Sunday." He would add that the weekday daily mass would also be canceled until peace and love were restored.

The confreres began to buzz and seemed to say how strong yet appropriate the words would be. Finally Lambert stood up and announced that he was late and had to leave immediately for Lutana. Tony was taken back by his words since he had hoped that his calmness at the meeting was a sign that he had changed his mind and had decided to stay. But he walked Lambert out to his car. The regional said he thought that Jose would co-operate but that even if he didn't, Tony should go on with everything as planned. They then shook hands. Jean wished him luck and God's blessings and drove off to Lutana.

As Tony turned around to go back to the meeting room, he saw Jose walking down the outside corridor heading for his room. Seeing Tony and feeling his stare toward his direction, Jose shouted that he was late and had planned to go to a far-off area. Tony did not respond since Jose seemed to be in such a hurry. It vexed him to realize that Jose considered a rosary more important than a decision made in common that would effect the whole area. He wondered if Jose was offended by their words at the meeting and if he would oppose what they had been planning. The putter of Jose's motorcycle *'pikipiki...pikipiki...pikipiki...'* could be heard as he drove away. Tony felt relieved with all that had taken place at the meeting and supported by Lambert, the diocesan officials and at least two of the three men with whom he lived. What would happen to Jose would be anyone's guess. The gesture of Sunday morning was of prime concern, more important than Jose's feelings!

Tony found himself in his room for the rest of the afternoon trying to put Kirundi words together to express the ideas he was reviewing in his mind. He wanted to underline the tragedy that had happened as hundreds of lives had been lost over the past weeks. He would express the senselessness of this hatred among so many people who were all christians and roman catholics, attending the same church every week, reading and listening to the same scriptures and receiving the same Jesus Christ in the Eucharist. He wondered how people could be so faithful about attending church yet so unfaithful in betraying their fellow christians who shared the same faith as they did! How could this be? Who is behind all this damn foolhardiness? When will this calamity end?

As Tony looked for the answers to these questions, it occurred to him that the Batutsi had the Bahutu killed because they believed that they would be killed themselves if they did not take the initiative. When the attempted *coup* started, they must have been made to believe that they and their families were being annihilated. So before they were to suffer that fate, they had to exterminate the enemy first. Every Mututsi was involved because he believed that every Muhutu was a potential killer. So better to kill than to be killed! And it was so easy since the government soldiers, all Batutsi, were already in place at Puma. All one had to do was get the police to arrest and bring a neighbor to Puma. Then in an open trial, he would be accused, found guilty and placed in a truck later that afternoon and driven to the common graves near the military camp of Vurura.

The game was like the plight of thieves in Africa. If a thief is caught stealing, he is killed by the people with whatever instrument they can find. They take the laws into their own hands. So the thief, even if he is doing wrong, knows that if he fails, if he is caught, he will be killed. So his best defense is a good offense. He decides that he must kill anyone in his way for if not, he will be killed himself. The Batutsi offensive was to protect them from the Bahutu, whom they were now destroying in astronomical quanities. So their tactic is: execute rather than be slaughtered! As Tony reviewed this system in his mind, he realized that there were not enough people in the country who were thinking as christians should think. They remained more tribal than catholic, more offensive than vulnerable, more Batutsi/Bahutu than Children of God. The gospel was the only answer. The gospel was the word of God and Tony's role the following day was to convince as many people as possible to choose God and a gospel way of life rather than hold grudges and kill others out of fear, misunderstood as 'self-defense'. Fr. Tony now could see the tragedy clearly as it continued to unfold. In the short time he would be permitted the following day, could he convince the people to change, to convert, to accept the gospel of christianity? He was more than willing to give it a try.

It was important for Tony that he announce there would be no mass that day and mass, both daily and on Sundays, would only begin again when peace and justice had been returned to the area. He realized he was taking away what was most precious and important in the lives of his parishioners. But it would be in denying them what was most precious, the Body of Christ, that they would understand that their actions already dissociated themselves with their Lord. They could not receive Someone they were already desecrating. He tried to find the Kirundi words necessary to express how he felt about church practice on Sunday being valueless if people's attitudes would not be any different during the rest of the week.

He jotted down the reference from Isaiah about the liturgy being 'lip service' and the people having hearts far from God.

At supper, the missionaries decided not to talk about the local happenings but let the conversation center around stories and anecdotes unrelated to the present situation. Luc welcomed the *camaraderie* and led the conversation talking about the different villages in France and how French customs varied from province to province. The other three were willing to let him tell his stories and together they felt a welcomed distraction from their preoccupation with the politics outside. Finally their meal ended and it was time to have coffee in the common room.

As he did every evening, Cypriano Kitwi set up the cups, saucers, sugar and warm milk and then brought in the decanter containing coffee. Luigi got up and started to pour a cup for himself, Tony and Luc. Jose never drank coffee in the evening and went out of the room as the others continued to engage in friendly conversation. This was always a relaxing moment of the day as they sat back and shared stories and jokes and teased one another about different habits and idiosyncrasies. It seemed a long time before Jose returned. The coffee cups had been drained and all the dishes had been returned to the tray so that Cypriano could come for them and take them back to the kitchen before retiring. Tony asked Jose if everything was all right. He was assured that all was fine even though Jose didn't offer any explanation for his absence. Finally they all took up their breviaries and prayed compline together before Luigi went out to shut off the diesel-motor giving the others a short time to light a candle.

With only candlelight, Tony felt compelled to review his homily one more time. Although Jose had not been available to help him with the different expressions in Kirundi, he felt confident that all would understand his message the following morning. He dropped to his knees beside his bed and prayed for courage to proclaim the gospel message. He was overwhelmed with a realization that what he was about to do was the correct decision having been approved by the *bakuru*. The only thing that could go wrong would be a counter-message by Jose's failing to participate and he prayed that God would not allow that to happen. God would not be that vile! Finally he rose from his knees, got into bed and blew out the candle. Would that with a short breath he could blow out all the horrendous quagmire in Burundi! 'Good night cruel world,' he thought, 'Good night, sad Butova' he heard himself say and he fell quickly into deep slumber.

16. The Fire Of The Holy Spirit

Tony always rose early on Sunday mornings since many details had to be attended to before the first mass at 7:15. He felt anxious as the alarm sounded at 5:00 o'clock and rose from his sleep to meet the challenge of a new day. He said a brief prayer, asking God to bless his work and efforts, as he realized the importance of this Pentecost Sunday. Tony loved Sundays at Butova. There was always a large crowd at church and they could be seen from the priests' house coming up the road and through the fields, over by the Teachers' Training College. They would arrive from all directions. It was a spectacular sight to see the women dressed in the most colorful impuzu and walking with babies on their backs and a wooden kneeler on their heads. In years gone by, the missionaries always wore their white cassocks on Sunday mornings. However the church was starting to change and Mathias had set the precedent of wearing a suit and white shirt and tie to receive the people. Tony only had one suit, a bluish-dark green, double-breasted ensemble that he had received as an ordination present from his parents. He always wore it with pride on the Sundays he was staying in Butova and not traveling to an outstation for mass. He enjoyed looking neat and clean for his parishioners, showing them that Sunday mornings were special moments to encounter God and each other.

As he finished washing, Tony went back to his room to dress. He came out feeling clean and ready to deliver the special message he had prepared. He walked down the corridor towards the chapel and looked out at the rising sun. The horizon was a beautiful pink brilliance and he saw the bright color as a positive sign. From the rising of the sun, to its setting, God would be blessing this community in a very special way, he thought.

Tony looked over to the hillside of Piga and he could already see the President's House, as the darkness of night gave way to the brightness of the day. Dawn was always a special time of day, when the gift of life broke free from the macabre doubts of night. He turned down the corridor and entered the chapel for a time of personal prayer to ask special blessings on the day.

After some time, he was joined by Luigi and then Jose came into the chapel. The three men prayed Lauds together and then exited. It was breakfast time and they were about to start the vigorous activities of the day. Tony already felt behind schedule, so he skipped breakfast and went right to the church. Usually it was the duty of Bernardo Inzu to unlock the church and prepare the mass and vestments but Bernardo had been arrested a week before and no one knew about his whereabouts. Tony thought of him as he approached the big church, remembering how hard Bernardo worked to support his family. He had a bicycle and would travel many miles to the surrounding markets and purchase all kinds of food and trinkets and then bring them to sell at the marketplace either at Puma or the bigger market of Ruhweza every Tuesday and Friday. When Inzu was accused and arrested, Tony realized that it was because he had made so much money through his hard work, blood, sweat and tears that the Batutsi were envious of him and accused him so that after his death they could claim all his possessions since he was officially considered a traitor. Bernardo had now 'disappeared' and his wife, Mariya, who was pregnant, had come the previous week to tell Tony that her husband would not be available for sacristy work. Tony gave Mariya Bernardo's pay for the month with something extra to help her in her grief in hope that she would be able to eat well and look after the baby. He promised to continue to help but reminded her that the others' needs were great as well since there were now hundreds of new widows in the area. Tony shuttered at the thought of all these widows and thousands of orphans.

But now in the sacristy, he turned his attention to preparing the service and altar. The most important part of their church equipment on this day was the public address system. He would not be approaching the altar so there was no need to check that microphone. However he made sure all was ready with the pulpit mike and that the electricity would work as soon as they turned on the system. All seemed ready to go.

People were already starting to come into the church and pray silently before the Blessed Sacrament. Tony looked out, beyond the sacristy door, and thought how pious the people seemed to be. He wondered, as he saw them from afar, if they were praying for husbands or fathers or brothers who had been killed this past week. Or, on the contrary, were they the ones who had born false witness, told stories and made accusations of their neighbors and thus were directly responsible for their demise. If they were Batutsi, they would feel justified and supported by the police and soldiers. Yet they feared the future when there would obviously be revenge. If they were Bahutu, they were grieving so many murderous deaths, fearing for their very lives and regretting not having been able to kill their Batutsi neighbors first. Tony wondered how they could possibly pray. Were they praying for peace, for forgiveness, for unity, for love? Hardly. They were praying with regrets that they hadn't done more to kill every Batutsi they ever knew. If they were Batutsi, they came into the church with a certain arrogance but overpowered by fear. They would never know when there might be a Muhutu hiding somewhere with a machete in his hands ready to pounce on the Mututsi. Never again would the Batutsi or Bahutu ever be free of suspicion of each other.

Tony calmly placed the Bible at the ambo making sure that it was opened to the exact page for the first reading from Deuteronomy. Then he found the second reading from I John. And finally he turned to John's Gospel and quickly slid past the story of the Good Samaritan in Luke, deciding on John's account of the Last Supper rather than the story of the helping one's neighbor. He slipped the copy of his homily under the shelf below the bible and thought of how special this area of the church was to him. When he would proclaim the gospel and preach the message, it was Bishop Moulin and Monsignor Ruyaga speaking to the people. No, it was even more! This was the Word of God! Therefore it was the Father, Jesus Christ and the Holy Spirit speaking to these christians. He began to feel confident and even excited. He was anxious for the next hour to go by so that he could begin the service for the people. Then it dawned on him that he had more time than usual since the service was to begin somewhat later than on a normal Sunday. The BanyaButova were notorious for being late and he wanted the catechumens, who normally met in the catechumenate on the far side of the compound, to all be present. He had sent word for all the catechumens to come to the church and it would take some patient waiting before all would be displaced a second time. Since there would be no singing and the readings would be rather short, the gathering would not be long anyhow, probably only thirty minutes. As Tony looked up, he saw Sr. Maragarita walking through the sacristy door. She had come to prepare the musical instruments that accompanied the singing.

"*Bwakeye neza, Mama Maragarita!*" Fr. Tony went on, "but sorry, there will be no singing or music during the special service this morning."

The nun looked peculiarly at the pastor, expecting an explanation that was not forthcoming.

Tony responded to her inquiring stare with a command. This was the way he had learned to handle a situation he didn't want to respond to in any way whatsoever. 'Give them something to do and they will go and do it and you are off the hook!' That was what he had been taught in the seminary.

"Maragarita, tell the drummers not to put their drums out in the sun. We will not be using them today. Also tell all the Banyachoir not to come to the sacristy since they won't be processing today. The only ones who will be in the sanctuary will be us three priests!" he exhorted.

Maragarita often had an air of arrogance about her and this was one time when she showed it to the fullest. Embarrassed, thinking she had done something wrong, she turned on her heels and stormed out of the sacristy without uttering another word. She went outside and told the choir and musicians that they were not needed that day. The sacristy remained quiet and somewhat peaceful and then Tony heard footsteps and recognized them as Luigi's. As Tony turned to greet him he saw an exasperating look on the face that stared right at him.

"Jose has told me that he cannot participate in this service with us. He believes that we are handling the situation wrongly and decided, during the night, in much prayer and reflection as he says, that he could not be a part of not saying mass especially on this feast day of the Holy Spirit. He said that he would celebrate the 10:15 mass and would prepare a homily on Pentecost and the Spirit."

Tony exploded in anger. His ears seemed numb. His eyes grew larger with his fury. He clenched his fist and wanted to pound his closed hand on the sacristy table in front of him. Even though he had thought all along that Jose would betray him, now it was official, now the final trump card had been played. He tried to disconnect himself from the words he had just heard. Further he was dumbfounded that Jose didn't have the courage to have told him earlier that morning after prayer but had passed on the message through Luigi who was not in a position to question him. The ultimate in cowardice!

Tony made a mental image of Jose and wanted to rip up the picture. Hatred, despair and fear seemed to spill from every cell in his body. But being an extrovert, he tried to find a solution by speaking his thoughts and feelings:

"I can't believe that the jerk would do this to us. First of all he knows that this was our common decision and witness as a community. Secondly we have the support of the bishop and vicar general and Lambert. They are our superiors and thus they have not only supported us in taking this step but represent the Holy Spirit in this decision. That dimwit is turning his back on God Himself!!"

Luigi listened attentively as both men stared at each other in the otherwise empty sacristy. Then he said:

"Look, Tony, Jose is not important, especially at a time like this. We have more important things to do than to discuss him and his stupidity. People are always laughing at him: the way he walks, his dirty cassocks and clothing. He smells so badly that even the Africans comment on it. He has no respect from the people. If he did, would Bishop Moulin have appointed you pastor when you only had thirty months in the country when Jose had nine years? He knows the language well and the customs and culture of the people but he is very suspect, especially by the men. They don't consider him a strong *mugabo* and see him too free with the young girls. So whether or not he is with us or not will make very little difference to them."

"Oh, I know all that, Luigi and thanks for reminding me about his insignificance. Jose is a small little runt, both figuratively and realistically! However I truly wanted this to be a community decision... a stand that we were all taking together. Now I believe that our witness will not be understood as coming from the whole church the Gospel Christ, God Himself. If ever he speaks to the people and voices his disapproval of our witness, it will show everyone that we are divided! Then today will be seen as my own personal decision. I am not afraid to take the full responsibility but this will give everyone the opportunity of saying it is only one opinion and already another father in the community is opposing it. His decision nullifies ours. Oh, Luigi, I wish Lambert had stayed until this morning and would have been here right now. Luigi, go, get Jose and tell him I want to see him immediately. But he is so pigheaded, he will probably refuse and I can't leave the sacristy right now. If he refuses to come and talk to me, tell him I forbid him to celebrate the 10:15 mass and that I am announcing at this mass that henceforth mass will not be celebrated here in Butova until peace and unity come back to the area. If that coward doesn't want to come and talk to me, tell him I have no use for him as an associate here and that he can get on his *pikipiki* and leave the parish indefinitely as soon as possible. If we can't work together, then he's gone!"

As Luigi turned on his heels to go find Jose and deliver the message, Tony started to panic. What if the people rise up in protest to what he is going to say? What if they will be strengthened by Jose's stand and oppose Tony's message? What if they don't understand his Kirundi and misinterpreted the message? Further he thought, what if some important government officials be present, like the president, they could even have him arrested for insurrection or making public statements against the government? He dropped to his knees and asked the Lord for help. 'Please, Dear Jesus, guide me in this, the most difficult moment of my life. You, too, were accused of insurrection and even put to death for it. I join my death to yours and if you want me to offer my life as a sacrifice so that the people will understand divine love and justice, then I will gladly undergo whatever I have to, even death, for your greater honor and glory. Lord help me, I say 'yes' to you!'

As Tony rose to his feet, he become aware of murmuring in the church and the moving of benches and realized it was time to begin the morning prayers that the people always said 10 minutes before mass. He went outside the sacristy and saw Saverino Imbwa standing over by Sister Maragarita and the other Banyachoir.

"Saverino!" Tony called the catechist aside, "please go over to the catechumenate and tell the catechists that there will be only one celebration here today. They are to come over here to the main church as soon as possible. Mention that I have sent you."

Without asking a question, but raising his eyebrows, Imbwa turned and hastened toward the doors of the church. It would take some time to have them all in church. That would be the correct moment to start the service. Before going back to the sacristy, Tony went to the microphone and intoned: "*Kwa'zina"*...(In the Name of.....) The people picked up the intonation, fell to their knees on kneelers or on the cement floor and began the rhythmic recitation of morning prayers. The memorized prayers that all catholics in Burundi said before the common service in the morning were the traditional prayers of the church that they had learned by heart when they were youngsters. They said the Apostles' Creed, the Our Father, three Hail Marys, Acts of Contrition, Faith, Hope and Charity and many other rote prayers. The sound of their rhythmic prayers bounced off the brick walls of the church and hopefully found their way to heaven. This sing-song would continue for the next ten minutes before mass was to begin. However on this morning, Tony's plan was to wait an additional few minutes so that all would settle in and then he and Luigi would come out of the sacristy and lead the Liturgy of the Word. He'd read his short homily and then dismiss the people.

Morning prayer ended and the echo of the rhythmic sounds of praising God and imploring divine pardon seemed to settle on the people. Fr. Tony loved this building where each year the three priests welcomed over five hundred adult catechumens into the Faith at two Baptismal ceremonies: one at Easter time (Holy Saturday) and the other in the middle of the month of August. Even though over 1200 people could fit into the church, the normal Sunday congregation filled the nave and sides to the left and right of the altar conformably but seldom to overflowing. However today, with the catechumens and others making a special effort, Tony believed that the church would be filled to the rafters. He thought of the way he had been double-crossed by Jose and felt nothing but disdain in his heart. He heard himself asking God for forgiveness and thought how foolish life was that when the missionaries were admonishing the christians for hatred and rash-judgments, he had similar hatred and distain in his heart for the man with whom he lived! Tony felt better having shared his frustrations with God and experienced the calming effect of God's compassion and love. He, too, would have loved to celebrate the Eucharist on this Pentecost Sunday but he realized that if his people did not merit God's special love, then neither did he!

Luigi come back to the sacristy and he seemed ready to pick up the pieces broken by Jose. He said that he would give an introduction to each reading and do the readings himself. Tony thanked him and said that was the exact way he wanted it done since only the priests would be actively participating in the service that day. Tony asked Luigi if he had found Jose and he shook his head 'no' meaning that 'yes' he had spoken to him but 'no' was still Jose's response.

"He, however, wants you to know that he will say the second mass and looked surprised when I told him that you wanted him out of the parish as soon as possible since he had become a trouble-maker." Again Luigi took up the same battle-cry: "It is not important that we are seen as being in accord with each other. The important thing is that the people realize that we are presenting the love of Christ to them, a love that has been radically absent in their actions over the past many weeks."

Fr. Luigi vested in alb, cincture and red stole and then went over to Tony and gave him a great bear hug:

"I want you to know that I support this position completely," Luigi whispered to Tony, "and I will stand by you no matter what may happen! You have my total support."

The two men hugged again and Tony stepped outside the door to see if the catechumens had arrived in church. As they had, he then came over to Luigi. The two priests joined hands as the presider did every Sunday with the servers, banyachoir, catechists and readers. But today they were only two. They prayed asking God's blessing on the service they were about to undertake. Tony lead the prayer:

"Glorious Holy Father of heaven and earth," he went on, "we thank you for all the good gifts you have given to us over this past week. We ask you to send your Holy Spirit on both of us and on the whole congregation so that your message of peace and reconciliation may be communicated to all. Give those who are unashamed murderers a contrite heart and the grace of conversion. We beg your pardon since this message will not be as clear as it should be because we, your priests, are divided and sinners. Father in heaven open our lips and clarify our hearts so that Your Spirit may blow through our humanity and proclaim your Holy Gospel to all creation. We pray this prayer through God our Father, in the love of Christ, Your Son, and in the presence of the Holy Spirit, one God, world without end. Amen."

Father Luigi lifted high the Bible and went to the sacristy door. He asked Tony if he wanted the short entrance or the long one and Tony said he wanted as little pomp and ceremony as possible. Luigi and then the pastor, robed in white alb, red stole and cincture, left the sacristy and processed towards the ambo.

Usually the procession was made up of the servers, the banyachoir and the readers. They went out the side doors to the main entrance of the church. There they turned around to face the congregation and wait for the signal to enter the church and process up the center aisle to the sanctuary. The thirty or so members of the choir always walked proudly in the procession. They would all be singing and the musicians, especially those on the ten drums already in the sanctuary, would pick up the beat and the whole church would be one loud rhythmic expression of praise. The presider would come last and process to the altar where he would kiss the area where Christ's Body would become present during the celebration and then proceed to his chair. Only then would the singing and praising and loud drumming cease.

But today the ceremony lacked color and volume. Its tranquility was deafening! Before people had a chance to realize all had started, the procession ended. Furthermore when the congregation looked at the altar they found something strange. There were two priests, Father Tony and Father Luigi. Every Sunday, the priests tried to cover as many outstations as possible, so never would there be concelebration, not even on Christmas or Easter. In fact, many of the people had never seen two priests say mass at the same time! They also found it strange that there was no music, no singing, no catechists, no servers, no readers at the altar. The sanctuary looked bare... this huge area with only the two priests standing in front of two chairs at the back of the sanctuary.

Fr. Tony spoke slowly into the microphone. He welcomed everyone to the service that he called the liturgy of the word and he mentioned, in particular, the catechumens who were normally by themselves in the old church. He added how special it was to have them all together and added that the message of the Scriptures was for all, baptized and unbaptized alike. He invited them to pay special attention to the Word of God. Finally he mentioned that even though they had begun late, the service would be shorter than usual.

"Today is Pentecost Sunday, the gift of the Holy Sprint to the church. The same Holy Spirit, who descended on the Apostles 2,000 years ago, will come to us in Butova today in a very dynamic way."

He asked for a moment of silence before singing the opening prayer: "Oh God, Who did instruct the hearts of the faithful by the power of the Holy Spirit, send forth the same Spirit on us today so that we may be truly wise and ever rejoice in His Consolation. We pray to God Our Father in the presence of Jesus Christ, God's Only Son, Who lives and reigns with the Holy Spirit, for You are One God forever and ever. AMINA."

As the priests sat down, the whole church seemed to relax in anticipation of the Word of God that would now be proclaimed to them. There was always a low murmuring of voices in the church, between the prayer and the readings. One of the reasons for voices in the background was because people who were late would now be given entrance into the church and they would try to find a suitable place to worship. Greeting those in the immediate vicinity was essential. Also the people readied themselves to hear the message by clearing their throats so that they would not have to disturb others during the readings. In the *kirundi* tradition of the country, every word, every syllable was vitally important

Fr. Luigi calmly strode to the ambo. Tony felt vexed that his confrere was alone and thought how much more powerful the message would have been if Jose were also walking to the pulpit with Luigi. He tried to dispel these thoughts and heard himself whisper aloud in his native English: '….. and I'll be damned if he'll celebrate the second mass.....there will be no second mass!'

Luigi had only been in the country eight months. He had spent six months at the language center in the north of the country and then Bishop Moulin had appointed him to Butova to learn the pastoral system and ways through the White Father Missionaries who had been in the country for over eighty years. The bishop was a member of the White Fathers and believed that no missionary should be placed in a parish without passing through one of several of their model parishes he had in the diocese of Vurura. So Luigi had been appointed to Butova for the first year or two of his ministry. Then he was to join his own missionary community, the Francis Xavier Missionaries from Italy. So daily Luigi courageously plugged away at learning Kirundi, French, and the ways of the apostolate in the diocese of Vurura.

The Italian missioner began the introduction of the reading with a calm, tranquil voice. He mentioned that it was from the Book of Deuteronomy, the summary of the Ten Commandments, the Magna Carta of how we should live as human beings created by God. He made no reference to the political situation confronting everybody. Yet all would realize what was being said by glossing between the lines. When Luigi concluded the short introduction, he opened the Bible slowly and began to read from Deuteronomy, chapter 5 verses 6-21. His Kirundi pronunciation was excellent and he surprised Tony, who had never heard Luigi read in Kirundi. His speaking to people daily outside the parish offices left a lot to be desired. But when he read from the prepared text of the scriptures, he was loud, clear and very easy to understand. He soon got into the rhythm of each phrase and the words seemed to role off his tongue as if he were a true son of Burundi. Tony was delighted.

"I the Lord am Your God...and I will bestow mercy down to the thousandth generation.....You shall not kill...You shall not steal.....You shall not dishonor witness against your neighbor....." Luigi finally concluded the reading, held the book of scriptures high above his head and proclaimed: "This is the Word of the Lord!" He turned sharply on his heals and walked back to be seated beside Tony. Tony looked right at him and after Luigi had sat down, their eyes met and Tony whispered: "Great reading, Luigi." Luigi, accepting the compliment, beamed with pride. Without rising, Tony spoke into his portable microphone:

"Now over the next several minutes, let us reflect on these words of scripture," he exhorted.

There was dead silence in the church. It was an awkward silence, since it was not normally part of the Sunday liturgy. After a few minutes, people started to get fidgety and there was some coughing and clearing of throats. Tony waited a few more minutes before turning to Luigi, a sign to introduce and proclaim the second reading.

"Just continue as you did the first introduction and reading, friend, it was terrific!" Tony said to him, keeping a serene and serious demeanor.

Luigi could hear the sound of the heels of his shoes thumping the cement floor as he walked to the ambo. He explained that the New Testament reading that he was about to proclaim was a completion of the Old Testament values of a bygone era. God required justice from His People of Old. But now, in this time after Jesus Christ, God requires His New People to act accordingly to only one principle: unconditional love.

"We are the Body of Christ," Luigi continued, "so God requires us to love each other as Christ loves us, unconditionally and perfectly! Now, with the coming of Jesus in the New Testament, the message of love of neighbor goes over, above, and beyond justice. It is pouring out unconditional love upon neighbors and family, some of whom don't deserve it." Luigi concluded by saying that we are invited to love everyone as Christ loves us and love them in the way that Jesus, Who is in us, loves us: totally, unconditionally and absolutely. Then he turned to the back part of the Bible, found 1 John and began to read from chapter 3 verses 11-24. As Luigi read, there were some 'ohs' and 'ahs' from the people and Tony realized that they were responding to inner feelings of condemnation, regret and guilt as they allowed the Word of God to judge their personal lives. He wondered if the whole church would soon revolt and hadn't a clue as to what he might do, if they did. This was the Word of God and thus the plumb-line to measure us by! The plumb-line seemed very warped and twisted!

'God's Word will never pass away,' Tony thought.

Luigi began to read as slowly as he could, pausing briefly at the end of each verse. Every sentence seemed to condemn the actions of those who had hatred toward many of the other tribe. They had had them arrested, witnessed at their trials, sent them to burial in a dirty, dilapidated Arab's lorry.

> *"We are called to love our brother, unlike Cain who slaughtered his brother.....because his own works were evil, he slaughtered him.....everyone who hates his brother is a murderer and do murderers have eternal life in them?.....if a person with worldly means has no compassion on his brother, how can we say the life of God abides in him?.....we receive all we need from God because we keep his commandments.....and his commandment is to love one another just as He, the Lord Jesus, commanded us...and we know that He remains in us by the Spirit that He has given us..."*

As Luigi proclaimed the last verse, he thought how wonderfully considerate God is. Even though the first part of the reading was very direct and called the people to change their ways, the latter part was filled with hope. The invitation had been issued loud and clear for people to start living as *Bakristu* and not as Batutsi or Bahutu.

Luigi walked back to his seat and again, after a low whisper of congratulations, Tony once again called the community to silent reflection. This time the murmuring started earlier as the people were becoming more and more impatient. They felt judged and condemned by the Word of God. Their common response to this, as a large community, was to begin protesting by talking to others in whispering fashion. Nevertheless, Tony took the same amount of time as he had taken after the first reading and then, when the long time was up, he rose and walked slowly to the lectern. The whole church rose with him as they understood that this was the time when the reading of the Gospel would take place. Tony did not want to give a personal introduction to the Gospel for this was Christ's words and they stood by themselves. However he did comment of why the people were all standing. Because Jesus, God the Father and the Holy Spirit were about to address them, BanyaButova. He entreated them to listen to this Word, make it their own and allow it to seed new life into their hearts.

'Lord, be in my mind, and on my lips and in my heart so that I might worthily proclaim your Holy Gospel.' Tony prayed as he made the three-fold sign of the cross on his forehead, lips and heart.

He looked up and saw hundreds of adults before him make the three-fold crosses as they had been taught to do since the missionaries had come to that area of Southern Burundi in the early 1930's. He wondered if they knew what they were praying for: 'God, come into my mind, be on my lips and abide in my heart, so that I might truly experience You, think of You, speak of You, love You…'

Then in a loud, burly voice, the young pastor began to intone the passage he had chosen from John's Gospel, chapter 15. As he sang the words, he thought of how Jesus proclaimed these sacred words to His apostles and then later in the night, He went out into the garden, suffered His agony, was arrested and tried before Pilate and finally was put to death. Tony often had wondered if he and the other priests were not called to suffer the same fate! It was the Christ-Presence in them that would invite them to lay down their lives as Christ had surrendered His Life. He often feared where this thought would lead him. Since Tony believed with all his heart that his priestly ordination made him an *alter Christus* (another Christ) he accepted the fact that someday, somewhere, somehow, that Christ-energy in him would have to be subjected to the same fate as that of the Master over nineteen centuries previous. Tony continued to sing the Gospel message and once he was into a rhythmic-pattern, it all flowed very smoothly:

> *"This is my commandment: 'Love one another as I have loved you!'*
>
> *"No one has greater love than this, to lay down one's life for one's friends."*
>
> *"You are my friends, if you do what I command you."*

"It was not you who chose me, but I, who chose you, and appointed you to go and bear fruit that will remain."
"This I command you: 'Love one another'!"

As Tony completed the last words, he lifted up the Book of the Gospels as high as his big hands could lift it over his head and chanted: "This is the Gospel, the Good News of Our Lord and Savior, Jesus Christ." And he heard the people respond in unison:
"Thanks be to God!"

Some of the people who had brought kneelers now sat down on them while most of the congregation remained standing to hear the homily. Bunched together, it looked as if they were leaning up against one another. At the base of the walls all around the church some found a place to be seated and were happy to do so. Tony was always a bit embarrassed to speak at length since so many people had to remain standing upright. And that, after having walked for an hour or two or three coming to the church. But alas, today would be short and to the point. They wouldn't have time to get tired, neither at the service nor at the homily. He took his notes from the small shelf, a single sheet of paper with his handwriting on both sides of the page, and whispered to the Holy Spirit to take over his voice box and tongue and speak the Word of God to the parishioners. He began to read the message as slowly and clearly as he could:*"Bakristu,* The greatest gift that Our Lord and Savior Jesus Christ has left us, His brothers and sisters, is the gift of His Body and Blood in the Sacrament of the Holy Eucharist. He has commanded us to celebrate this sacrament as a meal of friendship, love and peace. The gospel message we have just heard is from St. John, chapter 15, which was spoken by Jesus at the Last Supper when He left us the gift of the Eucharist. So it is an honor to hear His words to us today.

However, Jesus spoke these words in love and peace to His Apostles at the moment when He celebrated the first mass. What a moment of abiding peace this must have been for all of them. He left us the reminder that mass can only be celebrated in an atmosphere where there is unfathomable peace and selfless love among those who celebrate the Lord's meal.

Yet we must admit that here in the church of Butova today, many of you are not at peace with others! In fact many of you have hatred in your hearts for those who oppose you, or who have done you wrong over the past weeks. I am not here to judge you but I want to believe in you and in the power of God's grace living within each of you. But a community such as this, that lives in hatred and seeks only revenge, cannot celebrate the eucharistic meal of the Lord. In fact it would be a sacrilege to bring the

Lord and the eucharist into your presence here today. Both Bishop Moulin and the Vicar General, Monsignor Ruyaga agree with this decision not to celebrate mass and they support it totally.

So we will now end this service by praying for those who have died over the past weeks and by asking the Prince of Peace to restore harmony to our area. But we will not have mass or holy communion since celebrating a mass in such an atmosphere of hatred and tribalism would be wrong. So please tell others there will be no other mass today and all weekday masses are cancelled. Please go home and pray that God forgive the dreadful acts of fratricide and genocide committed here over these past weeks and beg His Spirit of peace, love, joy and kindness to come back to our community here in Butova and throughout *Burundi Bwacu.* Only at that time, will we begin mass once again here in the church of God." Tony then took a deep breath and mentioned to the people that he would conclude with prayers:

"Let us Pray: O God of all grace, inspire our leaders and those who guide us, to rebuild our country in love and peace.....Take away our fears and desires for vengeance and give us the peace that we so yearn for in our hearts.....Let us now pray for those who have died and those responsible for their deaths (Tony left a long silence and invited the people to mentioned names out loud if they so desired).....And when this peace returns, help each of us to deepen our devotion to you.....And may Almighty God bless you all and give you an unquenchable desire for His Peace and Love, in the name of the Father, and of the Son and of the Holy Spirit. Amen."

As Tony turned and stepped away from the pulpit, he heard loud uncontrolled noise and shouting throughout the whole church. People were hollering at one another and they didn't try to keep their voices from expressing their fury at being judged and condemned. There was so much anger and ugliness building in all of the people that Tony believed it would soon turn into a riot. As he returned to the area where Luigi was, the Italian priest lead the pastor back to the sacristy. Both men genuflected before the altar bearing the Blessed Sacrament and as they walked away together their eyes met as they could never have imagined that their words and message were the cause of such wild uprising and loud show of emotion. They walked side-by-side into the sacristy, wondering if they had done the right thing, or if they had instigated a riot. They both feared that they might be attacked by the people. As they took off their liturgical garb, the look on their faces seemed to say: 'We thought we were doing the right thing but maybe we miscalculated!' Luigi was the first to speak:

"Maybe it would have been safer to have stayed with Jose!" he smiled slightly reassuring Tony that he understood the price they had to pay to preach the Gospel of Christ.

Tony responded: "At least if we are going to be martyred, we will die preaching the Gospel of Love!"

"Yes," Luigi replied, "we will be the first martyrs, killed by their own parishioners! Don't they realize the true Gospel when you preach it to them. What do they expect in church? That we congratulate them for having killed so many of their brethern?"

As Tony walked out the door from the sacristy and into the church, he passed Sister Maragarita who was bringing some songbooks back to the sacristy. As she passed him, she said out of the side of her mouth, only indirectly looking his way:

"The people are all saying, *Pati*, that they want you to leave the parish as soon as possible. They want another priest, anyone, but you!"

Tony wanted to grab her and shake her but he realized he would be attacking the messenger and not the message. He also knew there would be other opportunities to discuss all this with her at a later date.

Tony continued his steps out through the church that was now almost empty and nodded at the few people who had lagged behind in the church. Then some approached him to shake his hand. They were, of course, Bahutu and many said "*Urakoze, Pati*," (Thank you, Father) and walked away. It was then that Tony realized that 'Yes' the Lord had placed His Words and His Spirit in his heart and the Word of God had been preached to the people that day in Butova. Many didn't like the sharp two-edged sword because it cut deeply to condemn their murderous acts. But the sword also touched others' hearts, mending them and giving them the desire to seek forgiveness, reconciliation and mend the hideous hatreds that had culminated in tens-of-thousands of killings over the past three weeks. Tony realized, furthermore, that reconciliation had to begin with repentance and that many people had been humbly brought to their knees by God's Message that he had delivered. The reconciliation process was only beginning. It would be a long, long tomorrow.

As Fr. Tony went from one small group of people to another outside the church after the service, his fear of violence was dispelled and he realized that the outburst in church was only a primary reaction to their feelings after hearing the message. They had shown their annoyance for a scolding most believed was not deserved. 'It is sometimes difficult to differentiate between aggression and self-defense,' the priest thought..

Many people justified the flow of blood that had overtaken Butova the past weeks and they rationalize it as self-defense. But now, in church, they were forced to consider another option: violence is never justified as a christian response even when anger and fear dominate a life situation. 'Christianity isn't easy to live,' Tony thought, 'and it is even harder to preach!'

When only a few pockets of people remained on the dusty road in front of the church, Tony walked back to the priests' house that was about thirty meters away. He felt overwhelmed now as he contemplated life at the mission without Jose. Jose had been one problem after another, a constant thorn-in-his-side since Mathias had gone back to Europe. Yet he was a confrere committed to spreading the gospel to the peoples of Africa. How sad it was that their efforts had been crushed and that the chapter of their history together at Butova would be written with scorn and defeatism. The dryness of the warm, sunny day made him thirsty and it was only then that he realized it was past 9:15 and he hadn't yet had his breakfast. But before he went into the dining room, he had one score to settle.

As Fr. Tony approached Jose's office on the outside facade of the house, he realized that even though he had been tremendously hurt and even victimized by Jose, this was no time for angry words or threats. He would remain calm, cool and collected and explain his reasoning as logically as possible even though Jose often defied any form of sound reasoning. Tony knocked on Jose's office door but there was no response. So he turned and headed down the corridor, and saw that Jose's bedroom door was open. Since Jose looked after the money collected each day from the grinding mill, he always had substantial amounts of cash in his room. So the door was seldom unlocked, let alone open. Tony surmised that Jose must be in his room.

This small room was the most unhealthy area Tony had ever seen in his life. When he had to change money and Jose was not around, he would put a key in the bedroom door, take a deep breathe of fresh air outside, open the door, go in and find the money box as quickly as possible and bring it out on the verandah to count the change outside the room. Then he would repeat the process all over again making sure he took as big a breath as he could and then put the box back. He jokingly called his confrere's bedroom: 'take a breath or instant death!' Once Jose had taken the box to his office by mistake and Tony went looking for it in Jose's bedroom. He thought he would never recover as he went from one part of the bedroom to the other, under the bed, in the closet, by the window…..Tony could not imagine how any human being could sleep in such dirt, such odors, such stench.

"Jose," Tony called out, "are you in there?" he asked as he looked into the room. Jose came out and stood in front of the door:

"I would like to talk to you for a few minutes," Tony began. "Could we go into the common room to chat?"

Jose agreed but said that he was reviewing some notes for his homily and he would join Tony as soon as possible. Tony wanted to tell him he didn't have to worry about a homily that would never be delivered but held his tongue. Passing through the refectory, he cut himself a slice of bread, poured a cup of black coffee and went to the door that gave unto the kitchen, across the roadway. He called out: "Cypriano, *amaso!*" *Amaso* meant eyes and thus eggs with unbroken yokes. This must have seemed to the Africans like some *Muzungu* staring back at them from the topside of the plate. The only other alternative was "omileti" which needed no translation! Tony then opened the doors between the dining room and common room. If Jose went directly to the latter, Tony wouldn't miss him. He knew Jose would be slow in coming, so he thought it better to get breakfast over with while he waited.

As the pastor finished his frugal meal, there was still no Jose. So he got up. checked that it was now 9:40 and went back to Jose's room. The door was closed. Tony knocked as he walked by quickly. There was no response so Jose must have gone to his office. Now coming around to the front, Tony saw that Jose's office door was opened. He found Jose hard at work, writing notes taken from a thick book.

Without any sign of apology or remorse for not coming to the meeting, Jose looked up and said how the ideas intrigued him about Pentecost and its Hebrew meaning of fifty that he now would explain to the people at the next mass. Tony realized it was Jose's way of confirming that he would say the 10:15 mass and that he wanted Tony to know that he would not do any politicking. Indirectly he was affirming his position and Tony was reading him like a book. He silently prayed for patience:

"Jose" Tony began in a slow, harsh voice, "I have never been more disappointed in anyone as I now am with you today. We made an agreement, affirmed by the bishop and vicar general and approved by our White Father superior and planned by all four of us. We had meeting after meeting where you said you would go along with our decision. You sulked most of the time, but you never had the courage to say 'no' in our public meetings. Then you tell Luigi, moments before we were to announce our position to the people, that you are not going to participate. You didn't even have the guts to tell me in person earlier this morning when we talked after prayer. I have told the BanyaButova at the early mass that from now on, mass will be canceled here in Butova and throughout all the parish until peace and love and unity will have come back to the area. So there will be no 10:15 mass! That is clear. Ditch your homily. I prefer that those who come at 10:15 will hear the message from others."

"As for you personally, Jose, I know you have had a lot of trouble following our common decisions over the past weeks. This is a vital time here and I don't want the BanyaButova seeing us divided. So I ask you to leave the mission as soon as possible. Go wherever you want, to another parish, diocese, to Europe, wherever but just GO! As soon as I can, I will see Bishop Moulin and write to Jean Lambert to give them a detailed report."

Tony turned and left the room without a reaction or response. As he walked back to the *kigo*, he heard lots of noise in the courtyard. He turned the corner and saw Mathieu and Marthe Richard coming towards him with serious looking scowls on their faces.

"We have just received a message from our directors in Bujarundi and they have asked us to evacuate Butova as soon as possible." Mathieu began with a voice sounding as if he were out of breath. He continued:

"They have sent us orders to join them as soon as possible. The other two couples want to come with us, so we have decided to take all our belongings and go to Bujarundi. If we leave soon, we can be there before nightfall. So now we have a big favor to ask of you!" They both looked directly at Tony, with their fingers entwined together as a sign of their special love for each other. Only a week before, Mathieu and Marthe had come to Tony and shared with him the exuberant joy that they were pregnant and were expecting their first child sometime before the end of the calendar year. Tony looked at them. They both knew his love and admiration for them which meant that they already had whatever they were asking of him!

"We only have our car and we are six with our belongings, books, furniture, wardrobes and so on. We need a truck to get everything to Bujarundi. I'm sure a brother would come with us and drive back tomorrow if you would lend us the van." Mathieu concluded his request with a slight, shy smile. Tony had always thought how close Mathieu resembled classical pictures he had seen of Abraham Lincoln. Mathieu, like the slain American president, had a long black beard, was very tall and walked taking high steps with his work boots flaunting in the air. When he wore a three piece suit on special occasions, Tony could see nothing in Mathieu but the great American from yesteryear. For all these reasons, he liked Mathieu very much and trusted him without question. Finally Marthe added:

"You will have the truck back tomorrow, we assure you!"

"It is yours for as long as you need it," Tony replied not missing a step or giving them time to blink.

"However there is no gas in it and we don't have any here at the mission. Maybe Brother Louis can get you the key to the pump at the school?" he suggested.

Mathieu looked at Marthe, reached out with one hand around her waist and said:

"Let's go to the brothers' and see if anyone is available for the *safari* and if they have some gas." With that Marc and Lise Hendrick, a Belgian couple who also taught at the school and who would be leaving with the Richards, came out to the *kigo* and said they would start loading the truck while Mathieu and Marthe were organizing things with the brothers. Soon the other couple, Canadians Emile and Raymonde Lacroix, appeared and said they had finished all their personal packing and were ready to help the Hendricks load the truck.

These three couples had lived in three separate but inter-joined apartments in the back of the mission. It was novel and pleasant to have married women walking around the back cloister of the rectory and all the priests had enjoyed the pleasant exchanges in the *kigo* with these three couples. Often the wives would do some baking and would send over a dessert for the clerics which now would be dearly missed. Raymonde Lacroix often baked them a carrot cake which Tony told everyone 'was to die for!' When President Sabimana was visiting earlier that year and there was a carrot cake in the 'fridge, Raymonde had offered him a piece. The delicacy found favor on the presidential palate and Mathias spent a long time explaining to the chief-of-state that this cake was made from carrots!

But the three couples' security had to be assured above all else. Because Marthe Richard was pregnant, Mathieu seemed to be very anxious about her safety and that of their baby. They returned within a half-hour saying they could get gas anytime since Mathieu had been given the key to the pump. Brother Louis, everyone's favorite brother with his sense of humor and gregarious laugh, had given Mathieu the key and accepted to drive them. He told them to pass the message on to Tony that he would surely be back the following afternoon with the van.

Tony remained in the *kigo* with the three couples and helped them carry their belongings to the van. The year before, when they arrived in Butova, the couples had hired three local teenage boys to work in the kitchen with whoever did the cooking on each particular day. Since all three women taught, they normally decided in mid-afternoon who would prepare the culinary delights that evening. Then they would all eat together.

The three boys were Alfredo, the son of the catechist Samueli Sumura, and two of his friends: Luduvico and Osicari. On this clear May day, the boys looked anxious and withdrawn as they carried many of the heavier articles to the van. Mathieu and Marthe called Tony aside and said they had something further to ask of him. They started to whisper, so Tony lead them over toward the mission house where they would be able to speak normally. Marthe started by explaining:

"We really are attached to these three boys who have rendered us great service over the past year. However each of them has expressed to us that he is a Muhutu. They all are fearing for their lives. Over this past week, they have not been going home at night after work, but we let them sleep in our living rooms or kitchen according to each couple's availability. They say that they have been accused and if they weren't protected by us, they would have been killed already. I presume you know that Samueli, Alfredo's father, has been taken ten days ago and all believe he is dead. So our plan is to hide them in the trunk under the truck and fill the outside space with boxes so that when anyone tries to look in at a checkpoint, they won't be seen. We want to know what you think about this idea and seeing that it is your vehicle, we felt obliged to tell you."

Tony did not hesitate to respond. After taking a deep breath he congratulated them for being so generous and kind in thinking about these African young men that they loved so much.

"However, I have to disagree with your doing this. If you were caught, what do you think the Batutsi would do to you? I thought you wanted to escape to Bujarundi while you were still able? There is every possibility in the world that many checkpoints will have you take out everything just to be mean to you and show their authority over you. They will most surely find the boys and arrest all of you for trying to hide them. Further if they were to discover your plan, they would consider the boys guilty of treason since they were trying to escape. Don't you realize that it is situations like these that they are looking for to accuse us *Bazungu* of being on the side of the Bahutu? They would come down so very hard on you for meddling in their affairs as Europeans and make you an example for others. They might even kill you. And the reason why you have been called to Bujurundi as soon as possible is because your safety is in question. I'm sorry, Mathieu and Marthe, you deserve better, but I know it would be making a mistake."

The three walked back to where the others had continued the loading of the van. The Richards then told the other two couples the result of their talk with Tony and there was much whispering and murmuring. Then they all got back to the work at hand. As Emile Lacroix passed Tony along the common path to the truck, he asked;

"So you don't think it would be good to take the boys with us?"

Tony looked at him, put down a chair he was carrying and said:

"Are you crazy? There is more than a chance that at one of the roadblocks, they will stop you and ask you to take everything out just to see what you *Bazungu* have and if they might persuade you into giving them something. When they would catch you red-handed like this you would be arrested immediately, I thought that you wanted to get your wives and yourselves out safely. That would be the silliest thing you could do. No! No! I say emphatically, No!" Tony was surprised at the clearness of his voice and the absoluteness of his thought. As he repeated 'No! No! No!' he realized that he, like all the other missionaries, had taken to repeating a word over and over again to give it emphasis. This was the *genre* they had all picked up from Bishop Moulin who continually repeated the words and expressions he wanted emphasized over and over again. The good bishop spoke very flamboyantly both in French, his mother tongue, and in Kirundi, his adopted language for the past forty-five years. Tony often thought of imitating the bishop in Kirundi but was afraid, when speaking spontaneously to people, that he would make a mistake in grammar or pronunciation and then repeat the mistake over and over again. So he stuck with imitating Bishop Moulin in French only! He picked up the chair again and walked towards the truck.

Slowly they came to the end of the loading and Tony invited them to come to the priests' dining room for something to eat before they left.

"You never know when and where you will be getting another meal". he said rather jokingly and all laughed nervously, realizing there were four or five hours of unknown happenings ahead of them.

"We don't want to disturb your cook and it is a short time before lunch. Let's just go in, sit, have some coffee and a few bananas and we will be on our way," Marthe Richard said as Tony ushered them into the refectory.

As he held the door open for his six impromptu guests, Tony noticed some singing in the distance. It was a familiar hymn that they always sung at mass, and it was coming from the church building itself. As he heard many voices, his chin and jaw dropped so much, he thought his head would hit the floor. Quickly Tony asked his guests to sit down at table and went over to the other door and called out to Cypriano who came running out as he usually did when the priests beckoned for him. Tony shouted "*Kahawa, Imiwi*, Cypi," (Coffee, Bananas) and he went back into the dining room, crossed over to the other door and excused himself from his guests, all in one movement. Walking quickly towards the singing voices in the church, he passed Luigi's room and knocked on the door. A loud "*Avante*" came from inside, so Tony opened the door, peaked his head inside and said:

"Luigi, would you mind going to sit with the couples? They are leaving permanently for Bujarundi and I invited them for coffee but now I must go over to the church to investigate something. I don't think I'll like what I know I'll find! Just stay with them a few minutes and I'll be back as soon as I can."

He was gone in a flash and Luigi went out immediately, locked his door and joined the couples in the refectory. He, too, heard some singing in the background and was glad Tony had not asked him to accompany him to church but simply to remain in the dining room and entertain the three couples.

Tony entered the church from the side door and stopping, stared at what was happening. There were about 50 young adults in the church, sitting on the floor in the front. They were so close to each other, squeezed into that small area, that Tony could hardly differentiate one from another. Jose was in the pulpit, reading the Gospel for Pentecost Sunday. He had white vestments on, obviously forgetting that the color of the day was red to reflect the flames of fire the Holy Spirit was to bring to this community. Tony smiled when he realized Jose's error. He was so determined to say mass on Pentecost, yet he hadn't even consulted the *Ordo* (Latin for order: ritual of liturgical codes, signs and symbols of a particular day) for the color to wear at mass. That was typical of Jose. A one-track mind, often derailed!

Fr. Tony had a choice to make. Either interrupt the mass and send Jose back to the sacristy to devest. This would publicly embarrass his confrere beyond repair. Or let things go and deal with the situation later. He remembered Bishop Moulin defining the role of the missionary in Burundi at this time of so many killings. So Tony understood that this strategy applied to the present situation as well. He walked to the front of the pulpit and Jose automatically looked down at him distractedly. Tony stood there, listening, his arms crossed over his chest, looking as stern as he could. Maliciously, he wanted to put as much pressure on Jose as he could. But Tony couldn't bear to interrupt the service. It was the grace of God that was passing through, even though Jose was doing something Tony considered wrong.

As the proclaiming of the gospel came to completion, Jose left the pulpit and walked down the steps to be closer to the young people. Tony saw this as a move to get away from him. So he, in turn, walked out behind the gathered congregation and stood behind them and listened to what Jose had to say. He thought: 'I will not interrupt him, as long as he chooses to talk about the Holy Spirit, the gifts and the power of God. However if he dares to get political or say anything about the decision we have made, then I will intervene and send the young people packing. That will be the end of 'his' mass.'

Jose began with a great smile and he started telling a story about himself riding his *pikipiki* the other day and how he scared some chickens. Jose laughed so loudly that smiles came over his audience, not because of what he was telling them about himself, but because of the loud volume of his voice and the tremolo in his voice box as he described the scene of frightened chickens. This reminded Tony of the many evenings when Jose would present the *akasinema* (cinema) and the confreres would come from the surrounding parishes to listen to the way Jose was listening to the sound track in French and immediately translating it into Kirundi. All considered his descriptions more entertaining than the movie!

Tony stood in the back for five, then ten minutes and finally Jose came to an end. When the prayers of the faithful were over, and no one had mentioned praying for peace and unity amid the political turmoil throughout the country, Jose went to the altar to begin the liturgy of the eucharist. Since all these prayers were not spontaneous, Tony believed there would be no problems with politics, and quietly tiptoed out the door he had entered some twenty minutes earlier. He went back to the mission house and heard the three couples with Luigi coming out from the refectory, their voices echoing as they walked along the enclosed corridor toward the *kigo* and the parked mission van. Their three cooks: Alfredo, Luduvico and Osicari were standing by the truck looking very sad. Someone or something had already made it known to them that they would not be going with the Europeans. Their faces looked drawn and their eyes were filled with fear. The three women said they wanted to go back to their quarters for one last look and to pick up their purses. Tony could tell that they had other needs since they all were very teary-eyed. The three men went over to their cooks and started to shake their hands. Alfredo asked with tears in his eyes:

"Can't we go with you, *Monsieur* Mathieu?"

Tony believed it was his duty to reply since he had sabotaged the plans of the three couples:

"Alfredo, Luduvico, Osicari," he whispered in a very low voice, "you know how difficult and dangerous it will be for these *Bazungu* to drive to Bujurundi, through all those road blocks. Someone would surely have them disembark and inspect all their belongings and if they were to hide you, you would, no doubt, be found. Then you all would be killed, without any defense or mercy. Furthermore since the roads are so dry you would suffocate in that small space near the ground before you would get to Bujurundi. No, that is not a choice anyone can undertake. You can stay in these apartments where the Bazungu have been protecting you and we will try to do as much as we can for you."

As he was concluding, the three ladies joined their husbands. Brother Louis arrived and put smiles on everyone's face. What cheer this beautiful man brought with him wherever he went. The hugs were very tearful and heart-wrenching. The women hugged each of their cooks and the men came over to Tony and Luigi and shook hands with them with vim and vigor and Tony gave each a big bear-hug. They all realized that these people had lived a traumatic experience together over the past weeks and they would remember each other and love and support each other for as long as they would breathe air on the same side of planet earth. One by one the couples climbed into the vehicles, rolled down the windows and waved fond 'good-byes'. Brother Louis went first with the Richards and the two other couples followed in another vehicle that had been given to the Lacroix by CUSO (Canadian University Students Overseas). They would drive the volkswagen to Bujarundi and return it to the organization there. Since both the Lacroix and the Hendricks were all small featured people, they decided to risk having four persons in the car all the way to Bujarundi. As they all drove out of sight around the priests' residence, Mathieu put his head out the window on the passenger's side and whistled a shrill loud sound. Tony couldn't believe how much it resembled the *induru*, the Kirundi cry of death. He wondered how many more cries of *induru* would be heard here in Butova and throughout Burundi before the rest of this terrible nightmare would end.

Fr. Tony turned back to the three young men who were looking at their last chance to safety disappear around the building. He encouraged them to go back into their quarters and stay there.

'Hopefully all will blow over and they will not be arrested,' he thought to himself more wishfully than realistically. Tony then asked them if they wanted to go to confession, leaving it understood that death could be imminent for these three Bahutu youths. They answered in the affirmative and Tony told them to prepare themselves and he would come back after lunch and meet with each of them individually. As their human *kizungu* protection moving farther and farther away, their hours were now numbered.

17. A Fairly Peaceful Afternoon

Tony and Luigi started to walk back and forth in the kigo and Tony complained how the little clay stones would always get into his sandals. They walked out toward the garden, to the brick fence that walled them from the outside world all around them. They talked in gratitude about the different workers who had helped them put in these gardens, the other workers at the grinding mill and those who washed and ironed their clothes. One of the most difficult realities for the missionaries was that they were never certain who was Mututsi or who was Muhutu. So they remained uncertain if their workers, absent on this Sunday afternoon, would be alive and ready for the activities of the following day. Thus was life on this Pentecost Sunday in Butova.

Finally they looked up and saw Cypriano running towards them announcing that lunch was ready. The two men walked toward the dining room and Luc came in the other door from the corridor to join them. Tony said a short prayer and the three men sat down. They never waited for Jose as he was always late and could keep them standing for a long time if they were courteous.

Luc was first to speak as Luigi dished out the soup.

"I heard singing in the church at ten-thirty. Did Jose go over and say mass?"

"Yes, he did." Tony replied in a monotone voice. "And I will deal with that as soon as I can. I have already told him that he is to be leaving here this afternoon. I presume he is in his office or room packing."

"Not at all," Luc replied. I just walked by both his office and his room and they were locked. He must be out with the youth groups. He never comes to lunch with everyone else on Sunday noon."

Tony felt a headache coming on so he said:

"Let's change the subject and not talk about him or what is happening all around us. We have made certain decisions and Jose has contradicted them. Thus there is no way for us to continue as a team and therefore he has to go. I'm more than sure the bishop will take our side. In fact, he has already taken our side and will be very angry at Jose's lack of cooperation. He has never trusted him and I'm sure he will ask him to leave the diocese after the latest incident. I don't think there will be a problem getting along without him, especially now since there will be no sacramental activity.

Mass has been celebrated in our parish church for the last time for quite a while. These people are in no way ready to forgive each other. I'm afraid the genocide, horrible tragedy that it is, will continue until something drastic happens."

The three missionaries sat around the table as the conversation went from the way Europe was preparing for the Olympic Games in Germany to the news about the missioners' different families. Since they were all young, Luigi and Tony in their late twenties and Luc, still a teenager doing his military service, the family news was always bits and pieces about what their parents were doing or what was going on in the lives of their siblings. Tony was proud to announce that his sister's two little girls were growing stronger each day. One was one-and-a-half and the other three months. In his heart he longed to be back to Canada to share life with them. Even if it still was May, Christmas would be a possibility and now that he was so upset about the savagery, his desire to leave, vacation with his family and come back to another country of Africa was always distracting him from the reality of life in Burundi.

'Healthy thoughts!' he had concluded.

Luigi also talked about his family and said he too, wanted to be with them in Italy as soon as possible. He saw little reason to stay in Butova, especially now that they were not giving the sacraments. However he knew that the priests couldn't abandon the mission and that their job was to be seen, and embarrass the soldiers and police into doing things honestly and correctly. He saw the community as watchdogs without a specific mandate.....except from God!

Luc mentioned that he had recently received a letter from his 'patron' as he called him. M. Lucien Catoire had his office in Paris and had come to Burundi and Bujarundi and then Butova when Luc was appointed to the mission. All the community had met him and found him to be a charming and courageous individual. He introduced Luc to them as if he were leaving them his very own son and Tony had fond memories of the two days Catoire spent with them before going back to the capital and then returning to Europe.

"He says '*salut*' to you all and has heard that there was some trouble in the country." Luc continued, "However he didn't indicate that the people of Europe were startled in any way by the happenings. He concluded that it was not serious but his letter was dated in early May which was around the first slaughters here. A lot of water has gone under the bridge since then!" Luigi jumped in: "And most of the water has been polluted and turned to blood with thousands of *cadavers* of the poor Bahutu thrown into it."

After lunch, Tony asked his colleagues if he could be excused since he was very tired and coffee might just keep him from a needed *siesta*. Luc and Luigi thought it would be good for them as well to go to their rooms and rest. As they headed out the doors, Tony asked them if they thought it a good idea to come together with the sisters and brothers and celebrate a common mass towards the end of the afternoon. The two replied that they though it a great gesture of solidarity and Luigi said he would prepare the music and play his guitar, believing the decision had already been made. Tony marveled at the ease with which they made decisions when Jose wasn't there. Luc said he welcomed the prayer support with all the religious in Butova. Tony went directly to his office and wrote two notes: one to the sisters in Kirundi and the other to the brothers in French. He then went outside and saw a young student from the TTC and asked him to take both letters to the respective communities.

"Put the responses under my office door when they give them back to you and here is something for your efforts," he said as he handed the student a ten franc paper note. Finally he went around the corner to his room, unlocked the door and fell onto his bed. He was so exhausted mentally and physically that he could not move. Quickly he went into a sound sleep, still fully dressed and lying diagonally across his bedspread. This would be a comfortable sleep and Tony relaxed better than he ever had over the past strenuous weeks. He would certainly need the extra rest.

An hour and a-half later, Tony awoke, startled by the barking of the two mission dogs who, during the day, were tied up in the kennel in the corner of the yard facing the fathers' bedrooms. Normally the dogs slept soundly during the sunny days and were released to prowl the *kigo* at night. They were both female German Shepherds and took pride in protecting the mission and the fathers. But for them to bark continually during the day meant something or someone was disturbing them. Tony picked up both notes with positive responses and went out on the verandah and met Luc and Luigi who were already there. People from outside the walls were shouting:

"You have three traitors there, and you must turn them over to us. If not, you are not a friend of *UPRONA*."

Tony motioned to the other two to join him inside and he walked down the corridor to the hallway leading to the dining room. He wondered if these people, trying to attack the mission, were also upset at what he had said in church that morning. Luigi said that he had not heard any reference to the morning service but the attackers were really angry that the fathers were hiding the three young men. Tony breathed a sigh of relief and went back out to calm the dogs who were still barking. They were so upset that they hadn't even eaten the food that had brought to them. Finally they quieted down and went over to the food and started to eat. The three missionaries went in to the living room for a cup of coffee that would compose them as they discussed what they had to do concerning the three boys they were hiding in the couples' apartments.

Luigi looked at Tony and asked him a question that had been on his mind over the past few days:

"Now that we have stopped giving the sacraments," he went on, "what are we doing here? Our work from morning to night has been saying mass, teaching the people, hearing confessions and giving the sacrament of the sick. There were marriages to prepare and bless and confirmation classes and preparation for baptism. I have never realized more that all our work-day is centered around the sacraments!"

Tony responded, hesitatingly, since he, too, had been thinking in exactly the same way. He really didn't know what they would do from day to day now that the sacramental ministry was being placed on hold. But he would stay put as he had promised Moulin and Ruyaga.

"I was thinking that we are now like the first missionaries who came to Central Africa eighty-years ago. Before they made any converts to the faith, they had to encourage people to live according to the natural law without telling anyone about God. Then when their message seemed to be received by many, they explained the roots of christianity. So we, too, will have all the time in the world to teach them the essentials of our faith which is love: of God and of neighbor. They need to hear that more than anything else. I don't think we will be bored now that we are back to a meaningful method of pre-evangelization. So let's be free to go to their homes and their hillsides and talk to them individually about the principles of human living. In a sense, I am happy, with tears in my eyes, that this all has happened. It is like the '*felix culpa*' that we sing about on Holy Saturday at the vigil. We are not happy about the sin that caused Jesus to die. But we are happy that sin has brought us the Savior, Who has obtained salvation for us. So it is a 'happy fault'. Similarly here in Burundi, we are not happy about the murders by the thousands but we are happy that now there will be a new way of living and evaluating whether people are believers or not. So many catholics have rejected their faith by killing others or having their neighbors killed. We must now begin a new era where we can question the authenticity of our catholic faith."

"The catholic faith does not consist in going to church on Sunday and following all the external rules. But it is contradicted by false-witnessing telling lies and committing perjury or allowing innocent people to be murdered. They must realize that because they are on the side of the government does not give them a free hand to assassinate others. If they have killed another or caused his death they are guilty of the greatest of all evils. Never before have I refused catholics holy communion. But today a whole church was refused, thousands of them, because their hatred was stronger than their love. How could anyone say that they love Christ? 'Love?' 'Christ?'…." Fr. Tony heard himself repeat, as if he had made an error. These two words could not stand beside each other in the Burundi that he now knew. What had gone so terribly wrong with this largely christian population?

Walking back to their rooms, the missionaries encouraged each other. Tony mentioned to Luc and Luigi that he had received positive responses from both Brother Alex Labine and *Mama Mukuru.* Both communities would gather together for an evening mass in the church side chapel at 5pm. He added in retrospect that he had toyed with the idea of scheduling the mass later, at 6pm when it would be dark outside and no Africans would be in the immediate vicinity of the church. But he had thought better of it since he wanted mass to end before nightfall. He felt somewhat embarrassed that the *Bazungu* missionaries could have mass with the African sisters and missionary brothers when the eucharist was denied the entire parish! That was an issue he was confronting in his own conscience. He felt very unworthy, in his own sinfulness, of celebrating the eucharist.

'However, the state of urgency dictates that we religious have the strength of the eucharist,' he justified.

Fr. Tony Joseph had one promise to keep......a debt to render. He had given his word to Alfredo, Luduvico and Osicari that he would hear their confessions. And so now he must go and help these three young men prepare themselves for almost certain death.

'Prepare these mere boys for death,' he heard himself say and distain overwhelmed his whole person.

As Tony walked down the two steps from the corridor in front of the priests' rooms and over the clay stones of the *kigo,* he spit his disgust on the ground and noticed his saliva was thin and putrid. He believed this was a sign that he had absolutely no energy left in his body. He braced himself, not knowing that this day would be more and more difficult as it progressed. Before he would be able to retire to his bed that night, things would be worse than he could even have imagined.

As he came to the back apartments, he didn't have the faintest idea where the boys might be although he figured they would be together, hiding somewhere for fear of the angry people outside. They certainly had heard the attackers a short time earlier and feared for their very lives. Tony trusted that the soldiers or police would not enter this private property and thus the boys were better protected than any of their friends hiding out in the *mihana*.

"Alfredo, Luduvico, Osicari," Fr. Tony called out, *"ni jewe Pati Antonio* (it is I, Fr. Anthony). Please come out to see me. I am alone and won't hurt you or let you get hurt."

He saw the kitchen door open gradually and he heard a squeaking sound as the door widened larger and larger. Tony felt like he was watching a horror movie on TV. A dark-skinned hand appeared on the outside part of the door handle and then he saw Alfredo come forth. He truly was the son of the catechist Samueli Samura whom Tony had liked so much because of his honesty and simplicity. Tony had enjoyed Samueli and found the catechist to be a special friend. He often laughed heartily with him. The pastor had become distraught ten days earlier when he heard that Samueli had been arrested and had 'disappeared'. People recounted how he was seen going out on one of the trucks to the common graves near Vurura. In most families, when a father was arrested and murdered, either by machete, sledge hammer or transported to the common graves, the police normally pursued the rest of the family in a very hostile way which often lead to the arrests of sons and brothers and the confiscation of all material possessions that the police were interested in stealing for themselves. The Batutsi *bakuru* could not and would not believe that a father would act independently of his sons. If the father were a traitor, then his sons were guilty as well! So. many wives had to morn not only the loss of their husbands but subsequently three, four, five or six sons as well. So many wives became widows by their husband's murder but also experienced other family members pass by the machete, sword or sledge-hammer.

As Tony looked at Alfredo, this young boy who had learned so much from Marthe Richard about cooking and France and European styles and how to set and decorate a table and what foods to serve together, he realized that the three boys' chances of survival were very minimal. He wondered if the boys blamed him, since he had absolutely forbidden the couples to take the boys along with them to Bujarundi. The pastor stood by his decision since he was convinced that they would never have made it to the capital without being discovered at a roadblock somewhere. The idea crossed Tony's mind that the couples could have let the boys off in some barren area. But eventually they would have been picked up by a Mututsi and when they would not have been able to produce a *laissez-passer*, they would have been killed instantly. Tony reasoned that the three boys were still alive here in Butova and thus there was still a smidgen of hope that all might miraculously blow over and these three boys would be free.

Osicari and finally Luduvico came forward and all three young men, approached Tony with their right hands outreaching to greet the pastor.

"I have come," Tony began, "as I said I would. I promised to hear your confessions. It is not easy for me to say this to you. This is a very dangerous time for all Bahutu and I want to make sure that God is with you. Thousands of people have died in Burundi over the past weeks without having the opportunity of receiving the sacraments, namely confession that would take away all their sins. I asked Kizungu to allow me to meet with the prisoners to hear the confessions of all those who were being taken out by truck and he reassured me that they were going to Vurura and thus Monsignor Luduvico Ruyaga could hear their confessions. Then a priest followed their truck and came to tell me that they never went near the area where Ruyaga lives. Rather they went and dumped them in common graves and gave them the *coup de grace* with a sword and watched them die.....obviously without a priest. So I am very pleased that I can give you the opportunity of confession. If afterwards, you die, then you will go straight to heaven. So thank God that you are here at the mission even if you would have preferred going to Bujarundi with the *Bazungu*. Maybe God wanted you to stay back and be ready to die rather than have you taken from the van with no opportunity to receive confession.

The three young men, like sheep being led to the slaughter-house, nodded their heads and said a common '*Egome*' (Yes) to the priest. Tony went into the kitchen and readied himself to hear their confessions. He had already suggested that they take the necessary time to examine their consciences and confess not only their recent sins, but every serious wrong of their past lives. Then he closed the door. For a second, it was like closing the whole world out, away from himself. He thought only of these three young men and asked God for the grace to be attentive to their needs and besought Divinity to give them strength and courage to live the last moments of their lives in peacefulness. But deep within himself, his feelings were colored with deep dark despair, as he realized the boys would probably soon be arrested and taken to the common graves shortly afterwards. His reflections, sadly, were correct, not premature in any way!

'Cursed be these hypocrites,' the pastor thought, 'who are ruining their whole country by killing their able-bodied men and so many of their young boys.' Tony was very angry and his abhorrence seemed to come through every pore of his body. The only way he could try to bring about peace of heart and patience of mind was through prayer. He tried to allow God to calm him, sat on a chair and after about ten minutes felt some peacefulness and serenity. Then he got up, went to the door and invited the three young men to come in one-by-one.

Tony was rather surprised when Luduvico was the first to enter the kitchen. He knelt at Tony's feet, blessed himself and started the formal words of confession. What Fr. Tony was about to hear, he would seal in his heart forever. He had been taught in the seminary that what a priest hears in confession is so secret, so private, so personal that he must forget it as soon as he has finished dealing with it in the sacramental experience. Tony knew that was merely theory. He had tried to make abstraction of what had been told to him under the sacred seal, but it sometimes was very difficult. Especially for Tony. His memory for minute, insignificant things seemed so exact that he always had to make an effort to try to forgot. This really was a burden that should not have been put on the shoulders of any human being! If he didn't know the person, then it was easier to forgot the whole incident. But if that penitent were a catechist, a teacher or someone else he knew personally, his memory would recall the sins over and over again when he was with the person outside sacramental intimacy.

Tony knew that what these boys would now say to him would remain with him for a very long time since their hours were numbered and their murderers were close at hand. He realized that they, like him, were contemplating that this would be their last confession of their lives.

Luduvico started telling his sins:

"I was late for mass many times, I swore often, I hated those who came to arrest and kill my father, my two uncles and my older brother and I had many bad thoughts. And, oh yes, *Pati*, I missed mass today, Sunday."

Tony allowed a long silence to follow Luduvico's sins, imagining them dissolving in Christ's Precious Blood on the Cross. Then he began to counsel him:

"Listen to me, Luduvico. God knows you. He knows your every thought, every desire of your heart. And God wants only one thing. That you be happy with Him some day in heaven. Don't think of these Batutsi who can kill your body. They can't kill your soul, your inner spirit, your true self. You were made to live forever with God and now that I will give you forgiveness for all your sins, I want you to ask God to fill you with love for Him and to take you home to heaven with Him." Tony went on:

"God cannot refuse you such a request, to love Him more and more each and every moment of your life. I am now going to give you forgiveness of your sins and never think of them again. Never wish evil on anyone and love your enemies, love those who want to kill you, those who killed your father, uncles, brother and others of your family who have died. Forgive, in advance, those who want to kill you and ask God to have pity on each and every one of them for their ignorance and sinfulness If you fail, ask God to forgive you and by the absolution I will now give you, God will forgive all your failures and sins from now until you die. So straight away, thank God for His love and allow Him to clean your heart perfectly."

Father Anthony Joseph continued with absolution:

"By the power given to me by God and lived out in and through the church, the Body of Christ, Luduvico, I forgive you all your wrongdoing, failures and sins and I absolve you in the name of the Father and of Jesus, God's Son, and of the Holy Spirit." Both men replied: *"AMINA"*.

Tony then concluded the sacramental experience by telling Luduvico that his penance was to read a beautiful passage of Scripture, 1 Corinthians 13. The priest then took out a small bible in Kirundi that he had tucked into his back pocket, turned to the end of 1 Corinthians and began to read and pray the penance with Luduvico:

"If I speak the language of men and angels, but do not have love.....I am a blaring brass and a clanging cymbal. If I have faith to move mountains, but do not have love.....I am nothing. Love is gentle, love is kind, love is not boastful. Love never keeps track of evil but love rejoices in the truth..... There are three things that are important: faith, hope and love, but the greatest of these in LOVE".

He blessed Luduvico, took his two hands into his own and held him tightly:

"Be strong, son, you are walking into a new life, a life so beautiful that you have never dreamed it possible. The Batutsi can give you true freedom in death: for the moment you leave this earth, is the moment you will enter eternal life in heaven and be totally happy with God, Who is Love. So rejoice, your name is written in the book of heaven! Go to the Lord and continue to pray for all of us who are left behind."

As Tony stood and hugged the young man, he felt as if his arms were stretching beyond the whole universe and reaching to heaven. He realized that he was hugging a saint and believed that the body he was touching and the soul he was ministering to would be in God's glory in a very short time. Tony allowed himself to be carried away by the emotions of the moment and his eyes welled up with tears. Although his whole body was shaking, he felt a calm come over himself, knowing that through the priesthood he had prepared another person to spend eternity in the arms of God. What a marvelous gift God had given him in this extraordinary grace called 'priesthood'. He was living a mystery so great and so magnificent, yet he would never be able to tell anyone about it. But that did not matter. It was his secret with the Lord and Savior, Jesus Christ and no one else on this planet would ever enter into their bond of intimacy.

Tony stood up and Luduvico moved toward the closed door. Tony had a strong desire to hug this young man once more. He needed to show his support again since he doubted if he would ever see Luduvico alive, this side of heaven. He thought of how God would want to hug all three of the boys for their bravery and strength and he reached out and put his arms around Luduvico once more:

"I want to tell you, as God's representative, that He loves you very much and this hug means that He supports you because soon you might be drastically humiliated by the soldiers, the policemen and your neighbors. Never question that God is on your side and no matter how they might hurt you, God will lift you up and give you strength to overcome all prejudice and hatred. Never stop loving those who despise you and even want to kill you. Jesus said: 'Love your enemies.' And I say: 'beg God to help your enemies, pray for them that they receive grace and spiritual help.' Luduvico stepped back and Fr. Tony opened the door, peeked his head outside and said:

"We're through. Who will be next?" He preferred to grin rather than be solemn and pompous. Besides he needed the added smile himself, for most of the muscles in his face he used to grin hadn't been exercised in weeks. He was totally depressed.

Alfredo came next. Tony welcomed him into the room. As the young man knelt at the priest's feet, Tony was impressed at the way he knew his prayers and the introduction to confession so well. Certainly this man was the son of Samueli Samura and his father had prepared him well for the sacraments. Obviously he had also prepared him well for other trials of life as well.

Alfredo knelt very straight and it was heartwarming for Tony to hear him say each prayer with deep devotion and respect. He confessed his sins with marked humility, describing each act and gesture in as much detail that Fr. Tony could understand both the degree of knowledge and the amount of remorse in his heart. Tony gave him absolution and prayed a blessing over him. He talked to him as well about his own difficulty in not being able to love and forgive some people who have done him wrong:

"They have killed your dear father and that has made it hard for me as well to forgive them. Yet I was only one of his friends. He was your relative, your flesh and blood, your father, your lifeline. So God knows that it is very hard for you to forgive them, Alfredo. Please say these words after me:

"Lord, God, Our heavenly Father. You looked down from heaven one sad Friday afternoon and saw some of your children, that You had created, put to death Your Only Begotten Son, Jesus Christ. How irate you must have been to see your own creation killing your Beloved." Tony reached out his hands, palms downward and placed them on Alfredo's head and continued:

"Look down on us, this afternoon and give us the grace to pardon and forgive those who have been responsible for the demise of Samueli Samura. And I pray to you, Heavenly Father, for Alfredo his son. Give this young man the grace of forgiveness and reconciliation. Help him not to be resentful, but allow him to forgive all those who have killed his father."

Tony again walked the second young man to the door and embraced him, telling him he would always be there to love and support him. He then opened the door and ushered him out. Sadly, this was the last time Fr. Tony would ever talk to Samura's son.

Osicari seemed to be very anxious as his turn arrived. He came through the door like a burst of wind and Tony sat down in his chair while the young man knelt beside him. He went through the introductory prayers rather quickly and not with the same clear articulation as Alfredo had done previously. Tony noted his struggles and empathized with him. Osicari began his confession of sins:

"I stole many times from the market place because my family was hungry and my father couldn't find work. But, Pati, I only stole food and just enough for our family to eat for a few days. I have not gone to mass for three weeks because I feared going out and being arrested, for many of my friends have also been killed. I was afraid of getting caught myself and put into prison or even murdered. I once attended a meeting before Easter and I gave them some of my money to buy machetes. I knew this was for the attempted 'coup' and I am a Muhutu. We are so many that we should be rulers and not slaves to the Batutsi. At times I fear them, I fear for my life and I wonder if they will kill all of us. I sleep with a knife under my bed and if someone were to enter my room here on the compound and try to attack me, I would spring on him and stab and kill him. I confess this because I believe these are wrong desires, wanting to hurt all the Batutsi, but I don't care. They have killed many of my friends, my father and brother and they will end up eradicating me. I hate them so much that I want to get them before they have the chance of getting me. Please don't tell me, Pati, to give up the knife. It is my only protection and the only way that I will stay alive."

Fr. Tony listened attentively and shook his head from side to side:

"No" he responded to Osicari's query. "I will never tell you not to protect yourself. We all need to look after ourselves. Charity demands that we begin with ourselves. So you have the duty and responsibility to protect yourself first and above all. So don't feel guilty about having a knife. Nonetheless there is a big difference between willingly killing another and defensively protecting yourself. However if the soldiers come to accuse you and arrest you, what will you do?" Tony asked.

Osicari pondered the question quietly and realized that he had to be honest both with the priest and with himself:

"Earlier they came to get us to come out of the compound and they would have arrested us….I have heard that they have gone to arrest some of my family and my father has 'disappeared'…..they accused them falsely of plotting to burn houses of the Batutsi and steal their cows. So you are right in predicting what will happen. But most of those who allowed themselves to be arrested also allowed themselves to die and were carted off by trucks to the common graves. So I have pondered this question for a long time. If they come to arrest me, I will do everything I can to free myself before they tie me up and lead me to Puma. Once they have me there, they can accuse me of everything and I will not be able to defend myself. Obviously I will be carted off in the truck the following day. Therefore I will attack them when I can, which is the moment when they come to arrest me. Yes, I gave money to buy machetes. But that is justice. We Bahutu form most of the population of this country and we must rule ourselves. So I gave money to bring this about. But the coup failed!"

Tony felt a slight smile come over his face. He stared at Osicari and realized that finally he had met a Muhutu who was not taking this genocide sitting down. He had thought that their amorphous and pessimistic attitude, this fatalism was a kihutu trait, that they had all inherited from their ancestors! But finally, here, encountering Osicari through the sacrament of reconciliation, Tony felt the passion, the unquenchable thirst for justice that this young man had and he was filled with pride.

"Osicari" he said to the penitent. "I have rarely heard anyone speak so well about his wonderful people. You really are aware of the situation and I can see you have suffered much for the way the Batutsi have treated you and your family. Further I understand that you want to murder all those who have injured your father and your brother. But remember you are a christian and God does not want us to have hatred, jealousy, or murder in our hearts. As for the weapon, if they send armed soldiers to arrest you, it will be difficult for you to respond to their accusations with a mere knife. Maybe it would be better for you to flee from here and go find protection among some friends who can hide you. The authorities know that you are here and that the Bazungu left this morning. They also know that we, priests, are the only ones to protect you. When night falls, why don't you run from this place, stay off the main roads and seek indaro from some friends where you know the soldiers wouldn't look for you. I would even be willing to drive you in a certain direction if you so desire. I know where the checkpoints are, and I could drop you before we get to one and you could make your get-a-way on foot. Talk to the others and decide if you all want to go together or separately or not at all. You know that you are welcome to stay here for as long as you so desire. But in that they know you are here, they will soon come looking for you. I don't know how long I will be able to hold them off. Let me know before nightfall so that I can take the time to drive you if that is what you want, Osicari." Tony didn't realize that he would be driving over the roads of the Bututsi all night long, but the three young men would not be his passengers.

Tony then reached his hands out to Osicari and with admiration in his heart and a small crackling in his voice, gave the brave young man absolution for all the sins of his past life and said penance with him which was, once again, a reading of I Corinthians 13. He saw him to the kitchen door and assured him that he would be there to drive him wherever he needed to go. Tony then opened the door and the two men went out together. As they walked side-by-side, Tony's admiration for this young Murundi continued to grow as he realized how much courage and strength it took to live this god-forsaken life of a Muhutu.

It was already 4:15 and in a short two hours darkness would hover over them all. Tony went into the chapel where the fathers kept the Blessed Sacrament in the tabernacle. He loved this little area smaller, than his bedroom, but containing the Bread of Life for the world. Tony knelt before the Risen Christ and asked him for strength as he reviewed his day. The decision to not say mass was something he never thought he would ever have to make in his priestly life but he now was totally sure that it was the right choice. Then saying 'goodbye' to the three couples that he had come to know and love so much was traumatic. But one of the hardest decisions of all, yet clairvoyantly the easiest, was insisting that the Bazungu leave the young Bahutu teenagers behind. He believed his decision was 100% correct but at the same time, he knew they all, the young men as well as the three couples, blamed him. Yet he was protecting them from what might have been a total disaster if they had been stopped and searched, which was inevitable. He wondered how far the three couples had gone by now and said a little prayer that they be safe. They had come to Burundi to educate and help and not put their lives in great peril. He sympathized especially with the Richards' and prayed that their unborn infant be safe in Marthe's womb. Tony looked at his watch. It was 4:40, time to go to church and set up for mass at the side altar. He got up, genuflected at the presence of the Living Lord under the simple form of Bread: God was prisoner in his own tabernacle. He left reluctantly for it was time to join the larger community.

As Fr. Tony walked over to the church, he heard Jose's pikipiki in the distance on the other side of the building. Then he heard him shout:

"Nagasaga, bagenzi, tuzobonana!" (Good-Bye, Friends, See you again soon.)

Tony recognized Jose's voice and, turning around, walked across the corridor and then saw his confrere, on his motorcycle, overcoat flying from his back, a green painted metal trunk on the back of his moto and some twenty young people running after him and waving goodbye. They finally stopped running and turned back to the mission house. Tony read the expression of sadness on their faces. Pati Jose was leaving Butova and they would miss his enthusiasm and commitment to them, the UGA of the parish. Jose was driving away for good, he was going and his life in Butova was now a thing of the past. Tony breathed a sigh of relief and yet despondency crept in all around him. Why didn't his colleague of the past two years and two months have the decency to come and say 'good bye' to him? In his heart he heard himself whisper: 'Thanks be to God!' But externally he was sad and downcast. He closed his eyes and said out loud: 'You fraud!' However he realized that he was not cursing Jose, but rather himself! He could easily find the words to condemn the Batutsi but he had to take the beam out of his own eye first. Tony would go to church for the eucharist, but never did he feel more worthless, more disgraceful, more despicable, a walking contradiction between God's love and human frailty. How could he ever preside over this eucharist?

18. Calm Before The Storm

Fr. Tony walked quickly toward the church and went directly to the sacristy. Some of the brothers and all of the sisters were already in the side alcove and when they saw him enter, Sr. Maragarita got up to accompany him into the sacristy and start the mass preparations. Quickly she had everything set up. They would have mass in both Kirundi and French since the brothers only understood French and the sisters knew only Kirundi. The readings would alternate and the hymns would be in Kirundi since the brothers loved to hear native singing. Luigi joined the pastor and both men prayed silently and then together, before leaving the sacristy in procession towards the side altar.

The side area was an alcove in the arm of the church. The building had been built by Walter De Winter who had done a magnificent job in constructing this church in the late '50's. It was built of solid reddish brick, the color of the clay in the area. There were three tons of glass that made up the colored windows all shaped in the form of triangles, in honor of the Trinity. Mathias had reorganized the church's side area so that there were enough kneelers and benches to hold 200 people as they often had that many at morning mass. This was a perfect area for smaller liturgies and even Monsignor Luduvico Ruyaga enjoyed sharing with the school teachers when he celebrated special masses for *les Equipes Enseignantes*. On Sundays, the people in that area would turn the other way and face the main altar.

When Tony and Luigi arrived at the altar, the pastor saw that the religious brothers and sisters in front of him were scattered throughout the area. 'Just like lost sheep, each going astray and doing his/her own thing!' he smiled to himself. The religious all feared intimacy so very much. He invited them to come forward and occupy the front benches which they did slowly, each hopping over the benches/kneelers as they went.

"Usually you sit in the back of the church and leave the first places for your students," he went on, "but today we are all by ourselves. This is our special mass! Let's show each other that we're united and supporting one another."

As he looked up, he was surprised that a special friend of his, Petero Tumba, was among them. Petero lived in a room which had a back door given onto the fathers' back yard. There he called home, living with another catechist, Saverino Imbwa. The two young men had followed a three-year course in the catechists' school near Bujarundi. When Mathias succeeded in getting the two catechists for Butova, he prepared a room for them in the walled area that separated the mission from the outside. So when Petero and Saverino went out their front door, they were in the village with all kirundi life around them. When they went out their back door, they were in the fathers' kigo, protected from life outside. The young men liked the two different lifestyles. They could be completely with their Barundi brothers in one area and yet they were among church leaders at the other part. They enjoyed their home and especially the fact that they were not charged rent for their room.

Jose had told Petero to stay in his room at all times and never go out the front door among the people where he would not be protected. If he really needed some fresh air, he was to go out the back door to the fathers' yard and be as discrete as possible.

Even though Tony was happy to see Petero in the church, he feared for his life and would have preferred that Petero would have not come out at all, ever for mass. He was sitting between two of the sisters, Maragarita and Domitila who were both rather robust. Petero was thin and small in build. Tony surmised that between these two big ladies, he probably would not be seen if any spies from Puma would meander into the church. Petero was very well protected by the nuns.

After Tony welcomed everyone very warmly, Sister Maragarita led them in the opening hymn. Tony alternated from Kirundi to French as they dialogued the penitential rite. They took the texts from the mass of Pentecost and the pastor readied himself for the homily. Yet there was nothing to sermonize about except encourage each other to go on living in this difficult situation. He mentioned that at the first Pentecost, the Spirit was poured out upon the apostles and they received the gifts of the Holy Spirit. He asked all to pray for themselves personally and for the whole group collectively that each and every person receive the gifts of the Spirit and be able to carry out his or her function according to the plan of God.

After the homily, Father Tony went right into the prayers of the faithful, leaving the apostles' creed for the last part of the liturgy of the word. He invited them to form their own petitions and for the next ten minutes prayers came from all directions: for the teachers of the college who had been arrested and most likely were killed, for the workers of the brothers, the sisters and the priests who had been arrested, for the catechists, so many of them who had been arrested and never seen again, for the spouses of all the above who were in deep depression and despondency, for many nuns of the sisters' community who were Bahutu and whose lives were in danger especially in Gisumu, for the direction of the church, the bishops and the leaders of religious orders that they make decisions that witness the Love of Christ amid the present turmoil in Burundi, for Jose who had now left the mission that he find his way and for the three couples the Richards', the Lacroix' and the Hendricks' that God be with them and guide them to safety in their trip to Bujarundi.

The prayers went on and on and every time Tony tried to bring them to a conclusion, someone else would speak up with a particular intention. It was a beautiful kaleidoscope of how their hearts were feeling and how much they needed each other. They concluded that the situation had become so tragic and the deaths so numerous that only the Divine Power could bring about peace in their *Burundi bwacu*.

After the profession of faith, the community sat to offer the bread and wine and they then stood for the preface and knelt for the consecration. As Tony genuflected before the host that he believed with all his heart had become the Body of the Lord Jesus, he stayed for the longest time in adoration of his God. If God could perform the miracle of coming down from heaven at this sinful man's persistence by saying the words: "This is my Body, given for you", then why did He not come down at the prayers of all and establish peace in Butova and throughout the whole country? With his head bowed in adoration towards the Risen Christ, Fr. Tony still questioned the plan of God: so many untimely deaths and so much hatred among these two tribes. He kept hearing the word: why? Why? WHY?" The reality of the Risen Christ in quiet solitude and seclusion on the altar contradicted the pain, suffering and violence outside.

After the consecration of the chalice filled with wine, Tony bent in adoration once more. He realized this gold plated chalice limited the blood of Christ to one shape, one area, one dimension. How could God allow such limitations on His Physical Presence and yet not answer their prayers. Tony genuflected in adoration and yet he wondered if Christ were truly present as the church had taught him all his life. How could a God be so cruel, so unconcerned, so aloof? He wanted to believe and prayed for hope but adding to his confusion was a diminished faith in a God, he once thought 'Almighty' yet now a 'god' who was totally incapable of doing anything to stop this atrocious situation. Did he really believe? And if he believed in a three-fold presence of God, past, present and to come, did he really believe that God is Love? Did Fr. Anthony Joseph, pastor of hundreds of innocent people murdered by government soldiers over the past three weeks truly believe that a God who is called love could stand by and allow so many innocent people go to their horrible deaths? Where was this god? Where was the god of these catholics? Tony wanted to talk to him and tell him what a horrible experience he had been having and if god, as he understood him to be, truly cared, he would and should intervene.

Fr. Tony rose from his position of adoration and the thought went through his mind that his life had been wasted here in Butova. He wanted to leave, to get out, to bend down and kiss this bloody ground '*nagasaga*' forever. Maybe the three couples, who probably were now very close to their destination of Bujarundi, were the only sane ones he knew. His heart, that had always been filled with love and joy, was now overcome with sadness and sorrow. He resented his priesthood, his vocation, his wanting to serve the Barundi and, above all, his god who stood by, oblivious to the whole situation. His heart pounded within his chest and amid the 'thump, thump thump' was a mysterious voice crying within him: "God damn this wretched country, these miserable Barundi, this bloody mission. God damn this whole abominable world! He did not realize that this moment was his Garden of Gethsemane. The Lord suffered his agony there and then left and was arrested. They were all suffering their agony at this mass and when they would go out, the young men and Tumba would be arrested. This supper-time eucharist was so similar to the Last Supper of Jesus: Osicari, Luduvico and Alfredo who had snuck into the side of the church were about to be arrested just as the Lord had gone out to the Garden of Gethesemni to await capture by those who hated him.

Having dug himself into the extreme depths of pessimism, Fr. Tony said the prayers after consecration that he had memorized long ago as a young priest. Luigi was still standing beside him and Tony heard his confrere echoing the words as well. The utter emptiness in his spirit started to be replenished and he felt a flash of guilt for having allowed himself to be so distraught. He tried to make light of his guilt and say that his load was very heavy, as was all of their struggles. He thought of the congregation before him. The sisters of which three were Bahutu and knew many of their family members were in great danger, maybe even murdered already. He thought of Petero Tumba and realized that his life was in great peril. And he thought of the brothers and how their lifetime project of building a catholic school of students caring for each other and living as one large family was now destroyed

Fr. Tony decided to put aside judging God and tried depending on God. God didn't owe him anything. He was a mere creature and God never promised to be on his side, to turn things in his favor. That thought consoled him. He realized that God would not answer his prayers simply because he prayed them. He felt relieved, but alone, lonely, truly celibate. No one in life loved him and no one even cared. He was a celibate for God. But now he realized that God didn't care either. He was not coming to his aid. He remained aloof, uncaring, unconcerned, indifferent. He felt like the prophet Hosea who was betrayed by his wife Gomer.

Once Fr. Tony had given his life for Africans. His priesthood was to build the church in Africa. In the seminary he had prayed many tines each day: *'We shall perform this exercise with the intention of obtaining from Our Lord, the Master of the Apostles, the grace to work effectively for Africans.'* He had made a missionary oath to serve the church of Africa until death. But now he thought of how he had been betrayed. The spouse that he had committed his heart to had stabbed him in the back. She had become unfaithful. She had sought and laid down with foreign gods. She, too, had turned her back on him, she had become indifferent, uncommitted, disconcerted. She had become an adulteress! But then he thought of the meaning of the prophet Hosea. It was an analogy to use marriage and betrayal as a sign that we, God's people, have been unfaithful to God. We were the culprits, the wrongdoers, the unfaithful spouse. We were the Gomer, the adultress. Fr. Tony turned his heart to God and begged for honesty and truthfulness to himself in realizing he was no better than the worst Mututsi. In the silence of his heart he thought of Jose and begged the Almighty for forgiveness for the way he had treated his brother.

It was time to distribute the eucharist. The brothers, always gentlemen, allowed the sisters to proceed first. Fr. Tony extended his fingers and placed the host in each sister's hand. Fr. Luigi took the cup and an altar linen and stood to the other side of the small sanctuary and said loudly to each communicant: 'The Blood of Christ' and offered each the Cup of Blessing. In the background they heard, first Tony and then Luigi saying: "Maragarita, The Body.....The Blood of Christ..... Gloria..... Terezita..... Anunciata..... Ana..... Alex..... Jean-Guy..... As Tony placed the Living Host in the hand of each religious, he wondered if each was going through identical traumas of faith as was his case.

As they went back to their places, Sr. Maragarita led them in song and they all joined in, physically witnessing that they really and truly believed. But Tony was still asking himself: Believe in what? In Whom?

His God had left Burundi! He just couldn't stay on the same plane. On the one hand, he was condemning the Barundi and on the other hand he felt more and more guilty about his own attitude of sinfulness. Why could he not have made it work with Jose? Why could he not have been understanding and open to his brother? Why did he have to set such a bad example? He imagined Jose on his *moto* going farther and farther away from Butova and tears of failure came to his eyes. Then a profound thought dawned upon the priest. He had first become angry at the Batutsi. Then his anger was transferred to God. Finally he realized his despondency led him to be angry with Jose and everyone else. Anger begets anger. He felt himself swirl and descend deeper into the bottomless pit. How could he ever escape? Then he realized that the answer was love. If he turned back over his current dilemma, and examined love in his life, he would realize that love of God would beget love of friends would beget love of all, Batutsi and Bahutu as well. He decided to make the decision to love everyone.

Luigi remained at the altar and purified the chalice as Tony sat in silence trying to find thoughts and words to initiate prayer. After the communion hymn was completed, he wanted to lead them in a spontaneous prayer, but his emptiness denied him the words. He had nothing to say, no prayers to voice, his tongue was silent, his voice-box was mute. Finally he got up, went to the altar where the sacramentary awaited him and read the final prayer. Without enthusiasm, he said the final salutations and blessed them and, with Luigi, kissed and then walked away from the altar of sacrifice. More than ever before he felt that it had been his sacrifice, his sufferings, his tragic life that he had offered to God. They walked up the steps, into the sacristy and disrobed on opposite sides of the room. The two men said absolutely nothing to each other for there was nothing to say. Tony walked out the door as quickly as his feet would carry him. They could put away the vestments tomorrow. There would be lots of time for that since all liturgical activities had been suspended. This mass had been one of the most difficult and strenuous experiences of his life and he did not believe he had the strength to ever do it again. His spirit had been so dampened by the mass that just thinking of saying another mass under these conditions made him feel rather ill. He walked quickly to the side doors of the church as Luigi locked the heavy steel church door.

As the two priests walked towards the front gate of the mission, they heard loud voices and much commotion. They hastened their steps and as they approached the gate of the mission compound, they both were struck with fear and horror.

Once during the mass Tony had looked up and thought he had seen Alfredo, Luduvico and Osicari at the side doors of the church. It had started to get dark in the big building so he was unsure if it were they or not. They had remained far in the distance and had not approached the community nor had come to communion. Tony's thoughts at that time had been so self-searching that he had not focused on what he was seeing. Now he realized that the three young men had come to the mass and as they were leaving the church and returning to the mission to stay in the houses where the couples had stayed, they were being apprehended by the police. There were at least ten policemen and two soldiers with rifles in their hands accusing them of attending political meetings. Each of the boys was being held by two policemen and the sisters and brothers were screaming at them.....the sisters in Kirundi and the brothers, led by Brother Alex, in French.

"How can you arrest these young men," Alex shouted, "they are innocent. They lived with our teachers and they didn't go outside these houses to attend political meetings . You just want to take them away and kill them because they are Bahutu." Alex' voice reached an unbelievable high decimal point. No one from the police or soldiers responded to his clamoring as they started to lead the boys away. Tony and Luigi came into their midst, and one policeman, whom Tony knew as Martino Kupiga, turned to him and said:

"We have been sent to arrest these men and are taking them to Puma. They will be tried tomorrow and returned to you if found innocent. However, we also want to arrest your teacher, Petero Tumba but he ran away from us and is hiding in your house. We did not go after him as we know you have vicious dogs. So we are telling you that you must bring him to us in Puma as soon as possible. *Bonsoir, mon Pere*." Kupiga turned to depart as the policemen turned and ushered the young men to the road which would lead to Puma and evident death.

Tony could not believe that the drama was continuing and that a tragic situation was becoming even worse. How could he hand over Petero? How could he drive him to his death? Yet if he refused, the authorities would attack the mission. That he knew for sure. He always feared them on Sunday evenings more than any other time during the week since the soldiers and policemen walked around the *'mihana'* all Sunday long, drinking as much banana beer as they could get. They were often drunk, out of their wits, as the evening approached. If they were feeling no pain and wanted to be mean, they could surely come and attack the mission since they knew Petero was hiding there and the priests were hiding him. As they all walked away, Tony and Luigi went through the gate and closed it and locked it. Then Tony said to Luigi, in a voice loud enough for all to hear:

"Let's go and release the dogs so they can protect us throughout the night." He said this to give them all something to think about if they were contemplating an attack. The missionaries had two large German shepherds who were very vicious to intruders. Once it got dark and someone released them, they were on the prowl during the whole night until they were put back in their kennel the following morning. They were two females. The dogs had been trained to attack anyone who came into the yard after the gate had been locked. Petero Tumba and Saverino Imbwa along with the two cooks were the only persons besides the fathers that the dogs were friendly towards. When a car came to the gate, the driver would honk until the fathers came out, opened the gate and allowed the car to enter. Then the occupants drove to the *kigo*, parked, and stayed in the car until the fathers came and protected them from the dogs. So all impromptu thieves were discouraged from invading the fathers' property.

Luigi went toward the wall between the fathers' house and where the couples had lived and opened the cage. The dogs came running out and Tony called out to them: "Champ, Ace, come here." The large strong beasts came running as fast as they could and even though Tony knew they would never attack him, his back straightened up rigidly fearing a rush of muscled flesh against his hips and legs. They stopped almost on his command as he and Luigi patted them on their heads and necks. The priests felt peace and security all around, something they had not felt in a very long time. At least no one from the soldiers or police would try anything at night while these strong, well-fed dogs were at their watch. Luc came out of his room. He had joined them at mass and had returned quickly to do some personal work before supper.

"What is all the commotion about?"

"The three boys have been arrested by the police and two soldiers after mass. They have lead them away to Puma." Luigi said with disgust in his voice.

"It sounds similar to what happened to Christ after His Mass" Luc responded. "Those sons-of-bitches!"

Tony tried to control his emotions from getting the best of him.

"Luc, you come to mass one time and now you are spiritualizing everything. You will make a great priest someday!" He teased him helping all of them to lighten up a bit. "Never, not for these people. I would prefer to be a vagabond or wretched beggar before I would do anything for these Batutsi. If you think I would waste my life being a priest for these miserable bastards, you are mistaken, one hundred percent. Never, Never, Never" he said with insistence.

Luigi laughed:

"You can never tell, Luc. When God calls you, you can never resist. Look at Tony and me. We said 'yes' and here we are, priests of the magnificent, powerful church in Burundi," he said sarcastically. Luc was well aware that both the priests he was living with had planned to leave Burundi permanently as soon as this tragedy ended. Their priesthood had been a disastrous calamity in Central Africa.

"Let's go into the common room and sit and talk about this whole problem," Tony went on, "we have some big decisions to make about Petero. We'll tell you about it, Luc, when we are together. Let's meet in ten minutes. I would like to go and chat with Petero first to make sure he is OK." Luigi said he would go to the chapel and pray for Osicari, Luduvico and Alfredo.

The three missionaries went off in different directions with Tony going over to the catechists' back door and *hod*ied by knocking on the wooden frame.

"It is I, *Pati* Antonio. I am alone. Can I come in?"

"*Mon Pere*, I will open for you." He heard one lock being unbolted, then another latch and a final key in a large padlock. When the three operations were completed, Petero opened the door and invited the priest into his room. "Saverino is not home yet, so I am all alone. I came to mass but was afraid to be seen. So I didn't go to holy communion. I have felt so far away from my Lord and Savior Jesus Christ these past days that I needed that time to pray. Mass means the world to me! I went walking this afternoon and Sister Maragarita told me there would be mass." Petero talked in a very confused state.

Tony wanted to scold him, for his imprudence in leaving the house and going for a walk along the roads where he would be seen. But what the hell? Petero was an African and they were all born out-of-doors! Even if Tony had warned him on three different occasions this past week not to go out for any reason, Petero was African. What else would someone do but walk through the *mihana* on a Sunday afternoon! It was just too much to impose that sanction on him!

So as could be imagined, Petero told Tony that he had been accused and some men wanted to apprehend him and take him to Puma but he managed to escape and ran as fast as he could back to his room before they could catch him. The door on that side was steel so they could not break it down. Petero had escaped with his life. He further had another narrow escape from the police and soldiers after mass. When he had seen the soldiers and policemen, he never had run faster in his life. Into the *kigo* he had sprinted to his back door that he had left unlocked for obvious reasons.

Petero spoke in a slow a whisper. Total fear was written all over his countenance. He ended by shrugging his shoulders and mentioned that he was wrong in going out and should have followed the priests' advice.

"Petero, thank you for telling me that the mass means everything to you. I can come to your room from time to time and say mass here. But please don't go out for any reason whatsoever. I command you, stay in here at all times. If you need anything, ask one of us and we will get it for you. Luc will bring you the food you need from the co-operative. And Saverino can get you other things."

"*Mon Pere,* " Petero went on, "I cannot trust this man with anything. I am also afraid that he will allow the police to come in with him and then they will take me away."

Tony reassured his friend that he would have a talk with Saverino and that nothing would go wrong. What a large error of judgment the pastor was making in putting his trust in another racist Mututsi: Imbwa (name means 'dog') turned out to be a real son-of-a-bitch, more kitutsi than Christian or catechist! He was out for blood and even that of the man with whom he was sharing life and food and blankets and debts. How deep was this tribal hatred in Burundi. A Muzungu like Father Tony Joseph would never understand their tribalry.

Tony walked back to the common room and found Luc and Luigi there chatting casually. Tony sat with them and they all took a moment of silence to reflect and ask God's help on the decisions they would be making. Tony was so distraught that he couldn't find words to pray and he knew the two other men felt the same way. He told them that he had seen Jose leave and asked if either of them had spoken to him. They replied negatively and Tony thought how mean he was to leave without saying anything to anyone.

"He must have been so hurt that he didn't care to talk to any of us. I'm truly sorry that it had to end this way. How sad! But it is probably good for all of us since we certainly weren't giving much of a christian example to the Barundi. I hope that God will help him find his way. But I must say that I am relieved." Tony said sympathetically but realistically.

He then asked for advice on what they should do about Petero Tumba. He explained what he and Petero had just been chatting about. They debated the different positions back and forth. Luigi explained that some priests in other parishes had hidden Bahutu who were being sought by the soldiers and they had saved many lives. Luc interjected:

"But if we were to hand him over to the *bakuru*, the soldiers could kill the detainee without cause. But in other similar situations, they would allow them to go free." They all concluded that it was extremely difficult to know who to trust and who would be a renegade. Leading someone to the wrong Mututsi could mean automatic death. Yet if those sought out were placed in the right hands, they would be protected. It all seemed so insane, so irrational. Their goal was to protect Petero as long as possible and hope the soldiers and police would go away to bother someone else. Luc added that it was imperative that Petero not be seen in public:

"He is really asking for it if he continues to go out and mingle with the people. Someone will surely hate him enough to have him killed." he noted.

After they had all expressed themselves about the dilemma, they agreed that they were in a difficult predicament and that more prayer and discussion should be put into it before a common decision be reached. Luigi had been physically closer to Osicari, Luduvico and Alfredo and thus he had seen more of the anger of the soldiers and policemen as they arrested the young men. Luc worried that they would probably come back at some ungodly hour of the night and demand that Petero be turned over. They all agreed that they were in immanent danger and Tony suggested that they spend more time discussing what their personal priorities as missionaries should be.

"We have heard how our superiors from Vurura want us to stay with the people. It wouldn't be advisable that we do anything to prejudice their wishes. We are not called to be martyrs, but rather prophets." Luigi added.

It was clear to Tony what this exchange was suggesting.….then the door from the dining room opened without a knock and they realized it could only be one person, the cook Cypriano Kitwi. They were all alarmed when he interrupted their conversation for it was abnormal for a Murundi to barge into a meeting of *bakuru*. What could possibly be so important as to intrude on the priests?

"They have come to the window in the kitchen, *Bapati,*" the cook went on, "and they have insisted that I tell you that if you don't hand Tumba over this evening, they will attack the mission with machetes and clubs and take him by force. They said you are hiding a person who is under arrest and you do not have the right to do this. You are guilty of treason and if you don't bring him down to Puma by four hours (10 o'clock), they will attack during the night and all of you may be killed." Cypriano said, putting emphasis on the important words: 'all' 'you' 'killed'. Tony thanked Cypriano for relaying the message and told him to put dinner on the table. The cook, in respect, backed to the door and asked:

"What shall I tell them so that they will stop pestering me in the kitchen?"

"Tell them we are discussing the situation and we will decide soon." Tony called out to the cook. "Now be-gone!"

"Be-gone!" He said to the two others quoting himself. "Isn't that the word Jesus used in the gospel when he knew that there was a devil in St. Peter?" he smiled.

"Cypriano is certainly acting like he is inspired by the devil. Do you think the police have really come to him? Why would they not break down Tumba's front door, rather than go to the kitchen beside his room and work through Kitwi? Do you think that Cypi is inventing a story so that we will hand Petero over? The Batutsi really despise Tumba and are jealous of him, his good looks, his way with women and the respect that we have for him. All the Batutsi workers here at Butova would love to see him dead." Luigi said.

Tony went on:

"Maybe I should go to Alberto Kizungu and see what he, the administrator, thinks. I have to trust someone and maybe I should start with him. I could go down and explain that I believe Petero is innocent and that we are not 'hiding' him since he has not done any wrong. I would not be afraid to say that to Kizungu and see his reaction." Tony added pensively.

Both Luc and Luigi thought this was a good idea to confront the administrator with their belief of Petero's innocence was the best way to initiate a dialogue. The three men rose and went through the door as Cypriano was placing a big bowl of hot soup on the table. They sat down quickly and helped themselves to the soup. Finally Cypriano appeared once more and this time he had a note in his hand that he handed to Tony. He opened it while Cypriano was still removing the soup and bowls from the table. Kitwi said to Tony:

"They are still at the kitchen window, awaiting a reply." Cypriano backed to the door, paused and then turned to exit.

Tony read the note aloud. It was written poorly in Kirundi but he was determined to make it understandable. It was signed by the soldier Samueli Kufa.

"Fathers, Greetings. You are aware that Petero Tumba is wanted for trial at Puma, accused of treason. He is being protected by you in your mission. You are ordered to hand him over before four hours of this night or we will come and remove him by force.

We insist that you co-operate with these military orders. Our highest regards and deepest respects to you, Dear Fathers.

Ni jewe, (It is I), - *Chief of Police, Samueli Kufa."*

Tony's reaction, at first, was to laugh. His plan was now sabotaged and his ace was trumped. He really believed that Cypriano was incapable of writing such a letter and the penmanship was totally different from Cypriano's scribbling. Furthermore he now realized that the administrator would not have the power to contradict the military authorities. Alberto Kizungu had been told what awaited him if he did not go along with the plan. He was a weak man, and rubber- stamped all that they did and said.

Tony meanwhile thought how significant the soldier's name 'Kufa' was as it meant 'to kill'. Kufa was bound and determined to live up to his name for he wanted Petero's head because he knew Tumba was so well loved and respected by so many. It would certainly be a way of showing the clergy and religious at the mission how important the authorities were. Thus was another case of the Batutsi showing the Bazungu that they were in charge of their own country and very capable of handling all situations that came their way. 'Neo-colonialism', Tony had once thought 'is the scourge of Africa. Colonialism will never be put to rest until Africans cease trying to colonize Africans!'

Tony read the note aloud and the others tried to understand the Kirundi. Tony translated what he understood and it was enough to send the three a clear message. Cypriano again opened the door and brought in the meal. It was fried beef , mashed potatoes and beans with gravy on the side. A large bowl of salad was already on the table and the three passed around the serving dishes. Cypriano had baked a Japanese prune pie that sat at the end of the table. As Kitwi departed once more, the three missionaries looked at each other and no one seemed to be interested in eating. The events of the day which culminated in this horrible letter, had totally taken away their appetites. They passed the dishes from one to the other and each took a little food on his plate but eating was impossible for all of them.

"What shall we do?" Tony asked no one in particular.

"We are not hungry," Luigi added, "so let's get up and go and sit in the common room where the chairs are more comfortable." He had wanted to say this for the last two weeks as he had had no appetite himself. But alas the others seemed to enjoy their food. Now no one was eating. The three rose and went into the adjoining room and sat in a small circle where they could see each other. Finally Luc broke the silence:

"I am so angry at that damn soldier," he went on "The other day he flagged me down on the road and made me drive him to a *mihana* about ten miles out of my way and he even had the gall to ask me to wait for him while he visited with a girl, whom he called his cousin. I took off as soon as he was out of my truck and I am sure he was pissed off at me for the extra miles he had to walk. He went for physical comfort but I bet he ended up with sore feet!" Luc laughed sarcastically.

"It is for reasons like this that he is trying to get even with us in every way he can and Petero will be the one who will have to pay the price" Tony responded, and then went on:

"But they are in charge and they mean what they say. We cannot afford to take the risk and have them come and massacre all of us. They are probably all drunk from their rounds today. Sunday is their day to get loaded and they are probably all well on their way. This is a serious threat and it only takes one bullet to kill each of us and they have many left!"

"Now I have a suggestion to make!" Tony went on:

"I sadly believe we have no other choice but to hand Petero over to the right authorities. We cannot risk an attack especially during the night when visibility would be sparse. They could do damage that would cost us dearly. Actually I fear that we have given them an excuse to attack the whole mission. They have a justifiable excuse all ready and able to be used. Maybe this is the reason why Ruyaga insisted that we stay. If we were not here, they could come in and ransack everything as the rebels did in the Congo a few years ago. So my suggestion is that I talk to Tumba and after suggesting that he give himself up to the authorities, I drive him to Kizungu. I will suggest that he receive the sacraments first to prepare him for his awful ordeal."

"What if the administrator is not at home, or they won't let you speak to him?" Luigi raised his voice forcefully.

"Remember they are as mad as hell at you for the message you proclaimed in church this morning that totally condemned their actions." Luigi said, trying to help Tony clarify the serious danger that he would have to face.

"If Kizungu is not there," Tony responded, "I will take Petero to Vuvoga where Libori Mihaga is in charge". Now Libori Mihaga was a good friend of Tony's and they had often talked at length about different subjects when Mihaga had been school commissioner, located in Butova.

Tony trusted that if he left Tumba in Mihaga's care, the catechist would not be tortured during the night, as happened at soldiers' watches at Puma.

There was a short moment of silence as the three men reflected on the different options that were theirs. Soon all three agreed that, even though this was a painful and almost unforgivable feint towards the catechist, yet it was the only solution to their dilemma. The three men looked at each other and felt peace about the difficult decision.

Tony walked out the door, down the corridor and in front of the small chapel. He paused a few seconds to pray for courage now that he knew the decision had to be carried out. He cut through the back courtyard and over to the catechists' back door. He called out to Petero who came to the door.

"I need to speak to you, Petero" said the priest, "Be assured that I am alone." Petero went through the process of unlocking the door again and opening all three locks for Fr. Tony.

"Come quickly with me, Petero. Don't be afraid. I will protect you from the dogs. The dogs came running quickly and Tony told Petero to walk slowly and carefully and go directly to the fathers' chapel. The two men entered and the dogs turned around and went running to another part of the big yard where they had heard a disturbing noise.

Tony fell to his knees in front of the Blessed Sacrament contained in the tabernacle on the altar and Petero genuflected to the same general area and knelt on a stall to the right of the room. Tony thought the best way to inform Tumba of the decision that had to be made was to pray out loud to the Lord whom both men believed was in the Living Bread, silently dwelling within the tabernacle.

"Lord, Jesus, bless Petero and bless me as I must share some big problems with him tonight. Help him to understand the seriousness of the situation we are in right now. He knows that there have been many accusations toward him from Puma and now the soldiers are saying they will attack the mission if he does not surrender within a few hours. Our backs are against the wall, Lord. We cannot allow them to come and ransack our mission and put all our lives in danger. Bless Petero and help him to realize that he must surrender for the common good. I will take him to the administrator and, only if I feel comfortable that he will be well-treated, will I leave him there.

Tony then turned to look right at Petero Tumba:

"If you would like to receive the sacrament of confession, I will give you a few minutes by yourself and then come back to give you God's pardon." Tony said, showing his priestly caring for Petero's soul even if he couldn't do much to save his body. He got up and walked to the door.

"I'll be back soon," he added as he closed the door leaving Tumba in the silence of the small chapel. Tony walked up and down the corridor in front of the chapel, past the refectory to the common room door and back again. He continued this little path over and over again trying to make some sense out of this ugly nightmare. His thoughts ran in all directions. Were they making the right decision? What if he were in Petero's place? Did he think that Petero was guilty? ....guilty of what crime? Would the soldiers torture him throughout the night, bringing his body close to the night fire and singeing his bare skin? If he kept Petero in the mission, would the soldiers attack?.....would they all be killed? He asked himself millions of questions that seemingly had no answers.

Luigi had heard Tony's footsteps and came out to see who was walking back and forth. The two men spoke in whispers outside the dining room door and Luigi reassured Tony that there was no other choice but to turn Petero in to the authorities and try to save him by handing him over to those they trusted. Tony insisted that that was Mihaga but he had to try approaching Kizungu first so that all would know that Tumba was no longer at the mission house.

Fr. Anthony Joseph reentered the chapel and asked Petero if he wanted the sacraments. He nodded 'yes' and Tony sat down, put his purple stole around his neck as a sign of the sacramental actions that were about to take place. He readied himself to hear Petero's confession.

Tony had never seen fear as he now experienced it on the face and in the trembling body of this young man. He knelt before the priest and said the introductory prayer for confession with a voice that was very low and crackling. At no time did Petero confess hating people or having enemies or wanting revenge on the people who were out to kill him. The priest reveled in the sincerity and caring love that this young man had as he spoke words of self-condemnation. Tony had been told when he was a seminarian that confession does not tell you how bad a person is but rather the contrary, how very good one is striving to be. The priest prayed over the penitent and placed his open hands on Petero's head to invoke the Holy Spirit. As he prayed, Fr. Tony took Petero's dark-skinned hand into his own. He prayed with him for courage and strength and if he were to die, he prayed that Petero forgive his accusers and his murderers.

Tony thought: 'What a hypocrite I am. I am sending this man to his death and I help him to pray for those who are maligning him. Yet I will probably hate them for the rest of my days as they are going to willfully hurt and kill my friend! Tony led Petero in the prayer that would be his penance. The two men held hands as Tony said and Petero echoed the *"Dawe wa Twese"* ("Lord of all": Our Father). Tony then went to the side of the altar and took the vessel that contained the holy oils for the Sacrament of the Sick. Surely they both realized that Petero was in danger of death. The priest said the prayers over his catechist, who had seen many persons being anointed but never had received this sacrament himself. Then came the anointing. Tony traced a cross on Petero's forehead and once again, uttered the words of forgiveness of all the sins this young man might have committed throughout his short lifetime: 'By this holy anointing, I pardon you from all the sins you have committed by your speech....hearing.... eyesight…..'

As Tony returned the oils to their place, he turned back to the tabernacle and genuflected in respect for the living presence of the Lord in the sacrament of eucharist. Unlocking the tabernacle, he took out the ciborium containing some hosts that both men believed were the Body of Christ, the Lord. Tony turned toward Petero, holding the ciborium in his left hand and one small host in his right;

"Behold, Petero, this is Jesus, the Lamb of God, Who went to his death for the sins of all of us. This is He Who loves you and I so much, that He died for us. How happy are we invited to His Banquet." He heard Petero respond:

"Lord, I am not worthy that you come under my roof. Say but the word and my soul shall be healed."

Tony held out the small, pure white, motionless Host and offered it to Petero:

"Petero, Catechist, Teacher, Man-of-God and Believer-in-God, this is the Body of Christ," and Petero held his right hand over his left to receive His King and make a throne for His God as he said: "AMINA". Then Petero did something so beautiful yet so unexpected. He reached out his tongue and touched the Host as he held it in his hand.

Two months earlier when the priests and catechists were in the common room preparing for the holy week services, Mathias had mentioned that they would have three crucifixes and invite the people to come forward. as usual, and kiss the cross as part of the Good Friday service. Petero had spoken up and said that kissing is not the *kirundi* way of showing love and respect. Tony had asked him to explain. Petero related that if a Murundi wanted to show affection, he would stick out his tongue and touch the loved object with the end of this small organ. It was more of a tongue-kiss than an exchange of affection with the lips. A few weeks later, at the Good

Friday service, Tony was holding a crucifix and people were approaching trying to do something so very foreign to them. They had observed the Bazungu kissing the body of Christ on the crucifix with their lips and they were awkwardly trying to imitate them. But when Petero approached, he felt totally accepted by Tony as a Murundi and touched the body of Christ with his tongue.

On this night, Petero, once again, felt enough at ease with Tony to be himself. So he embraced the image of the crucified Christ with his tongue. Then he took the host, placed it in his mouth and closed his eyes in a prayer of total commitment and surrender to the will of God. Tony, although he had received the eucharist at mass a few hours before, felt the need to be close to his God and reassured and strengthened by Him. He, too, took a host from the ciborium, and touched it with his tongue and then placed it in his mouth as the two men were finally united in the sacramental presence of their Lord and God , Jesus Christ.

Tony returned the ciborium to its place, locked the tabernacle door, and knelt in silent prayer. He breathed tensely and could also hear Petero's heavy panting as well. The catechist then spoke a prayer out loud:

"Lord Jesus, you forgave those who destroyed your body as you went to your death. I ask you for the courage to forgive all those who hate me and want me dead as well. I have received You at this time into my heart. Please receive me at the moment of my death into Your Heavenly Home and make me happy with You and all the angels and saints in that heavenly bliss that is my true destiny. I love you Jesus and please help *Pere* Tony to be strong and help all the people of Butova to do Your Holy Will. AMINA"

Tony felt a tear come from one eye and then another from the other eye and they traced a wet path down his cheeks. He was never prouder of anyone than he was of this beautiful man and he implored God that He keep them both safe and somehow right the wrong Peter was receiving. Tony then went on again:

"Petero, it is time to go. You have prepared yourself perfectly, in the case that you might die tonight, If you do, you will know that your last breath on the face of this earth, will be your first breath in heaven. Before we go, is there anything else I can do for you?"

Petero stood up and put his right hand into his front pants pocket. He took out ten maroon colored 50 FrBu notes and handed them to Tony. This money was the equilivent of $5.00 or one month's pay for a worker in Burundi.

"Would you see to it that this, my only-remaining money, gets to my mother in Muka?" Tony reassured Petero that he would and took the money and realized, very painfully, that this was all the poor man had to his credit going to his death.

"I have one last favor, *Pati*" Petero went on, "I would like to go and say 'good-bye' to the sisters. Could we stop at their convent on the way to Puma?"

Tony, smiling, put him at-ease by mentioning how much he respected him for caring for the sisters. Then he added;

"I want you to lie down on the back seat of my VW. It is dark out, and if anyone stops us, they will not see you. But first, let's go to the sisters'."

They drove around the mission house and Tony told Petero to stay hidden in the car at all times. He got out, opened the gate and chased the dogs away. Then he drove through the fence and getting out again, closed and locked the gate. He then drove in front of the church and turned right, onto the main road and down the few hundred meters to the sisters' residence. He got out and took Petero with him. But the sisters' door was locked and loud singing was coming from the chapel. Common politeness, especially in Burundi, dictated that one wait at the door for their hosts to come when they had finished their spiritual activity. Tony said:

"We don't want to disturb them. Let's go around to the back and the sister who is cooking supper will surely be in the kitchen and will let us in. The two men walked around the right side of the house. Tony would not know until a week later when Petero would already have been killed, that there was a soldier in the lay teachers' residence. He had been drinking all day and now he had forced himself on these four unmarried girls who taught at the girls' school run by the nuns. The soldier was doing crazy things as some people do when they have had too much to drink. He was ordering the women to stand up, to sit down, to raise their hands, to move their feet. They never told the priest if his commands became more brazenly sexual in nature as the booze effected him. However Tony knew the *kirundi* mentality well enough to understand how fearful and embarrassed these young ladies must have been.

At the time the two men started to walk around the house, it looked to the soldier as if they were heading to the teachers' residence. He panicked at the possibility of getting caught and cocked his gun, getting ready to shoot at the on-coming seeming 'intruders'. The teachers looked out the window and Maria, a short-stocky, fun-loving Muhutukazi from the north of Burundi, who helped Fr. Tony every Saturday to put his homily into good Kirundi, recognized the priest even in the dark and she shouted at the soldier: "Don't shoot! it's the priest!".

As the soldier looked out the window again he finally noticed that the two men were turning towards the back of the sisters' house and not coming to the women's residence at all. Tony never knew how close he had come to death that night until Maria told him the following week what had happened.

Sister Domitilia was in the kitchen and received Fr. Tony and Petero with her normal *kirundi* courtesy. She said that prayer was almost over and invited them to stay for supper. She thanked Tony for the mass earlier that evening and then the sisters started to come into their small dining room. They were pleasantly surprised to see the pastor and their favorite catechist. However they did find it strange that the men had come to visit them after dark. It was now about 8pm. Tony told the sisters the purpose of their visit:

"Petero has been called to Puma and the soldiers will attack the mission unless I take him there. So I have just given him the sacraments and his final wish was to bid you all 'good bye'. You are more than friends to him. You are his true sisters. So please hug him and tell him you will pray that God spare him and bring him to safety."

The commiseration that these sisters showed Petero would touch Tony for the rest of his life. Each sister, Maragarita, Ana, Domitila, Gloria, Anunciata and Terezita came forth with tears in her eyes. It had been a strenuous three weeks for every one of them. Most sisters of the Beneteresia Religious Order were from the center of the country where the Bahutu predominated and certainly in that area, most Bahutu were catholics. Needless to say, it was overwhelmingly painful to bid their brother *"Genda n'Amahoro ya Kristu"* (Go, in Christ's peace).

These women-of-God, so simple in their lifestyle, sharing a small house with white-washed walls and cement floors, had a common room that was decorated with homespun-baskets and colorful wall artisan that had been hooked by sisters of the past, decorating their home with African artifacts. Each sister now approached her 'little brother' and hugged him tightly. Some even gave him encouragement by speaking words of appreciation and strengthening him with heartening, cherishing words of wisdom. Finally when all had completed their salutations, Tony took a step toward the front door as he felt the need to exit quickly. His heart was heavy, witnessing this sad farewell and he wondered how he would handle the final 'good bye' to Petero when that inevitable moment would take place. Joking seemed to be the only way he could deal with the tragedy. At least, he hoped, he would change some tears to laughter. He looked at the sisters and jokingly said they could now drown their sorrows in *inzoga* (banana beer). However he made a pun and said they would have *inzoka* (a snake) in their stomachs. The sisters all laughed but Tony surmised that it was polite pity approval since they were all overcome by the melancholy spirit that was in their hearts.

The two men walked to the front door where Tony's VW was parked. The sisters accompanied them to the car and Petero got in the back as Tony explained to the sisters that he was going to hide Petero until he could have a meeting with the administrator at Puma. Sister Maragarita, always outspoken, could be heard to respond:

"It is Sunday night. He will be drunk if he is at home at all," she remarked as they drove away, with Petero waving from the back window of the car.

19. Petero Tumba Surrendered, Turned-over

The drive to Puma, just a few miles away, was made in quiet and solitude. Tony's mind was still revisiting the beautiful but sad 'send-off' from the sisters. He knew they had not cried their last tears for their beloved country, as so many Bahutu were still to fall. Tony now feared the worst. Petero, on the other hand, was focused on the situation he would soon be encountering. Would he be beaten? Would he be tortured? Would he be mistreated in so many other different ways? He had heard how the soldiers tortured other Bahutu who had been arrested: lighted cigarettes in their mouths, beating them on the head with a billy-club until they became unconscious, dragging them over to the area of night watch, to a position beside the fire with the flames touching their skin and scorching them continuously. He panicked as he thought of what was awaiting him and finally he blared out to Tony:

"Is there not something you can do to prevent me from being arrested and tortured this night?"

Tony replied:

"Don't fret or worry, Petero. I will see to it that you will be placed in the hands of someone that I can trust. I will hold him totally responsible and make him promise to defend you. You are being accused, but you are not guilty. There is a difference and I hope your prosecutors understand that.

"I don't trust Kizungu, *Pati*, and besides he is only nominally in charge. He merely has a title. It is the military that have the final say in everything." Petero said sounding very dejected.

Tony remembered that he had heard some 'Mututsi' recount that if Kizungu did not go along with everything the soldiers wanted, they had a hole in the ground for his burial. He realized that the administrator was powerless and the ones who had all the power were the ruthless soldiers.

As they arrived at Puma, many memories went through Tony's mind. He remembered the day President Sabimana had come to the Town Center and the priests were so proud of their friend who spoke powerfully to the crowd of thousands. He revisited many Thursday afternoons that were spent with the town population overflowing and hearing speech after speech from some of the members of the L'UPRONA Party as they tried to influence the people to support their efforts. He recalled, during the influenza epidemic the previous year, how he met with the *Muganga* and asked to visit his supply room to be assured that he was not keeping medicine that could be used on those who were already dying. He remembered coming to visit his catechist and secretary Deogratias Pungu in the infirmary when he was dying. And now Tony wondered if more memories, more morose feelings would be created that night. Of his many recollections of this place, he wondered if this night would be the most tragic Fr. Tony knew that the chances of all ending well were very slim.

Keeping his head focused straight ahead on the bumpy road, Tony whispered to Petero that he stay low and he wouldn't be seen. He then got out, locked his car, lit his flashlight and proceeded toward the path that would lead to Kizungu's house. He heard a door open in front of him and a figure came out and walked down the path toward him. In the dim reflection of the torch, he could make out that it was a man with a long coat over his body, flowing down to his knees. He saw the man's bare legs and surmised that he was wearing short pants. The man was of average height and so he knew it wasn't Kizungu, for he was very tall and slender. Finally the man spoke to him and Tony recognized him as a policeman who often came to the mission accompanying Alberto Kizungu:

"Good Evening, *Pati*. Can I be of service to you?" he asked politely.

"I have come seeking the Administrator. Is he at home?" Tony asked.

"I am very sorry, *Pati*" the man continued with even greater courtesy, "he has gone on a long trip and will not be back for some time. Is there something I can help you with?"

Tony showed his disappointment and mentioned that he sought the Administrator since the soldiers wanted to arrest his catechist and employee Petero Tumba:

"I wanted to talk to the Administrator so that he could invite the soldiers to come to the mission and get him. However that will have to wait I cannot agree to any hand-over until I talk with Kizungu." Tony wanted to out-think them all so he planted the thought in their minds that Tumba was still at the mission house. He smiled to himself wondering what would have been the reaction if it had been known that Petero was only a few meters away, hidden in the car. Finally two soldiers, armed with rifles, came out of the same door that the policeman had come from and took up standing positions on both sides of the policeman. Tony recognized one of them as Samueli Kufa but did not know the other soldier by name.

"We have heard that you played a very sharp political game in church today." Kufa went on, "I don't think President Sabimana, who everyone says is your friend, will be very pleased with you not having the mass. I advise you, *mon Pere*, to return to normal as soon as possible. You are sending a very dangerous message!"

Tony thought it best to ignore the comments. That would be the best way to show him his words was unimportant. So he spoke up before Kufa could add anything else:

"I have come to talk about many things with the Administrator. Is he in his house?" he asked ignoring the response the policeman had previously given to him. There was no reply and Tony looked right at the policeman who seemed irritated by the question. Then from the inside of the house, Tony heard a loud laugh that he knew it was that of Kizungu. He looked straight into the eyes of each soldier and then at the policeman and snickered:

"Oh, I guess I am not important enough for him to come away from his partying. Please tell him I have come by and awaited his welcoming me into his home without any luck. I would like to speak to him when he is available about the arrest of Tumba. In the meantime I will travel about the check points making sure the enemy has not come to attack any of the night watchmen." Tony turned around, did not shake hands with any of the three, which was a true insult to treat them as if they did not exist, and walked back to his car aware that there was no margin for making a mistake. For a few seconds he panicked, wondering what he would ever do if they had the politeness to walk him back to his vehicle. Then he realized that they had been insulted and hurt and definitely would not do anything to show him politeness. They didn't want him to believe that he had got the best of them. Tony reached the car, took out his key, opened the door and got in. He drove away, around the square and back up the road to Butova.

As he went, he told Petero about his confrontation and the brave man-of-God told him that he had heard every word each had spoken. He thanked Tony for not handing him over to that dreadful trio of murderers as the priest told him that he was now going to drive him to Vuvoga and see if Libori Mihaga were there so that he would be left in the hands of someone reliable.

Once again they drove along in silence. The night was clear yet dark and the air was light. Tony rolled down his window for a few minutes to breathe in the night air and he felt refreshed after the hot and strenuous day that this Sunday had been. The drive down to Vuvoga started to be monotonous as they descended one hillside after another. On the other side of this outstation, was the valley of the Boso and beyond that the two parishes of Lutana and Muka. It was a wide-open area in the valley where many Batutsi shepherds would come with their flocks in the dry season and stay until the rains and then return to the upper regions. They often remained there for five months, from May until October. The Boso was a beautiful area where undomesticated animals still flourished and most of the fathers and the president went hunting for gazelle.

Tony was uncertain where the barrier-checkpoint was and if Mihaga would be there. However he knew it had to be on the main road for its purpose was to halt and check cars. So he calculated that if he drove along the road that went from Butova to Lutana, somewhere in the middle around Vuvoga, he would find the night watch. He just hoped and prayed that Libori would be there.

About ten or twelve kilometers after Luconi, the cutoff to Vuvoga, he saw a fire burning on the left side adjoining the road. That would be the checkpoint! Again Tony stopped his car about thirty feet in front of the area where many men were gathered. He got out and walked towards them, shouting his name: "*Pati* Antonio, *Pati* Antonio, *ni jewe, Pati* Antonio" (It is I, Father Anthony). The men all approached him and there was a mixture of Batutsi among the larger Bahutu. Most of the men had heavy gray blankets around their shoulders that draped down to their knees. There were others who had on long winter coats. Tony always wondered where they had received such gifts as this was Central Africa and people who wore heavy winter coats would never believe they could be used in Burundi. But they were ideal for night wear here in the high mountains. Who in Europe or North America could have surmised that these would be of great value to the people of Central and East Africa where nights in the mountains were extremely cold, especially as they approached the dry season? But they put warm clothing and blankets to good use, especially in night watch when they stayed up and awake during the whole night looking for an enemy that never was!

Fr. Tony exchanged greetings with them all and extended a hand to each one. One of the men, obviously a Muhutu, said:

"I was at mass this morning, *Pati*, and you truly did the right thing and said the right words. God is angry with all of us in Burundi for the way we are carrying on. But we hope that you will soon be able to give us the sacraments again. We have wronged God and each other very grievously over the last weeks and God cannot be pleased."

Tony responded by thanking him for his words of appreciation and said that he would be very pleased to give them the sacraments when peace was restored. Then he looked up and Libori Mihaga was approaching the group. He was rubbing his eyes and Tony surmised that he had been sleeping. He came right over and stretched out his hand to join it with Tony's and looked very surprised to see the priest at this time of night:

"Can I see you for a moment, M. Mihaga" Tony asked. Libori beckoned for him to come aside from the group and follow him. The two men walked up the side of the road in privacy and Tony began by telling him that he had a serious problem. He explained about not saying mass that morning and Libori responded by mentioning that he had been at church in Butova and had witnessed the whole situation. His comments were encouraging to Tony since Mihaga seemed to compliment him for taking such risk. The pastor remarked that he had only taken that stand since he was totally supported by the bishop and Monseignor Ruyaga. Tony understood how important it was to mention Ruyaga since he was a Mututsi priest and all knew he was going to be the next bishop someday when Moulin would retire.

Then Tony continued: "This evening, a strange thing happened. The soldiers came to arrest Petero Tumba, our very special friend and catechist who has studied at the Catechetical School near Bujarundi." Tony continued, as Libori nodded that he knew Petero and the school as well:

"They were afraid to enter our compound since we had released the dogs for the night. So they, and to be specific the soldier named Kufa, sent a note via our cook saying that if Petero is not handed over by 10pm tonight, they will attack our mission and anything could happen. I am afraid that if I hand Tumba over, they will torture him throughout the night, without any trial whatsoever. And I know he is innocent!" Then Tony borrowed a line from the bishop and spoke a Moulinism. He repeated his last words for emphasis.

"He's innocent! Petero Tumba is innocent! He is innocent! Tumba is innocent! And I won't allow an innocent catechist to be arrested and maybe executed simply because the policemen and soldiers are jealous of his talents and popularity. Do you follow, Libori?"

Mihaga nodded in the affirmative and Tony finally trusted him enough to tell him the rest of the story:

"I have talked seriously to Tumba and have concluded that he is not guilty of any crime. So there is no reason for his being arrested except that his Batutsi enemies can be appeased. I can imagine what kind of a public trial he would have! So many men would be out to have him killed because the women find Petero so handsome and such a spiritual man. So I put him in the back of my car and brought him to the Administrator's house in Puma. I left him in the car and a policeman and two soldiers, one of them Kufa, came out and talked to me as I tried to see Kizungu. But I heard *M. l'Administrateur* laughing in his house and yet they told me he was away traveling. So I concluded that the best thing to do was to keep Tumba in the car and bring him down to you. I know you are a just and kind man and you can arrange it that no one will torture him during the night," Tony concluded.

Having spoken in Kirundi, Tony wondered if he had been understood clearly and completely. Even though they discussed in the dark of night, he felt Libori's face drop and he knew a question mark would be decorated all over his features if he could penetrate the darkness. Before Mihaga could respond, Tony stopped talking in circles and came forth with the truth:

"Yes, Libori, Tumba is still in the back of my car and I trust only you . Please take him for the night and promise me that he won't be tortured by any of your watchmen. Come quickly for Tumba has been hidden in that car for the past few hours."

Mihaga, mesmerized, accompanied the priest over to his VW that Tony opened with his key. He reached inside to open the lock on the passanger door as he whispered to Petero in the back:

"Are you all right?" Petero grunted a reply as his voice was beyond speaking clearly. He was so overcome with fright and emotion:

"I have Libori Mihaga with me, Petero," the priest went on, "he has given me his word that you will not be intimidated this night. In the morning, he will see to it that you are brought to the authorities at Puma since they still want your arrest. I, for my part, will do all I can to plead your innocence to the Administrator and whoever is in charge of your case on behalf of the military. I am giving you my word, Petero, that we, at the mission, will do all we can to obtain your release. We believe that you are innocent and if you truly are, then you should be released." Finally Tumba spoke up, his voice crackling:

"*Pati*, these men are savage beasts. They hate us, Bahutu, and all they want is to kill us. You can do as much as you can, but once they have me, they will do everything to kill me. But try to do all that is in your power for you are my only hope."

Sadly, Tony went around to the passenger side of the VW and opened the door, reaching into the back of the car to give Petero a hand and help him to come out of the *motocari* by the front door. He stepped out, a grey woolen blanket still around his shoulders. As Tony shined his flashlight on Petero's face so that Libori might recognize him, he could see his eyes were red and full of tears. This was the most trying time for this young man, being handed over to the authorities, who had his decision to live or die in their hands and who hated his tribe and thus him, viciously. Mihaga greeted him kindly, extending his hand to shake Petero's in *kirundi* greeting, as he remarked:

"Welcome, Petero. I know you very well for all the time you have spent teaching the christians here at Vuvoga. I promised the Reverend Father that I will take care of you and see that you are not harmed throughout the night. In the morning, we will have to follow orders from higher authority," Mihaga's remarks sounded stern but comforting.

Libori Mihaga then called two of the night watchmen who came running quickly. He had Petero's hands tied and they lead him away to a hut on the side of the road. As he was leaving, Tony reassured him:

"Courage, Catechist, all will be well. I will see to that," and he embraced him with both arms outstretched. His eyes welled up with tears and he felt the fast beating of Petero's heart. For the first time in his life, he knew the beating of two hearts into one, the crying of tears mingled together into one, the common brokenness, the oneness of pain, unity with another. Two friends embraced who would never be with each other again this side of heaven. "Petero, I will remember you 'til the end of time. I love you my brother, my friend, my other self-in-Christ." Tony turned back to Libori, visibly shaken. He shook his hand, approached him and face-to-face, looked him straight in the eye:

"Mihaga, I have come to Vuvoga tonight, because I trust you above all others. If anything happens to Tumba this night, I will hold you personally responsible. When these events are all over, there will be prosecutions for the war-crimes and atrocities committed. I would be very disappointed if I had to add your name to the list I already have prepared in much detail. I hope I have not trusted you in vain!"

Libori reassured him once more that he would do all in his power to protect Petero. Tony thanked him, got into his car, turned it around and drove back to Butova.

While he drove, his mind meandered back over his day. It had been one of the most horrible of his young life. But mostly he focused on Petero Tumba. Had Tony done all he could have to save Petero from this fate? Had they looked at every possibility or were there other options they could have taken? Was Petero in the safest place to spend a peaceful and restful night? And finally, were the missionaries unwilling to take the risk? Why was he so fearful of hiding Petero safely in the mission? Was he afraid for his own skin and felt better that Petero be handed over so that the mission would not be attacked?

Father Tony tried to pray for Petero but could not concentrate on his thoughts. He blamed God for this horrible fate. He wondered how a country that was so catholic, could commit such atrocities. He wondered what would happen to Butova now that they had stopped celebrating mass or giving the sacraments. He wondered what he and Luigi would be doing in the future, since there would be no church services to prepare, no outstations to visit, no confessions to hear, no children to baptize, no couples to prepare for marriage. Their whole life in Burundi was centered on giving the sacraments and yet now there were no sacraments to be given. A thought came to him. Since the priests had taken such a strong stand that morning, many people, especially the Batutsi in general and the authorities in particular, would not want them back in this parish after the events would subside. So Tony would be moving on to greener pastures elsewhere. His days in Butova were numbered! Going back to Canada for home leave was all he desired. So he would spend his spare time over the next weeks, when this African holocaust would be over, packing his cases and getting ready to depart from Butova. That would be an enjoyable time and along with seeing the widows who would be still coming to him by the hundreds and helping them, he would be kept busy. The interesting thing about being pastor of Butova Parish was that there were so many people in the area, helping people never ended. The work load would continue to be overwhelming. He looked forward to helping the widows and orphans but did not particularly relish the time and energy it would take hearing in detail all the ferocious crimes that the Batutsi had performed on their fellow countrymen. Yet all of a sudden, his work had become tremendously simplistic. The stories would be the same. All that would differ would be the details.

As Tony drove along, he found it strange that there were no other checkpoints between Vuvoga and Butova and wondered why the authorities did not want more protection for the Bututsi area of Butova and defense from the strongly Bahutu population of Vuvoga. He surmised that either the authorities had missed that area in their planning or people responsible for the checkpoint had not come out. The latter was close to impossible since it was a man's duty, under accusation of treason, not to show up for night watch. So he concluded that, once again, the soldiers and police had miscalculated. They were probably too busy hunting down and killing throughout the day to spend much time on positioning checkpoints strategically for night watch.

It was after eleven o'clock when Tony arrived back at the mission house. The dogs came barking to the fence and he knew that this would probably wake up his confreres. Sure enough, as he unlocked the gate, he saw a flashlight shining in the distance and opening the gate heard the deep voice of Luigi calling:

"Is that you, Tony?"

Tony answered right back in the affirmative not wanting to startle Luigi since a person could not see the car in the darkness for the bright head lights were shining in front of the vehicle. Luigi approached, held the dogs back while the car drove right through and then closed and locked the gate. Tony drove the car around to the back and as he disembarked, saw another flashlight coming from Luc's room. He came over to the car, yawning and wiping his eyes. As the three men met outside the dining room door, Tony asked Luc to start up the generator so that the mission lights could be seen. Even though it would cost three evenings' mazout-oil, it would be worth it to have the lights on all night for their safety and protection. The two men went into the dining room and Luigi lit a candle and they both sat down. When the electricity came on, Tony got up and cut a couple of slices of bread. Then he got some margarine and jam that Cypriano had made from Japanese prunes and came back to the table. He had already started telling Luigi about his adventures in Puma and the discussion with Mihaga on the road to Vuvoga when Luc joined them. Tony detailed the happenings: the good-byes at the sisters, the cold reception at Puma and finally his trust that leaving Petero with Mihaga was the only sound solution. Finally the three men said a short prayer at table, asking God to protect the three boys, Tumba, their mission and themselves. Tony then said he would put a note on the front gate saying that Petero had been surrendered to Mihaga. Since none of the military had a vehicle to drive the forty minutes to where Mihaga was, Tony knew that Tumba's safety was assured. He put the note on the fence, fastening it to the handle that anyone would use if trying to open the gate. Then he went back to his room. He wondered if he would sleep this night because of the tragic events of his day and also because of the noise of the motor turning. In any case, if his eyes would not close, he had electricity in his room, a first for him outside the capital. He might be able to catch up on some reading he had neglected over the past weeks.

But despite all the distractions, Tony did fall asleep quickly and woke at dawn. He stumbled out of bed and, still in his night clothes, meandered out to the courtyard behind the toilets where the motor kept turning. He turned it off and retruned to his room. He thanked God for having been kept safe. There had been no attacks on the part of the soldiers or anyone else during the night and he prayed that that would remain the same. He walked to the gate and saw that the note he had taped to the handle was still in place so he tore it off with another echo of gratitude.

It was always peaceful in the African morning when life came back again and people were thankful for having come through another night. He wondered about the four others: Osicari, Luduvico, Alfredo and Petero, who had slept at the mission the previous nights and were now under arrest. He squirmed as he thought of the agony they could have been going through and, although he believed Petero had been kept safe, he wondered how the three other boys were doing. His sacerdotal reflexes wanted to say a prayer for them but wondered if that would really help. He just hoped beyond all expectation that these four friends were not suffering.

Another day had begun in Butova, Monday the 22nd of May. Fr. Tony hoped this day would not be as taxing as the previous had been. In fact he believed that if the pace were to continue, he would go stark raving mad.

20. Tumba Arrested, Brought To Puma

As Fr. Anthony Joseph came out to greet the widows that were in front of his office door that morning, he was surprised to find a man from Lusaga who approached him rather abruptly as he turned the corridor to walk to his office door. Tony recognized him as Artimo Kiganda, a member of the Lusaga church council and a person who would always come and spend time with Tony when he went to that outstation. Tony even recalled going to Artimo's home the last time he was in Lusaga and drinking beer with him and all the members of the parish council. As he welcomed Artimo into his office, he asked him if he had come directly from Lusaga that morning. He realized that there must be an issue of great importance for him to have walked the long distance so early. Artimo said that he had been on the road before dawn. The short stocky man, whose build revealed his kihutu ancestry, sat down quickly in the chair in front of Tony's desk and blurted out his story:

"Last night some men arrived at the home of our distinguished catechist Eusebio Bitega," Kiganda went on, "and they told him they were going to beat him to death because he was a friend of the Bazungu, the priests at Butova." Tony closed his eyes, lifted up his head and felt his eyeballs rolling inside, heavy against his closed eyelids. He wondered how things could get even worse when the situation had become catastrophic so long ago. Now his reflexive reaction was to blame God as he heard one horrible, gruesome story after another. Better to say, the priest wasn't hoping in God anymore. If there were a God, then why would He allow one tragedy of this sort after another to take place without a hint of justice. It seemed exasperating:

"Is he still alive?" asked the priest.

"Thanks be to God," the laymen witnessed to the spiritual guru, "there was a doctor, Anastasio Bugana, visiting his family, neighbors of Eusebio, and he came over and treated him. His head was cut with a machete and his mouth as well. They were transporting him to the hospital in Vurura when I set out to bring you the news. Bitega has spoken very little and his body would not move but we are praying that he will not die." Then the robust man added:

"These Batutsi must be seeking revenge with you. When they called Eusebio a 'friend of the Bazungu', we realize that you are the only Bazungu that Bitega has ever known. It is obvious that they were trying to hurt you by killing the catechist."

"Who were those who attacked him?" Tony asked.

"The leader was a former soldier who has left the military service years ago. He wore his soldier's uniform and came to Bitega's house with about ten other young men. They are all Batutsi and they said that they would harm others if he or any others of the church showed that we were friends of yours." Artimo went on: "*Pati,* what did you say or do that has made them so angry?"

Tony did not answer this brave man who sat in front of him, risking his own life.

"You have to give me the names of all those that you know who were part of the attack. I will report them but don't worry, I will never mention your name nor where I received this information. Can you write, Artimo?" The man answered in the affirmative, and Tony gave him a pencil and some paper and led him to Jose's old office and locked him in from the outside telling him to write down all he knew about those who had attacked his friend. He then walked back to his office door a beaten and defeated man and heard the widows all vying for the first places to come and see him. They hoped that if they were first they would receive more than the powered milk, cooking oil, flour and 100 FrBu that he was giving each on them.

The rest of his morning was spent in listening to stories of murders, massacres, arrests and beatings. Each widow seemed to have a different story yet the conclusion was always the same. Their husbands, the fathers of so many children, had been lead away and tried very quickly and never heard from again. Those widows who were courageous enough to go to the soldiers or police and ask for the whereabouts of their husbands were told that there was no record of them and that they must have 'disappeared', having taken flight because they were guilty of some crime of treason. So it was concluded that they had fled the area. Yet everyone knew that flight was not an option for if a Muhutu was found outside his local area without a paper of *laissez-passer*, he would be executed immediately. Yet the soldiers had them believe that their husbands had run away! All the killings were done in private and many a widow surmised that her husband was so tortured during the night that he died from these wounds and never got a trial.

Tony heard a commotion about eleven o'clock that morning. He got up and went outside his office where many of the women were gathered waiting for him. He heard loud voices from many of the *bagore* and understood that they were becoming verbally aggressive to a man who looked nicely dressed but could not be recognized by Tony since his back was to him. When the man finally turned around, he saw that it was Lazaro Ndigi, teacher at the Brothers' Teachers' Training School. Lazaro had moved up quickly in the education hierarchy and was now the assistant to the Brother Director of the School. Tony remembered the trip they had made ten days earlier and the way that he was well received when the soldiers, with their rifles hanging over the back of the truck, had recognized him as one of their very own. But now Lazaro was showing his haughty side by telling the women that they had no right to seek compensation from the priest since their husbands had been murdered and thus they were all considered traitors.

"The proof that your husbands are traitors" he said, "is that they are now dead."

And Tony thought 'dead men don't lie! The very fact that they were dead meant that they were dangerous for the government to deal with and not necessarily 'traitors'. He then approached Lazaro and asked him if he could help him with anything. When Lazaro responded that he had come to talk to him on official business, Tony invited him to have a seat outside and wait for him to finish with the women in his office. Lazaro agreed, but added that he had a class coming soon at the school and Tony let him know it wouldn't be too long. He wanted to make sure the teacher understood that other people were busy as well and that even though he might think himself superior to others, especially these wives of the Bahutu who had been killed, nevertheless they had been waiting longer than the teacher and deserved, in justice, to be seen as soon as possible.

When that group of widows left his office, Tony stood by the door and invited the teacher in. It was only then that he noticed that Lazaro had a handgun stuck in his belt as he walked past the open door and sat on the bench that had been most recently occupied by the widows. Tony froze for a few seconds when he saw the gun. Then he stood up and pointing to the weapon, he asked Ndigi:

"Where did you get that fire-arm?"

Quick to reply, the teacher said that he had received it from the military for his personal protection.

Tony responded by asking him:

"Ndigi, what have you done that you need such security? You are carrying a gun for self-protection? Why would you think that anyone would want to hurt you, unless you believe that you have done some horrible crimes? Carrying a gun proves that you are condemning yourself." Tony scoffed at Ndigi as he continued:

"*Musenuri* Ruyaga gave me a rifle two weeks ago, but that was to protect my parishioners. I hope he didn't think I needed it to protect myself! Furthermore I would never feel the need to go about carrying a fire-arm. I would think that the people would see me as needing protection, and thus would judge me as guilty of some crime if I carried a gun. So Ndigi, what crime are people saying you committed?" Tony asked, aggression clinging to his every word. He disliked this egotistical Mututsi and saw absolutely no reason for him to be able to take the law into his own hands simply because he was an educated teacher and self-appointed *mukuru*. 'If he truly were an educator, he should be acting very differently,' Tony construed.

"*Mon Pere*," Lazaro responded in excellent French, "I have committed absolutely no crime. But this is a time when all of us, faithful and loyal citizens, are called upon to protect our beloved Burundi. The military know that I am an important person and have entrusted me with this fire-arm."

Then something funny happened that made the priest almost burst into laughter amid the horrible scene he was contemplating. Over the next few weeks he would tell this anecdote over and over again to friends and colleagues alike to put a smile on their faces. Lazaro moved his left foot a few inches and crossed his right leg over it. But as he did this simple gesture, Tony noticed that the gun was almost falling out of his belt. One more jerking motion..... and bang! And sure enough: 'bang!' it fell on the floor. Tony scrambled to reach it as Ndigi was overcome with surprise. He walked over to the teacher and said:

"My good man, Professor Ndigi, you had better look after that fire-arm so that you don't execute yourself! It would be a shame to tell people that you were the cause of your own death!" he added looking at an embarrassed Lazaro Ndigi, trying to hide the incident by affixing the firearm back on his belt as quickly as possible.

Tony continued speaking since he wanted to embarrass the teacher one more time:

"I have seen many military in my home country and many people with fire-arms. I have never seen or even heard of one who allowed his gun to fall to the floor. It could be picked up by an enemy and the owner killed instantly. Oui, M.le professeur, you had better watch out or you could be on your way to heaven! You might not always have the soldiers around you to protect you. If some of those Bahutu widows had been here in the office with you this afternoon, you would now be DEAD!" he added, accentuating the last word and making it sound utterly acerbic.

Ndigi decided to change the subject and said that he needed to talk to the pastor professionally, about the decision Tony had made the previous day. Tony pretended to not understand. So Ndigi told him that he was disappointed with the decision he had made Sunday and that he had come representing the whole population of Butova, asking the priest to begin celebrating masses as soon as possible so that all would be in order the following Sunday.

"Were you at mass, yesterday?" Tony asked the teacher whom he had never seen in church. His reply was in the negative with an explanation that he had a meeting with the soldiers.

"What have you heard, about what took place in church?"

"You have said that because there is so much hatred between the races here in Butova, you will not pray with us." was the teacher's reply.

"Well Lazaro, let me explain the situation to you a little better than others have told it to you. You were ill-informed! I have judged absolutely no one. But in a country like Burundi, where in a very short period of time one-hundred-thousand people are murdered because of tribal-hatred, then I believe that it would be a sacrilege to bring the presence of a loving God into that state of affairs. In fact, Ndigi, I am going to say one thing to you and only say it once. Then you can get up and leave my office because I have some very poor widows to see who need my help. They don't come to tell me what to do. Nor do they carry arms. They come because they are poor and they will be poor for a long time because dimwits like you are going around killing their husbands, fathers or sons. So this is what I have to say to you, Mr. Professor: I have no intention of celebrating mass for you murderers. You may think that this does not concern you personally, for you are not baptized catholic. But you, Ndigi, are a tyrant and if you drop that gun someplace, someday, where there are Bahutu, they will rid the earth of your existence. Now get going, I have work to do." Father Anthony Joseph stood up and walked briskly to the door. Without speaking one more word, but looking at him with fury written all over his face, Lazaro moved to the door and exited faster than he had come in. As he went down the stairs to the footpath, he heard the pastor call out to the widows, still waiting patiently:

"Whoever are the next three, please come into my office." Lazaro walked away knowing that the priest was very angry at the situation and the killings and wondered what he could do to seek revenge for all that Tony had done to embarrass him. Tony, for his part, had remembered something Jose always said: 'The Barundi don't get angry.....they get even!'

Soon it was nearly 1pm and Tony left his office for lunch. Once again he had had a disastrous and painful morning and longed to be free and share his experiences with his colleagues and to draw strength from them. "I can't believe that he said that!" Luc exclaimed when Tony reiterated his encounter with the teacher. His voice was so loud that Tony thought people might hear it on the other side of the offices. "I cannot believe it! The wretch! How could he, a baptized-pagan, dare come to you, pastor of the parish, and scold you for not celebrating a catholic mass? I hope he understood every word you said to him!"

"I know he did," Tony went on, "and I hope they stay etched on his soul forever. Yet I don't think he was attacking me personally, but rather making a point politically"

As Tony returned to his office after lunch, a policeman from Puma was waiting for him. Tony went over and greeted him. The policeman said that he had come from the prison and that Petero Tumba had been apprehended and was now in jail. Tony answered in astonishment by saying that he had left Petero at the checkpoint near Vuvoga the preceding night.

"Tumba was being lead to Puma this morning for trial," the policeman went on, "and he escaped from those who were leading him. They screamed and ran after him and people started chasing him from all directions. Finally he was apprehended, and handcuffed, his watch and clothes were stolen. He arrived at Puma almost naked. It would have been better for him if he would not have tried to escape" the policeman told Tony.

Tony, thinking of the ordeal that Jesus had gone through centuries before, responded knowing the calm, disciplined person his catechist was:

"It was probably those who were bringing him to Puma who attacked him themselves because he had a watch," he responded, disappointed in himself that he had not taken the watch the night before and held it for Petero's mother. 'What a nice keepsake it would have been for her,' he thought. Then he turned back to the policeman:

"Would you take a note to the person-in-charge at Puma. Who, by the way, is in charge?" he questioned.

"The administrator, as usual," was the response and then Tony realized once again that he had been tricked by those at Puma the previous night. He wondered why this policeman had come to give him the news about Petero. Taking a pen and paper, Tony wrote to the administrator knowing that his action was useless but it was the only chance he had to save Tumba. In his nicest, politest Kirundi, he addressed Alberto Kizungu. He mentioned nothing about Sunday evening but said that it was his responsibility as a priest to see his catechist and give him the blessings and consolation of the catholic church. He mentioned that he would do the same for him, the administrator, if the need ever occurred. He signed the copy and put a note on the bottom saying that he was sending a copy to the Vicar General, Msgr. Luduvico Ruyaga, just to keep the Mututsi honest. He knew that the administrator was a coward and more afraid of the Batutsi leaders than of any Muhutu.

Fr. Tony was a very practical man. So he asked the administrator when he could visit the catechist, and invited a reply by the same policeman. It was not the kirundi or polite way of acting, but he was trying to put Kizungu on the spot as much as he could. Within a few minutes, the policeman was away with the message and Tony wondered, as he watched him go out the door, if his efforts were not utterly futile. At least, Kizungu was now aware that Tony knew Petero was being held in prison.

Fr. Tony went back to his office for the afternoon and undertook the drudgery of listening to more and more widows tell their stories of how their husbands were arrested and executed. On one occasion he asked one woman about her husband and he noticed that when she spoke, the other women put their impuzu up to their mouths to relieve tension and show that they were embarrassed about something. The woman didn't answer the questions very quickly and in the beginning, Tony thought she was intimidated or nervous or very saddened by the situation. Finally one woman spoke up. She said that this woman was telling lies and that she was only coming because Tony was giving away free supplies to those who were widows. Tony ordered her out of his office when she admitted the truth and went outside to publicly denounce her. He told her that her penalty for lying would be paying one blanket for the poor. She went away calling out that she would bring him the money but he knew well that this was the last time he would ever see this poor wretched soul. He figured she must have felt justified and was probably a widow and thought that, since her husband was dead, she, too, had a right to the help that Tony was giving to the widows of the genocide killings.

As the afternoon wore on, the pastor received less and less women. After four o'clock many of them would not think of coming to the mission since it was time to be home and darkness would come before they could walk back and forth let alone spend time in front of the priest's office door. That could wait until tomorrow.

Finally by five o'clock Tony walked out of his office and around the back courtyard and got into his VW. He would drive down to Puma and see what was happening. Over the past three weeks, he learned to fear such trips for he would always receive some surprisingly bad news when he went to Puma. Now his apprehensions became greater since he knew that Petero, Osicari, Luduvico and Alfredo were part of those held in the Puma jail. He had never been through the jail to visit since most of the prisoners in the mornings and afternoons would sit unguarded outside. They would never run away since there was nowhere for them to go..... nowhere at least until they would be found by someone and returned to jail and given more time. The only way that they would eat would be if someone from their families would come and stay in that area, live with a family and prepare food daily for the husband, father or son. As Tony drove to Puma, he thought of this policy and realized that he had to be the one who should organize food for his friends or else they would not live through the week. He drove straight ahead and the jail was on his left. Many of the prisoners were milling around outside preparing to go back inside and ready themselves for the night. Tony had never seen more prisoners at Puma than on this day. Furthermore he saw many wives, mothers or daughters walking around with food stuffs for their particular prisoner. He realized that when someone was arrested, the whole family had to suffer and was disunited.

Tony parked his car in front of the jail and got out, locking the door on the driver's side. Many of the people came over to him and he recognized two or three policemen who were watching over the prisoners. A few of the women shook his hand in great kirundi fashion. Tony had learned the meaningful symbol of how the people shook hands. They would extend their right hand and at the same time, they would hold their right wrist with their left hand. In this way they showed respect, for it was the whole body, the whole person, that was exchanging the greeting. Most had sad looks of panic and stress on their faces and a few of them even said he had spoken the truth at the Sunday service. He knew that they all were Bahutu and thus appreciated what he had said since it seemed to condemn the Batutsi government. Tony greeted one of the policemen very politely. He asked if he could see Petero Tumba and the policeman told him that that would be impossible. Tony responded:

"Why isn't he and the other boys that worked for the Bazungu outside where we can see that they are healthy and still alive?" he asked with an impertinent look on his face.

The policeman took a step backward and stated that many of the prisoners were in solitary confinement and were not allowed an access to public privileges. Tony retorted quickly and asked him: "Why? What have they done that merited such restriction?" The policeman backed away and another came forward:

"Your speech, Pati, in the church yesterday has shown us that you are a friend of the bamenja. Better not to speak too clearly by words or actions" he went on. "So all prisoners that have been taken from your house are considered traitors because you have condemned the government."

Tony responded immediately: "These are unforgivable acts that you are performing. God will damn you to hell forever if you destroy his little ones." He walked back to his car and low and behold as he lifted his dejected head to look forward and see who was coming toward him, he found himself face-to-face with the soldier Kufa! So he seized the opportunity and said to him: "I have come to ask you a very special favor. I would like to visit with four friends of mine who are being held as prisoners here. I, as their priest and spiritual mentor, seek permission to minister to them. I have asked the administrator for permission, but he is not at home." Tony lied, staring directly into the eyes of the soldier as he continued: "Now I would like to ask you for permission to pray with them."

"Mon Pere," the soldier answered him, "your friends are among the most dangerous arrested prisoners. They were part of your household and we are trying them before the courts for having performed acts of treason. There is no way that we can allow you a visit."

Tony felt defeated. He knew that they were only too willing to trump him for they saw a way to get back at him through those he called his friends. He thought it better to leave as soon as possible or the situation could get worse for the four young men. As he drove away, Kufa stood at the front side of his car. Tony rolled down the window and mentioned that he believed that the four had no one to prepare their food. He asked if he could bring it to them, hoping that he could give it directly to them. This would serve a two-fold purpose: he would be able to talk to them and it would prevent the soldiers from stealing the food. Kufa responded:

"I want to inform you, Reverend Pere, that those needs are being addressed. Some other people have brought them food and they don't need your help. If ever they are in need, we will call you."

Tony, realizing they were insurmountable, rolled up his window, glared at the monster and drove back to Butova. Again he thought: 'How bad can it get, when it had gone far beyond everyone's threshold of grief and painfulness?'

21. Doomsday Gets Closer

The pastor awoke on May 23rd with renewed hope in his heart. He was always surprised when the new day dawned that he was able to rise and put behind him the troubles of yesterday. The dawn seemed to bring new expectations and heal the past.

In mid-morning, Eugenio Mugera, the mission woodcutter said he had been given an important letter for Fr. Tony from someone he didn't know who had come from Puma, He thanked Eugenio and went back into his office to read the note. He was overjoyed that it was from Petero Tumba who had signed in the *kirundi* way: *"ni jewe, Petero"* (it is I, Petero). As he smiled, he recalled what a droll expression this was that the letter-writer would conclude with 'it is I' as if the letter were written by a ghost who only revealed its true identity at the end of the letter. The letter read as follows:

Pati nkunda cane, (Father, whom I love very much)

I send you greetings from the jail in Puma where I have been held since yesterday afternoon. I know your concern for me, so I wanted to write this letter to you. This jail is overcrowded and the smell and lack of hygiene is unbelievably vile. Furthermore, there is no one to give me food since my family lives far away and they don't even know that I am in prison. I need your help. The best solution would be to have me released since I have never committed any crime. Yet the authorities are accusing me of treason and are saying that I did terrible things. The people are lying and falsely accusing me. I have never been involved with politics since, as a catechist, I believed my role was not to take sides but to help both sides see how much God loves all of us.

Secondly, if it is not possible to free me, would you try to get me some food? I am very hungry and thirsty since they have not made any rations available to us. But do not give it to the guards for they, themselves. will eat it. I end by sending you my fondest regards.

Ni jewe,
Petero.

Once again Father Tony felt the heavy responsibility that had been laid on his shoulders when Mathias was reappointed to Germany. He knew that he was the only person capable of speaking to the authorities in vain hope that they would look after Petero's needs. Yet Tony had calculated all this the previous day when he had asked Kufa and the policemen to release Tumba or at least have his needs for food and drink met. He realized that they failed to comply with the stipulations made in so many international agreements regarding the treatment of prisoners. Yet the Barundi authorities were probably not aware of any of these stipulations and, even if they were, they would absolutely never comply, especially since it involved a Muhutu. Fr. Tony at least would sit down and write a return letter to Petero and hope that he could get it to him without it being noticed by the soldiers and policemen. But there were great possibilities that it would fall into their hands. So the pastor had to choose his words carefully and not even say that he had received a letter from Petero, for this would surely stir up suspicion that someone in the jail was helping the catechist get news outside the prison walls. The priest's letter to Petero, in French well known by the catechist and very little by the guards and policeman, read as follows:

My Dear Friend and Beloved Catechist Petero,

I send you greetings from Butova where we are doing all we can to have you released from jail. Yesterday (Monday), I went to Puma and asked to visit with you. But that was impossible. So I was very pleased to hear you are well and I pray that you will soon be reading these words. Never give up trusting in God, Petero. God is on your side and He will not allow you to become discouraged or despondent. We become depressed when we don't realize that God is working all around us and that He will save us from every danger and peril. I am aware that you have neither food nor drink and I will do all I can to get you what you need materially. In the meantime, remember St. Paul was thrown into prison many times because of his love for Christ. So when you are suffering, know, dear friend, that you are doing this as an Apostle of the Lord. Continue to witness to Him and His Love while you are in jail. I will also try to get a Bible to you so that you can read the Word of God and draw strength from the Scriptures. Jesus understands what you are going through since He was arrested and kept in prison on Holy Thursday night. Talk to Him and draw strength from Him and His tremendous love for you. Again, I will do all that I can to have you released or at least to get you food and drink.

Ni jewe,
Pati Antonio.

Tony thought it best that he try to deliver the missive himself. He drove to Puma and, on arriving, saw the Administrator, Alberto Kizungu. The priest was pleased, since he thought somehow it would be easier to get him, representing the civil and not the military authority, to approve a visit from the pastor to his catechist or at least agree to pass the letter to Petero. As Tony got out of his car, the administrator came over to greet him in fine *kirundi* fashion. After some brown-nose small talk about how nice it was that the administrator was back in Puma and how much he was missed in his absence, Tony mentioned the events of the past days and how he tried to leave Petero Tumba with Kizungu since he considered him the chief in the area. He wanted to see Kizungu's reaction when he told him that he had been informed that he was not in his house Sunday evening and yet had heard laughter through the walls. But the sly Mututsi never spoke to give away any trace of the fact that he had been there all the time.

"*M. l'Administrateur,*" Tony went on, "I have a very special favor to ask of you. I know I have been very helpful to you over the past weeks, driving you to the outposts for night watch, bringing the police and soldiers to Mundi, and making our vehicles available for you whenever and wherever possible. It has been an honor to respond to your needs since we are very good friends, *M. l''Administrateur.*" Tony went on, his mouth flooding Kizungu with unearned compliments: "But, furthermore, I represent the Roman Catholic Church as pastor of Butova Parish and the vocation of the catholic church is to help the local government and authorities when there is any need whatsoever. But now, I would appreciate you doing something for me and our catholic church, for I know that you are also a very fervent member of the church and disciple of Christ. You know that Petero Tumba is a catechist and highly trained by the diocese of Vurura. I would like, as his pastor, to visit him in jail and organize his food and drink as he has no mother, wife, sister or child to prepare food for him here in the Bututsi."

As he spoke, Tony looked up at Kizungu and saw him already shaking his head. Tony stopped in his tracks and allowed Kizungu to make a comment:

"I am sorry, *Mon Pere,*" he said emphatically, "but Petero Tumba has been arrested for treason towards the government and is not permitted any visitors. Besides, if he were to be found guilty, he would go to Vurura and there Monsignor Luduvico Ruyaga would be available to give him spiritual consolation." Tony was startled by the directness of the reply and the firmness of Kizungu's voice. He reciprocated with his voice filled with repulsion: "*M. l'Administrateur*, you once tricked me by telling me, when I asked you permission to hear the confessions of my parishioners that were being killed, that they were going to Vurura and there they could obtain the services of Msgr. Ruyaga. Well, I asked the Monsignor the other day and he told me categorically that he has never been approached by anyone from Butova or Puma or Vurura to give the sacraments to the condemned! And therefore, since the bishop and monsignor have appointed me pastor here in Butova, I demand to see all my parishioners to give them spiritual counseling and meet all their personal religious obligations."

"I am sorry but I must insist that you cannot have the permission," Kizungu interjected.

Tony couldn't believe that his life had become so painfully sterile over the past weeks and now a total impasse with a man he had helped and wanted to support. He went on:

"*M. l'Administrateur*, I regret both your decision and what I now have to say to you. You are following the civil law of the country. I, on my part, am following the law of Christ and the laws of the Roman Catholic Church. I will never again make myself or our mission vehicles available to you under any circumstances. Please never ask, for the answer will always be as negative as the one you have just given to me. Furthermore, *M. l'Administrateur*, in that you have made this decision, respecting your civil responsibilities to the detriment of your christian ones, I forbid you from receiving the sacraments in our church until you realize what offense you have committed in not allowing me to speak spiritually with my catechist. We. priests of Butova, will not hear your numerous sins in confession because you refuse the gift of the same sacrament to those that you audaciously have condemned to death. We priests will never be available to you nor your family for any spiritual needs whatsoever. So please do not call that I will have to refuse as clearly and as directly as you have refused me today. Alberto Kizungu, consider yourself excommunicated from the practice of the Roman Catholic faith." Tony terminated the conversation without another word.

Alberto Kizungu looked at the priest with anger visible all over his face. Once again Tony thought of the African axiom that all the missionaries laughed at since it was so true of the Batutsi: "I don't get angry, I get even!" There would be a day of reckoning, but right now Tony was satisfied with what he had said and how he had communicated it. The priest walked away, got into his car and drove back to Butova with the letter to Tumba still in his pocket. He was annoyed at himself since he had become so involved talking about the visit that he hadn't remembered to get the letter to Petero. But now all that counted was Petero getting some food and drink and knowing that the priests in the parish were trying to help obtain his release. A visit from Tony was not that vital since Tumba had gone to confession two nights earlier. But Tony had another strategy: Plan B! He decided to try it as soon as he was back to his office.

The pastor remembered one of the policeman whom he considered a close and helpful friend. His name was Paulo Bihondi who lived across the valley on a hillside near Ruhaha. Furthermore, he was the product of a Mututsi mother and a Muhutu father. Tony had once talked to him about his job in Puma jail. He had said that his responsibility was guarding the prisoners, especially in the late afternoon and early evening.

On arrival back at the parish, Tony sent a young boy with a note inviting Paulo to come to the mission to see him as soon as possible. Within the hour, Bihondi was knocking on his door saying he was stopping by on his way to work. Tony praised God under his breath for granting him this favor and hoped that it would provide food for Petero and even for Osicari, Luduvico and Alfredo. Paulo sat down in front of Tony's desk and the pastor offered him some tobacco since Paulo seemed like the kind of man who would smoke a cigarette. Bihondi reached into his pocket and Tony recognized the piece of paper he took out. It was the original note that the pastor had the young boy take to Paulo. Now that he had responded to the *rendez-vous*, there was no need to retain the invitation! The policeman proceeded to cradle the paper in his left hand and put the tobacco on it with his right. He licked the paper of his cigarette so that it would stick together and looked at Tony who was ready with a match.

They small-talked for a while and then Tony, without telling Paulo anything about the confrontation he had just had with Kizungu, asked him matter-of-factly if he would give this note to Petero Tumba when he saw him in prison. The policeman took the letter, folded it and placed it in the same pocket that once contained Tony's note that was now burning smoothly between Paulo's fingers. Pocketing the missive seemed the most natural gesture a person could ever do. Bihondi said he would give it to Petero as soon as he saw him later that afternoon. Tony switched back to the small talk, gave Paulo more tobacco and finally Bihondi stood up and said he had to be on his way. Tony thanked him and couldn't believe his good fortune. Maybe his luck was finally changing or the balance of power was spinning his way. He realized that if Paulo got the note to Petero, he would be reassured that the fathers were working for his release and would regain hope that food and drink would soon be coming as well. God was surely on their side with His small favors. As Bihondi opened the door to leave, Tony mentioned that he had a different brand of tobacco that was still sealed in a back room. He invited Bihondi to return to his office the next day and try some different tasting "itabi ya Bukanada" (Canadian tobacco). In that way, Tony planned to convince Paulo to be his secret messenger to his catechist. He thanked God for his parents and the many pouches of pipe tobacco they sent to Butova through the mail. Maybe the tobacco could be used to get Petero food and drink, or even still better, to free him. But alas, Fr. Tony's plans were merely dreams that would never come to fruition. Tumba's enemies would see to it that his demise would come very quickly. On leaving his office, Tony went to the dining room where Luc and Luigi were already at table for the afternoon *collation* (snack) and tea. This was a European custom that Tony had grown to appreciate very much. In the afternoon, the confreres gathered around the dining room table for a *tartine* (jam on a thick slice of bread) and a cup of coffee or tea. Since supper was so late, after 7 pm, the afternoon snack was an enjoyable break in the many activities.

As the three men were finishing their snack, they saw a small VW drive in along the road between the dining room and the kitchen. When the car stopped, Tony and Luigi went out to see who it might be since the missionaries were somewhat anxious about people coming on their compound close to dusk. Relationships between the government authorities or the soldiers and the church leaders were often strained lately. But the realization that it was a VW took most suspicion of a threat away. Normally African leaders didn't travel in the small beetle bug, but most economically-minded missionaries did. Furthermore those Batutsi that the Bazungu feared the most didn't have the means of traveling in their own personal vehicles anyway. So the confreres were more curious than anxious.

As the two priests turned the corner and went out to the back *kigo,* they were surprised to hear the voice of an estranged neighbor: Father Angelo Bertuzzi from the nearby parish of Mutwe. He was walking toward the verandah with Lorenzo his favorite African boy by his side. Lorenzo had been hand-picked by Bertuzzi many years earlier to work as a cook in his mission when Bertuzzi was parish priest of Bumeza. When the Italian White Father was appointed to build the new mission of Mutwe, he took Lorenzo with him and taught him everything: how to serve table as it was done in Italy, how to repair tires and change motor oil, how to build a church and catechumenate and outstations. Lorenzo soon became Bertuzzi's "Jack-of-all-trades" and could oversee just about everything at Mutwe Mission. The other missionaries and especially Pedro Sanchez and Raphael Saturnino who lived with Bertuzzi were totally averse to the way Bertuzzi included Lorenzo in everything. He would eat meals with the fathers and guests and he would accompany Bertuzzi whenever and wherever he traveled. . But the other fathers were angry at the way Bertuzzi brought the African boy into the inner sanctum of their community where no African without holy orders was welcome. But Bertuzzi had his own set of rules so Lorenzo always accompanied him. That was another reason why Bertuzzi was reviled by all his confreres.

Tony shook hands with the older priest and invited him into the sitting room. He felt ill-at-ease about the presence of Lorenzo since he understood French very well and thus it would be difficult to tell any stories that should remain among confreres. Luc came in and welcomed him as well and the conversation went from one horrible story to another. However as they spoke, Tony noticed one thing. The Butova missionaries were telling stories about how so many innocent people were being murdered. However Bertuzzi always took the part of the Batutsi and was blinded to the evil his favorites had done. So he kept talking about how gracious the Batutsi were and how strong and powerful the army. Finally Tony asked Lorenzo if he would like to go out to the kitchen and talk to the cook, Cypriano. He didn't question where Lorenzo fit in racially. He was obviously a Mututsi. His good looks, his suave way of talking and dressing and his overall smooth disposition gave it all away. Alas, if he had been a Muhutu, Bertuzzi would have disowned him years ago.

The founding pastor of Mutwe never tried to cover up what he considered the differences between the Batutsi and the Bahutu. The former were more intelligent, cleaner, more cunning, better business people, more educated and better christians! In fact, Bertuzzi believed that the Bahutu were imbeciles, dirty, uneducated and weak christians. Oftentimes he would say as much, never relenting in his praise for those with longer noses (Batutsi), and his disdain for those shorter! (Bahutu).

With Lorenzo out of the room visiting in the kitchen, Tony asked Bertuzzi how things were going at Mutwe. The old man flashed a bright smile and said he had a fine story to tell them, all about the president. Bertuzzi gave everyone the impression that he was the president's best Muzungu friend and confident. And that probably was so. But the more he said it, the more other confreres wanted to prove the contrary. President

Sabimana often stayed with him in the priests' house at Mutwe, and arrived sometimes without being announced. He felt more secure when no one knew his plans or whereabouts. Even telling Bertuzzi in advance might lead to a plot to assassinate the national leader. Usually Bertuzzi and Sabimana would be alone but still Lorenzo would be invited by the pastor to join them. Seldom did Bertuzzi ever invite Sanchez or Saturnino to come and chat, but never failed to invite Lorenzo This just showed how callous he was about his confreres feelings.

Bertuzzi started his anecdote by telling them what Tony had heard during the first days of the Bahutu revolution in late April. It was a badly-kept secret. The rebels had gone northwest from Vurura and had taken hold of the catholic mission of Bitoke. Then they realized that if they climbed over the Mutwe mountains they would be right at Bertuzzi's doorstep. Since Bertuzzi made sure that everyone, Batutsi and Bahutu alike, knew of his personal friendship with the president, the cry of the Bahutu rebels was: 'Let's climb the mountain and attack the mission of Mutwe on the other side and cut the throat of *Pati 'Tuzi',* the friend of Sabimana.' Others said: '.....the priest of the Batutsi, let's cut off his head...." And they mimicked him by rhyming the short nickname the people gave to the priest "Tuzi" with "Tutsi", the root for Batutsi. Others made fun of the name of his mission, Mutwe, (head) and cutting off his head, which was translated by *mutwe.* 'The head of Mutwe needs to lose his head!'

Tony was appalled and angry that Bertuzzi would tell such a story, flaunting it in front of everyone that he loved the Batutsi more than the Bahutu. But what really angered Tony was Bertuzzi's attitude, full of conceit running all over his round face. So Tony thought he'd better make light of the whole thing or he would say something to the older priest that he would regret afterwards:

"So, Padre, did they cut your throat?" he mimicked sarcastically.

Bertuzzi responded with a hearty laugh: "They haven't been able to do it yet!" he replied.

Then Luigi jumped in as well: "You better not be too sure. Things are not over yet and the Bahutu are very angry at the cards they have been dealt," the younger Italian reprimanded his older countryman.

Bertuzzi was always ready for a challenge: "The Bahutu are too stupid!" He went on, without even lowering his voice but rather raising it at the word 'stupid'.

"They are not intelligent enough to lead a revolution when they have 85% of the population. These events have shown us the difference in the two tribes: the Batutsi are intelligent, enterprising, sharp, good looking, polite and fine organizers. Whereas the Bahutu are dumb, dumb, dumb.....

All that they can do is make and drink *inzoga*!" This was Bertuzzi's credo on the anthropological variances of the two tribes that had lived side-by-side in Burundi for the last four or five hundred years! There was some truth in what he was saying, but hearing the categorizations from his harsh, earsplitting- voice was almost unbearable for the three men of Butova.

Everyone was getting very upset, which was usually the case when Bertuzzi came calling. A visit turned into taking sides and defending the poor Bahutu against his outrageous and biased comments. But then the old man went on to tell them another story, which, once again, arrogantly showed his own importance and personal relationship with the Batutsi President.

"President Sabimana came to stay with me a few days ago and I so enjoyed his visit. When he arrived, he was with two other cabinet ministers and, as usual, I welcomed them into my living room. Lorenzo was there and I asked him to get us a bottle of Italian wine. As he got up to get it, *M. le President* started to smile and laugh and the other ministers followed along with him. I asked Etienne what was so amusing. Then he told me. The other day they were all together for mass in St. Francis Xavier church in the capital. They were outside, small-talking in a large circle when the mass had ended. The president was teasing the missionaries of the parish as is his way of showing us affection.....You know how much President Sabimana likes to banter with the Bazungu." Then Bertuzzi turned directly to Luigi and added:

"That parish is run by your community, Luigi, the Xaverian Missionaries, and your provincial Superior, Giovanni Bartoli was there." Luigi nodded at Bertuzzi that he knew the name of his religious community and the man who was his superior!

"As they joked, and you know the way the president always likes to put us at ease by teasing us," Bertuzzi repeated what he had just mentioned beforehand. "Well, Bartoli asked him if he could have a word with him in private. When the president obliged, they walked away from the group and Bartoli declared with great rage in his voice to the leader of our country: 'If you are president of a country where 150,000 people have been killed by your soldiers in three weeks, then I don't think that you should come to pray at mass or to receive holy communion any longer, certainly not in our church. *M. le President*, you are not welcome in our parish any longer.' And he walked away from the president leaving him alone. Sabimana returned to his group of friends and they all left immediately. The president told me the story himself when I invited him to have a drink of wine. He said: 'At least there is one priest in Burundi who is not refusing me wine!'

Could you believe that this man was so impolite to the President of the Republic? And he is your Superior, Luigi!" Bertuzzi concluded, oblivious to the factual reality of the story he had just told, but rather dwelling on Sabimana's hurt feelings at being told that a catholic without a conscience could not be welcomed at the Holy Table. The three Butova missionaries looked at each other and Luigi and Luc were ready to explode but they left the first word to Tony:

"Bertuzzi," he said, with absolutely no respect of age or rank for the older man, "I have to be honest with you. We refused to say mass two days ago, on Pentecost Sunday, for our people and we are refusing all the sacraments until 'LOVE' has come back to the area. I am glad someone has said the same thing to the president for he is more guilty than all the Bahutu who need the eucharist at this time of tragedy and national mourning. Sabimana goes to mass to feel good about himself and the country. I rejoice that Bartoli has stood up to him and I agree with him entirely! How could Sabimana allow such a massacre to happen and then think that he is still in perfect relationship with God? May God condemn him and all those who are encouraging these killings and this genocide. He is the person in headship of this country. Therefore he is responsible for every and all altercations. As for you, we cannot understand how a priest of God can be so prejudiced! Will you only be happy when you see that every Muhutu in Burundi has been murdered? Stop encouraging these raging maniacs, these outrageous Batutsi."

Luigi picked up the conversation and continued the bantering:

"Bishop Moulin agrees with what Tony is saying for he has helped us prepare our message to the people Sunday." Immediately, on hearing the name of the bishop, Bertuzzi cut in:

"Moulin has learned nothing in his forty-five years in Burundi! He doesn't understand the people or their needs and likes to talk and talk and repeat himself, yet says nothing. I have stopped going to him for advice years ago and he doesn't come my way very often," Bertuzzi continued, setting up a red herring chase to save face from the three who obviously wanted to pursue more reflection on Giovanni Bartoli's strong bias-Batutsi stance.

"We are not talking about Bishop Moulin, Bertuzzi" Luigi replied. "We are talking about a people who are massacring another, a tribe of 14% who are murdering another of 85%. The only reason that you can commit such genocide is that you have all the arms and ammunition." Luigi made the smooth transition from "they" to "you" totally implicating Bertuzzi in the Batutsi reprisals. He went on: "The power is in your guns. Somehow you, Batutsi, have to realize how anti-christian, how blindly pagan, you are. You are nothing but murderers and looters and liars and you make me want to throw up in your face!" Luigi concluded, startling his confreres who had never seen him so outraged.

Bertuzzi was on his feet. He walked over to the dining room door and opening it, went through to a second door leading out across the road to the kitchen. He opened that door as well and called out to Lorenzo and said they were going. When he came back to the living room, he found the three missioners still sitting and talking to one another quietly. He said rather harshly, with a voice starting to tremble:

"We must be going. If all you have to offer us in coffee, we prefer to go back home and have some wine. I will remember how you treated me and will be as discourteous to you when you come to visit me." Bertuzzi showed his angry not by debating the issue but rather changing the subject to talk about hospitality which he considered to be his *forte.*

"Don't hold your breath, Padre" Luc said as all three men looked at each other. They couldn't bare to make eye-contact with the racist. In the Kirundi tradition, they knew it was expected of them to walk a guest to his car. But Tony, Luc and Luigi stayed glued to their chairs.

"Let's send him a clear signal that we cannot be polite when someone is so blatantly biased," Tony said.

The proud Italian drove away seeping in anger. As they sat sipping their coffee, Luc remarked comically:

"I'm sorry the Bahutu never succeeded in crossing the mountain and slitting his throat. At least we wouldn't have to listen to that eardrum-piercing voice anymore! Bertuzzi doesn't deserve the name 'missionary' or 'priest', the narrow-minded wretch!" They all chuckled, for if not they would all have cried.

The following day, Wednesday, was the most peaceful of the week, if any of the days could be considered stress-free. Tony continued the strenuous task of receiving the widows and listening to their stories. It was a strange feeling for the missionaries to rise in the morning with no mass to celebrate and no catechism to organize and teach. But when the events would all be over and the soldiers gone from Puma, Tony wondered if the missioners would become bored with so few challenges in life. He certainly looked forward to those days but couldn't allow himself to hope that they would come about very soon. 'When this is all over, I am going to take a rest,' he continued his fantasy......'I want to leave Burundi and get away from this dreadful experience and rethink my life. I can't imagine continuing my ministry in this country, to these scornful quacks!'

In mid-afternoon, Tony decided to go to Puma to see if anything new had developed. When he arrived, he went directly to Kizungu's house and this time, he thought it might be appropriate to mention the president and Bertuzzi when he would chat with the local administrative chief. Flaunting the president's name certainly couldn't hurt. And Bertuzzi would be seen as a friend of the Batutsi and a confrere of the missioners. But once again, they told him that the administrator was away on official business and the 'muganga' was in charge.

Tony walked up the side road about five hundred feet until he came to the house where Jacobo Karini lived. He called out 'hodi' and soon he saw the muganga come toward him from a back room. Tony enjoyed talking to Karani since the infirmarian always laughed heartily when he spoke. On the other hand, the priest never let down his defenses nor trusted anything Karani told him. Karani had been trained as a nurse in his native Rwanda and had come to Burundi some years earlier since the Bahutu were now in power in Rwanda and caused many Batutsi to flee as refugees. The Rwandan Batutsi were even more volatile, violent and vicious toward the Bahutu than were their counterparts from Burundi, since they had been so humiliated by the Bahutu in their native country. How amazing it would be when all the horrendous stories would be told after the May '72 reprisals and genocide. They would tally the number of vial attacks led by Rwandan Batutsi! Rather than settle in the north that was mostly Bahutu, Karani came to the south, the Bututsi, with his wife and small children to have a future for themselves similar to the status and power they once had in Rwanda. When Kizungu traveled, he often left Karani in charge and so many people joked about this position of 'non-power' he had.

Jacobo Karani greeted the priest and invited him into his living room. The room was to the left on entering the house. It was painted a light color of pink with a high baseboard of dark wood all around the four walls. There was a two inch boarder around the middle of each wall running parallel to the baseboard. The walls were dirty with the wear-and-tear of five small children visible all over them. There were pictures drawn and words misspelled all over the lower portions of each wall. The room was filled with four armchairs and a sofa that seemed dirty and well used. In the middle was a coffee table filled with a large knitting pouch and a sewing kit. This obviously was Mrs Karani's work station. As in most African homes, there were many pictures of family and friends but all hanging from the ceiling of each wall and only lowered about one foot from the ceiling itself. Tony often wondered why Africans hung their pictures so high. Maybe they never had enough wire or they didn't want anyone to recognize their family or friends? The Karani family had a picture of the Sacred Heart of Jesus with a rosary circumventing the outside frame of the picture. Beside it was a gory picture of Jesus, His blood-stained body hanging from the cross and His eyes looking out as he uttered the words: 'Follow Me'. Most of the photos had lost their brightness and sharpness over the years and had been bleached in time by light and sun. As Karani pointed to an armchair he welcomed Fr. Tony gesturing for him to sit down. The priest recognized a picture of President Sabimana on the opposite wall. He looked quite young as the photo had probably been taken when he had become president in 1966. Tony at once realized how the past six years had made the man age, even though he was now only in his early thirties.

Karani's children, three girls and two boys, were running back and forth coming into the front room and then running out again. The two youngest were a boy about ten-months-old, crawling everywhere, and a girl two years old who walked very well and talked gibberish. The three oldest children seemed to be amused playing with the two babies. Finally Karani told them to go outside and stay there and asked the eldest girl to bring him and his guest two bottles of beer and two glasses. Tony and Jacobo started with some polite small-talk. Finally Karani cleared his throat as if priming himself for something difficult to say:

"Mon Pere," he began, "it is not good for you to come here every day and ask us to release your catechist. He has done wrong and he will have to pay the price for being a traitor to our country," he spoke in patriotic overtones.

"Has he been tried already and found guilty?" Tony asked raising his voice so that Karani would notice that the priest considered the accusation both unjust and unproven.

But Karani gave a pattern response:

"We cannot tell you what we now know based on the proven evidence. It is confidential and private," he said with an attitude of superiority.

Tony started to get very agitated but he thought that for Petero's sake, he should try to be more relaxed and restrain himself from further implicating Tumba.

"I just wondered, M l'Administrateur," Tony toyed with him by rolling the title over on his lips, "if there would be any chance of seeing my catechist for only a few minutes?"

Karani responded directly and without hesitation, as if he had been awaiting the question:

"That is impossible!" Karani answered: "He is kept in solitary confinement day and night and is allowed no visitors. That, of course, includes you, his parish priest."

As they continued their discussion, there was a young man who came running into the house, telling the infirmarian that someone had been carried to the dispensary with serious burns all over his body. Karani, making the most of his professional image, excused himself and his wife, Maria, came in as Tony followed Jacobo towards the front door.

Maria invited the priest to return to his armchair, as he hadn't finished his beer for she had an important problem to discuss with him. She flattered Tony by saying how much she respected his judgment. Then she mentioned how the country was in such disorder and disarray. Moreover things were getting worse for now even the church, which meant so much to her, was closed. Tony quickly responded by informing her that the church was always unlocked in the daytime and everyone was invited to go and pray for their particular needs and those of the whole country. Only masses and all other liturgies had been stopped. He said further that he would be unwilling to celebrate the sacraments until true love and God's peace came back to the area.

Then Maria told him how nervous and anxious she had become over the past weeks since, as she put it, she was a 'Rwandakazi' (lady from Rwanda). Actually Tony realized what she was really saying. She was a Mututsi and now that her tribe had killed so many and her husband was considered one of the ringleaders, she feared for their lives and for all the members of their family if the Bahutu themselves tried reprisals. Tony shook his head silently. This was a scar that the Batutsi would have to carry with them for a long, long time, especially where they were not protected by the military: in Europe, Asia, North America and other African countries. But the pastor became very cunning now that Maria had shown her vulnerability:

"Maria," Tony began, "do you ever question the many evil acts that your husband has done? Is he not responsible for many tortures and killings? Do you think he has been kind to the Bahutu over the past month? By the way, do the people see you as true Rwandans?" Tony asked her, insinuating that those who had left Rwanda were now the most vicious Batutsi in Burundi.

Maria did not lift her head to face the priest, but kept her eyes lowered to the floor. She tapped her sandaled feet on the floor creating a continuous rhythm that seemed to echo loudly in the embarrassing silence between them. All she could manage to say was:

"It is unfortunate and very unsafe for our children. I wonder if someday, in the future, they will be harmed or even killed for the way their father has acted over the past weeks. Jacobo has been the administrator's assistant for a long time but lately many very bad situations have developed. I wish we were back in Rwanda where it used to be so peaceful," Maria said disclosing her many disjointed thoughts.

"It was very peaceful here as well, Madame l'Administrateur," Tony said unequivocally, letting her know that her husband's title was also hers and that she had much to be accountable for as well as Karani. Again Tony rose and walked to the door. He bid the lady adieu and she thanked him for his visit with polite kirundi mannerisms and shook his hand. They walked outside and she accompanied him in silence to his car. Tony got in and drove away. As he looked back in his rearview mirror, he saw the large tall woman walk back to her house, her head still bowed in shame. 'Those wretched Batutsi will pay for their crimes!' the pastor thought as he drove back to Butova.

When Tony arrived at the mission house, he told the others about his adventures. A common distaste for Karani and his wife was felt by Luigi and Luc and they told story after story about the vicious hatred that was in this man. Certainly the Bahutu were badly treated in the dispensary since he was the man-in-charge of all the medicines. Now they were also crudely treated by him as acting administrator. The Bahutu were not a vindictive people but somehow a price would one day be paid for the many lives that had been snubbed out by the brutal Batutsi leaders. The missionaries knew that even though they would never see equality between the tribes, there would come a day sometime, somewhere, when the Bahutu would overthrow this domination and, by murdering and killing, would revenge their fallen fathers, brothers and sons who had died at the hands of Batutsi guns in this month of May, 1972. As for Maria, the missionaries confirmed that she had reason to be sad. Maria, wife of Jacobo Karani, mourned her children already because someday they will fall as symbolic-revenge for the evils of their forefathers. The Batutsi will always be outnumbered by the Bahutu everywhere in Central Africa. Tony said he knew that the Bahutu were watching and calculating: "We don't get angry.....we get even!" he smirked, "now there is an axiom that might just describe the next two or three decades in Burundi."

The three confreres talked about Jose that evening at recreation in the common room after supper. They were still disappointed that he had left the previous Sunday without saying 'goodbye' to any of them.

Luigi talked about how Jose loved to laugh and that he had learned much about Africans and their culture from observing him. Yet Jose was never willing to explain anything to him. He would use creative expressions in Kirundi that he had learned from the people, but was unwilling to explain his knowledge to a neophyte learning the language such as Luigi.

And Tony reminisced about when he had been with Jose and Mathias: Jose would depend on Mathias to help him through his bouts of depression and discouragement. He mentioned that Jose had told him many times over the past month how much he longed to go to Europe and spend time with Mathias Becker in Germany. Tony had discouraged him from pestering Mathias who had a very demanding job in Germany and didn't have time to spend with Suarez following him around with his personal problems. Tony believed that if Jose left Burundi and his problems there, he soon would have as many problems elsewhere in Europe. To the pastor, Jose Suarez was a walking enigma and created discouragement and anxiety wherever he would be. Tony went on:

"It was comical when we were here, just the three of us. Mathias and I were so big and burly and then the people saw Jose beside us, very small in build, even skinny. He walked with his body curved to one side and thus the people nicknamed him 'rubavu' which means rib! Isn't that ingenious? The people saw us as two big shanks of beef and Jose, the little rib, between us. Or maybe the name came from people imagining how we ate a meal together. Mathias and I would get all the big chunks of meat so that all that was left for Jose was the rib!" Tony howled as he reminisced and the others laughed long and hard with him for they all knew that Jose had 'une bonne fourchette'.

At night prayer that evening they prayed for Jose wherever he would be, and found the means to thank God for what Jose had accomplished in Butova. But each in his own words and each in his own way added a silent prayer in his heart, a prayer of gratitude to God that Jose would never be with them again to cause havoc and pandemonium at the mission. They prayed for the situation all around them: that they remain sane and do not loose their faith in God. They prayed for both tribes: that conversion to the Spirit of God come soon and that they be able to see an end to all this inestimable butchery. Then finally they prayed for Bertuzzi: that he find realism and compassion in his life and that the power of the Spirit control his tongue.

22 Hundreds Shot Outside Puma Prison

Tony rose early on the morning of Thursday, May 25th. It was foggy outside as he went to the wash basin to ready himself for the day. Back in his room, he dressed quickly and went to the chapel for morning prayer. Luigi was already there and the two men shared the prayers of Lauds and Matins, and also spent some time in mental contemplation. It was good for them to support each other and they prayed for strength. Unknown to them, this day would be one of the most difficult they would ever have to face in Butova. By the end of the day over two hundred men would have been murdered at the local jail of Puma. As they asked for strength to get through this day, they did not realize what extraordinary grace they were seeking from God.

After prayer, Tony went to the church as there were three couples to marry. He had met them the preceding day and had asked them to come to church early. He would meet them at 7 o'clock and have them exchange marriage vows. Matrimony was the only sacrament that was now given at the Butova Mission. The fathers believed it would be wrong to refuse those who had already prepared their marriage day and had put aside a great deal of money for the reception afterwards. However they were firm about postponing baptisms. Individual confession could wait until a serious conversion experience was brought about through community reconciliation. Sunday and daily masses were discontinued until peace returned.

Tony hurried over to the church and met the couples as he unlocked the door. When we will get back into 'regular church', he thought, we will need to hire a sacristan as Bernardo Inzu certainly won't be back. He really missed this man who had served him well over the past two years.

One bride was late in arriving so he chatted quietly with the others until she came into the church leisurely. She was dressed in a beautiful yellow-colored *impuzu* and was carrying her walking shoes on her head. Most brides bought plastic sandals for their wedding ceremony but found them painful to walk in to reach the church. So they carried them and for Africans that meant balancing them on their heads. The bride stopped half-way up the aisle and put on her shoes. She limped the rest of the way, wiggling her feet into the small sandals, and came to where the priest and the other couples were gathered. The couples with their siblings and friends were the only ones who came to the central parish for a wedding. The other guests went directly to the couple's new home and when the marriage ceremony was over and the newlyweds had taken possession of their home, they all celebrated with great jubilation. Each bride normally carried an umbrella that often was a present from the groom. They would hide their faces behind the umbrella, if they wanted to smile or laugh, as it was seen as very disrespectful for a bride to rejoice on her wedding day. She was leaving her family and the home of her father and mother and she had to show the external signs of sadness, grief and melancholy.

When the three couples had departed for their homes and the wedding celebrations, Tony went back to the parish house and entered the dining room for his breakfast. Cypriano came quickly with the eggs and toast that he always prepared for *Pati Mukuru* after mass. As he put the plate before Tony, he told him that there was someone in front of the office who had to see him urgently. Tony ate his breakfast quickly and five minutes later he was in front of his office where a man awaited him.

As Tony approached the office door, the man came towards him with a sense of urgency: "I must see you immediately, *Pati*" he began. "There is something important I must tell you. Can I have a word with you in private?"

Tony unlocked his office door, entered and motioned to the man to sit in front of his desk. The pastor was upset that this man insisted on speaking to him first and had already announced his presence through the cook. There were many widows waiting for him to tell their story and receive some oil, flour and a one hundred franc Burundi note. Yet Tony sensed that this man was not being impolite but had something very important to tell him. On the other hand, there were times when Tony would get frustrated by the way the men considered themselves more important than the women and would automatically go in front of them in the queue. He saw this man as an intruder and hoped that he would be on his way as soon as possible and allow Tony to get down to business.

As the man began to speak, Tony wondered if he were a Muhutu or a Mututsi. Sometimes it was very difficult to distinguish and Tony had given up guessing. The visitor said his name was Karoli Kabura and he lived near Puma. He had quite a story to tell.

During the night, Kabura had heard many shots from Puma along with screaming and yelling. His whole family awoke and finally when the noise persisted, he decided to go to Puma and investigate what was happening. As he got closer, he heard more gun shots and on arrival at the *arrondissement*, saw that the problem was at the jail. Many other neighbors had also left their homes and gathered in front of the prison. Dawn was breaking and stories were spreading that there had been unrest and riots among the inmates during the night and the soldiers had to use their rifles. Kabura whispered: "Many prisoners have been killed!"

Thoughts of Petero Tumba, Alfredo, Luduvico and Osicari went through Fr. Tony's mind as he imagined them lying on the ground, their bodies riddled with soldiers' bullets. Then Karoli continued with something that surprised the priest and made him very angry:

"The acting administrator, Jacobo Karani, told me to come and tell you the news about the riot and asked if you would take me to the military camp in Vurura to let the commander know what has happened. He said that if you drive me there I can take care of the rest because I was once in the military and I know the governor at Vurura very well. He is a personal friend. Did you know that he hails from Butova?" Kabura asked with a slight bit of pride in his voice. No doubt. Kabura was a Mututsi! Tony was very distracted and merely grunted that he had heard Kabura about the commander's background. His mind wandered from one thought to another trying to find some ounce of saneness in this slaughter. Once again he was being conned into driving. This time he would have to go for two hours so that the soldiers might get reinforcements. But then he reasoned: 'the soldiers do not need other soldiers. With their guns, the ten of them at Puma could easily handle two hundred unarmed Bahutu in jail.' Then he thought further: they had probably been drinking during the night and decided to go into the jail and amuse themselves by abusing the captives. Maybe they even let the Bahutu try to escape and then they had their excuse to shoot them in the back. But then Tony started to reason differently: if we make these killings known to the military governor, an official report will have to be filed and this will record their misdeeds. But I must make sure that everything is reported and recorded. Since Tony had now taken the habit of making a mental note of what was happening and writing it in a diary every day, he would have the exact sequence of happenings and be able to bring witness against many of the officials, soldiers and police when this nightmare would be over.

Tony did not like to be away from his office for any length of time. Furthermore dealing with the widows whose numbers were growing in leaps and bounds every day took up most of his time. He asked Kabura to step outside for a few moments and went to find his two companions. They were together in the dining room having coffee. There was so little for them to do now that all operations, except helping the widows, had been put on hold. So they had lots of time for morning cups of coffee! Tony sat for a moment and told them about what had happened at the jail. Luc was surprised that no one else had come to tell the fathers. He said it was unlike the Bahutu and recalled how they had come in large numbers when the first killings at Ruhaha had begun three weeks earlier. Luigi added: "The Bahutu are afraid of everything at this moment of time. They are not going to risk being seen telling us about what has happened. I don't know this Kabura but I presume he is a Mututsi and I wonder if he isn't barefaced lying so that you can drive him to Vurura. Nothing like having the parish priest as you own personal chauffeur!" he said with a light smile on his lips.

Tony could feel anger going to his face and blushed all over: "I will scream if they lie and trick me one more time. I am so upset at the way they have used me and our vehicles over the past weeks. The *muganga* will not even listen to me about seeing Petero and yet he dares to ask me for this… favor? Poor Petero, I should never have handed him over to them. He is probably dead now, " he expressed filled with guilt. Then he went on, "and Alfredo, and Osicari, and Luduvico and so many others. The list is endless, Bahutu killed by Batutsi! Murundi killed by Murundi, brother killed by brother! Innocence killed by vengeance!"

"But I think it is important that you get involved." Luigi said. "If you can save a few lives in any way whatsoever or at least discover more of their hidden agenda for your diary, it will be helpful."

"I'm going to go to Puma and see what happened and then I can talk to Karani and see what he wants and make a decision there. Do you both trust me with the decision?"

Luigi and Luc both agreed that this would be the best solution. They encouraged him to go to Puma and decide according to the way the spirit lead him. "I thank you for your input and I think I can make the right decision based on all that we have just shared. Thank you, brothers." Tony concluded.

He got up and left the two others at table. Luigi said that he would look after all the people that were coming with *majambo* (words i.e problems, personal stories, guidance, concerns, confession etc.) Tony was pleased since this was the first time Luigi ever offered to take over the office and be alone with the people. It would be a good lesson for him and his knowledge of Kirundi would grow in leaps and bounds.

Tony went right to his office and told the widows that Pati Luigi would serve them and listen to their needs and problems. He then called Kabura aside and invited him to come along to the backyard and get into the car with him. In a few seconds they were on their way to Puma. As they arrived, Tony heard gunshots coming from the area beyond the mud hut that had become a preparation station for the soldiers to manhandle the condemned and beat them before loading them into the trucks that took them to their graves on the road to Vurura. He could see many people beyond the hut looking into the horizon and he realized that this was the place where the soldiers were still shooting the prisoners. The people all around him who were looking on were speechless as he turned to look at those who were closest to him. It was one of those moments that transcends words. Their eyes would meet his and there was a communion of spirits as everyone seemed to be mesmerized that, one after another, as the bullets rang out, men, their friends and neighbors, their fathers, husbands, brothers and sons, were falling to the ground, never to walk the everlasting hills of their *Burundi Bwacu* again. Tony thought of Petero, Osicari, Luduvico and Alfredo and knew he would never see them alive again and his rage was bubbling up in his stomach, passing into his chest and moving up to his head, his face, his temples. Fury was in his eyes and yet there was nothing he could do about it. Fr. Tony tried to stay calm.

Finally he bowed his head and started to pray out loud.

"Lord, forgive those who are killing the innocent. And Father in heaven, come and console those who are dying right now and all who have died in prison this night. Be support and strength for their families, their wives and children and their dear mothers. And, Jesus, God of Peace, bring your grace to this area of Puma and Butova that hatred and abhorrence and rage might vanish and that your peace might come to dwell in all of us again. O, Christ, Jesus, you died that we might live. Help these men who, like you, are dying to someday live with you in eternal bliss."

Finally he lifted his head and saw Karani walking towards him. The *muganga* approached the priest slowly and put out his hand to greet him. Tony could not do the same. He left Karani with his arm outstretched, hand dangling and asked him what had happened. Karani said that they needed further protection because the soldiers had put down an uprising and had to shoot all those who were in jail trying to escape.. They now were running out of ammunition.

"They are all dead," Karani said, "but we still need more military from Vurura to protect our area."

Tony was beginning to understand kitutsi logic. They had arrested every Muhutu they suspected and then killed as many as possible in prison. Now they were starting to feel nervous and wanted further protection. This was exactly what Karani's wife, Maria, had said to Tony the previous afternoon. After the way the Batutsi had annihilated so many Bahutu, it would be the most natural thing in the world for them to seek revenge. If there were an increase in the numbers of military, that might usurp any thought of retribution by the Bahutu. They had gone to their deaths as "a sheep goes to the slaughter house." What a race of wimps! They allowed the Batutsi to arrest them, even in large numbers, but they never tried to escape or run away or attack all together like a pride of lions. Maybe one or other would have been killed. But the majority would have escaped. Tony yearned for them to make a statement that they were not fatalists waiting for some mysterious power, *Imana,* to come and snatch them away from this obvious peril, this dreadful massacre.

So now everything would change? Tony wondered. "Never! Never! Never!" he heard himself sputter to his inner thoughts. If it will take many generations, the Bahutu and the sons of the Bahutu and their sons will never even the score.

His thoughts were now racing faster than his mind could control them. "These Bahutu will never fight back, at least this generation has been so annihilated. They will never be capable of doing it. Only the *masakini* (disabled) are left. And the church has also contributed to making them into fatalists. 'Accept Batutsi suppression, like a devoted Christian.' 'Let the Batutsi soldiers hit you on one cheek and present the other to them.' 'If a Mututsi wants your coat, give him your shirt as well.' The gospel preached fatalism, to the detriment of justice, and thus genocide had taken over Burundi. 'Love your enemy. Pray for those who hate you. If your adversary asks you to go a mile with him, do more, go two miles.' Beautiful poetic words but very dangerous for the poor Bahutu. They had lived the gospel to the fullest and now they are dying for God's Word.

Tony thought of all the christian gospel clichés that he himself had used so often in sermons and teachings and he now realized that the beautiful message that he had given had been lived out by the Bahutu. The christian gospel can lead people to become fatalists, accepting their state even when they are being used, beaten, falsely accused and even murdered. They were being massacred and like the quote he remembered from the prophet Isaiah: "Like lambs led to the slaughter or sheep before the sheerer, they were silent and opened not their mouths." True spirituality but bad logic! The pastor came to an astonishing realization. They were like Jesus on the royal road of the cross. They, like the Master before them, allowed themselves to be destroyed so that the love for others might shine through their gestures. Then he weighed all his ideas and thoughts. It was either one or the other. They were utterly cowards and allowed themselves to be annihilated. Or they were the most characteristic of the signs of Jesus

Christ Who allowed Himself to be convicted and beaten, and mocked and slain so that defeat might engulf victory, so that innocence might overcome pride, so that frailty might conquer strength, so that pleading hands might defeat guns, so that silence might overwhelm anger. He decided to hope in the latter and saw the slain Bahutu as the reincarnation of Jesus-Christ Crucified.

The Batutsi would never believe that the Bahutu would revolt. The Bahutu leaders and organizers were now dead or had fled the country to Tanzania and the Congo. The Bahutu cause was a lost one since over the past three weeks over 150,000 men and boys had been assassinated. They were now doomed and totally defeated having lost most of their *intelligentsia* during the genocide.

Karani wanted more soldiers to protect himself and his family for he realized what he had done was grossly evil. But he knew in his mind that the Bahutu were totally defenseless. It was only his guilt that caused him anxiety. Finally Fr. Tony decided to go along with what the acting administrator was asking him, as this would give his diary more volume and he would see close at hand what sparked the Batutsi to do so much evil. He looked at Karani and asked him:

"Have your soldiers killed Petero Tumba, Alfredo, Luduvico and Osicari, M. Karani?"

"*Mon Pere,* I do not know everyone by name. However the prisoners had a revolt last night and the soldiers had to defend themselves. Many, I am sad to say, have perished."

"Are you talking about prisoners or soldiers when you say 'many' have perished?" Tony asked ironically.

"The military are all safe," was Karani's direct reply.

Tony questioned the acting leader looking him straight in the eye:

"Explain to me how the revolt started that I can believe that there was an uprising. However I feel compelled to believe that it was the soldiers themselves who started to revolt, if there ever was an insurrection. They probably went into the jail and upset the prisoners. Those men knew that they could not defend themselves and depended on their guards for everything. They would never have tried to revolt. Actually it is not *kihutu* (the way of the Bahutu) to rise up in revolt. If they had wanted to revolt, they would have done so before being put into prison." Tony replied looking at the *muganga* who stared abstractly into space not daring to make eye contact with the *mukuru.* Tony was reminded of the words Bishop Moulin had spoken two weeks earlier: "Our role as missionaries is to let them see us seeing them in the evil they are doing." There was no reply from Karani.

Tony said: "*M. L'Administrateur,* I have decided to go to the military camp of Vurura and tell those in responsibility what has happened here in Puma. Maybe they will be understanding and send soldiers to correct the fatal errors that have been committed. If not, I will have accumulated much positive information for my accusations after order will have been restored in your *Burundi Bwacu*". He said the final two words mocking the false loyalty that so many Barundi had toward their own country. Tony, himself, could only feel disdain for the Batutsi who were so cunning and immoral and the Bahutu who were so stupid and fatalistic. He called out to Karoli Kabura to get into his VW and the two men drove away from Puma in silence.

Tony thought of stopping at the mission but decided to go straight to Vurura for the two others would know that he was on his way. He felt sick to his stomach, slowly realizing that his best catechist, Tumba, was now probably dead along with the three young houseboys who had shown so much promise of succeeding with their lives. His melancholy showed in the way that he responded to Kabura's comments with one or two word grunts. He was a defeated man. He became very reflective and his thoughts kept him in his own little world. Fr. Tony was starting to hate every Mututsi that he had ever known. But his conscience pecked away at him as he realized that his hating the murderers did not help the situation at all. However he knew that he would never be able to care about a Mututsi ever again.

They made good time traveling along the road leading to Vurura in less than an hour. As they climbed the hill above the city, they saw the military camp below to the right and the town and mission to the left. Tony drove right to the camp and was stopped by the armed guards at the main gate. Kabura took the initiative to announce why they had come and they were waved through the three checkpoints and came to a parking area in front of the offices. Tony stayed in the car and Kabura got out and went into the office. He heard loud and joyous greetings being exchanged inside and then a few minutes later, Kabura came out and beckoned Tony to enter the office with him. He got out of the car slowly and Kabura held the entrance open as he invited the priest to enter. There were many men in military uniforms walking back and forth in the large unfurnished room. Tony felt such a disdain for the military uniforms and held back spitting on them. The military governor, a large stout man with a high forehead and long nose came over to him and greeted him. He introduced himself not by name, but by rank. There was no doubt about it. He was the man-in-charge, the military governor, *le chef clairvoyant*. After some unimportant small talk he asked Tony a fatal question: "How are things going in Butova?" he inquired. Tony was pleased he had the opportunity to respond. He realized that he was again fighting a lost cause, but at least he would speak openly and strongly and, who knows, maybe some lives would be spared over the following days.

"Your soldiers at Butova, actually as you know they are staying at Puma beyond Butova, are doing all they can to kill as many Bahutu as possible in our area." There was a stillness in the room as all ears turned to hear what the pastor was saying. "I want to protest with as much vehemence as possible because they have been permitted to come to our area and overwhelm the population with their quick trials, their nightly tortures and their many killings of innocent citizens. *M. le Gouverneur*, is it a crime, punishable by death, that people are of the kihutu race?" Tony went on with irony, "The Bahutu are a people who are simple and uneducated. They, who are being killed these past weeks, have never done anything to betray their country. But your soldiers are now afraid that there will be reprisals since so many innocent people have been liquidated. Their goal is to eliminate as much of the Bahutu population as possible. Last night was the ultimate in murder. The jail houses forty men comfortably. They had two hundred in jail and then during the night they said there was an insurrection. So the soldiers went into jail and killed most of them. We will never know how many. And then this morning, in front of all the citizens in the area, they killed those who remained. Many of them were my friends, a catechist and workers in our mission. We have spent tens of thousands of francs to educate and train them and now all that treasure both in money, knowledge and faith has been wasted. The *Muganga* Karani has asked me to bring Kabura to obtain more soldiers. Because Karani has been a villainous leader, he now fears what the Bahutu will do to him and his family when this is all over. But how can the Bahutu start a counter attack when all their strong men have been annihilated? Congratulations, *M. le Gouverneur*, your soldiers have set Burundi back eighty years and you will all pay the price over the years to come. You in the military, are all savages. There is no unity in the country. There will never be any progress. Peace is absurd." Fr. Tony concluded by disemboweling the three-fold motto of the *l'UPRONA* Party: Unity, Peace and Progress. The Batutsi had not only killed 150,000 males! They had succeeded in defeating the Bahutu's future and so many people who would never contribute to building this poor country. Tony was learning the underlining principle of any war: There are never any winners! Both sides loose!

The governor invited Tony and Kabura into his inner office which was large, with white walls and a green painted door and window frames. Three soldiers accompanied them, one entering the office and leaving two others standing at the door. Tony presumed they stayed outside to the left and right of the entrance. The governor's wooden desk was laden with piles of paper but all was neatly stacked to the front of the desk. The priest was surprised that the military leader had such a private area. He felt somewhat ashamed that he had been given to such an outburst outside when all he wanted to say could have been said in private to the governor alone. But he had been asked a question in public and chose to answer publicly. He did not regret the words he had spoken though since he had such an audience of *basoldat*.. At least all had heard with their own ears what he truly thought. He was glad to be able to wear both his heart and his tongue on his sleeve. So he decided to refuse the invitation by the governor to speak longer. To not drag everything painfully on might be an advantage to the kihutu cause, since the military governor had the power of life and death in the area. Tony knew that this top military soldier was not going to share any of his plans or strategy with him. So he concluded:

"*M. le Gouveneur*, time is running out on the situation in Butova. I was asked to make you aware of the situation and that, I have done. It is time for us to be on our way. I have many bodies to bury and widows and orphans to console. I do hope that peace will be restored to our area without the need of further military personnel." Tony concluded hoping the governor would heed his suggestion and not send more killers to Puma. The priest walked to the door and the governor accompanied him. They strolled to the car with Kabura. Karoli took the governor aside and they talked for some minutes before they both came back to find Tony in the car. Without another word, the two BanyaButova drove way. As they climbed the hill from the military camp back to the main road, Karoli asked Fr. Tony if he thought they would be sending further forces. Tony responded in the negative and again mentioned that the Bahutu were so fatalistic in accepting their doom that they would never cause any problems.

"Besides," he added, "you, Batutsi, have killed every educated and able-bodied *mugabo* (male) Muhutu. What is there to fear? An insurrection led by the *bagore* (women) in the *mihana*? (homes built around banana trees)" he asked sarcastically.

They continued the drive in silence and when they arrived in Butova, Tony drove past the church and the mission and moved on to Puma. As he arrived, he saw more people than usual in the square and then he heard shots ringing out from behind the hut. He found it shocking that while he had left three hours previously, there were still shots killing these so-called "revolting prisoners". All those jailed had certainly died long ago. It must be others that they have accused of being helpful to the insurrection that they have captured and are now murdering. He wondered how many men had been killed and if he or anyone else would ever know. With every gun shot, Tony felt a sharp pain go through his heart. He could not stomach the scene any longer and turned to get back into his VW. For Fr. Tony this adventure on this afternoon allowed him to feel the pain the disciples of Christ must have felt when they turned and walked away from the cross of Calvary. As he walked on, a policeman, whom he had known as Martino Kupiga, came running up to him and called out:

"Pati, Pati," Tony turned around and the policeman came closer and asked to speak to him privately. He began by telling him that there were great problems in the jail the previous night and asked him if he would go to Vurura and solicit the military governor for more troops to protect the area. Tony looked straight at him, eyeball to eyeball: "Why are you asking me to do this, Kupiga?" Tony went on, "there is no problem here. Your Batutsi soldiers have killed all the prisoners and there is no one left to disturb the peace. You have totally annihilated and utterly destroyed the Bahutu !"

"We have only murdered two hundred, all the men who were in prison, and some others who were helping them" he responded "there are lots of others who might disturb the order here," was the policeman's fearful reply.

"You have murdered over two hundred men and you are worried that others might rise up in insurrection?" Fr. Tony asked. "You have exterminated all your problems. I hope you are happy. I have just come from the military camp and have spoken with the governor. I hope he will keep his promise to me not to send any more assassins." Kupiga finally backed off and walked away without saying anything further to Tony. He realized how irritated the priest was and thought how wrong their decision had been to plan a false riot and thus be able to annihilate all the prisoners. But he justified the killings since many of the prisoners had not eaten for several days and were slowly dying of starvation. They didn't have the energy to stand up and walk. Yet they mounted a revolt!

Later that evening, Tony shared the news of his day with Luigi and Luc. Then they shared the happenings while he was away. Luigi mentioning that he had sat in Tony's office for three hours in the morning and four in the afternoon and had heard all kinds of stories about how the Bahutu men had been killed. He had hardly been able to eat since that day two weeks ago when he came upon the soldier in the hospital bayoneting a poor injured man to death. The disgust and disdain he again had in his heart after having heard seven hours of story-telling, detailing the most atrocious of murders, had caused him to totally lose his appetite. Luigi had a very small build and did not have too much weight to lose. Yet he had come to table most of the past month and would only sit and play with some food on his plate and drink a bit of water or coffee. Tony listened to his colleague and responded by encouraging him. He certainly did not want to have to deal with a deeply depressed priest on his hands besides trying to handle all the traumas outside.

"Luigi," Tony began, "is there some special food that you would like? We can have Cypriano prepare something that you might fancy. You must try to eat something or you will certainly fall ill and then we all will be in over our heads. I know you are very upset but please try to put your own needs above the drama outside. What about spaghetti or another Italian dish?"

"The way Cypriano cooks spaghetti, I would really get sick twice as much as I am now." he replied as both Luc and Tony chuckled.

"No, I will be all right and I will try to eat some soft desserts, some pudding or custard that Cypriano makes very well. But I just can't eat anything solid like bread, potatoes, or meat, ugh!.... just to think about it makes me sick to my stomach!" as he tapped his fork over and over again on the table.

The three missionaries crossed over to the sitting room for coffee and an evening of quiet relaxation. Tony lit his pipe and sat back wondering what was left for them to do. They had tried to witness to the gospel message of Jesus Christ but the tragedy continued to explode like a volcano. So many of their friends and companions of the church had been killed. Tony noted that every day he went to the office and took out so many cards of the status animorum (Latin: the state of souls). There he would write in large red print besides the name of one of the men who had died in the parish: evenements '72 (events of '72) and he made a huge cross and inscribed R.I.P. There were hundreds and hundreds of entries all with the same lettering. Then he would give a detail or two about the death, for example, the date and place of the man's arrest, the accusation, and the final place where he was last seen or was said to have been buried. The status animorum looked like a checkered cloth that many women wore as their impuzu. Since he did this with a red marker, the status animorum looked as if they had blood poured all over them. It was the blood of people who had been massacred and murdered and mistreated and hated until they had every drop of blood beaten out of their mortal bodies. Tony believed that the color of blood was very appropriate.

"What do you think is the estimated number of men that had died in our area?" Luc asked. "Your guess is as good as mine," Tony went on, "but there are between sixty and seventy-five people, dead or dying who have been driven to the common graves near Vurura every day for the past three weeks. That roughly is between 1300 and 1500 people. And then there have been exceptional days like today when over two hundred were massacred. There are 87 arrondisement in the country with an administrator in each. If they have had as many killings as we have had, that would be over 130,000. Then don't forget that most areas have more Bahutu than we have so I would add on another 20,000 and say that the total now would be around 150,000 minimum healthy Bahutu murdered in this horrible genocide. May their slaughterers someday be judged by Almighty God! Isn't that unbelievable? And this country is majority Roman Catholic. What went wrong when the missioners were so zealous? Maybe they forgot to preach and explain the fifth commandment? : 'THOU SHALT NOT KILL. These Batutsi have destroyed all the good that christianity and catholicism has brought to them. So many of them can't seem to understand the significance of our not celebrating mass last Sunday. For them God is part of their pagan culture and mentality and they don't realize how they have destroyed the hard work of missionaries, as well as the church's spiritual foundation and finances over the past eighty years. I'm relieved that those of us who are young can pack up and leave the tragedy behind." Tony said with disgust rolling off his lips. Then he continued: "When the killings finally stop and the country becomes civil again, those of us who are young and free, will leave everything as we found it and be off to another mission in another part of the world. Burundi will be part of our hideous past and we will bury feelings of fury and deception, interring them with all the cadavers that have been buried innocently over the past weeks."

After they prayed together, Luc went out to shut off the motor and Tony stood outside looking up into the dark sky. He could see clouds floating by and they brightened up the ugly darkness that seemed to dominate the whole skies. The pastor thought of his young friend Petero and wondered where his body might be. He imagined him lying in his own blood with no one willing to wash his broken body and bury it. He was considered a traitor and didn't deserve such courtesy and respect! He tried to open his heart to God yet still wondered if there really was a God who hovered over all this tragedy and Who could bring calm and peace into the catastrophe that Burundi had become. He asked God for a sign, something tangible, whereby he could believe in the Creator and the grandeur of His masterful Hand. Somehow, deep within himself his faith and hope had totally vanished. He would be loyal to the promise he made a few weeks previously when he had been installed as pastor but only until a replacement was appointed. He would leave this country and never look back on the years he had spent trying to help a people whose only passion was to destroy the other tribe. "Tribalry," he heard himself say to Luc who passed by going to his room, "shows us the most villainous side of a nation." Tony walked back to his room, turned the key in his door and entered with his flashlight shining brightly. He soon found his lamp and reached for the lighter in his pocket and soon the whole room was bright and he could see the outline of all his earthly possessions, circumventing the one area where he could be completely free and totally at ease. He sat on his bed and tried to pray to God for his friends that had died that day. Tony felt emotionally connected to all of them but in a special way to Petero Tumba. He recalled Petero handing him the 500 francs (equilivent of $5.00 USD) for his mother and decided that he would speak to the colleagues of Muka and arrange to have a house built for this woman who had given such a wonderful son to the world. Tony threw his hands up in the air and as he tried to persuade himself to pray, realized his efforts were useless. As he believed that he never again would want to work in Burundi, neither would he ever want to pray again. If there really was a God, then why did He not intervene. How could a God of justice and love stand by and allow all these good people to be massacred? He got up and undressed for bed. He got between the sheets, feeling the loneliness of celibacy. He needed a wife to hold him, to wipe away his tears and to whisper in his ear that all would be alright. He thought of how much he, at twenty-eight years of age had given up: a wife, a family, the joy of children's voices, the fulfillment of a meaningful job, a nice home, a car and on and on and on. His only consolation was that he still was only twenty-eight and the best was yet to come. During the night, Tony tossed and turned from side to side. Nothing would allow him to sleep soundly. It was a moonless, dark, dreary night with low clouds close to the ground and his body longed for morning when he would arise and with every tick of the clock be closer to his new life thousands of miles from this hell.

23 May 26,1972: Murders End, Genocide Continues

After breakfast, Tony went out to the front of the mission and to his surprise a truck, a Peugeot 504, was driving into the yard. Tomasi Muhwa, the organizer of the killings in the area, was at the wheel. Tony had developed a disdain for this man as he realized that he was the overseer, organizer and self-appointed *mukuru* behind all the nasty work carried out by the soldiers. Muhwa stopped his truck and got out, coming to greet Tony. As he walked up the steps to the mission offices and stretched out his hand, Tony stopped and stared right at him but did not extend his right arm. There were many women in front of his office door and Tony took advantage of the occasion whereby he could show all these Bahutukazi what he thought of the coordinator of all the crimes that had claimed their husbands, fathers and sons.

"I would like a word with you, *mon Pere*," Muhwa began. "I have heard that you refused to do the mass for the people here on Sunday. I consider this a judgment on the political situation of this area and I protest your action with much vehemence."

"M. Muhwa," Tony stared at him, "I really don't give a sweet damn what you think of my actions. I want you to know that your visit to this mission is most unwelcomed and I ask you to leave our presence as soon as possible."

Muhwa, aghast, took a step back and then turning again to Tony, shouted back over his shoulder at the priest:

"Go tell your lies elsewhere. You, at the mission, are not collaborating with the wishes of the government. You will pay dearly for this!"

"Muhwa," Tony was now screaming at the tall man in front of him on the verandah, "If I were you, I would not want word to get out that you have been the instigator of all these killings here in Butova. When the day of your judgment comes before God, I pray to have a seat in the front row. I will hold back nothing. I will be an eyewitness to all the evil you have done and all the lives that have vanished because of you. Be assured, Muhwa, that on the day of reckoning, with so many of us to witness against you, you will be judged very severely by the God of Justice. Tomasi, I call you by your christian name, if I were in your shoes, I would fear standing in front of Almighty God. You will be a most miserable and petrified person. And maybe, dear friend, your judgment will come soon. It will be at your moment of death, and after all the evil you have done, someone soon will blow your brains out. Watch out and keep out of the way of the Bahutu for they are claiming you as their very own prize." Tony turned his back and walked away. Muhwa had no other choice but to go back, get into his vehicle, backup and drive through the gate. He finally turned and sped back to the main road.

At one o'clock, as they were sitting down to their meal, a VW drove into the mission. It was Walter De Winter. He was always a welcomed guest at Butova since he had spent many years there and knew most of the families in the parish. He admired the BanyaButova and laughed as he often told stories about the years he spent in this mission. But he entered the back courtyard looking very serene and had an air of seriousness all over his face. He looked at Tony who had come out of the dining room to greet him and recognized Luigi and Luc with a handshake. They all thought he looked so bad because of his illness.

But his fatigued- figure was not due to his personal health problems but rather because of the news he was bringing from the bishop's house: "I have just come from Vurura," Walter began, "and all hell has broken out there. A Mututsi guard, I guess he was a policeman, has killed seven single female teachers who lived together beside the school. He went to their residence this morning and lined them up at gunpoint and took them outside the village and stood each up in front of a large tree and shot each young lady." Ruyaga asked me to stop and tell you because one teacher, whom he knew you considered a close friend, has been killed. Her name is Mariana. The older man saw Tony's face grimace and his chin drop almost to the ground. His knees started to crumble and he immediately felt faint. They all stepped up their pace and walked back to the dining room away from the mid-day sun.

"There is something dreadfully wrong. It is totally distorted, this story, Walter. Mariana was a Mututsikazi. I know for a fact that she was engaged to marry a soldier this summer. Any soldier has to be a Mututsi for they have killed all the Bahutu three weeks ago. A Mututsi soldier could not marry a Muhutukazi so Mariana has to be a Mututsikazi!"

"I know," Walter went on, "Ruyaga told me that as well. She was living with the six other teachers who were all Bahutukazi. When the soldier told them to go out with him, he told her to run away. She said she could not and made the decision that if her fellow teachers were going to be killed, she would die with them as well. What a martyr for the cause of the Lord Jesus Christ and His Kingdom here on earth."

Fr. Anthony Joseph became very silent. He could not utter a word. Luigi invited De Winter to the table and Tony turned and went into the chapel. He sat in the presence of the Lord, in the same area where he had given the eucharistic bread to Petero five days earlier, in the same area where he had forgiven his sins. He could not pray. God was no where to be found in Burundi. It was quiet in the chapel, but it would be a waste of time to mouth prayers to a God who could not, or what was even more laughable, would not, intervene. And in the quiet of the chapel he imagined Mariana, her body riddled with bullets, going up to heaven and entering into a place of peace, tranquility and refreshment. Yet he could not visualize God in the same image as Mariana. He smiled as he imagined the scene of this beautiful young saint rejoicing in her new life in heaven, surrounded by tens of thousands of other Barundi martyrs. Tony recalled talking to her so often during the weekend-retreats he gave to teachers. She always had her hair lifted up with a cloth binding it together and holding it high. Her eyes were so beautiful and her voice so cheerful and bright. The world would be all the less for having lost such a superb person. After twenty minutes in the chapel, Tony went back to the dining room and the men were having coffee and sweets and talking about other things seemingly so trite to Tony after the personal struggle he was experiencing. De Winter went on with his story in much more colorful detail than when he had merely given them the facts outside.

"When I arrived at the mission of Vurura, there were so many people hovering about. I got out of my car and started to talk to them. They told me that President Sabimana was coming to the mission to greet the bishop and they were waiting for him at any moment. Suddenly we all heard the sound of a helicopter and looked up to see it land. The president himself was flying the plane," De Winter paused to take a warm drink of Cypriano's coffee. President Sabimana had two French helicopter operators who had been lent to Burundi with the helicopter and one of them was always on board although the president often flew and considered himself to be an excellent pilot. He was the only person in the country, beside the two Frenchmen, who had learned to fly although there still were no particular licenses for flying in Burundi. De Winter went on telling the story with hubbub in his voice:

"What followed was something I never thought I would experience in Burundi. I have been here for 24years and never heard anything like this. The president got out of the 'copter and the bishop was standing on the verandah looking out at the plane. President Sabimana went over and extended his hand to Bishop Moulin, asking him how he was. All of us were astonished when the bishop would not extend his hand in greeting. He threw his head back, arms folded across his pectoral cross over his chest, and responded to Sabimana's gesture by shouting:

"M. le President, I am in mourning! I am in mourning!" and Moulin continued to repeat the expression over and over again until monotony proved he had made his point. It was embarrassing for me as a member of the clergy but I guess the bishop did what he thought was necessary. He meant probably that he was mourning for the seven teachers but also for the tens of thousands of catholics that have disappeared over the past weeks. I'm glad he said it for all of us. I hope the president won't take revenge out on us. It is his country and he can expel us for any reason. Maybe the bishop should have chosen his words more carefully or appeared less arrogant in expressing himself!"

Tony added a few thoughts of his own: "I am very happy that the bishop is finally speaking out. He must make himself the official spokesman for the church and not merely criticize in private. All the Barundi Catholic Bishops should issue a statement and denounce the violence and injustices."

"Most of the bishops and the Archbishop of Gisumu are Batutsi. Do you think that they will take a stand that is against their government?" De Winter asked. "Well, then, Bishop Moulin must speak out all the more since he is the only European bishop and sees all this in a very different light from the others." The men continued to discuss what should be done to give a christian perspective to all the events that had happened. Tony mentioned that if one parish stops celebrating mass and the sacraments but the others don't, it will be a fruitless gesture and a counter-witness since all the people will believe it is the local priests that are judging them and not the official position of the whole church.

Fr. Tony continued: "If Bishop Moulin believes that our canceling the sacraments was the correct gesture then he should get the message out to all the other dioceses and they in turn to their parishes to do the same thing. Moulin is our bishop and we have our priesthood through him. What strategy and witnessing that is taking place in one parish should be repeated throughout the whole diocese and thus the whole country." They all agreed with him but De Winter added that he would not do anything until a clear position was taken by the bishop and communicated throughout the diocese.

Walter stood up and said he had to be on his way. He still had to drive close to an hour to get back home to Lutana and he had a lot of things to share with his colleagues there. He drove off into the horizon and the confreres went into their rooms for a short siesta that would help digest lunch. Tony was back in the office within twenty minutes and groups of widows passed before him throughout the whole afternoon. He tired of hearing similar stories over and over again but was never bored. He would never have imagined the Batutsi soldiers and police to be such malicious villains. But he had to believe what the women were telling him as they shared in his office in groups of three or four. That certified the authenticity of each person and held each accountable for the story of her husband's death that she was sharing with the pastor.

Midway through the afternoon, Fr. Tony received a letter from Administrator Kizungu. He opened the note with some trepidation, wondering what could possibly be in the letter as Kizungu only wrote when he had a petition or request. Tony froze as he wondered how he would respond if, once again, Kizungu wanted to borrow a car or truck from the mission and, of course, a driver to go along with the vehicle.

The administrator began by saying that this was an official letter that he had written since he had just returned from a governmental meeting in Gisumu. Tony found it strange that he would go to Gisumu to a meeting since the provincial headquarters were at Vurura. Furthermore, the president was in Vurura.

In the missive, Kizungu related that the government had now passed a ruling that since all these widows and children were products of traitors of the government, they were traitors themselves, Subsequently, it would be a federal crime to help them in any way. If they were caught on the roads with food or blankets that they had received in charity, they would be taken into the woods and killed immediately. If foreign charitable organizations were found helping the widows and orphans, they were to be expelled from the country immediately. The letter concluded mentioning that he knew that Fr. Tony had been helping such traitors and said that this practice must stop as soon as possible or he would be reported, the soldiers would arrest him and he would be expelled.

Now in the depths of depression, Tony thought how nice it would be for him to be sitting in an airplane, headed anywhere in the world beyond Burundi. Then he came back to reality. What would he do with all the money he had been given by the American Embassy? What would he do with the food, the oil, the flour, the clothing? Certainly it would not be given to any Mututsi! They had won the war! Then Tony rationalized the situation: 'If I cannot give the widows anything personally, then, at least, I can see them and hear their stories. I can make a note of what they need and send a list along to the 'Meeting for the Poor' that Jose organized every month to help those in need. Then I'll give all the supplies to the Meeting and they will dole it out to the needy on the list. They are all poor and thus taking action this way can be justified,' Tony thought to himself.

Tony believed there was a solution for every problem and although the government made the laws, there was always a way to get around them in the spirit of christianity guided by the Holy Spirit. Immediately, he went out to the verandah and spoke to all the women. He explained the new ruling and that he couldn't give them anything directly but would have them taken care of in another manner. He did not want to make public that he would help each of them when the monthly distribution would take place in their local area at the 'Meeting for the Poor'. All he needed was their names and areas where they lived and the rest would be left to his good organizing skills. The remainder of the afternoon was spent in listening to the widows and making notes on their names and hillside and assuring them that they would not be forgotten. He made it very clear that he was helping them because they were widows and not because they were Bahutukazi. They all seemed to understand the new policy so all that remained was for them to trust.

Late in the afternoon, around 5 o'clock, Tony heard a noise and immediately realized that it was the helicopter and thus President Sabimana was about to visit them. The helicopter was used for one purpose only: to transport the president throughout the republic. As the radio station called him: President Etienne Sabimana, *Chef Clairvoyant et Liberateur du Peuple Barundi* (Clairvoyant Chief and Liberator of the Barundi People). The pastor's heart skipped a beat as he wondered why the president was coming to see them and hoped that it would not be a further difficulty. He left his office, went down the steps from the verandah and out to the large dirt area in front of the church where the helicopter normally landed. People were running from all directions congregating on the 'launching pad' that was used to land the helicopter. Enthusasm and excitement was the order of the day. It was always a beautiful sight to see all the Barundi running to the one area and shouting with exhilaration, clapping their hands and awaiting their leader with joy. President Sabimana was always happy to come back home where all his family and relatives and friends lived. He normally came once or twice a month, usually without any announcement for his own protection. The noise of the helicopter was so loud that everyone would hear it and come running to greet their favorite relative or friend. Tony looked around and wondered if there were any Bahutu in the crowd. He couldn't see any of the women he had received in his office that afternoon. He presumed that they had gone on their way and the last person in the world they wanted to see was the president of this devastated country. 'The widows,' Tony thought, 'must hate Sabimana with a passion he could almost taste!'

The President stepped from the 'copter and left the closing down and lock up to the French pilot who accompanied him. Tony was one of the first to be greeted and he congratulated Sabimana for a prefect landing. The dignitary shook hands with all the people who had worked up to the front row of the circle and then he turned to come back to Tony.

"Can we go into the mission and have a talk, *mon Pere*?" he asked.

Tony responded by leading the way and said how honored they were that he had come since he had not visited for awhile. As they walked up the stairs and along the verandah they entered the living room. Luigi and Luc were walking beside Sabimana and Tony took a few steps ahead of the group and opened the living room door and motioned for the president to enter first.

Sabimana drew back and said: *"Non, non, mon ami, je prefere que vous entriez le premier. mon Pere apres vous."* (No, no, my friend, I want you to enter first. After you, Father.) Tony at once realized that Sabimana was taking all the precautions possible and if there were a sniper waiting for him in the room, the pastor would bite the bullet. It was more than common courtesy. It was self-preservation. Tony was surprised that no one accompanied Etienne Sabimana. Usually he came to Butova with many of his male friends and ministers of the government. This was the first time Tony recalled seeing him alone. However there were two armed soldiers who had walked with them, one in the front and the other in the back. Now both stayed outside, one standing at attention beside the living room door while the other walked up and down the verandah.

Etienne Sabimana was rather short and pudgy. He had the build of a Muhutu, but surely was a Mututsi. He had the strangest mustache that Tony had ever seen. His sideburns came across his cheek bones that stood majestically out from the sides of his face. Then the hair ran across his face to the bottom of his nose, giving his countenance the appearance of a road map with lines running in all directions. His hair was rather thick and he was the most recognizable person in the country because of the shape of his beard. Tony recalled, as he looked at Sabimana, that the president had once told them that when he was studying at military school in Belgium, a man came up to him and said he would give him 200 Belgian francs ($4.00 USD) if he could touch his hair. It was then that Sabimana thought it would be special to have facial hair that would make him distinguishable and recognizable. Tony, Luc and Luigi all had beards and were rather proud of their famous parishioner making a stand for facial hair!

As they were sitting down, Tony went out to the dining room and called to Cypriano. He came running, having already been alerted that the president had entered the fathers' living room. Tony asked him to bring four bottles of '*Primus*' (European beer processed in Bujarundi) and four glasses and a plate of bread along with some cheese. Then he returned to the living room and was surprised when the president started talking about the country and different events that had taken place over the last month. They were waiting for him to say something about the bishop's remark or about how Father Giovanni Bartoli had condemned him. Luigi wondered if he knew that Bartoli was his immediate superior. He thought that maybe he would have to pay dearly since both Bartoli and Moulin were his superiors. But the president never broached that subject. Rather he talked about how, in the first days of the Bahutu revolution, their leaders made many mistakes that showed how foolish they really were. He told them two stories and went from sentence to sentence not leaving any time for any of them to interject a word, comment or question:

"When the 'coup' started, I was in my palace in Bujarundi. You remember that you visited me there when *Pere* Mathias Becker was returning to Europe. The rebels tried to attack the military camp in the capital and they were quickly put down by my soldiers. Those who had trained them in western Tanzania had tricked the imbeciles and they went to their deaths because of their stupidity. When they were being trained, they were told that a sheep could not shout: *'MI! MI! MI!'* the cry of the rebels in Zaire seven years ago. Then the leaders would take a gun with a bullet in it and shoot the sheep. Immediately they would take a man, have him shout: *"MI! MI! Mi!"* and would shot him with a blank in the gun. The man would not die. In this way they tried to show all these stupid fellows that if they were to cry: "*Mi Mi Mi",* they could not be harmed. As they attacked the military camp shouting: *'Mi! Mi! Mi!'* without any weapons whatsoever they fell in front of all the soldiers bullets as they defended our camp. What crazy people. They were so uneducated, so stupid!" The President went on with more stories, not giving any of the Bazungu an opportunity to place a word or ask a question.

"The Bahutu leaders had trained all the rebels over the border in Western Tanzania. We knew nothing about what was happening and what they were preparing. On Saturday, April 29th they drove truckload after truckload of rebels into Bujarundi. Then the leaders let them all out of the trucks and abandoned them and drove the trucks back to Tanzania. There they prepared themselves to take over my government but waited until the rebels would kill all the soldiers. They already had the new government formed, already appointing the president, prime minister and all the other ministers. The only thing that went wrong was the rebels, without arms and shouting: *"Mi! Mi! Mi!'* fell in front of our great military forces." As the President said all this, Tony shook his head in astonishment and became more and more angry as Sabimana praised the military. It was easy to shoot attackers who were defenseless. A soldier could take as many shots as needed.

Finally the President stopped his story-telling long enough to take a sip of beer that Tony had set in front of him. As he drank, Tony seized the opportunity to speak:

"*M. le President*, with all due respect, I have a question that I have toiled with over the past month and would like to share it with you and see how you would answer my query."

"Go ahead," Sabimana interacted as he licked his lips enjoying the fine taste of his Primus. Tony opened his heart to the leader of the country:

"I have become totally disillusioned with my missionary vocation since I became pastor of this your home parish, *M. le President.* Because I have witnessed so much hatred, numerous killings, so many beatings over the past weeks, I have had to look deeply into my heart and wonder why I ever came to Burundi. As you probably know, last Sunday I announced, with the permission of Bishop Moulin and the Vicar General Monsignor Luduvico Ruyaga, that until there is peace and unity in this area, we will not be celebrating any of the sacraments including mass on Sunday. I consider myself at the crossroads of my life. To spend all my energy working for reconciliation between your two tribes would take a lifetime of toil, hard work and total commitment to this extraordinary problem in Burundi. Anything less than that, *M. le President*, would not do justice to the enormity of your problem. I am only twenty-eight years of age. To think of spending the rest of my life bringing about reconciliation between your tribes leaves me with feelings of anxiety and the belief that I would not be listening to where God is calling me, obviously out of Burundi. On the other hand, as I am still young, I can leave your country, gȯ back home to North America and embark on another career, another vocation. I could work as a priest, building the church there or I could leave the vocation of priesthood, that, before Burundi, was so clear and exciting for me, and get married, raise a family of my own and admit that this life here in Central Africa was a totally unfathomable nightmare for a christian. In my place, *M. le President.* what would you do?" Tony sighed as he took a deep breathe. Etienne Sabimana was staring at Fr. Tony as he confessed his depression and the reasons why he felt so miserable. Now as Tony looked up after asking the question, the President of Burundi lowered his head and bent over with his right arm hanging to the floor. He made as if he were writing on the round rug immediately in front of him as he turned his eyes upward to see Tony:

"When Jesus was confronted by the people who asked him to solve a dilemma, he wrote in the sand and said 'let he who is without sin cast the first stone'. *Mon pere*, the situation of politics is not very much better in your own country, Canada, that is known as a so-called 'developed country'. You can criticize our situation but problems exist everywhere in the world," added the President of Burundi.

"But we have never killed 150,000 in a month, your Excellency," Tony responded with a spark of spite in his eyes. He was glad that he had blurted the problem out. He didn't care much about the answer that Sabimana had given him but Tony appreciated the opportunity of telling the leader, frankly and directly, that this genocide would discourage many missionaries and charitable organizations in the future.. The fact that Luc and Luigi heard how he was thinking was confirmation as well.

As the months and years after the Genocide of '72 went by, Tony pondered the dilemma that he had first voiced to the president. It would shape the rest of his life for month after month and year after year. He would continually ask himself if the grace of God could possibly support him in Burundi or if he were not wasting his time on a problem that would never heal. These two tribes hated each other, and the Batutsi had done so many horrible acts in May of '72 that peace could never be a reality. For the first time in his young life, the idealist, Fr. Anthony Joseph, had come face to face with a gigantic quandary that was so depressing that he believed God's grace and guidance would never be able to overcome the power of evil. He thought:

"I have finally come face-to-face with the mid-day devil and I have been swallowed up by the power of evil. From now on, I will look after myself and my own needs first. The priesthood is a beautiful vocation when you are working with people who believe in the Gospel Message of Jesus Christ: Peace, Love, Joy, Caring, Devotion, Tenderness, Harmony, Dedication, Understanding, Happiness, Honesty, Truthfulness and Selflessness. But if you try to change other people who live by selfish human ways, the Gospel will be of no value to those who hold that Tribalism, Language, Color of Skin or Religion, Lying, Cheating, Murdering, Torturing, Condemning, Beatings, Selfishness, Falsely Accusing, Hating, Threatening far exceed Christianity: the Love and Law of Christ."

He concluded: "If the work of the church after 80 years of evangelization has been totally defeated by this Batutsi-Bahutu entanglement, then life is unfair and I must move on to other people, places and things. How sad to realize that the fifth commandment is the weak link in the chain of God's gifts. He recalled how Bishop Moulin had said:

'You BanyaButova are not very good at the sixth commandment. (Thou shalt not commit adultery) You are even weaker at the seventh. (Thou shalt not steal) But your greatest downfall is the eighth .(Thou shalt not bear false witness, i.e. 'lies') 'No!' Tony thought, setting the record straight for Moulin and everyone else who might be interested: "Their weakest link in following the commandments is number five (THOU SHALT NOT KILL.)" The next generation of missionaries should start with encouraging them not to kill one another. When they get the scent of blood, they become insane and lose all possibility of reasoning. People like this don't deserve to hear the pearls of the gospel preached to them. They are acting like swine. They have acted as outrageous, violent, savage animals. I feel justified before God in departing, for didn't Jesus say: 'Don't throw your pearls to the swine?'

President Sabimana rose to his feet and walked towards the door. He reached out his hand to the three young missionaries. As he shook their hands with his left hand supporting his right by holding onto the wrist, (Kirundi sign of deep respect), he smiled and said:

"Before I leave, I have a funny story for you. What would you do if you heard that this great world was going to end in a few minutes because of some catastrophe?"

The three had recalled the joke but wondered why the president of a poor country that was a disaster politically as well as economically, would ask such a question. How would he end the story? They all responded politely: "No" in unison.

"Well I would go to Belgium because the Belgians are one- hundred-years behind times!" The President of Burundi scoffed! He walked out the door, the soldiers stood at attention and allowed the missionaries to walk him to his car that was now waiting in front of the gate. As he stopped, he turned to Tony and said:

"*Mon Pere*," his face became sober and deadly serious:

"Before leaving you, I do have one favor I want to ask. My old father is a pagan. He has never been baptized nor attended catechumenate or church. Would you be so kind as to baptize him in the catholic faith before he dies? I know he cannot or will not attend the catechumenate but I would like you to make an exception in this case."

Tony looked right at Sabimana and noticed his sincerity shown in a few tears that were trickling down the side of his face and into his heavy beard. The *mukuru* of *bakuru* shook hands with them again, got into the passenger side of the vehicle as the soldiers got into the back seat and then called Tony over to the passenger door:

"Mon Pere," Sabimana spoke rather in a whisper "If you have some time before you leave, would you prepare my father for baptism. I would feel so bad if he were to die without becoming catholic" the president of the gloomy country said as he waved, rolled up the window and was driven away. Tony walked away with Luigi and Luc and a mob of people following them: "I wonder how many tens of thousands of Bahutu have died who have never been baptized? I wonder how many people Sabimana is responsible for having killed, yet who have never had the possibility of making their peace with their Creator. How could I, in right conscience, baptize his father? Sabimana is a good example of how to be a Roman Catholic without being christian," Fr. Tony Anthony said looking at Luigi and Luc who shook their heads wondering how the president of this desperate country could be so hypocritical! "For him as well, religion is nothing but a fetish," they quipped.

THE END

Epilogue

Many events have taken place in Burundi since the genocide of 1972 and, sad to say, most of them detrimental to the unity and progress of the country. This beautiful land, with attractive green vegetation, high mountains and breath-taking valleys, has continued to deteriorate with continued Bahutu attacks on the Batutsi and reprisals of the latter on the former. Genocide is a normal way of life throughout the whole country since 1972. After the hideous events recorded in this book, other serious confrontations, dominated by Batutsi aggression, have become commonplace, over the last 34 years.

Colonel Etienne Sabimana was overthrown by his cousin Jean-Batiste Bagaza in 1976. Under his regime, most missionaries were expelled in 1979, without explanation or reason. The government was so repressive in this demarche, that many missionaries, who had withdrawn ten, fifteen or twenty years previously, were on the list of those expelled! This fiasco left the country void of clergy, and in the south, (Vurura) not one missionary has worked there four twenty-five years. Parishes of 15,000-20,000 baptized catholics were joined together into twos, threes, and fours with only one Murundi priest in charge of the whole area. Obviously these impediments have not allowed the church to function and grow over the past three decades of oppression

Now, forty-four years after independence and thirty-four after the sad events of 1972, the executive branch of government has tried to stabilize the situation, with very little success. A transitional government was inaugurated on November 1st 2001. A Muhutu, Domitien Ndayizeye was sworn in as President in 2003 to complete the second half of the transition. Since then, in 2005 Pierre Nkurunziza has won a democratic election and is presently the President

The future of Burundi looks very bleak indeed. A resource-poor, landlocked country, with little manufacturing possibilities, has little to offer the world market. 90% of the population lives on subsistence agriculture. The only foreign exchange that comes to the country is through the export of coffee or tea. This limits, tremendously, Burundi's foreign exchange earnings. Since 1993, continuous warfare has resulted in 350,000 deaths, 450,000 refugees fleeing into Tanzania and displacing 140,000 internally.

It is doubtful if peace and development will ever become a reality. 50% of children do not attend school, and 6% of adults have HIV/AIDS. Food, medicine, road repair, house building, electricity are all in limited stock.

A final word to update some of the characters of the story: Fr. Tony Joseph has worked as a priest in his home diocese for 15 years, spent four years in Tanzania and Kenya giving priests' retreats and was doing parish work in Mission Viejo, California where he met and finally married Melinda Marsden. They have a six-year-old son Anthony (ACE) who is the love of their life. The family now lives in Kelowna, British Columbia, Canada.

Jose Suarez still works in Burundi and is one of the dozen Missionaries of Africa with a working visa.

Bishop Bernard Moulin retired in 1974 and was expelled from Burundi in 1977. He returned the following year, was escorted to a local hotel and back to the plane leaving for Brussels the following morning. As he walked on the tarmac towards the plane, he was heard to say: "I have worked fifty years in Burundi and when I die, I will rise in the center of this country!" He died in 1982.

Bishop Luduvico Ruyaga has died a short time before the completion of this book. He became Bishop of Vurura in 1973, when Bishop Moulin consecrated him, gave him his miter, a sign of authority, and also gave him his bishop's ring, as a sign of love. Ruyaga administered the diocese for almost 32 years.

Luc Grange left Butovu and joined the Missionaries of Africa. He was ordained a priest and has worked in Zambia for decades. Angelo Bertuzzi died in Europe in 2004 at 88 years of age. Walter de Winter spent four more years in his beloved Lutana, and then 10 years as Treasurer General of two other dioceses. He died in his native Belgium on July 7, 2006 at 86 years of age.

Etienne Sabimana remained president of Burundi until 1976 when he was overthrown in a bloodless coup by his cousin Jean-Batiste Bagaza, who ran the regime until 1987. Sabimana accepted house arrest and then was banished to the Sudan where he drank himself to death in his early forties.

Glossary

A

Adriano: Muhutu. Youngest son of Gasipari Lubulu and Antonia.

Agusto, Guiseppe: Italian missionary and pastor of Ruziga parish on the Lake Tanganyikan coast. He was heroic during the genocide and protected a church full of Bahutu from the Batutsi soldiers by his own life.

Alb: White robe that a priest wears when celebrating Mass

Alfredo: Young Muhutu cook who worked for the lay Bazungu teachers of the TTC and was killed May 25th. His father was the catechist, Samueli Samura who was also killed the previous week.

Amaso: "Eyes" often used for eggs sunny-side up.

Ambo: A lectern in the church sanctuary from where God's word is proclaimed and sermons are given.

Ana, Sister: Mututsikazi: Benetereza Sister who taught grade school at the girls' elementary.

Antonia: Muhutukazi and wife of the boys' school principal, Gasipari Lubulu

Anunciata, Sister: Muhutukazi Beneteresia nun, helped Sr. Maragarita to teach catechism at the parish.

Arrondissement: French word for local government. In Butova the district covered 47,000 citizens and was lead by the Administrator Alberto Kizungu. There were 87 districts in Burundi.

B

Bahungu b'alitari: Altarboys.

Bakuru: The Kirundi word for authority. The root "kuru" meant head.

Bamenja: Traitors.

Banya: Those, who….

Banyabatisimu: Those preparing for baptism (last year of catechumenate).

Banyachoir: Those who sing in the choir.

Banyakonfirmatio: Those who were preparing for confirmation.

Bartoli, Giovanni: Italian, Provincial Superior of the Xaverian Missionaries from Italy. He lived in their parish in Bujarundi and was responsible for all missionaries in the Congo, Rwanda and Burundi. He planned to move his residence to the Congo after the Genocide of '72.

Basoma: Readers

Bashingantahe: "Shinga" means plant and "ntahe" means the lance. Thus those who plant the lance may speak and are considered elders.

Bazungu: Europeans. The root "zungu" means foreign.

Becker, Fr. Mathias (Matiasi): German former Pastor of Butova (1966-1972) reappointed to Germany in April, 1972.

Bertuzzi, Fr. Angelo (Tuzi): Italian White Father and pastor/ builder of neighboring mission of Mutwe. He had lived in the area for the past twenty-five years and loved the Batutsi and judged the Bahutu were unintelligent. Great friend of President Sabimana.

Bihova: Outstation to the west of Butova. There were two catechists: Arturo Tanze, a Mututsi who was the head catechist and betrayed of many catechumens who were awaiting baptism. His assistant was a Muhutu who fought for the rights of the murdered Bahutu.

Bikobwa, Superace: Muhutukazi whose husband was murdered in the second week of May. Husband died crucified to the earth. Her name "Bikobwa" means "girl" and "Superance" comes from French word for "hope", "l'esperance".

Binka Experimental Farm: On the road between Butova and Vurura where Tomasi Muhwa was director and many Belgian couples helped with the technical organization.

Bitega, Eusebio: Muhutu and head catechist at the outstation of Lusaga. He was brutally beaten May 21st

Bitoke: A mission near the coast, to the west of Mutwe. It was directed by the Xaverian Fathers.

Bora, Yohani: Mututsi and head catechist at the largest outstation, Mundi. The word "bora" means good in Kiswahili, a word often heard at the marketplace.

Borogoro: One of the closest outstations of Butova on the main road to Vurura. They had only one catechist since many people still went to Butova for services It was here that Fr. Tony built his first church.

Boso: the plains below Lutana where the Batutsi brought their cows to graze throughout the dry season. President Sabimana hunted there and kept the fathers in gazelle steaks.

Bucumi, Gaudentia: Muhutukazi whose husband was killed in the genocide. She said her husband died because he was a Muhutu.

Bugera: Middle Seminary where the soldiers invaded and killed three Bahutu priests, among them Michieli Kayoya, in the dining room on Wednesday May 17th.

Bujarundi: Burundi's capital on Lake Tanganyika. Hot and humid. Population of only 70,000 in 1972. Presidential palace was located there and many shops, hotels, military camps and office buildings were built there.

Bumeza: Parish to the north-east of Vurura where there were three priests: two Belgian White Fathers and one Italian Xaverian priest.

Bumonge: Parish in the diocese of Vurura on Lake Tanganyika. One of the places which the rebels held during the first week of the uprisings.

Burome: Parish to the south west of Butova which had two priests and many catechists. Burundi's leading producer of stinky cheese. Only southern area held by the rebels after the one night attempted coup.

Butano: Location where Deogratias Pungu and his wife Clementia lived with their eight children. About a thirty-minute walk from Butova.

Butova: Mission run by the White Fathers. There were four members in the community: Canadian Fr. Anthony Joseph, the pastor, Spanish Fr. Jose Suarez, Assistant, Italian Fr. Luigi Franco, Assistant and Luc Grange, young Frenchman doing his military service by establishing a co-operative in the parish.

C

Calcutta, Leo: Belgian Member of the Missionaries of Africa living and working in Muka Parish.

Catechist: A local person employed by the church to teach the catholic faith to adults and chidren preparing for baptism. Catechists worked two or four mornings a week (Tuesday and Thursday, or Wednesday and Friday or Tuesday to Friday) and were responsible for Sunday's service of the word as well as watching over all catholics in the area.

Catechumen: A man or woman who is attending teachings with the intention of being baptized in the catholic church.

Catechumenate: The place where catechism takes place. Also name for the group of catechumens together.

Catoire, Lucien: Frenchman who headed the Volontaires du Progres that sent young men and women to the poor world He was responsible for Luc Grange and his work in Butova.

Chiro: many young people gathered together at the parish after the second service on Sunday mornings. They wore distinct uniforms and played games, marched with flags and sung to celebrate their christian identity with other young people. Fr. Tony was the chaplain at Butova.

Church: Both the building and the community gathered together. In Kirundi, "Eklezia" means the community and "Isengeero", the building.

Cibikenke: One of the farthest outstations from the main parish situated on a hill before the descent to Boso.

Cincture: a cord worn on the hips which a priest wears at the celebration of Mass.

Clementia: wife of Deogratias Pungu.

Clara: Muhutukazi who came to daily mass and announced the death of Fr. Michieli Kayoya to Fr. Tony.

Collation: French word for afternoon tea, usually around 4pm in Burundi. A slice of bread (tartine) and butter, jam, fruit etc.

CUSO: Canadian University Students Overseas. A charitable organization founded in Canada that sends professors and students to the poor world to work for a year or two usually teaching or working in agriculture.

D

Diaspora: A community separated from the larger group.

Domitila, Sister: Mututsikazi Beneterezia Sister who taught grade school at the girls elementary.

E

Ego, Egome: Yes! The latter is longer and more emphasized.

Equipes Enseignantes: A catholic gathering of teachers both on the secondary and primary level who met regularly to deepen their spiritual outlook on life and prayer. They were founded by Msgr. Ruyaga and Fr. Tony was the local Butova chaplain.

Evangelization: The process of reaching out to others in order to bring them the message of God's salvation and the Good News of Jesus Christ and draw them to the Lord in the church.

F

Franco, Luigi: Italian priest and member of the parish community, lent by the Xaverian Fathers. He had come to Burundi the year before and was learning the language. He was deeply touched by all the violence and longed to return to Italy.

Freres de l'Instruction Chretienne (F.I.C): Brothers of Christian Instruction. Ten members of the community lived in Butova and taught as well as administered the Teachers' Training College.

G

Gisumu: second largest city in Burundi, situated in the center of the country, north of Butova and east of Bujarundi

Gaudentia, Sr: Muhutukazi, Superior General of the Beneterezia Sisters who lived at the General House in Gisumu.

Gloria, Sr: Muhutukazi: local superior of the Beneterezia sisters at Butova.

Gikobwa, Inocenti: Muhutukazi. The only female catechist at Butova. She taught children at the central parish school and survived the genocide by hiding.

Grange, Luc: A nineteen-year-old Frenchman who was doing his military service through the "Volunteer for Progress Organization" from Paris. Luc lived with the fathers at the mission house and was a member of the community. He started a cooperative that was very successful and persevered for his two years of service.

H

Hendrick, Marc and Lise: A Belgian couple who taught at the TTC and who were evacuated from Butova on May 21st.

Hodi: a greeting from Kiswahili to let the owners know when someone has arrived in their kigo. Of course there are no doorbells in Burundi.

I

Imbwa, Saverino: Mututsi trained catechist from Mutwe Parish and appointed to Butova. He shared a room and food with Petero Tumba. He was forced to give Petero the coup de grace when he was dying.

Impuzu: Very colorful outer garment worn by a woman. The hem was lifted and thrown over the opposite shoulder. She carried money (paper) folded into the corners of her impuzu.

Indaro: "sleep over" Since there are no hotels or hostels in Burundi, anyone needing to sleep and have food is given hospitality by staying with a local family.

Induru: Women's shrill cry when they have heard of death in the family and their way of announcing the death to the whole neighborhood.

Inzu, Bernardo: Muhutu sacristan at Butova. Inzu means "house". He also sold trinkets at the market to earn extra money. He was killed on May 11th and his wife (Mariya) was robbed of all their possessions since they believed Bernardo was a mumenja.

J

Joseph, Fr. Anthony: Canadian Parish Priest of Butova Mission and member of the Missionaries of Africa.

K

Kabura, Karoli: Mututsi who lived near Puma and witnessed the killings in prison early May 25th. He drove with Fr. Tony to the military camp at Vurura to report the "May 25th riot at Puma prison" to the Military Governor.

Karani, Jacobo: Mututsi "Muganga" (Infirmarian) at Puma and assistant to the Administrator. Originally from Rwanda Name means "secretary".

Kazi: the feminine gender added to the end of a word e.g. Muhutukazi, Mututsikazi

Kayoya, Fr. Mikieli: Muhutu priest of the archdiocese of Gisumu. He was killed by soldiers with two other priests who taught with him in the seminary of Bugera. Name means "little child".

Kebembo: Protestant mission outside Vurura on the road to the minor seminary.

Kigo: see Rugo

Kihutu/Kitutsi: The things that pertain to the ways and culture of being Muhutu or Mututsi. e.g what we would say in English: "That's German. That's American."

Kijiji: Tanzanian border city to the south of Lake Tanganiyka, where the lake, Burundi and Tanzania meet

Kitwi, Cypriano: Mututsi cook at Butova priests' house. He worked and lived at the mission for one complete month and then had the other month off.

Kufa, Samueli: Mututsi. The squad leader of the soldiers at Butova. He was responsible for many beatings and murders. Name means "to die".

Kupiga, Martino: Mututsi. Head of the police at Puma. He was a angry and violent man. Name means "to beat".

Kuramutsa: "walk home" A Bantu tradition. When someone comes to visit, the host walks the visitor part or all of the way back home.

L

Lacroix, Emile and Raymonde: A Canadian couple who taught at the TTC and who were evacuated from Butova on May 21st.

Lambert, Jean: Frenchman. He was the White Father regional superior and travelled throughout the country but had his base in Bujarundi.

Labine, Bro. Alex: Canadian, Superior of the Christian Instruction Brothers and Director of the Teachers' Training College.

Lorenzo: Mututsi and special friend of Fr. Angelo Bertuzzi. He started as his "boy" but then became his "chief-of-staff". Bertuzzi trusted Lorenzo with everything in Mutwe.

Louis, Brother: Canadian F.I.C. brother. He was chosen superior of the community just before the genocide.

Lubulu, Gasipari: Muhutu. Principal of the Butova Boys' Elementary School. Arrested on May 12th and killed thereafter.

Luconi: Village near the mission where the road from Butova joins two roads: Vurura and Mundi.

Luduvico: Muhutu cook who worked for the TTC lay couples. He was killed in Puma Prison, May 25th.

Lusaga: outstation to the northwest of Butova Parish. There were two catechists, including Eusebio Bitega, who ran the outstation.

Lutana: Mission to the east of Butova where Walter De Winter was the builder, founder and present pastor. There was a hospital in Lutana and the fathers would visit the mission every time they transported a patient.

M

Mabati: roof covering.

Maragarita, Sister: Mututsikazi. One of the Beneteriza Sisters from Gisumu. Directed choir and taught catechetics at Butova.

Maria: Mututsikazi, the wife of Jacobo Karani. Originally from Rwanda and very tall in stature.

Maria: Muhutukazi. She taught grade six girls and helped Fr. Tony put his Sunday sermon into good Kirundi by reviewing it with him Saturday afternoons.

Mariana: Mututsikazi. She was a teacher at Vurura Girls' Elementary School and close friend of Fr. Tony as a member of the Equipes Enseignante. She was killed by a Mututsi mukuru on May 26th.

Mariya: Muhutukazi, the wife of Bernardo Inzu, a merchant and parish sacristan.

Meeting for the Poor: Groups of men who came together, organized by Fr. Jose. They would bring the local peoples' offerings in money and supplies to the meeting and then discuss whoever was in need and bring them what was necessary to help them after the meeting.

Mihaga, Libori: Mututsi and former commissioner of schools. He was a well-liked by Tony. During the genocide, Mihaga was responsible for the barrier near Vuvoga.

Mihana: Groupings of banana trees, in the center of which the people built their homes. In this way, they could protect their produce from robbers and they had less sunshine and heat. This was also very practical as they had only a short distance to carry the heavy bunches of bananas.

Minani, Bernardo: Mututsi. Close friend of the missionaries who taught grade six boys. His wife was Pataricia.

Minani, Marita: Muhutukazi. One of the first widows to come to Fr. Tony for spiritual and financial help.

Minani, Paolo: Mututsi, former Finance Minister.

Mission: An area with a central church and many outstations. Usually it was close to 500 sq. miles. Normally there were three priests, sisters, many schools and forty-fifty catechists and the same number of teachers.

Missionaries of Africa: Also known as the White Fathers because of their habit based on the Arab gandurah and burnoose resembling Moslems. They still work exclusively throughout the African continent. In 1972, there were over 220 White Fathers in Burundi. Now there are 12!

Mizuri, Salvatore: Muhutu. Name is a positive response to a greeting i.e. "Very well, thank you" a greeting in Kiswahili. He taught grade five boys and was arrested on May 12th and subsequently murdered.

Moto: Abbreviated form for motorcycle.

Motocari: An automobile or truck. Any kind of vehicle from the British expression "motor car".

Moulin, Bernard (Bernardo): Belgian Catholic Bishop of Vurura and member of the Missionaries of Africa. He became bishop in 1949 and was appointed to the diocese of Zugozi. In 1961 he founded the diocese of Vururi.

Mugabo: man/manhood/manliness

Mugera, Eugenio: Muhutu. Woodcutter working for the fathers who prepared their woodpile everyday.

Mugore: woman

Muhwa, Tomasi: Mututsi director of experimental farm and tyrant/organizer of the massacres at Butova. Name means "thorn" and he was a thorn in the flesh of the missionaries.

Muka: Mission to the southwest of Butova from where Petero Tumba hailed. Fr. Mathias had worked there as a young missioner. Where Fathers Van Riel, Noker and Calcutta lived and worked. A large Bahutu population.

Mukuru: head, chief, leader, person-in-charge.

Mundi: An outstation to the west of Butova which was the largest in the parish. There were 2,000 baptized catholics at Mundi. It was the easiest to travel to and thus the fathers went there often for Sunday mass. This was where Tony heard about the seven Bahutu killed by the soldier at nightwatch (May 13th) and met the soldier the next day.

Murore, Daudi: Mututsi catechist at Butova and brother of President Sabimana. He still lived in Ruhaha.

Mupira: a round ball. The boys love to play soccer. They take old clothing and tie cord from the tree branches around it. When a missioner would got to an outstation, he would bring a rubber ball along for the boys to have fun.

Musaba, Jean-Bosco: Mututsi. He was the parish secretary, fired by Fr. Tony after all the murdering was over. No proof, but most likely involved.

Mutwa: Pygmy. A tribe apart from the Bahutu and the Batutsi that composed 1% of the total population of Burundi.

Mutwe: Mission to the northwest of Butova. Angelo Bertuzzi was pastor and Pedro Sanchez and Raphael Saturnino the assistants.

Muzoga, Stephano: Muhutu killed around May 9th. Head catechist of Bucari where he lived with his family. He had a wonderful sense of humor.

Mwiza, Nestori: Muhutu. Name means "nice". Assistant catechist at Mundi. He was arrested as one of the group of twenty-three, marched to Puma and killed on May 17th.

Myanza Lac: area on the coast of Lake Tanganyika where the fathers went for relaxation.

N

Nabi, Georgio: Mututsi. Teacher of grade 6 boys and assistant principal. He also lived in one of the houses rented from the mission and was the leader of all the other professors who lived there. He was very active during the genocide. Name means "bad".

Ndigi, Lazaro: Mututsi. Teacher and Assistant director at the TTC. He was a dominating force in the Bahutu genocide and is responsible for many deaths.

Noker, Franz: German. Assistant priest at the parish of Muka and best friend of Mathias Becker. They both loved motorcycle riding and were famous for their races against each other on the southern Burundi roads.

Ntware, Barnabe: Mututsi. He worked in the garden for the missionaries and also carried the mail to Vurura every Thursday. Fr. Tony was having him trained to be the new cook, replacing the older man, Cypriano Kitwi.

Nyandwi, Dieudonne: Mututsi Civil Governor of Vurura. Killed April 29th.

Nyabenda, Melechiori: Mututsi teacher of grade five boys who died of natural medical causes on May 10th.

O

Ordinary: Another word for Bishop, the man appointed by the Vatican to lead a diocese.

Osikari: Muhutu cook for the European couples who taught at TTC.

Outstation: A prayer chapel and satellite area where people had a Sunday service lead by a catechists since they lived too far from the parish church to get there on foot. Butova had eleven outstations. The major ones were: Mundi, Ruhweza, Lusaga, Vuvoga.

Oya, Oyaye: No! The latter is more emphatic then the former.

P

Pataricia: Mututsikazi. She was the wife of Bernardo Minani and good friend of the missionaries who taught grade 6 girls.

Pikipiki: Motorcycle: named after the sound it makes.

Piga: the hillside across from Butova mission where the parents of President Sabimana now lived. It was where the first murders took place on May 4th and was aptly called "beat".

Pre-evangelization: see Evangelization. The first steps leading to the evangelization process.

Proulx, Gerard: Canadian layman who lived with the brothers and taught French at the TTC. He tried to hide Professor Gregori Sumve and later had to turn him over to the authorities. Sumve was subsequently killed.

Punda: Outstation near the Boso to the south-east of Butova where one catechist worked alone.

Pungu, Deogratiaas: Muhutu catechist and parish secretary. Murdered on May 16th.

R

Richard, Mathieu and Marthe: A French couple who taught at the TTC since 1970 and were evacuated on May 21st.

Ruha, Bonaventuro: Mututsi from the outstation of Bihova who was Ambassador to the UN, USA and Canada and blood brother of the Administrator Alberto Kizungu.

Rugo: Also "kigo" The area surrounding one's house and fenced in usually. Private area where the animals were housed.

Ruhaha: hillside across from Butova Mission where President Sabimana had been born.

Ruhweza: Large outstation to the south of Butova where there were four catechists.

Rutega, Danieli: Muhutu. Head catechist of the large outstation of Vuvoga. He had taught there for thirty-three years.

Ruyaga, Msgr. Luduvico: Mututsi priest originated from Bumeza. He lived at Vurura with Bishop Moulin. He was appointed as the bishop's vicar general. Moulin turned all work in the diocese over to him at the beginning of the genocide.

Ruyigi, Petero: Mutwa. (Pygmy) Father of a young boy who worked at the mission. He died of interior stomach worms before Fr. Tony could get to him with medicine. He was buried by Fr. Tony and with his son.

Ruziga: Catholic mission on the coast of Lake Tanganyika where Father Guiseppe Agusto was pastor.

Rwagasore, Prince Louis: Mututsi Prime Minister who was assassinated in October, 1961 and was the founder of l'UPRONA. He is esteemed as the father of Burundi and his countenance graced the 100FrBu notes.

S

Sabimana, Etienne: Mututsi, President of Burundi. Born at Ruhaha, facing Butova mission and returned to his own parish often.

Sacristan: A person who looks after the church, especially the sanctuary. He will prepare the vessels for mass, marriages and baptisms, and keep all clean and proper.

Same: hillside where Melechiori Nyabenda lived and died.

Samura, Samueli: catechist at the home parish of Butova. He and his son, Alfredo, were killed in the genocide.

Sanchez, Fr. Pedro: Spanish Missionary of Africa and assistant priest at Mutwe. He planned to follow the trucks going to bury the cadavres, pass them and then return so he could be seen by the evil-doers.

Saturnino, Fr. Raphael: Spanish Missionary of Africa living in Mutwe who wanted to vest (dress in liturgical vestments), stand in the road and allow the trucks, carrying the cadavers to burial to run him over.

Shabaru, Arturo: Mututsi, Head of the Armed Forces and Minister of Defense and Foreign Affaires. He was the chief architect of the genocide coordinating the killings throughout the country. As Commander-in-Chief, he had all the Bahutu (600) soldiers killed in Gisumu at the beginning of the genocide.

Simba, Alberto: Mututsi. Head catechist of Ruhweza. Very old and vocal about his own opinions. Showed his arrogance often.

Stefano: A young teenager whom Fr. Tony asked to look for the truck going to Puma to pick up cadavers.

Stole: The garment worn by the priest during the celebration of Mass that goes around the neck and hangs over the chest to the waist.

Suarez, Fr. Jose: Spanish Missionary of Africa and assistant at Butova. He had first lived six years at Burome from 1963-69 and then Butova for the last three. He and Tony had many disagreements and failed to give the Barundi a true witness of love and peace.

Subira kandi: "repeat"

Sumve, Gregori: Muhutu professor of Kirundi grammar and literature at the TTC. He was handed over by Gerard Proulx (who had tried to hide him) on May 12th and subsequently killed.

T

Teresia: Mututsikazi. Wife of Yohani Bora, head catechist at Mundi.

Terezita, Sister: Muhutukazi. Benetereza sister who did housekeeping, cooking and gardening for the sister at Butova.

Tumba, Petero: Muhutu from Muka and trained catechist ministering at Butova. Arrested May 21st and killed May 25th.

TTC: Teachers Training College across the mission from the church. Over three-hundred-and-fifty male students, both Batutsi and Bahutu, in four levels of secondary school.

Twabasabwa, Domitilia: Muhutukazi who only had one leg. She and her disabled husband lived close to the mission and had three small children.

U

U.G.A. Group of young people to continue the experience of the Chiro. However rather than marching and playing games, they spent their time in discussion, reading scripture, singing and praying. Normally they met after the second mass every Sunday. Fr. Jose was their chaplain.

UPRONA: the first national political party of Burundi. L'Union pour le PROgret NAtional was founded before independence by the Prime Minister Prince Louis Rwagasore in 1961.

V

Van Riel, Kees: Belgian Missionary of Africa and pastor of Muka. He had been Bishop Moulin's vicar general from the foundation of the diocese in 1961.

Vicar General: Appointed by the bishop, the vicar general replaces him on different occasions. He also helps with the administration. Msgr. Luduvico Ruyaga was the full-time VG for Bishop Moulin and Kees Van Riel was another and pastor of Muka.

Volontiers du Progres: A French voluntary organization that sent young people to aid projects in the poor world. Luc Grange was one of them and Lucien Catoire was the person responsible.

Vurura: Diocesan Headquarters where Bishop Moulin and Vicar General Luduvico Ruyaga lived. The diocesan offices were there. Also the cathedral had been built on the upper hill. There was a community of three priests working and living there in their own quarters.

Vuvoga: Large outstation to the east of Butova where there were four catechists.

W

White Fathers: see Missionaries of Africa.

Z

Zugozi: diocese in the north of Burundi on the Rwandan border where Bernard Moulin was bishop from 1949 until he was asked to found the diocese of Vurura in 1961.

Printed in the United States
74231LV00004B/10-48